mage

AND THE ENDLESS UNKNOWN

SJ Miller

AUTHOR & ARTIST
SJ Miller

EDITOR
Clint Pereira

PUBLISHER • EDITOR-IN-CHIEF
C. Spike Trotman

ART DIRECTOR
Matt Sheridan

PREPRESS, ADDITIONAL DESIGN, PROOFREADER
Hye Mardikian

First Edition: July 2023
Printed in China

ISBN: 978-1-63899-119-9 (print)
       978-1-63899-120-5 (ebook)

strange and amazing

329 West 18th Street, Suite 604 | Chicago, IL 60616 | ironcircus.com | inquiry@ironcircus.com

Publisher's Cataloging-in-Publication
(Provided by Cassidy Cataloguing Services, Inc.)

Names: Miller, S. J. (Illustrator), author, artist. | Pereira, Clint, editor. | Spike, 1978- publisher. | Sheridan, Matt, art director. | Mardikian, Hye, designer.

Title: Mage and the endless unknown / SJ Miller [author & artist] ; copy editor, Clint Pereira ; publisher & editor, C. Spike Trotman ; art director, Matt Sheridan ; print technician & additional design, Hye Mardikian.

Description: First edition. | Chicago, IL : Iron Circus Comics, 2023.

Identifiers: ISBN: 9781638991199

Subjects: LCSH: Wizards--Comic books, strips, etc. | Magic--Comic books, strips, etc. | Voyages and travels--Comic books, strips, etc. | Monsters--Comic books, strips, etc. | Light and darkness-- Comic books, strips, etc. | LCGFT: Graphic novels. | Fantasy comics. | Horror comics. | BISAC: YOUNG ADULT FICTION / Comics & Graphic Novels / Fantasy. | YOUNG ADULT FICTION / Comics & Graphic Novels / Horror. | YOUNG ADULT FICTION / Fantasy / Dark Fantasy. | YOUNG ADULT FICTION / Fantasy / Wizards & Witches.

Classification: LCC: PN6727.M558 M34 2023 | DDC: 741.5973--dc23

PARTS

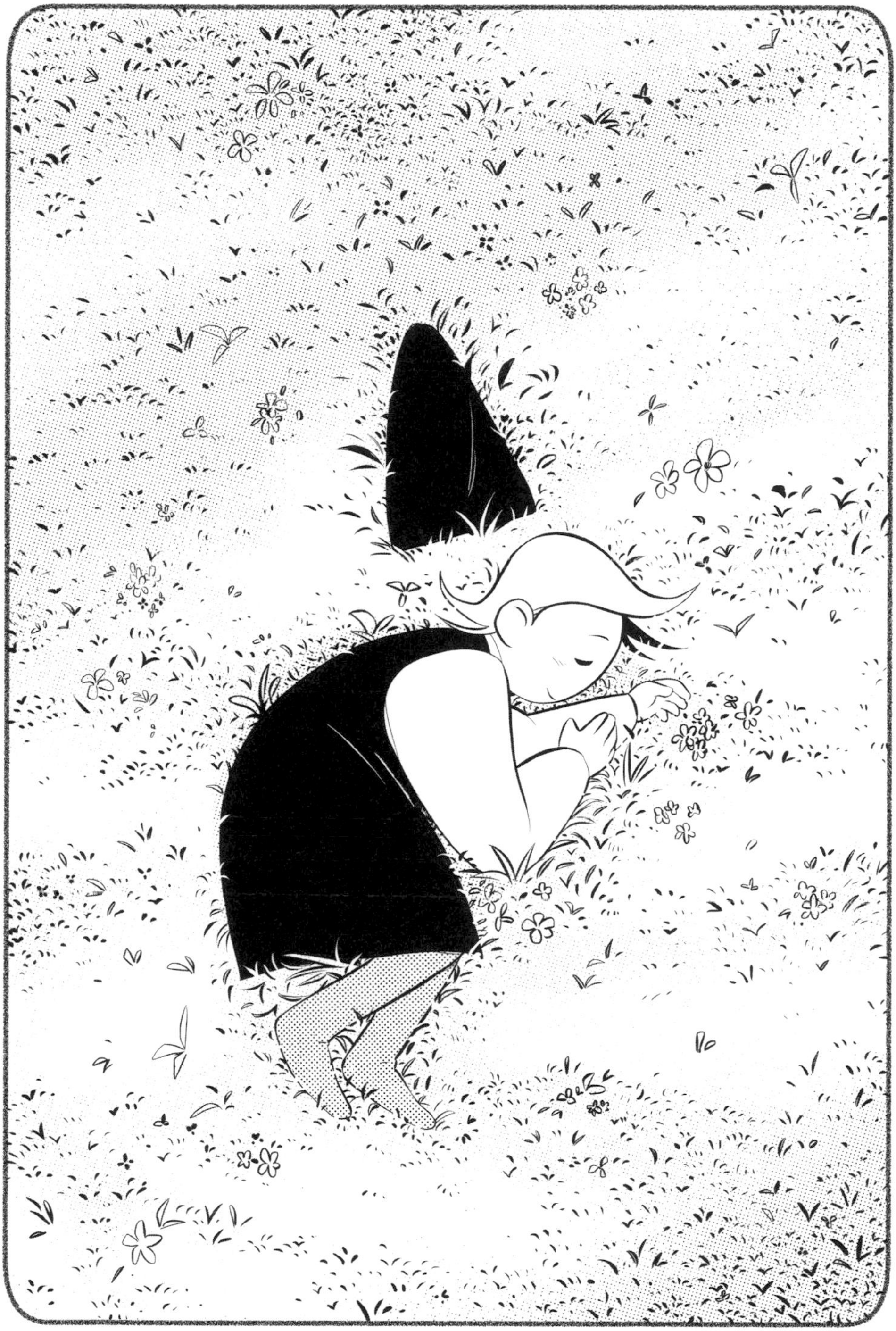

PART ONE

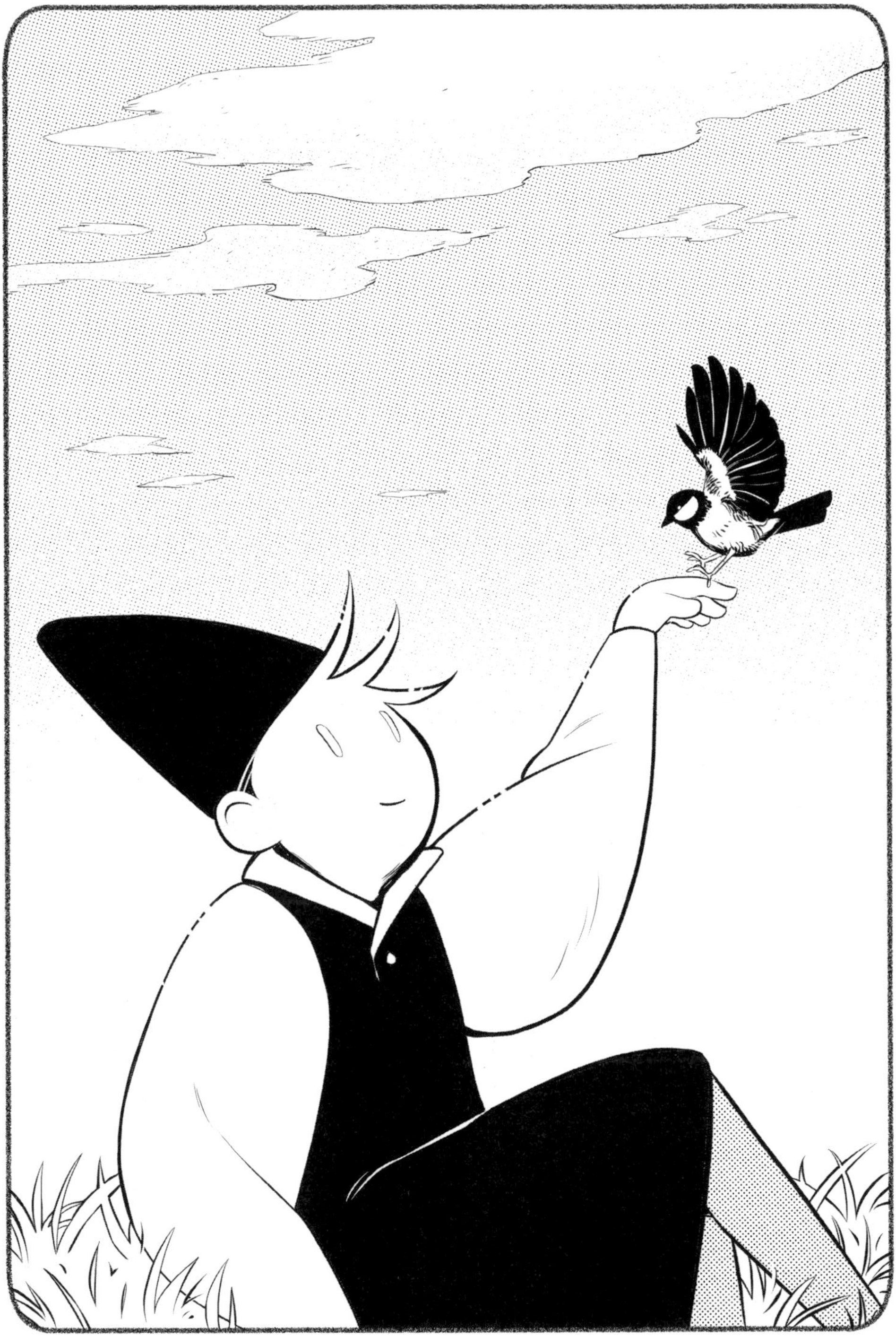

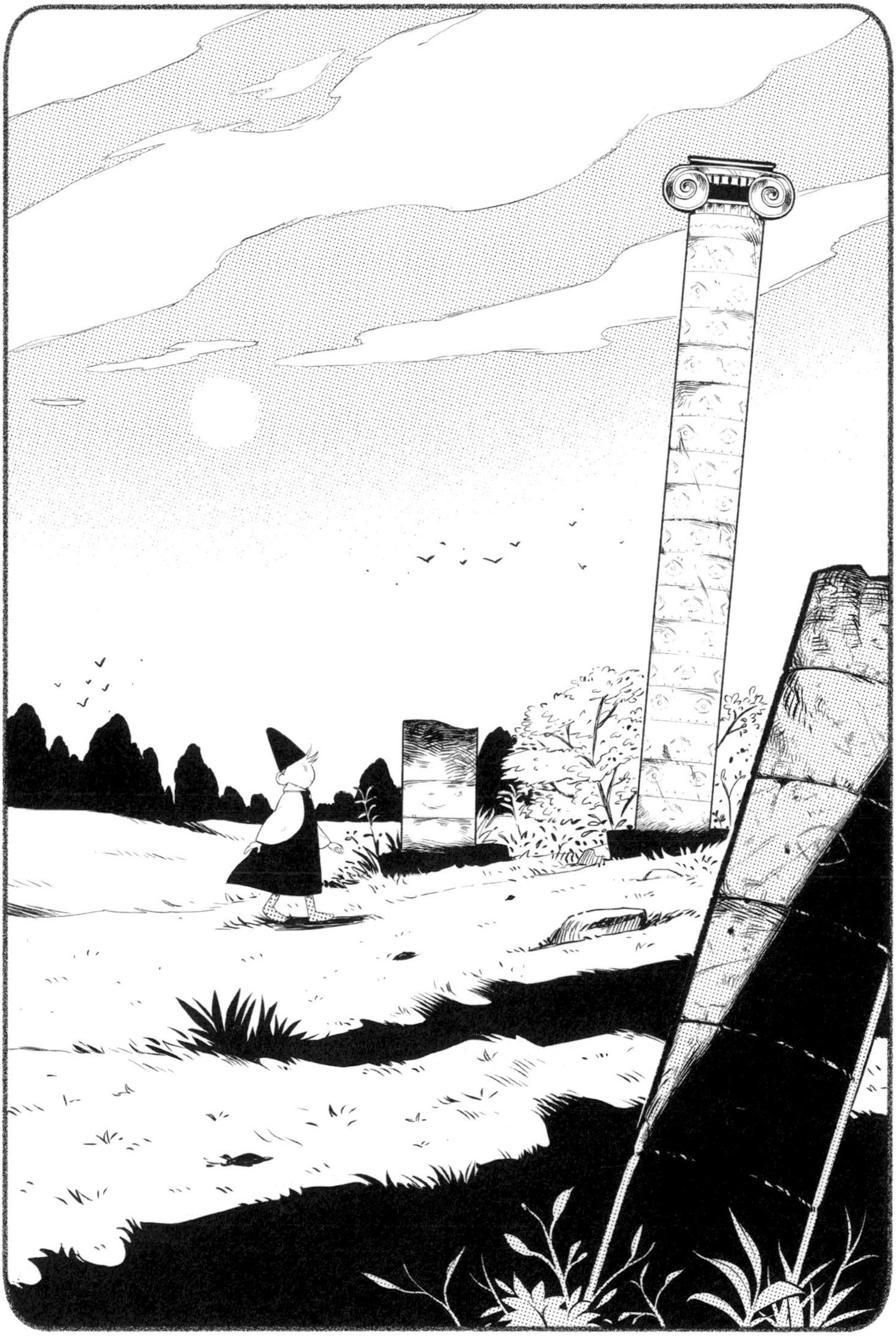

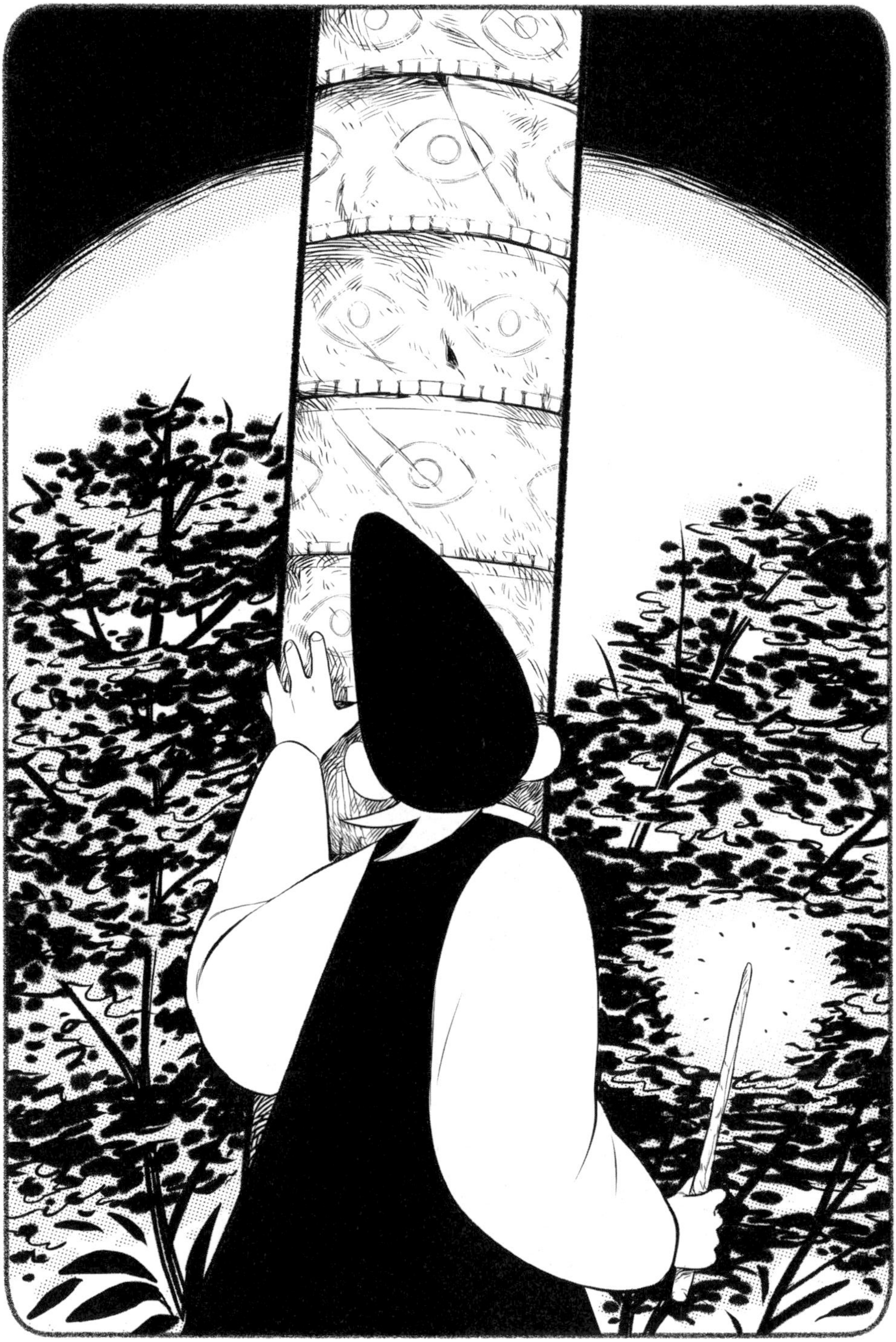

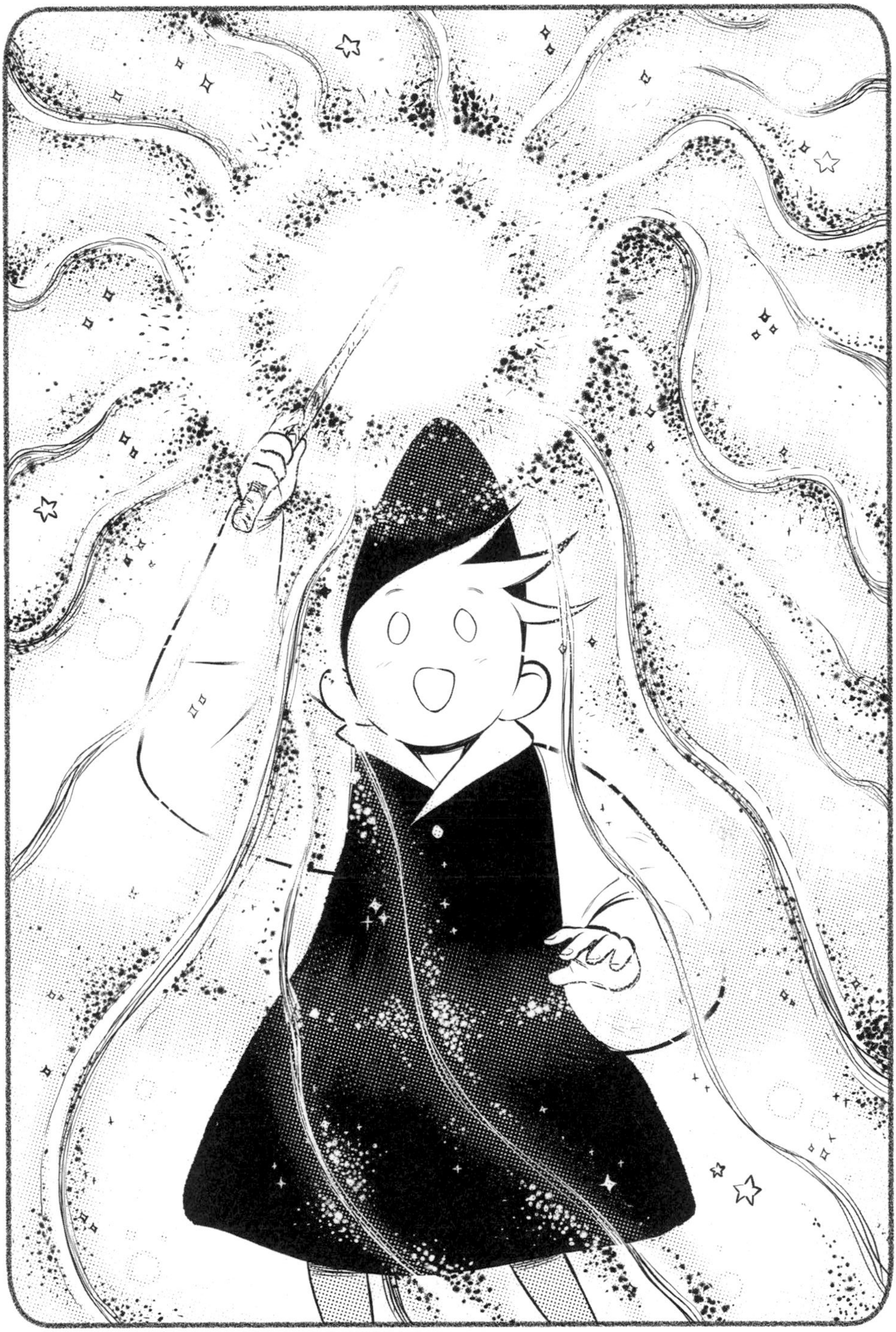

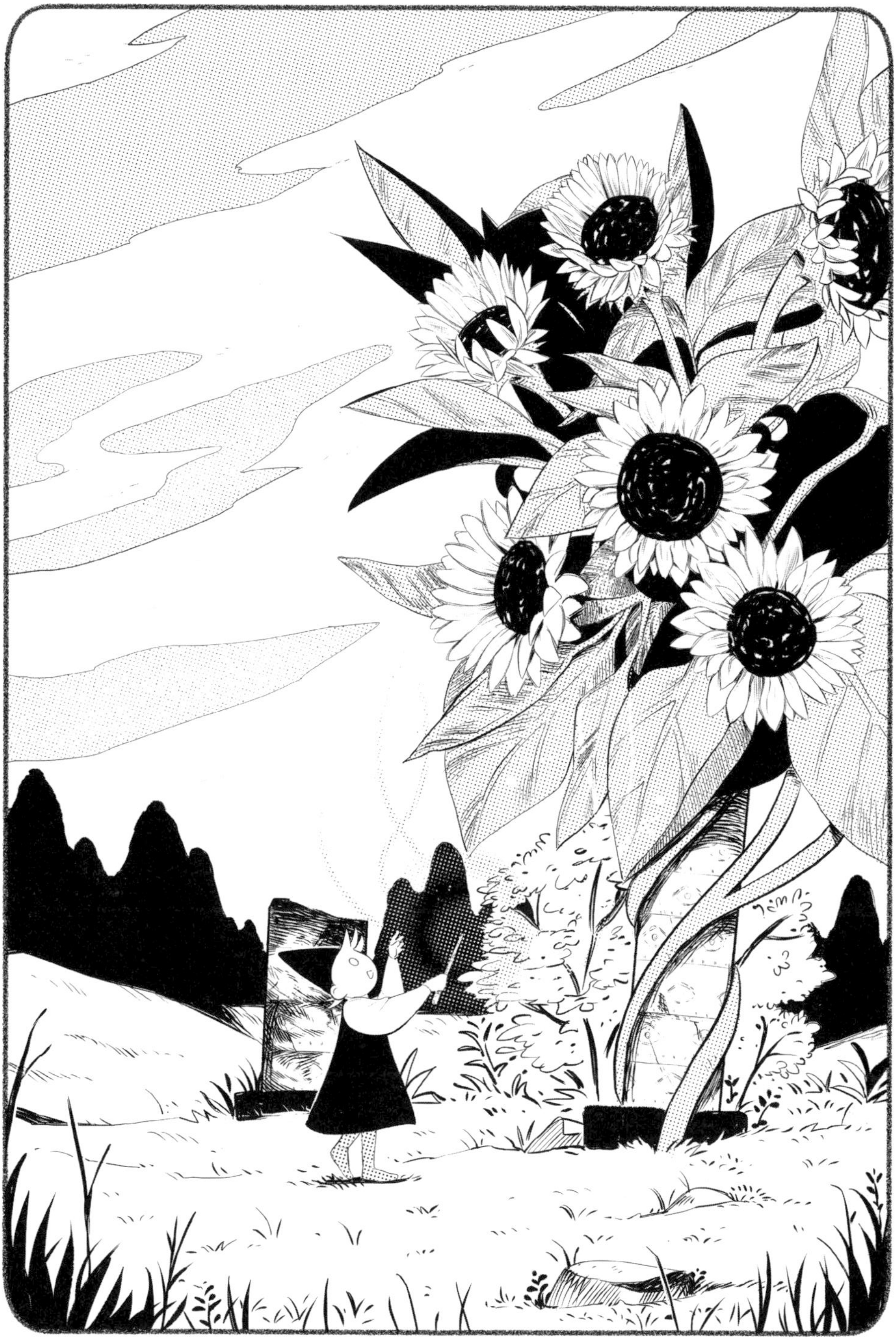

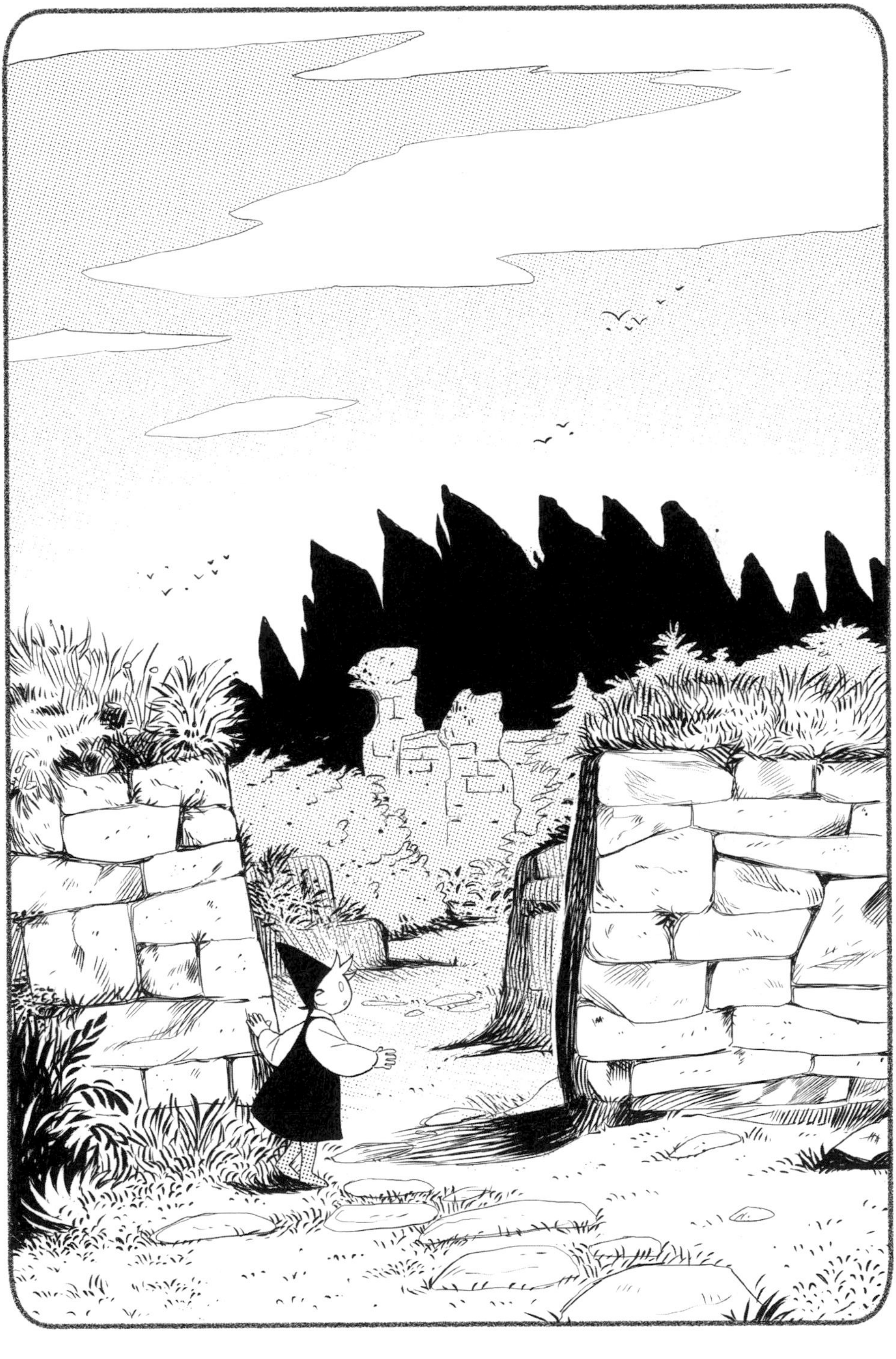

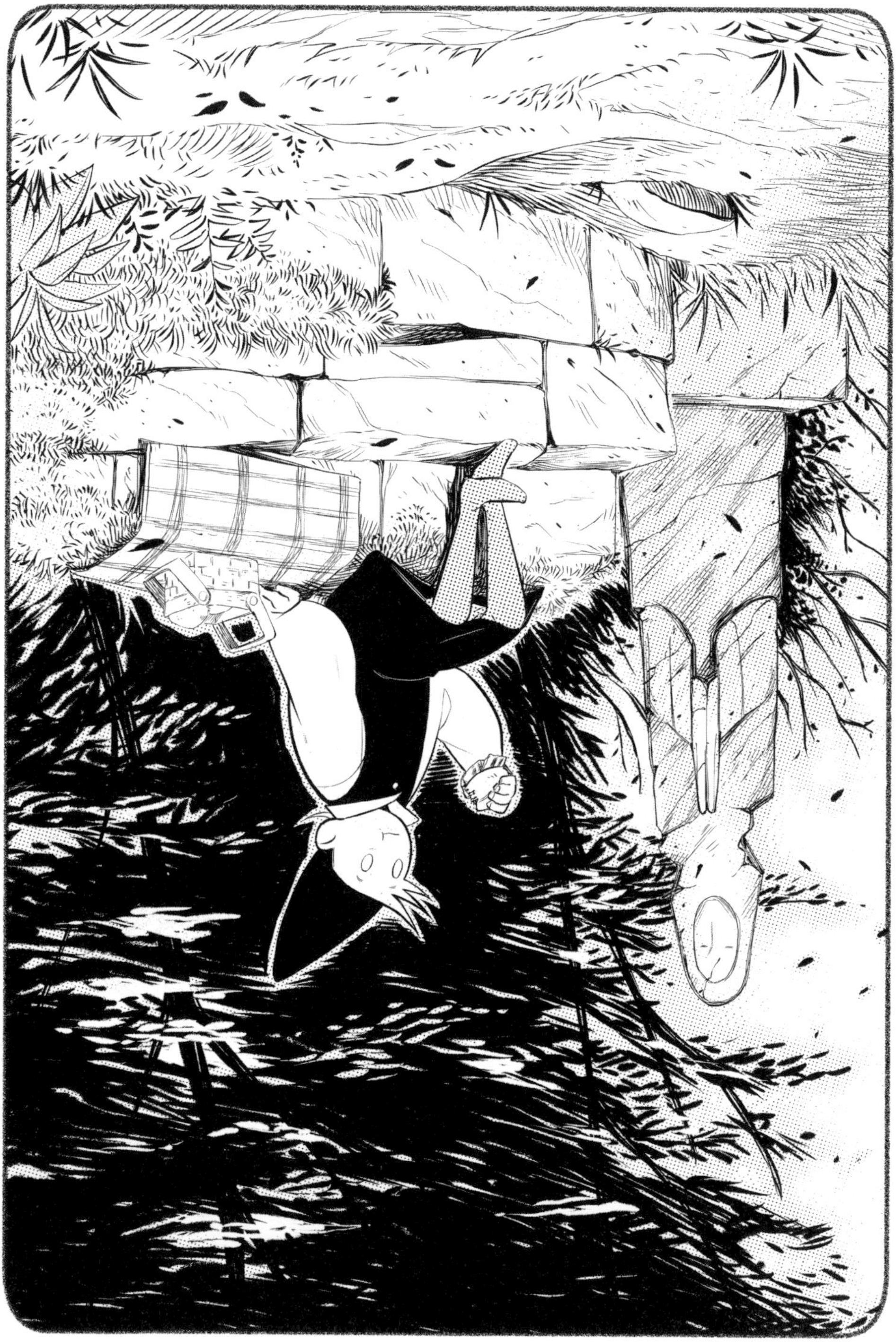

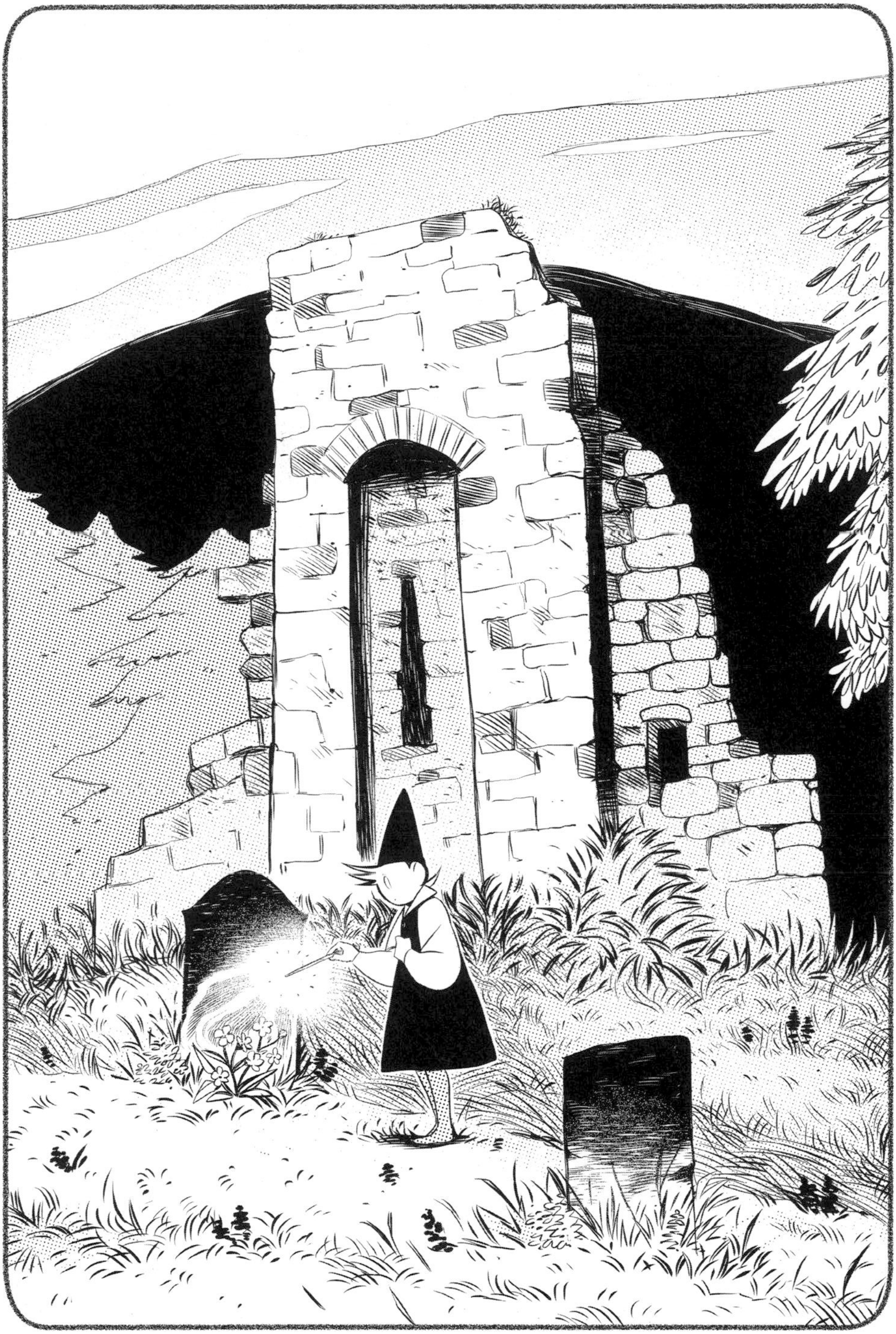

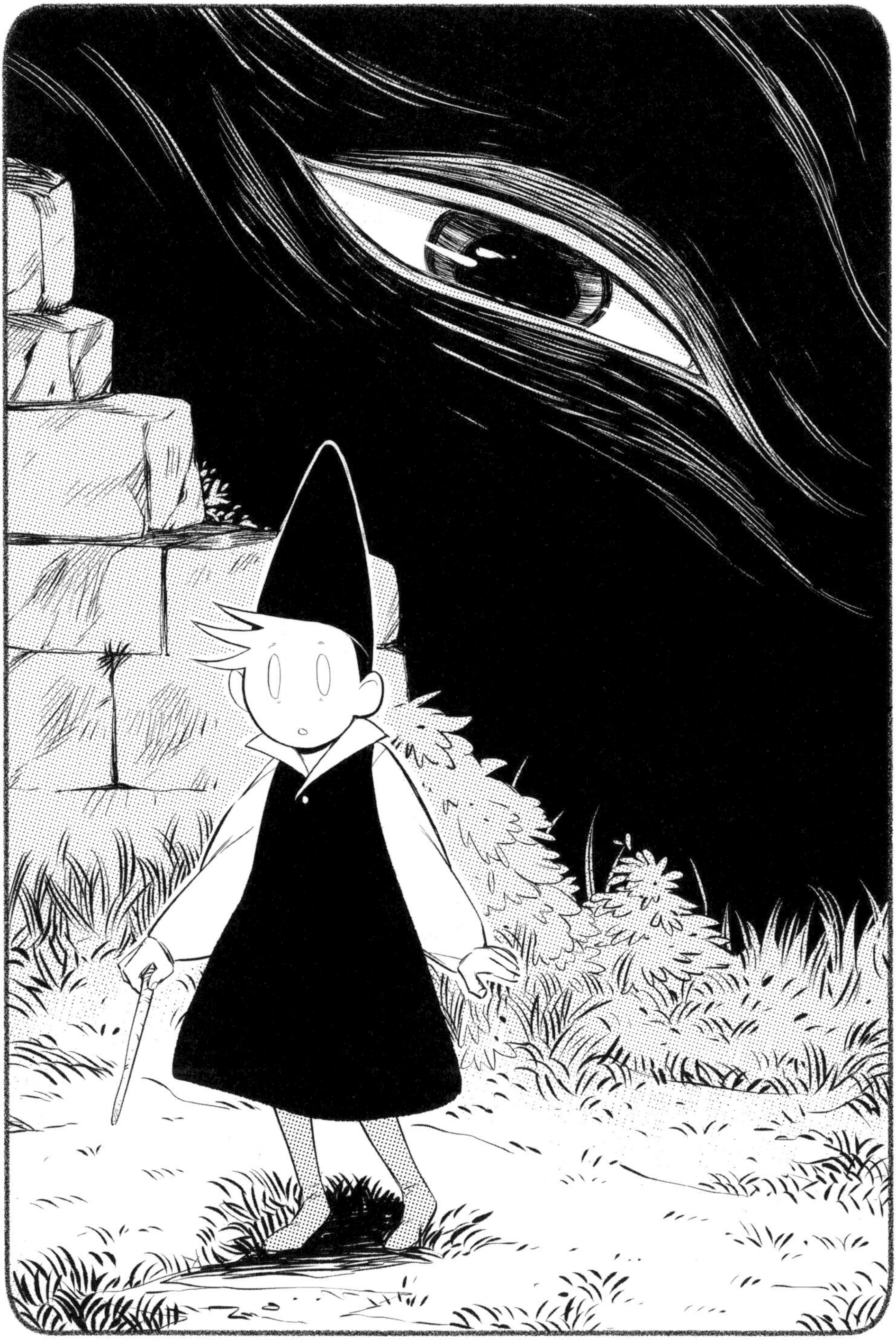

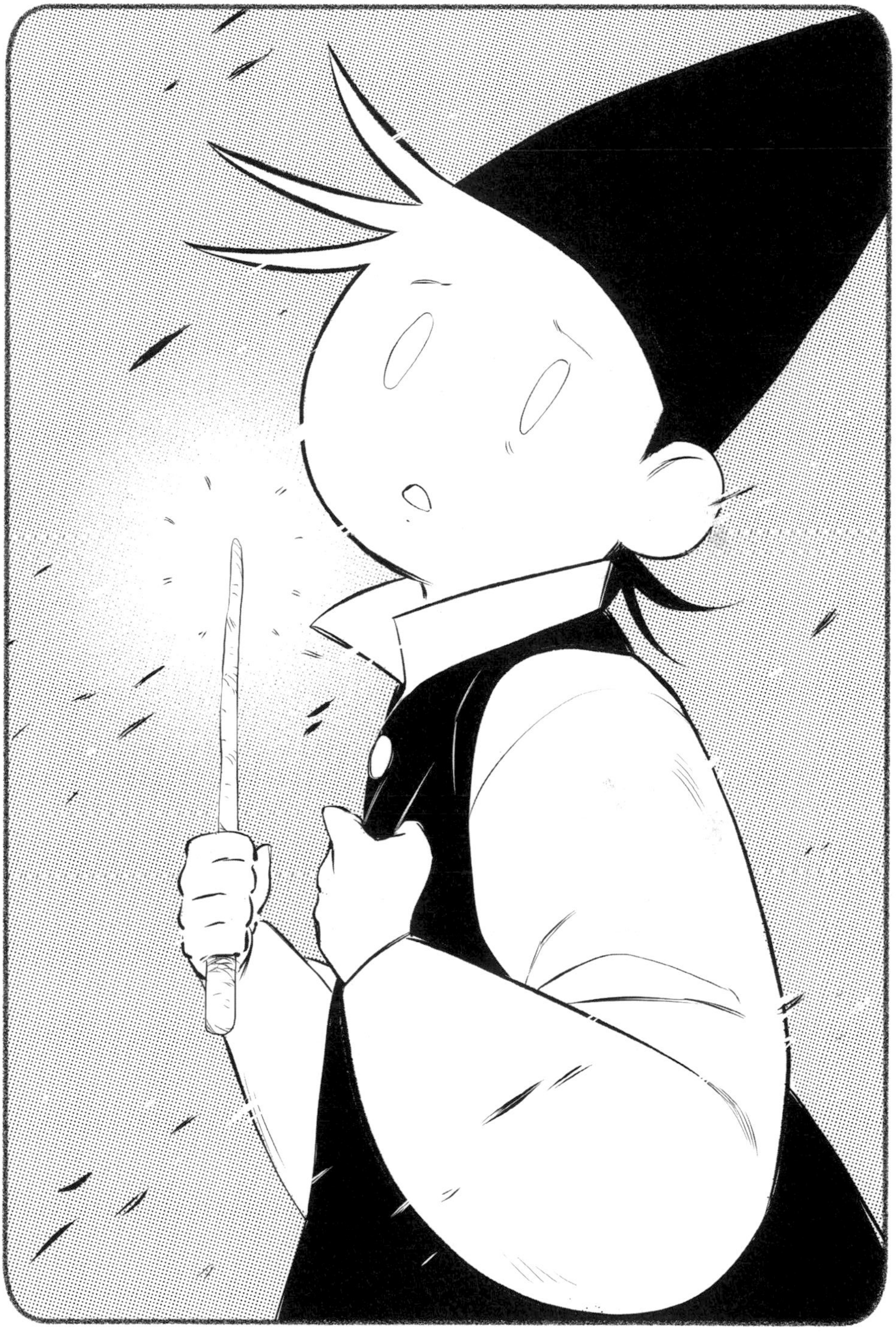

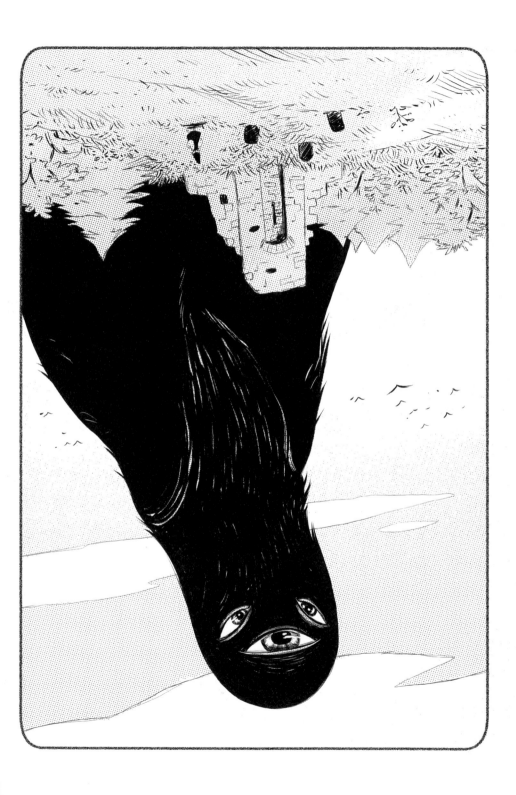

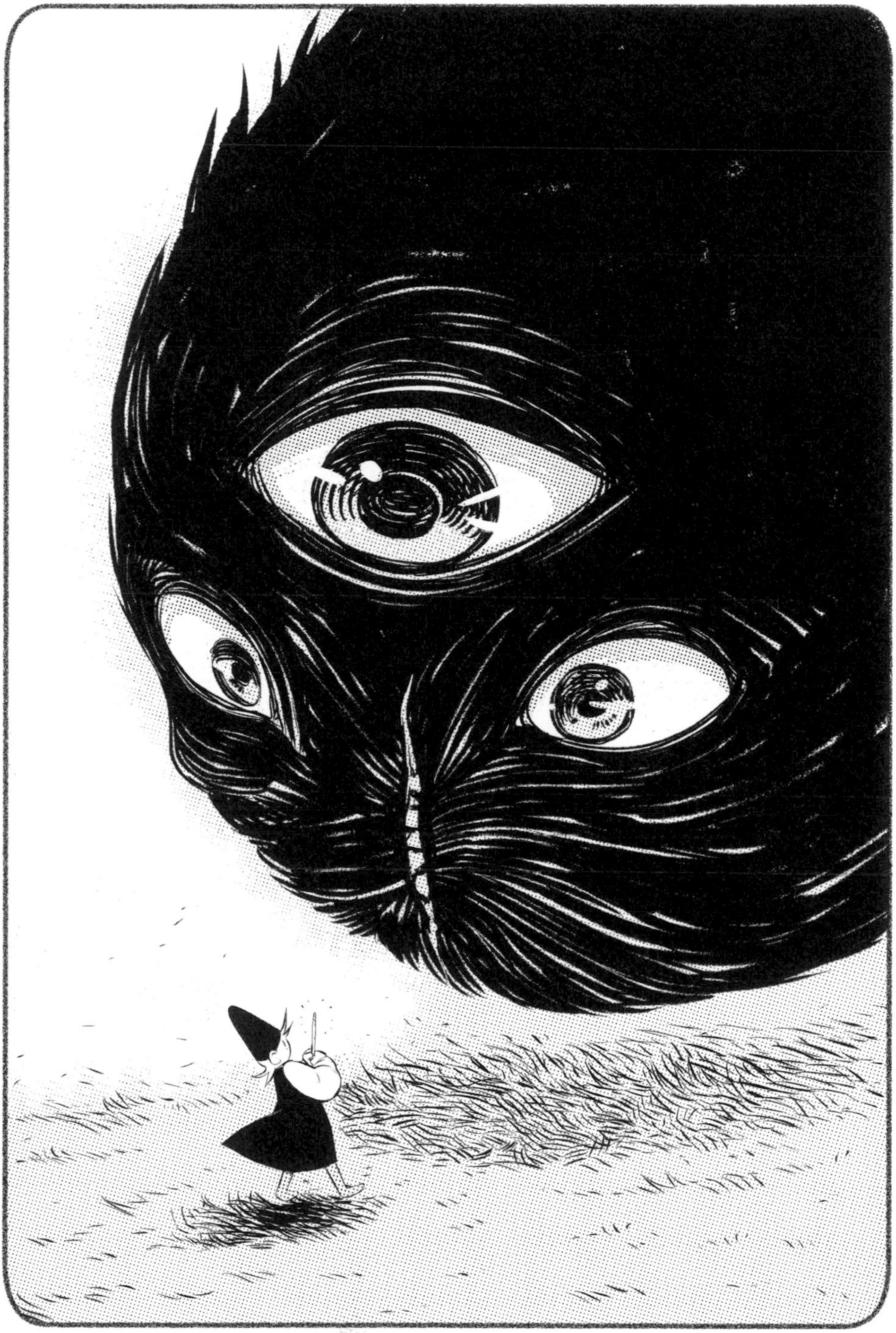

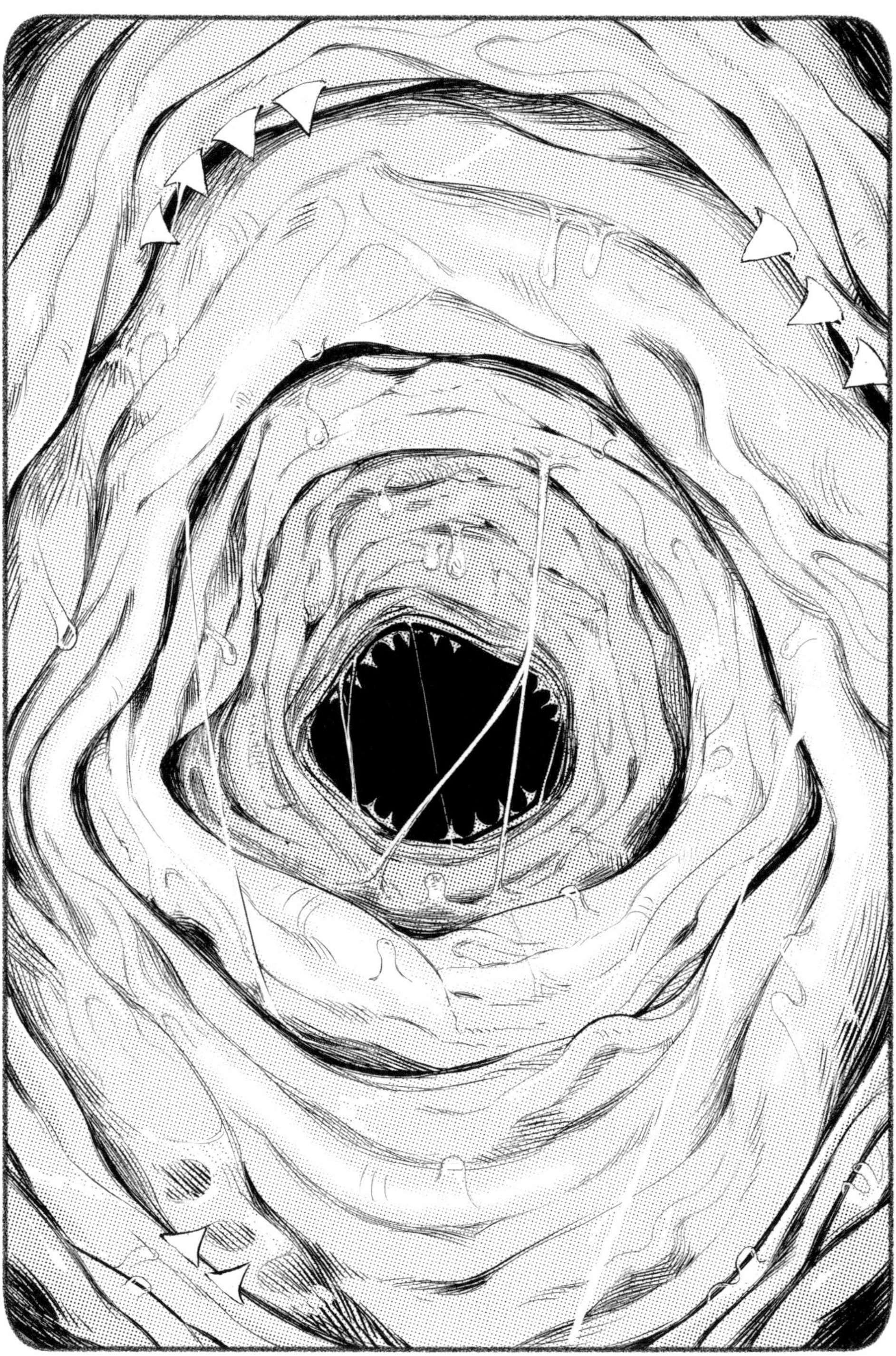

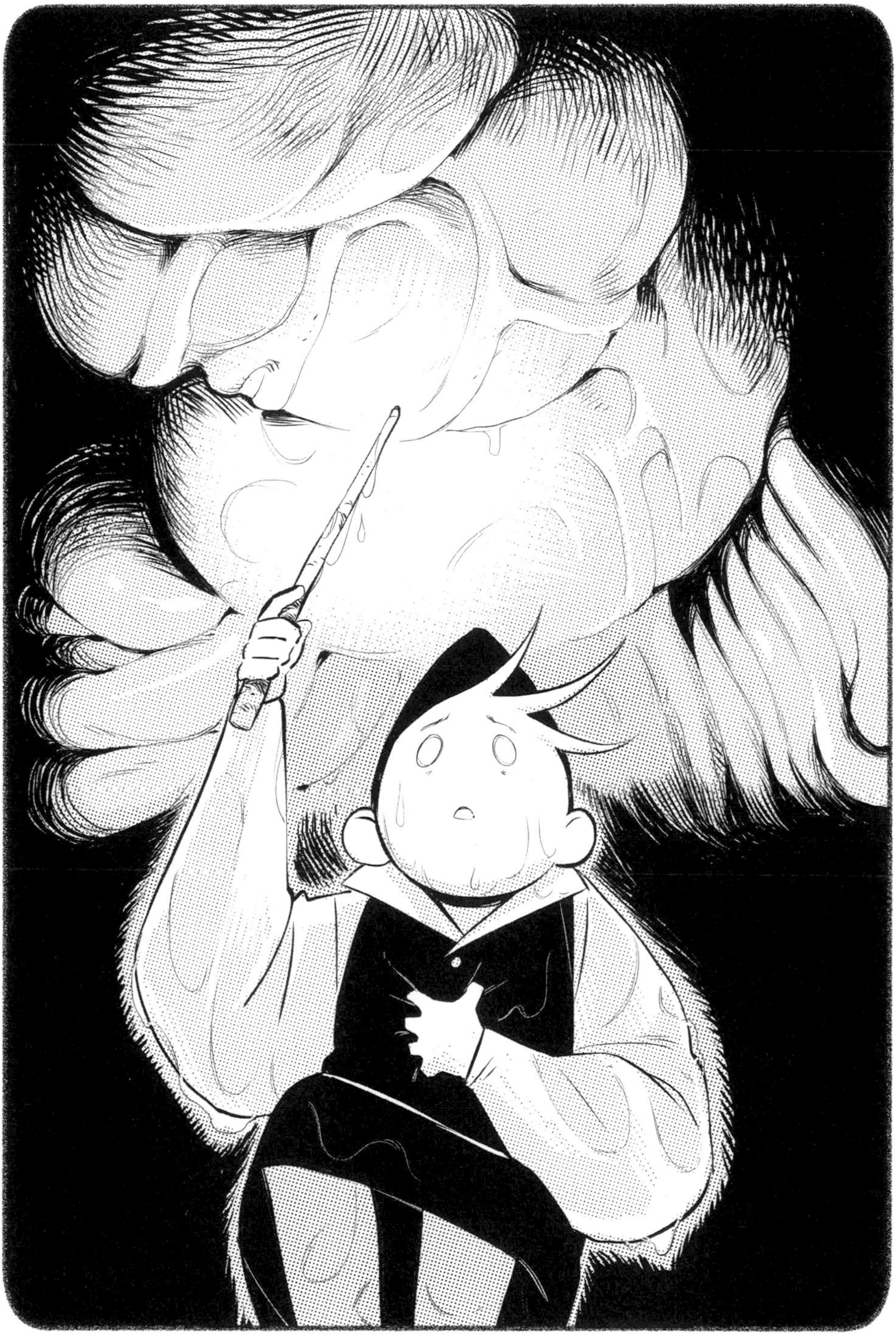

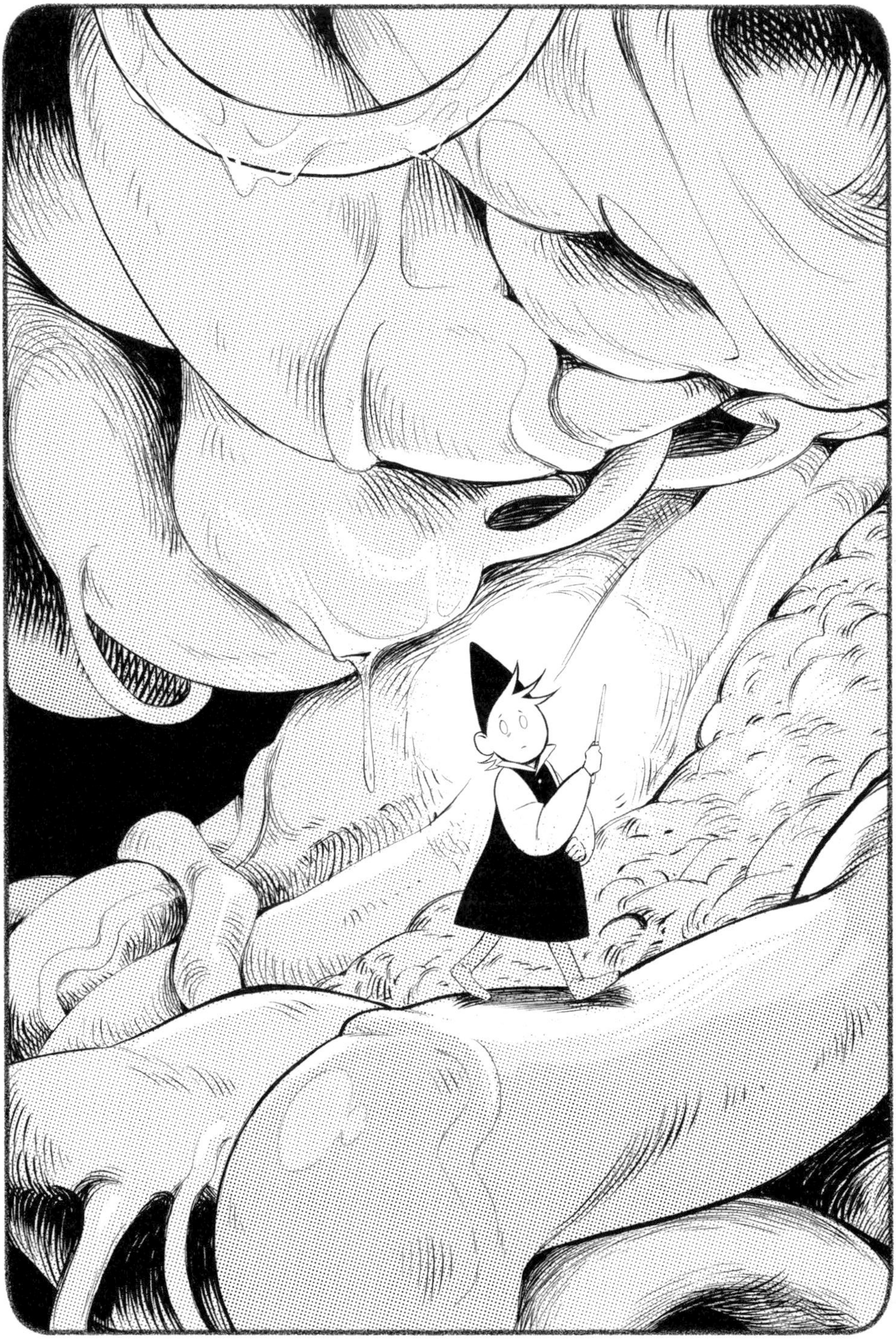

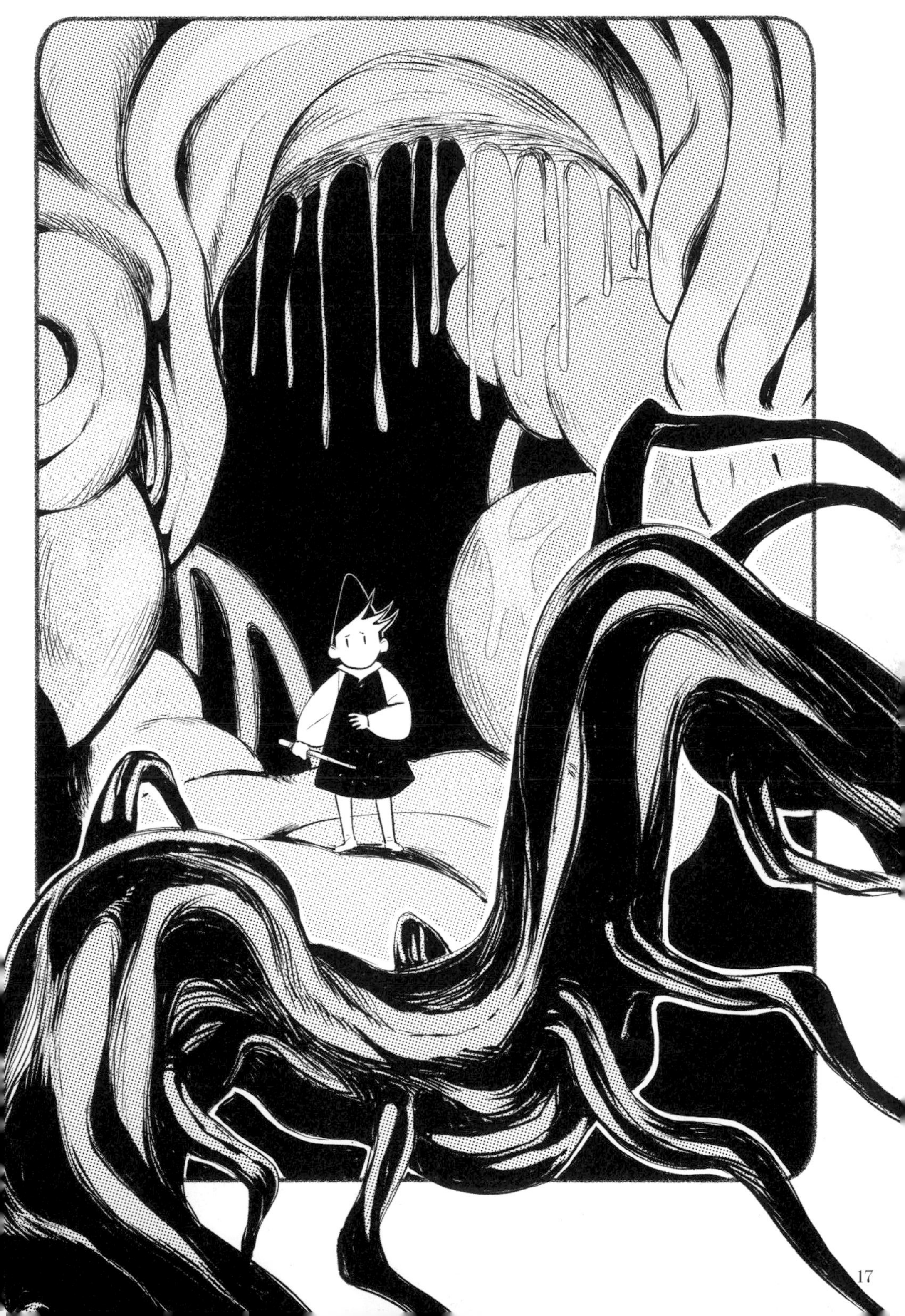

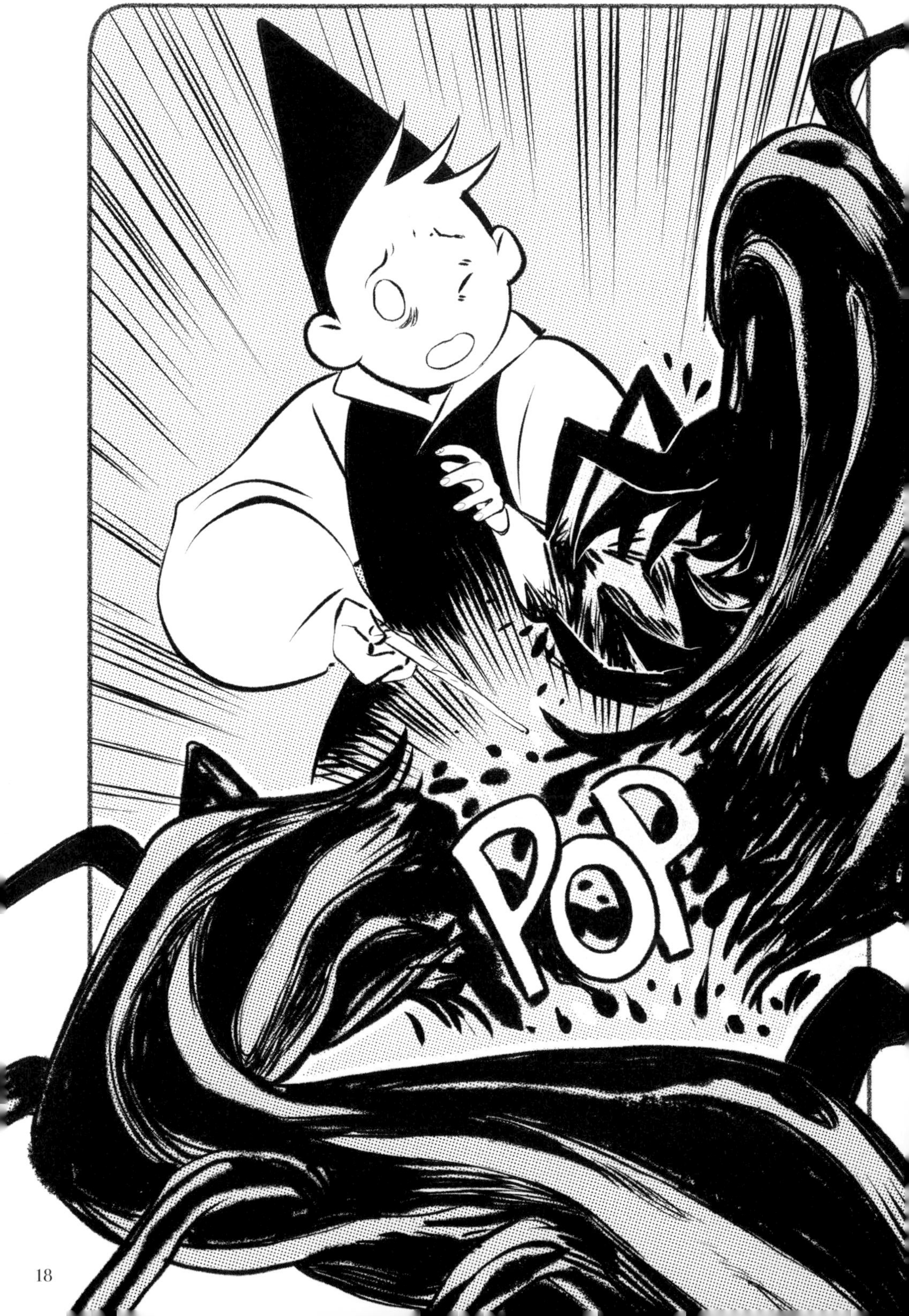
POP

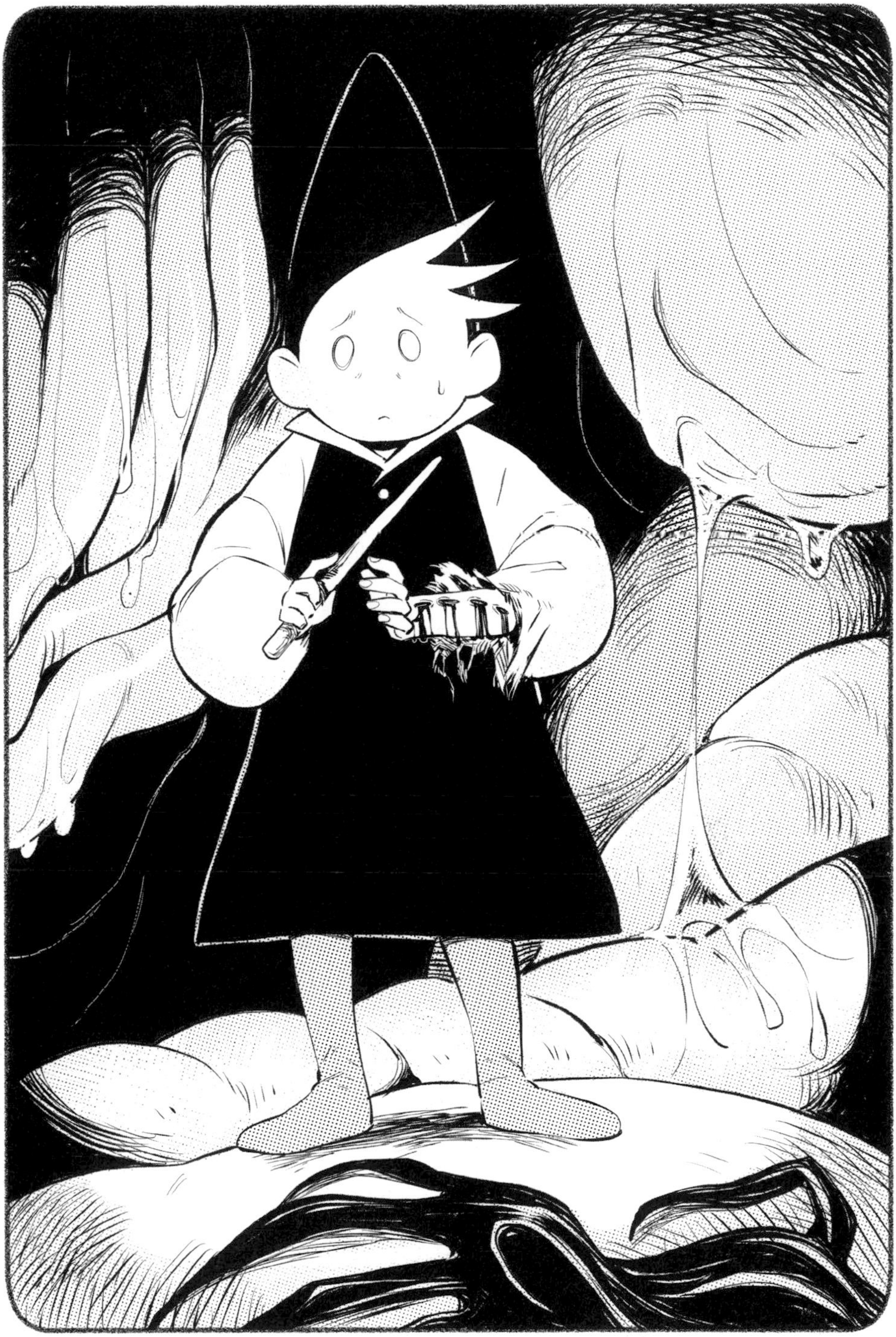

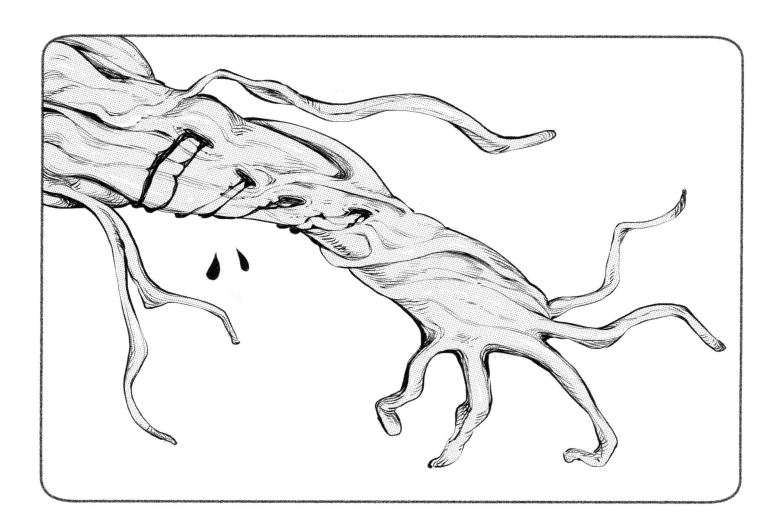

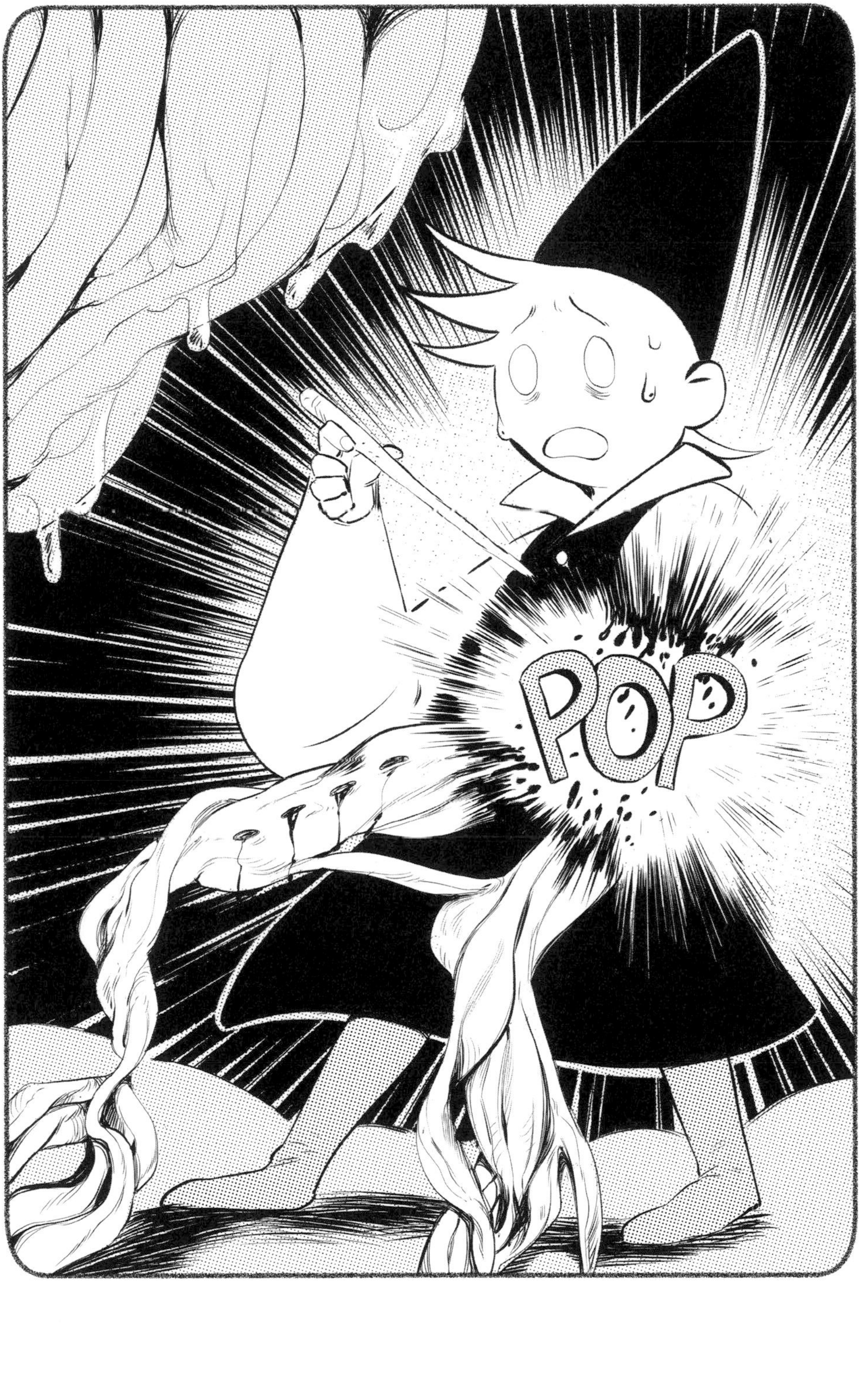
POP

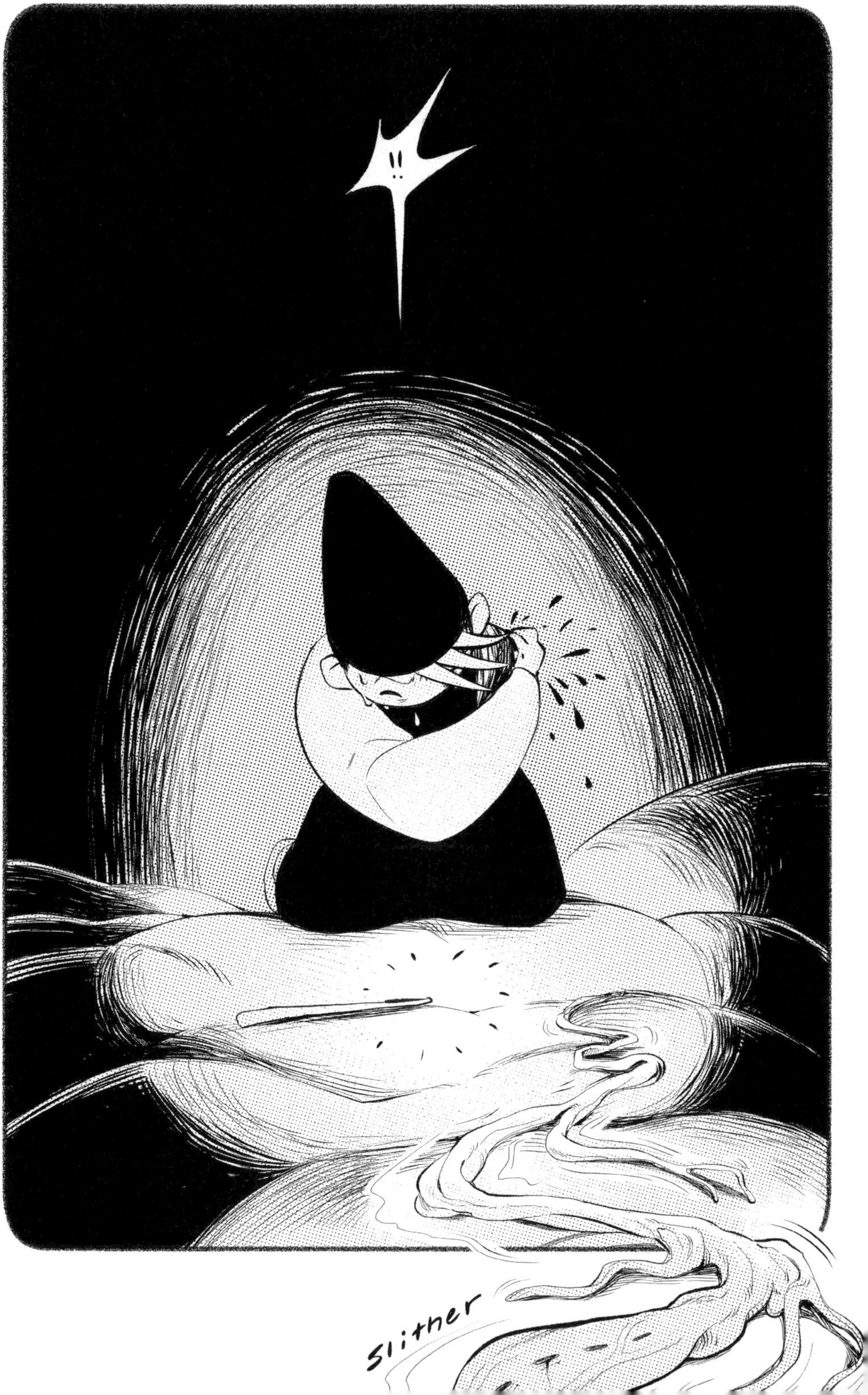
!!
slither

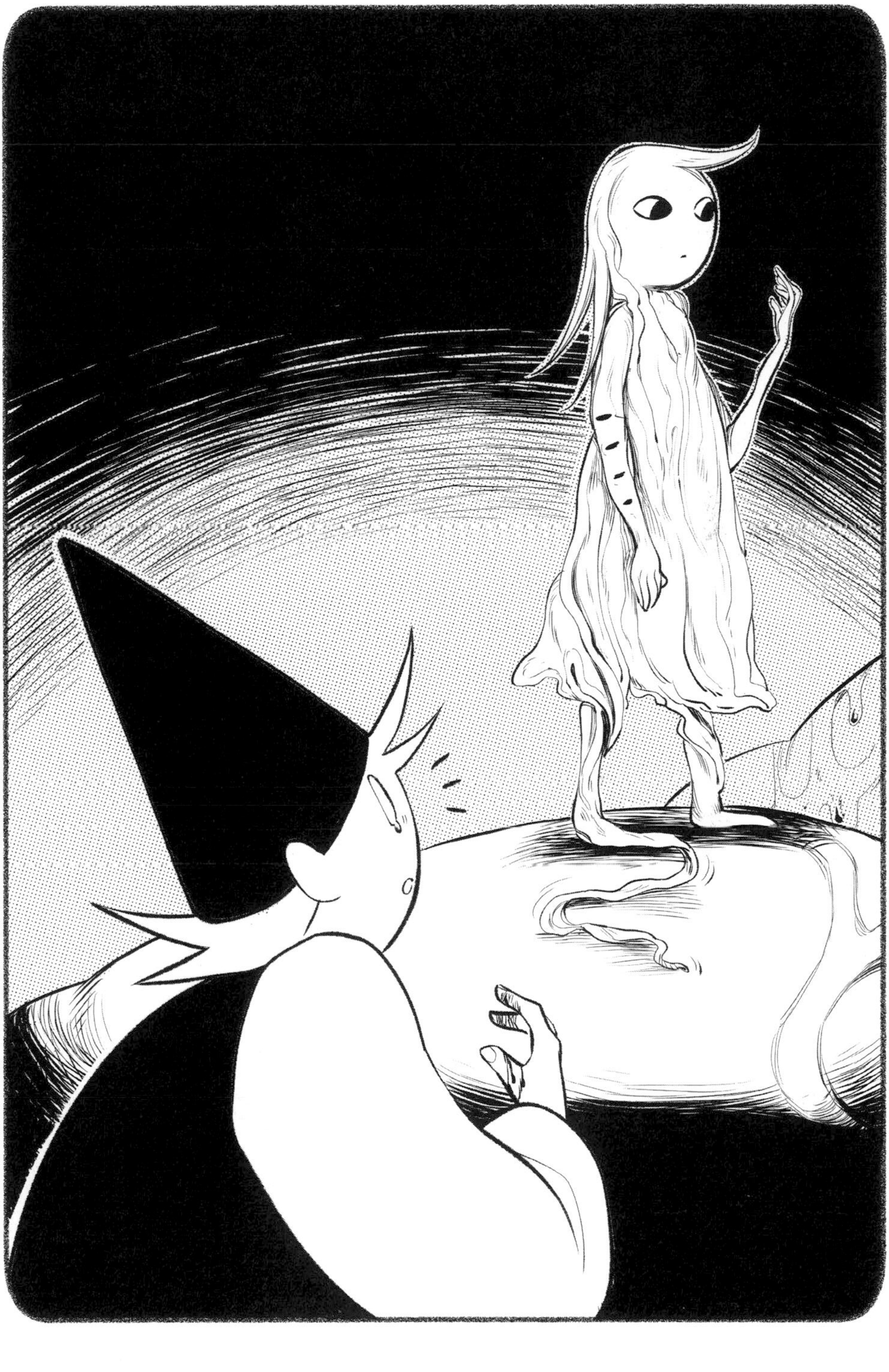

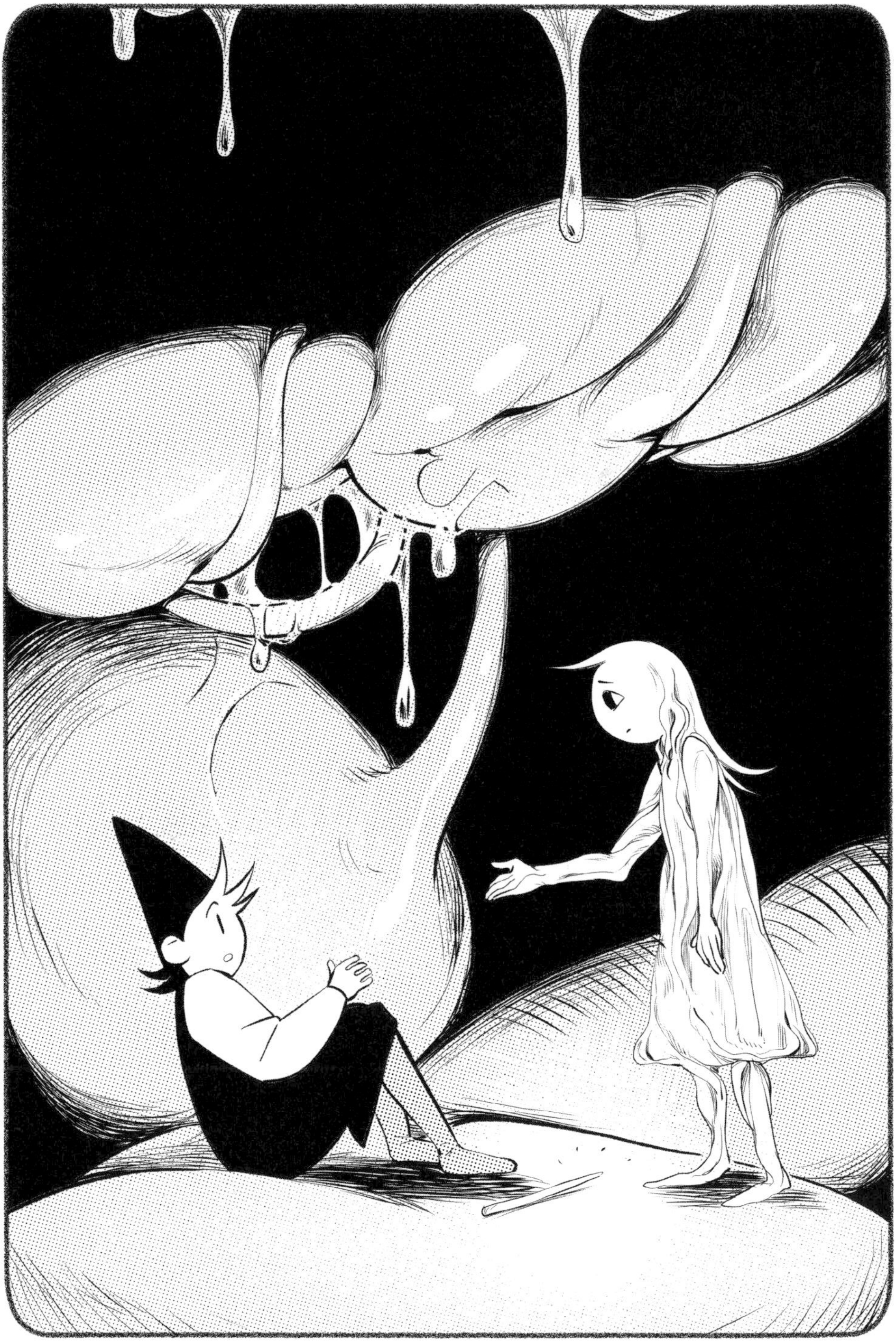

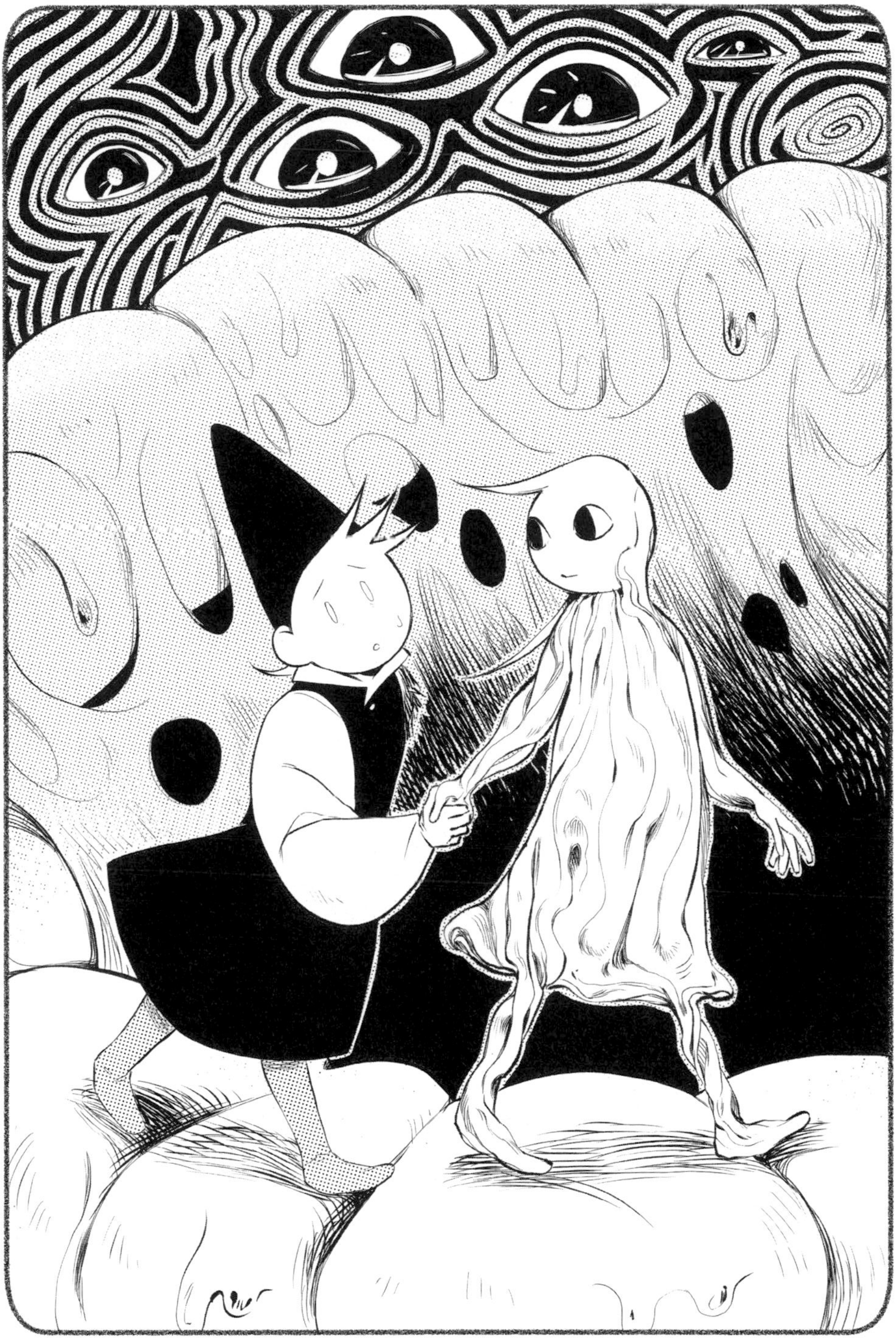

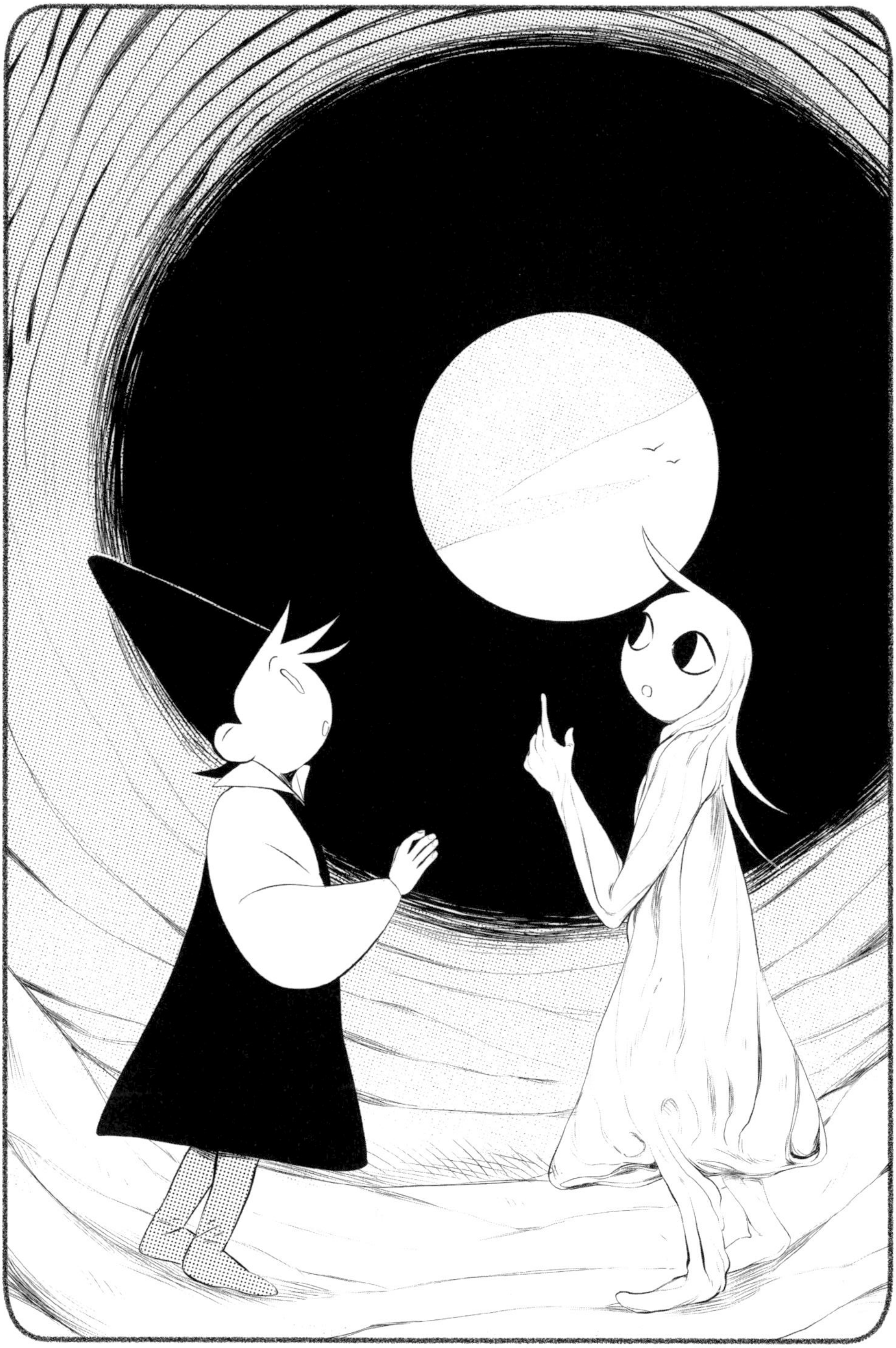

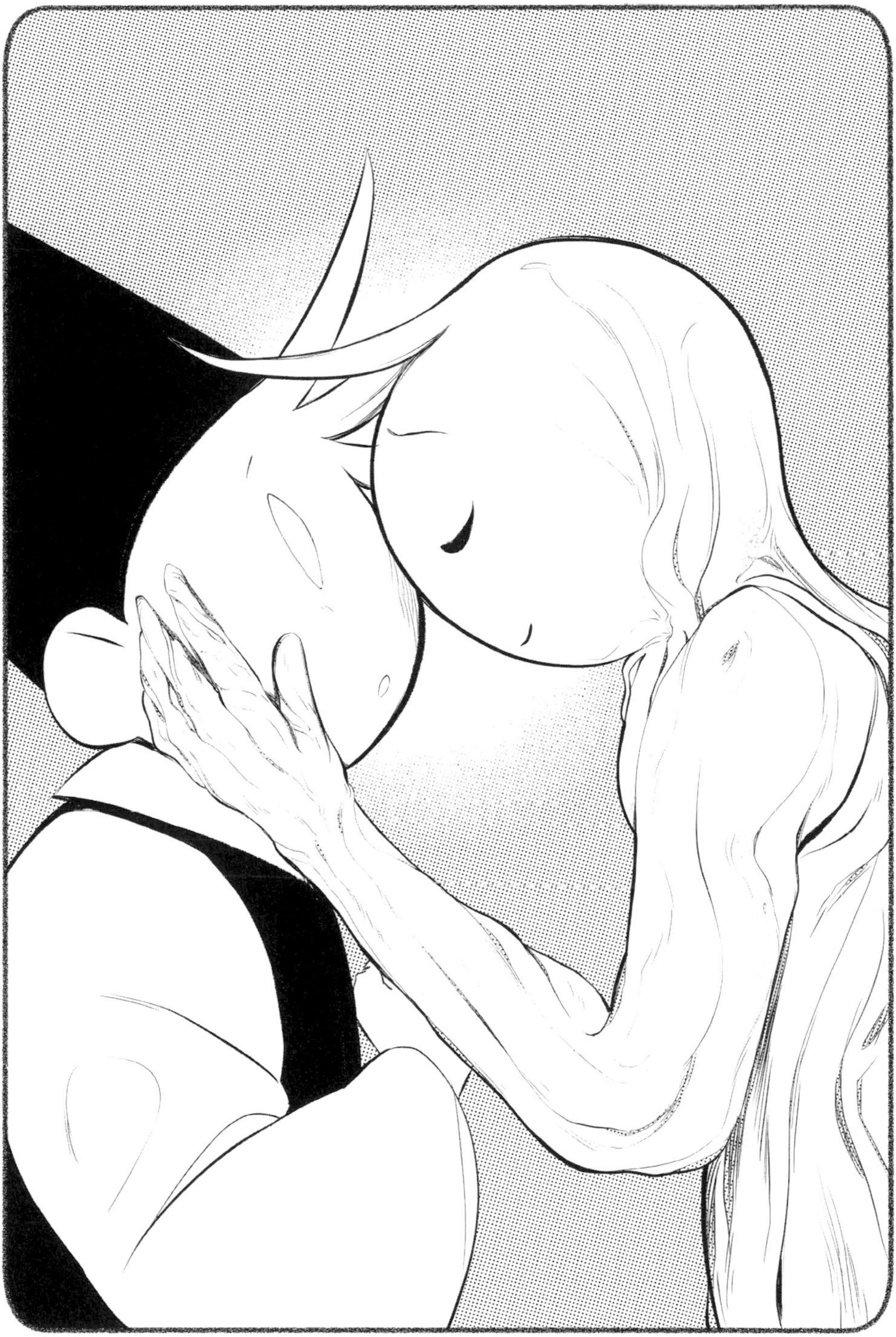

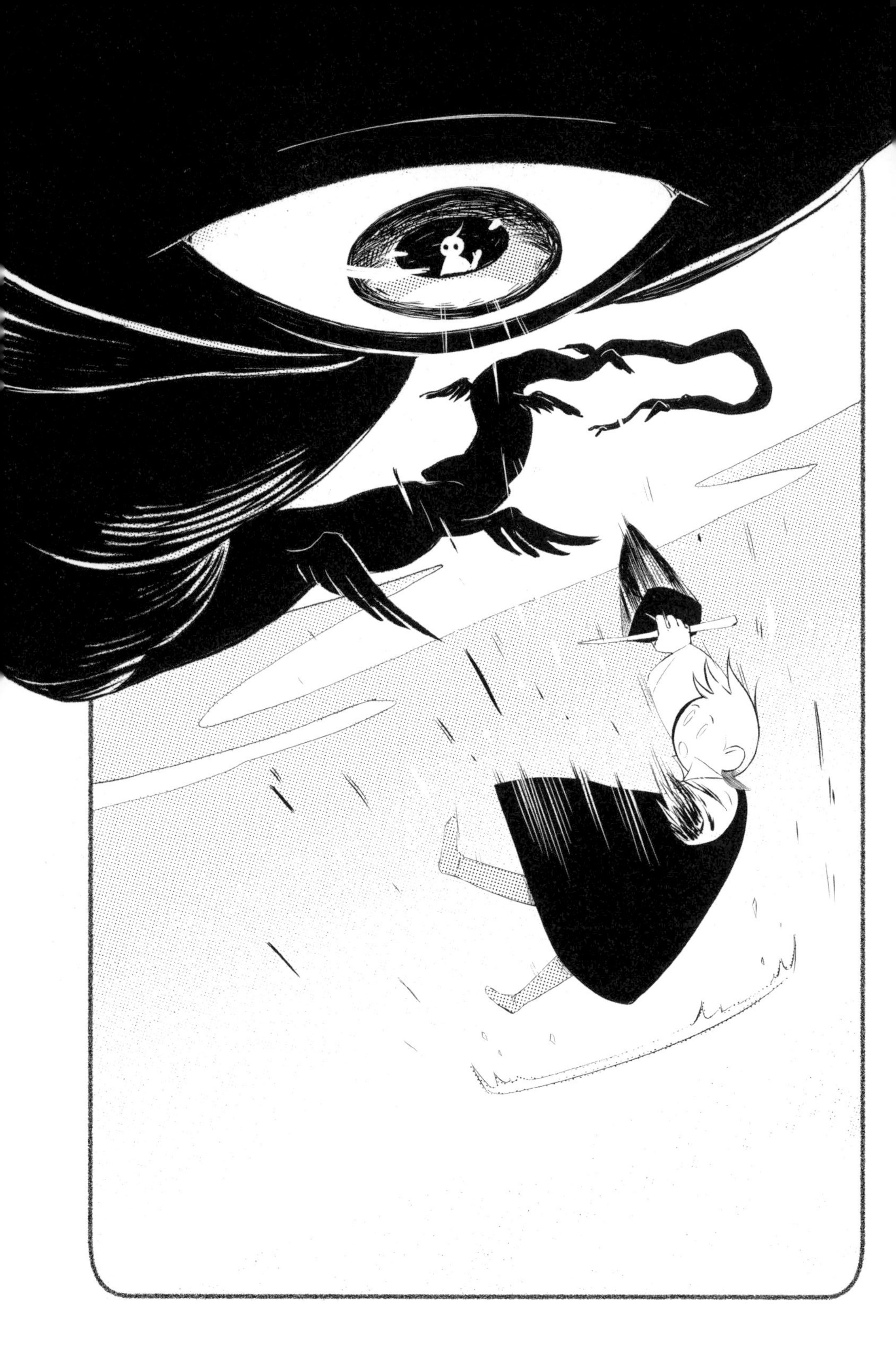

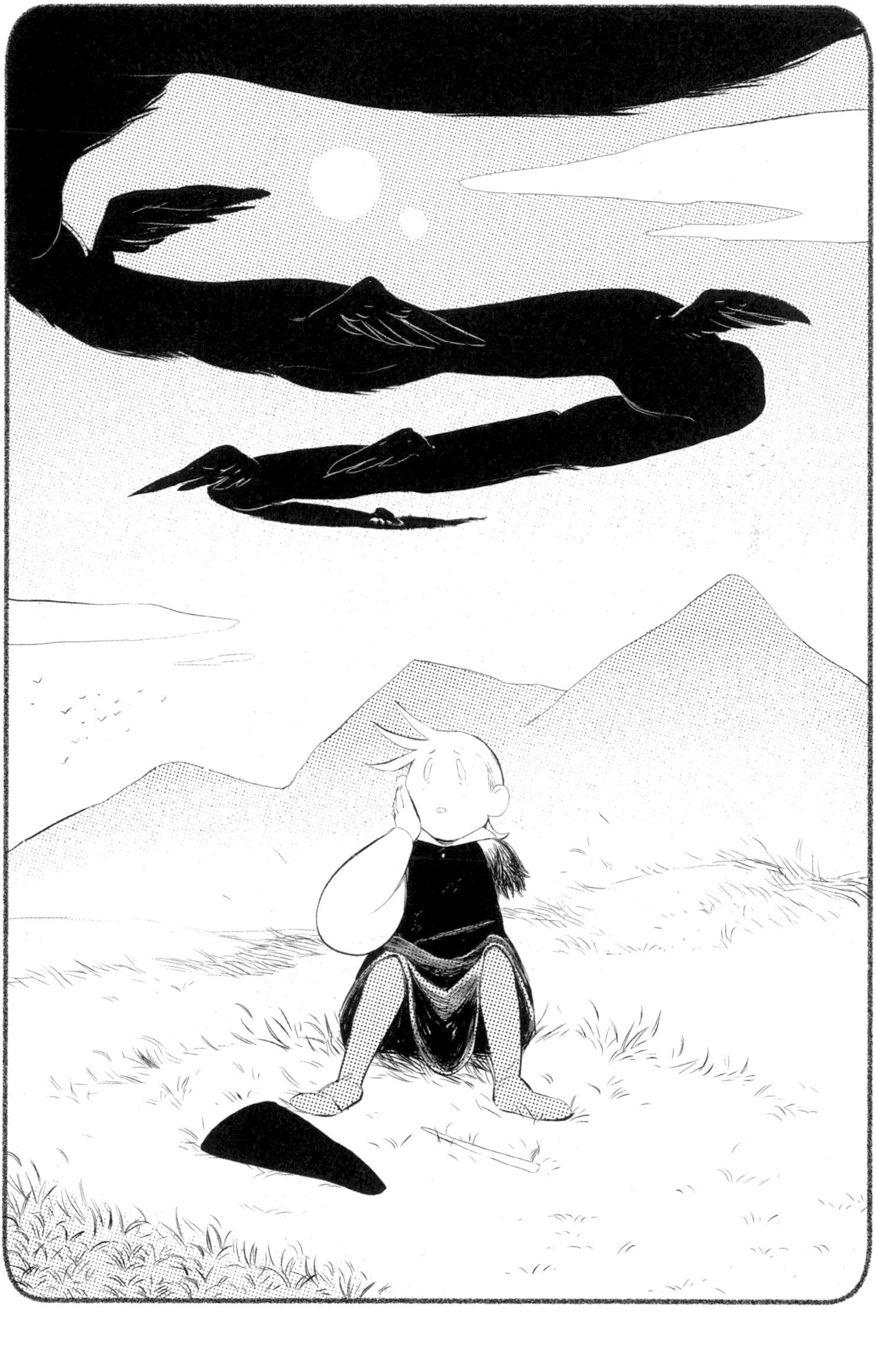

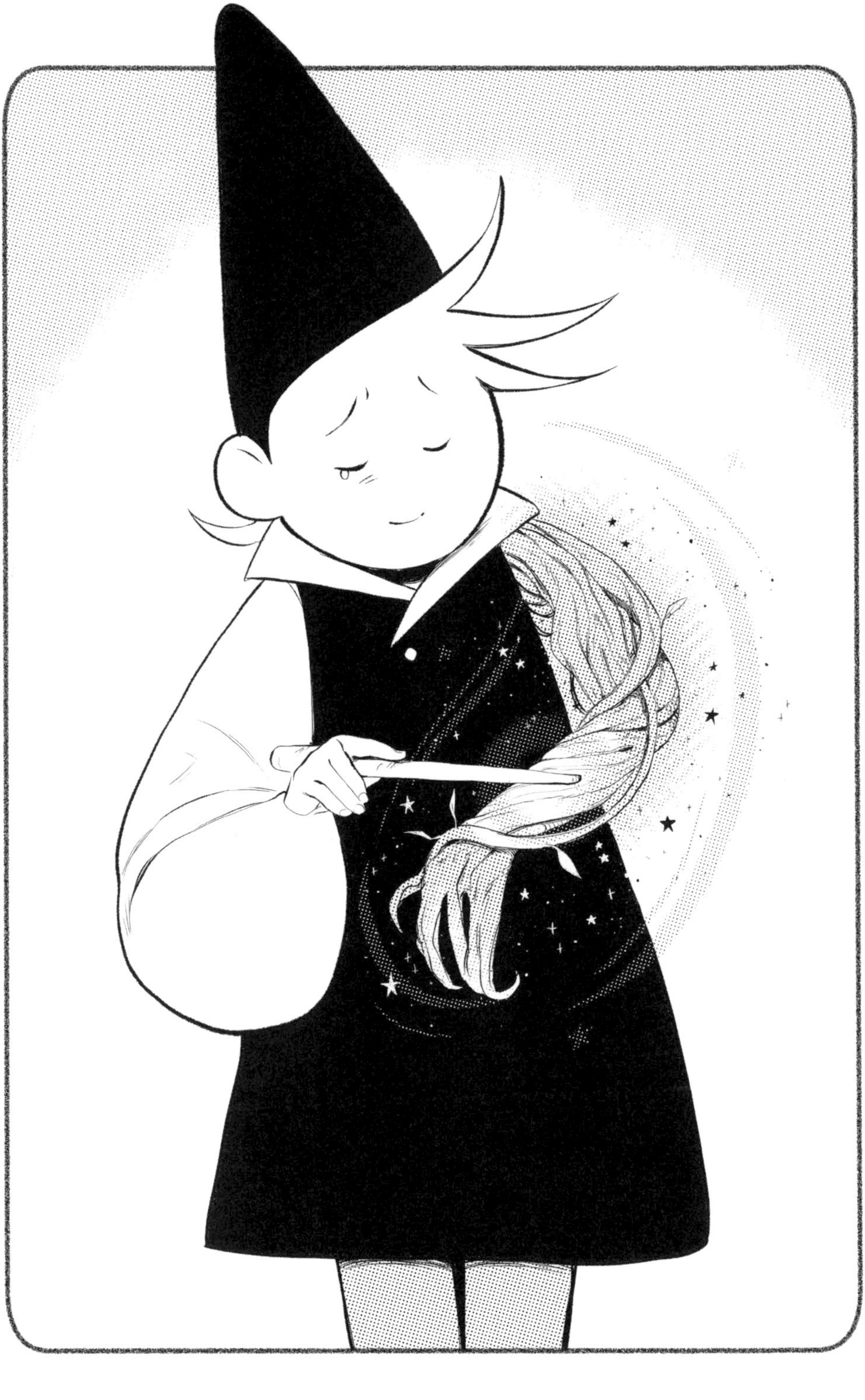

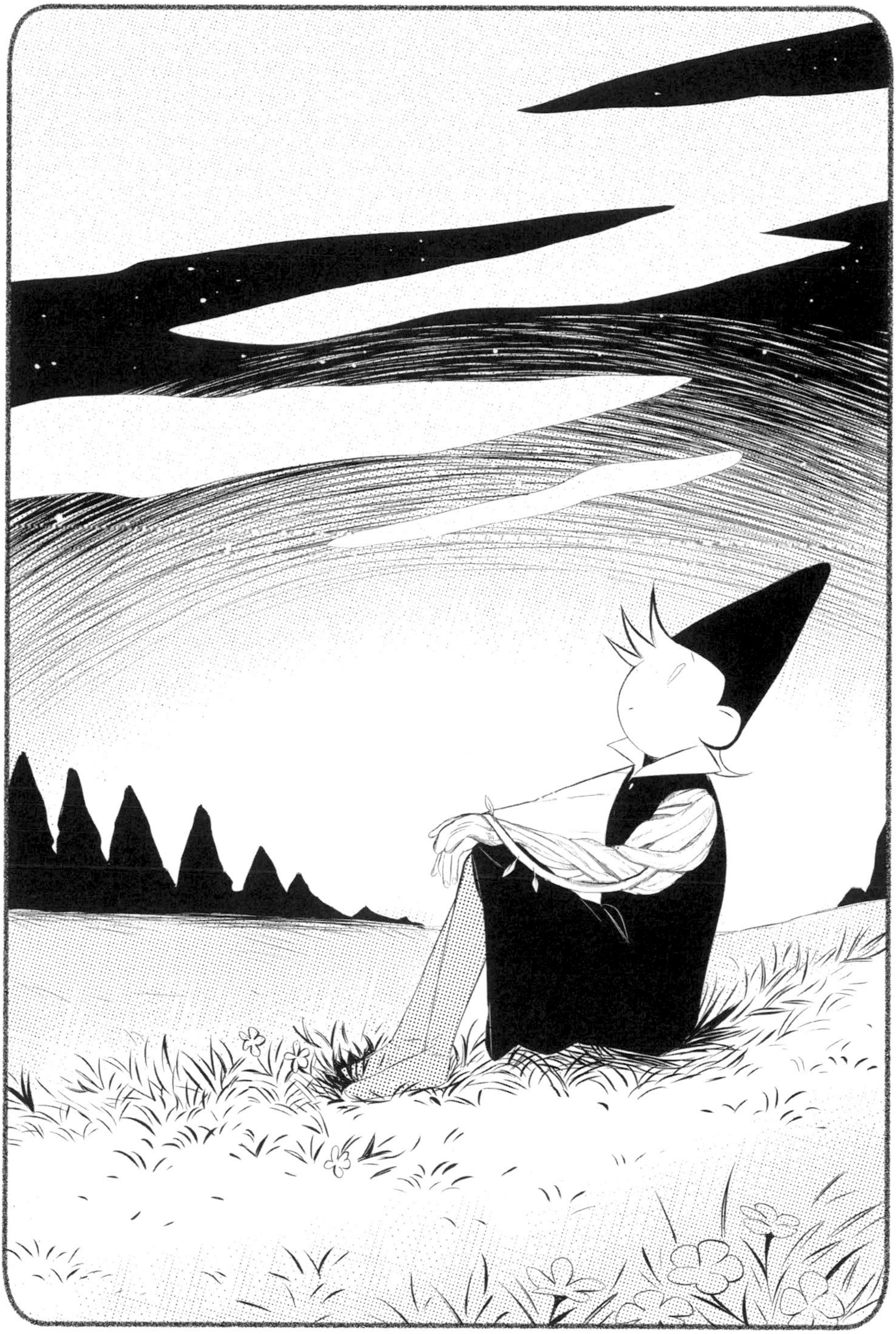

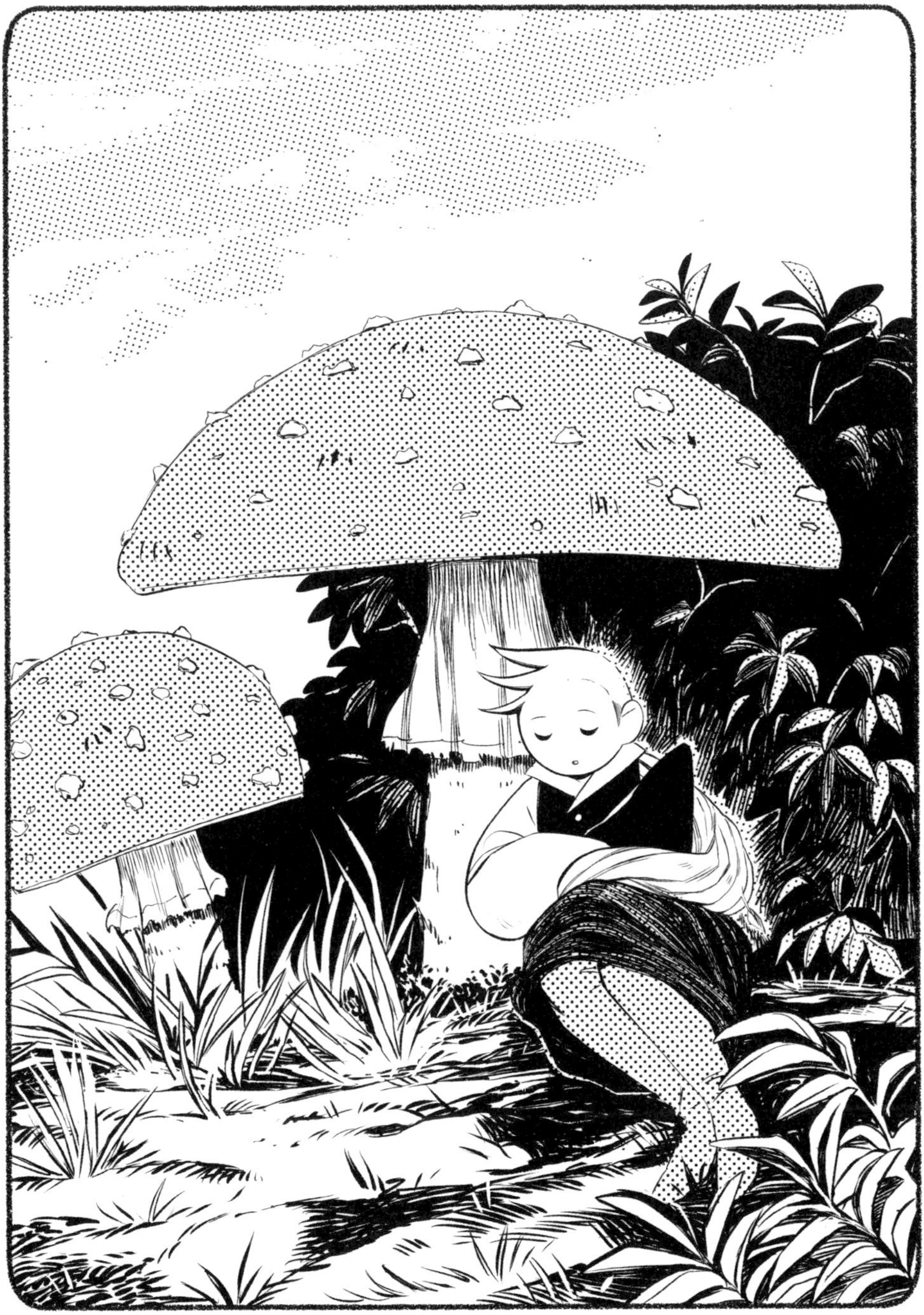

PART TWO

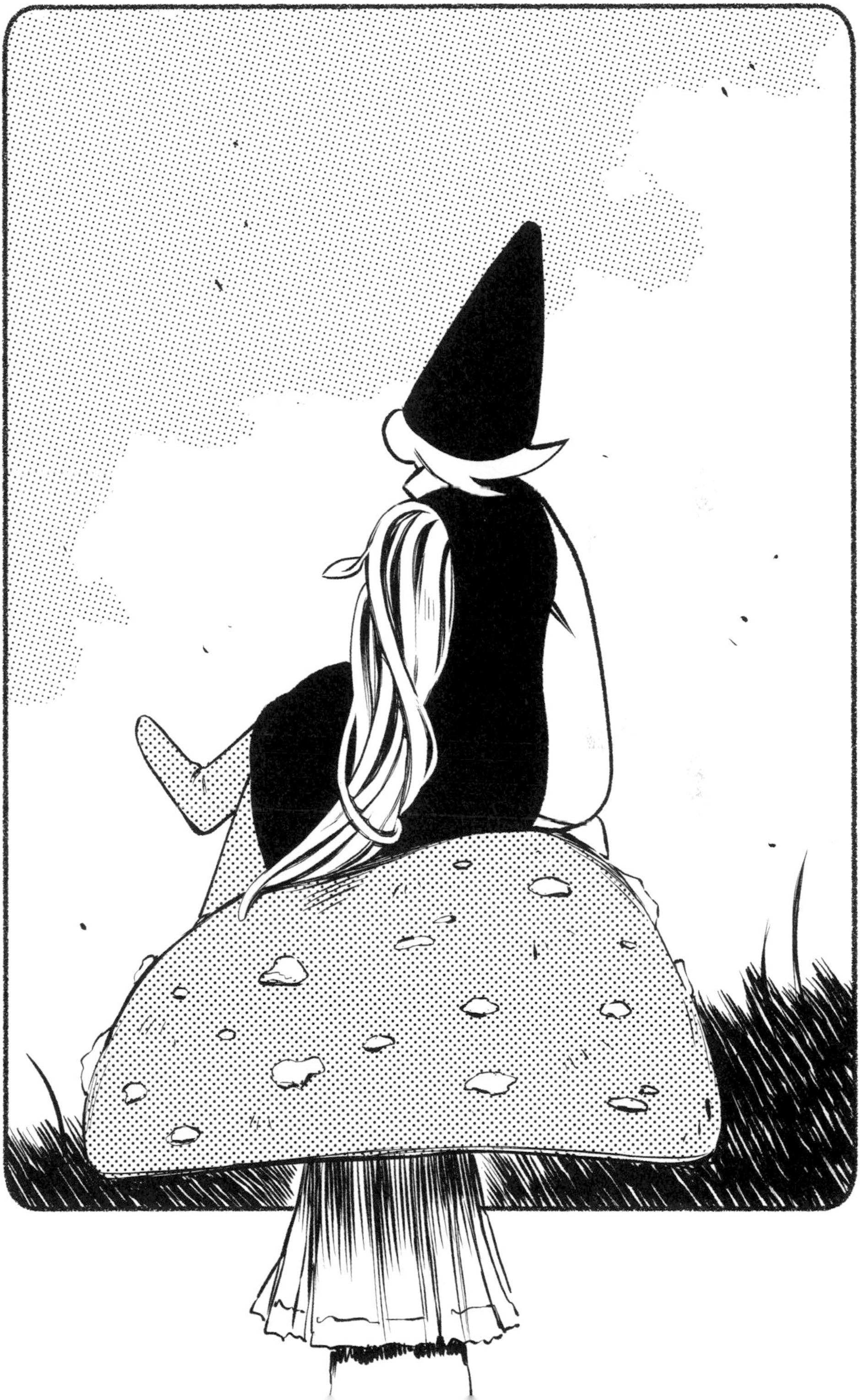

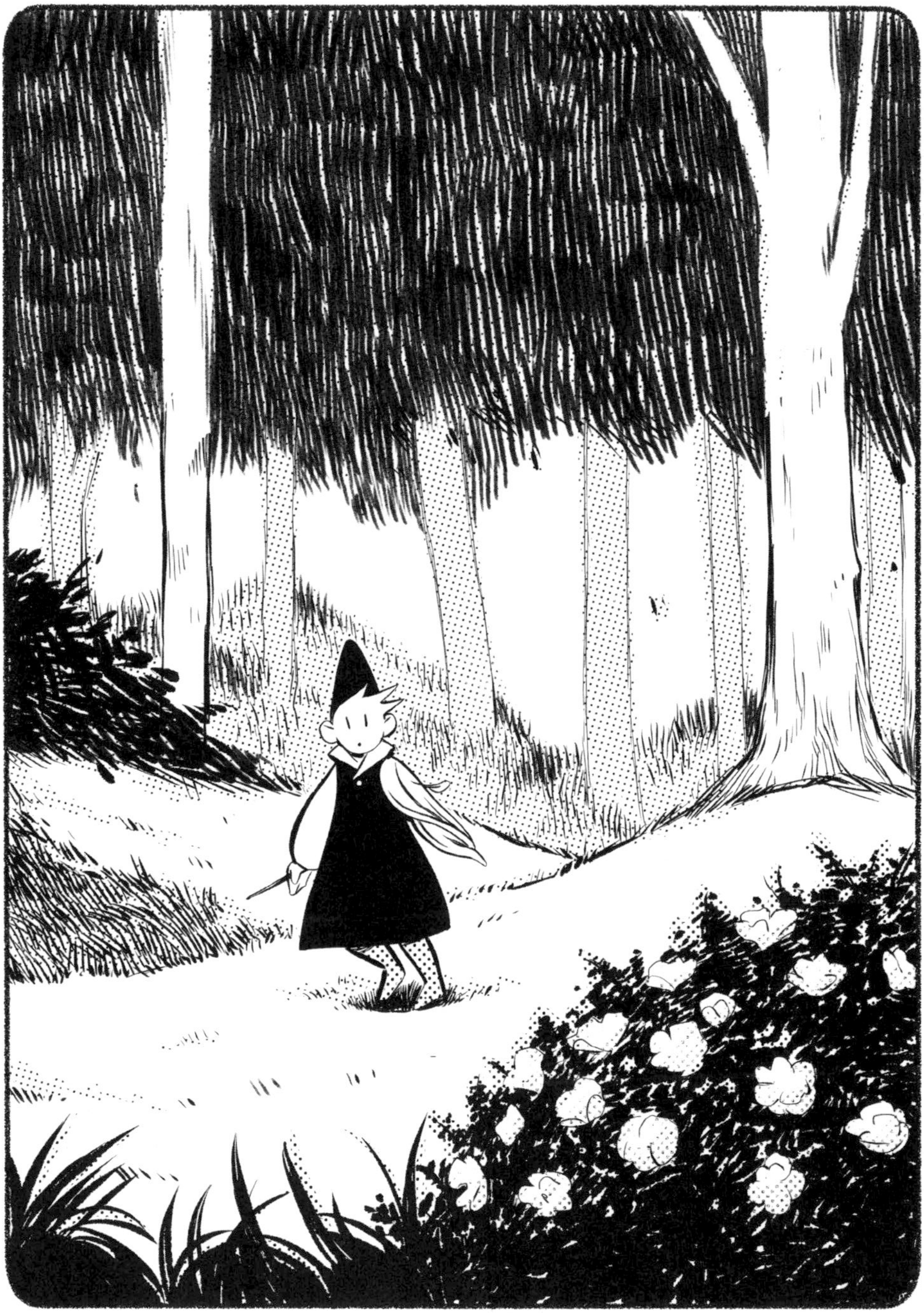

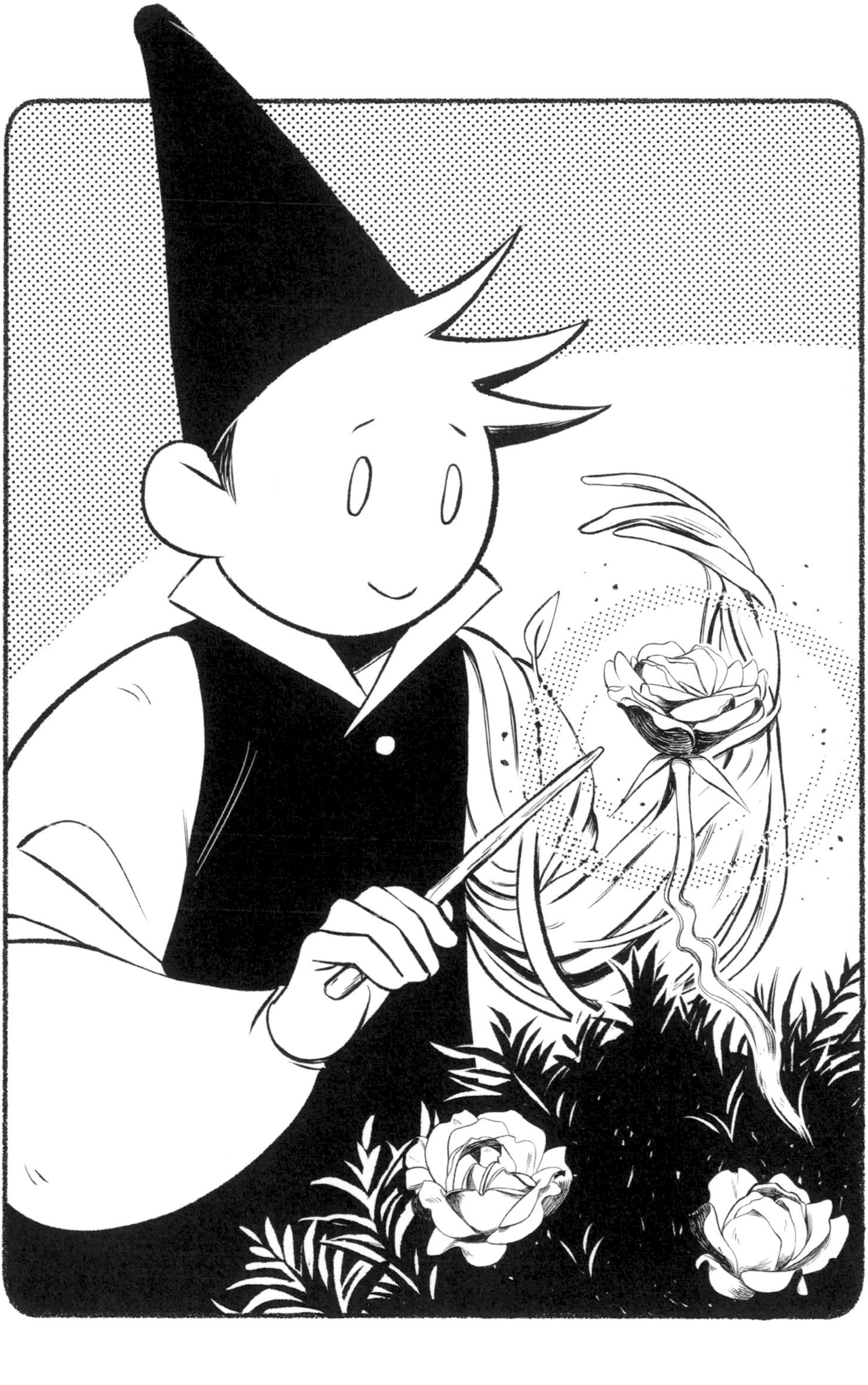

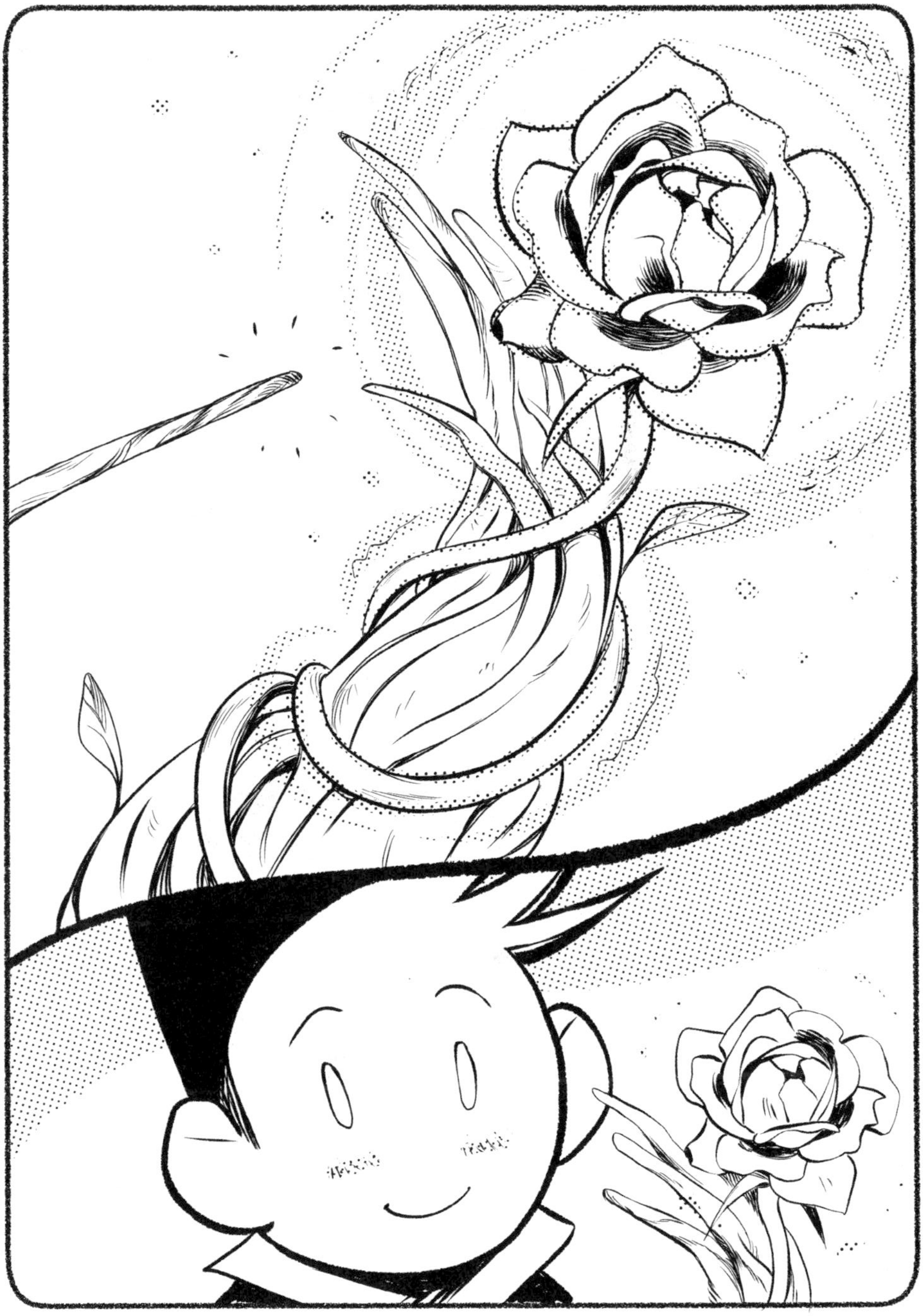

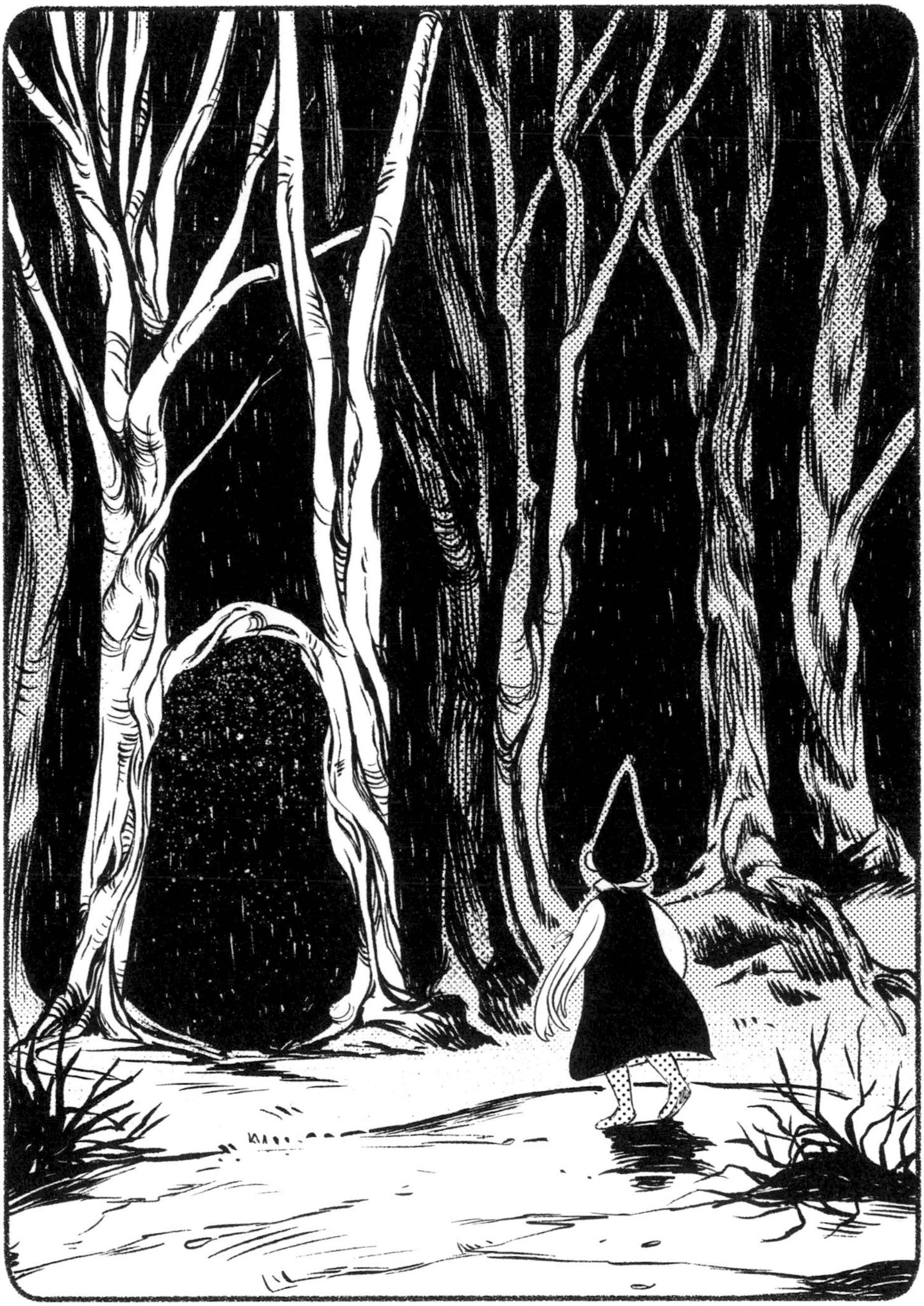

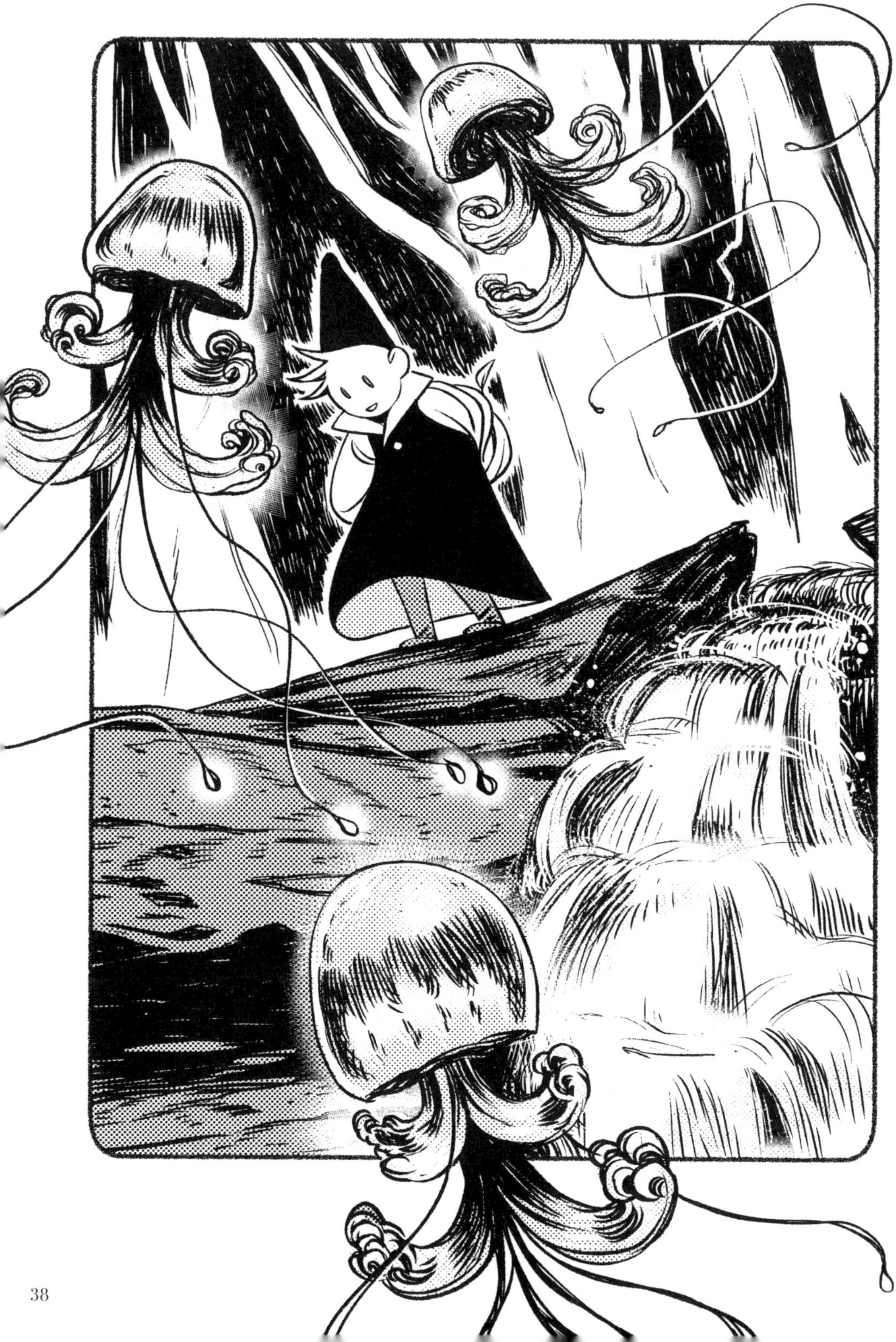

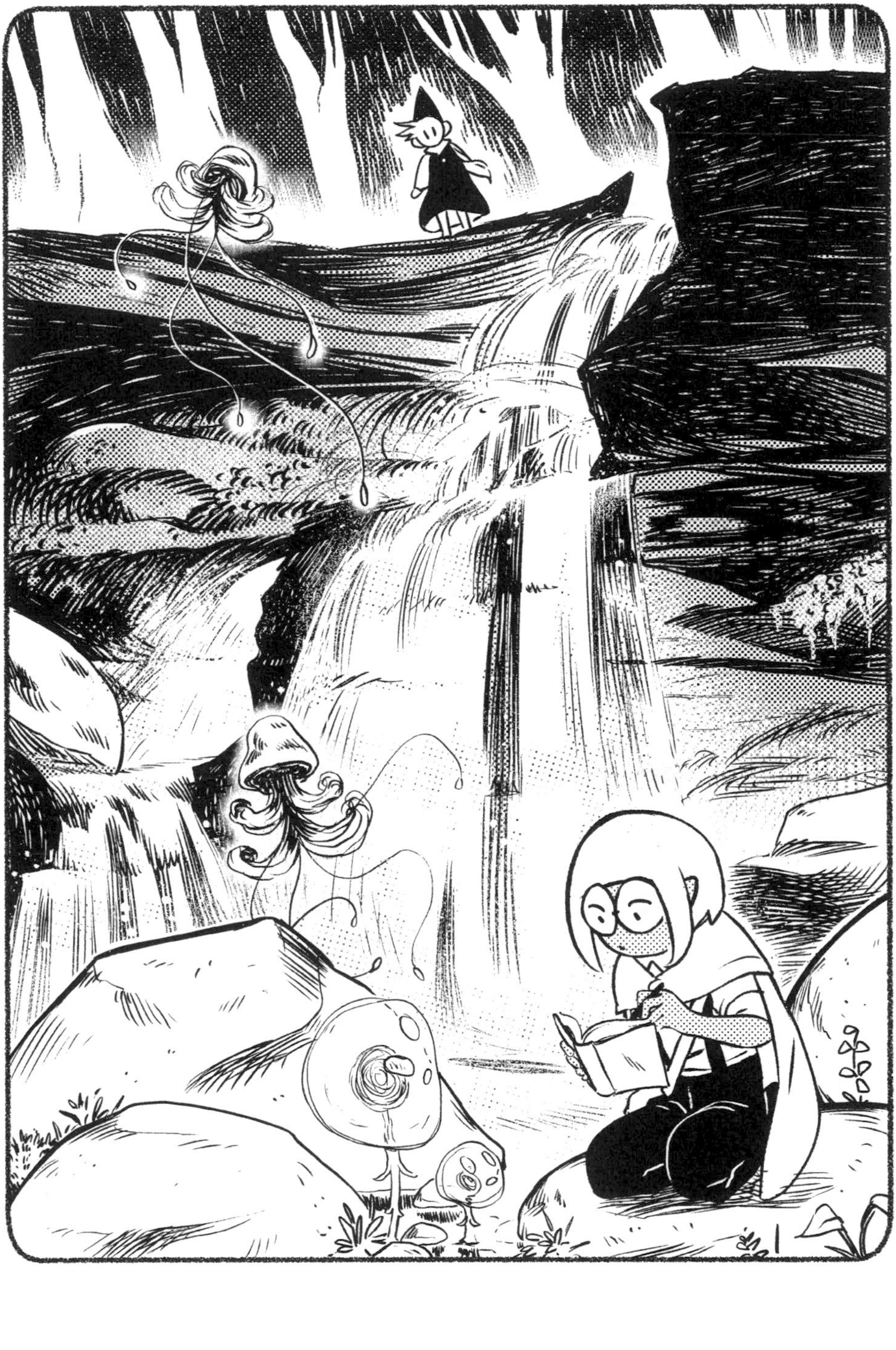

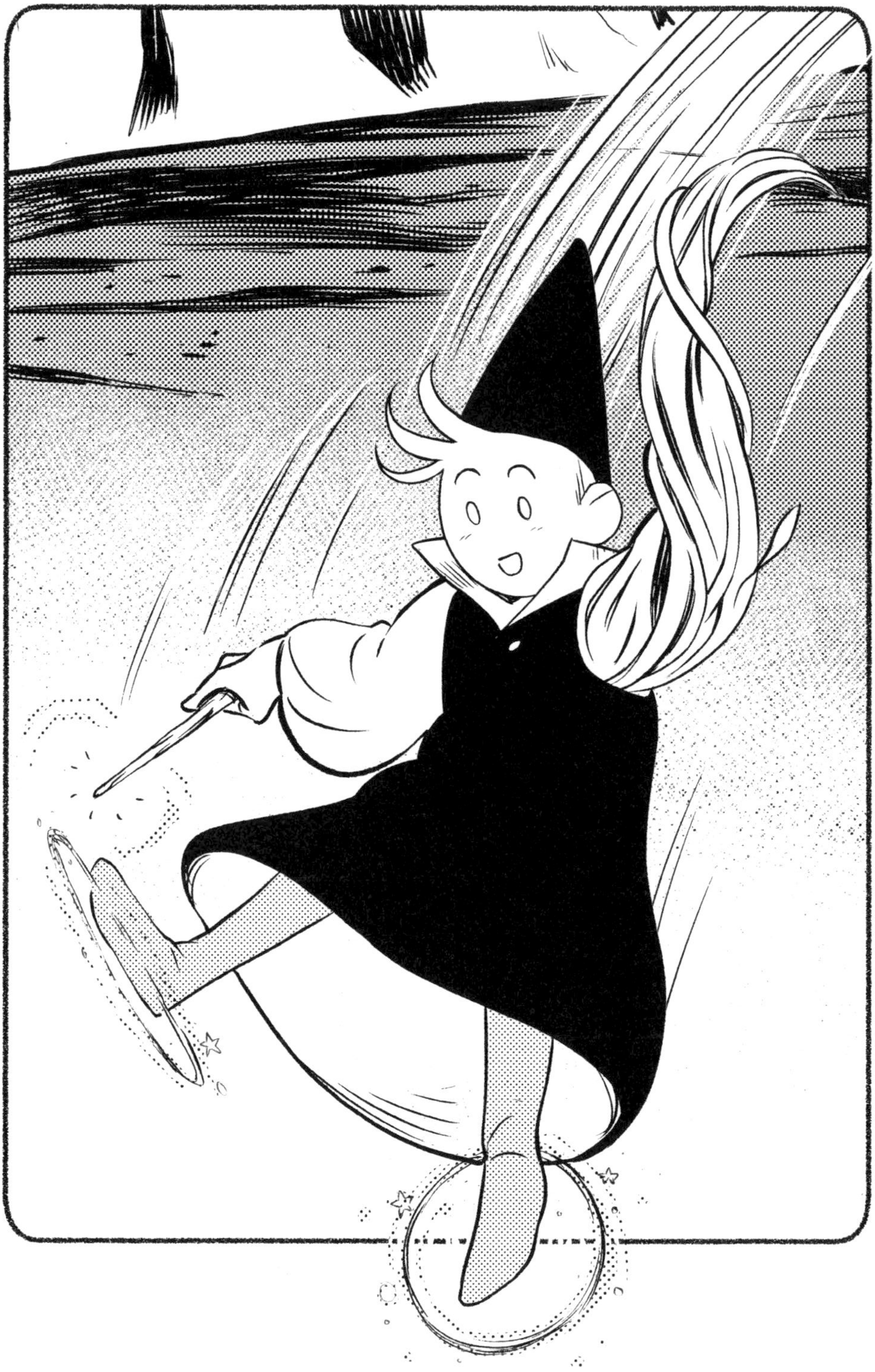

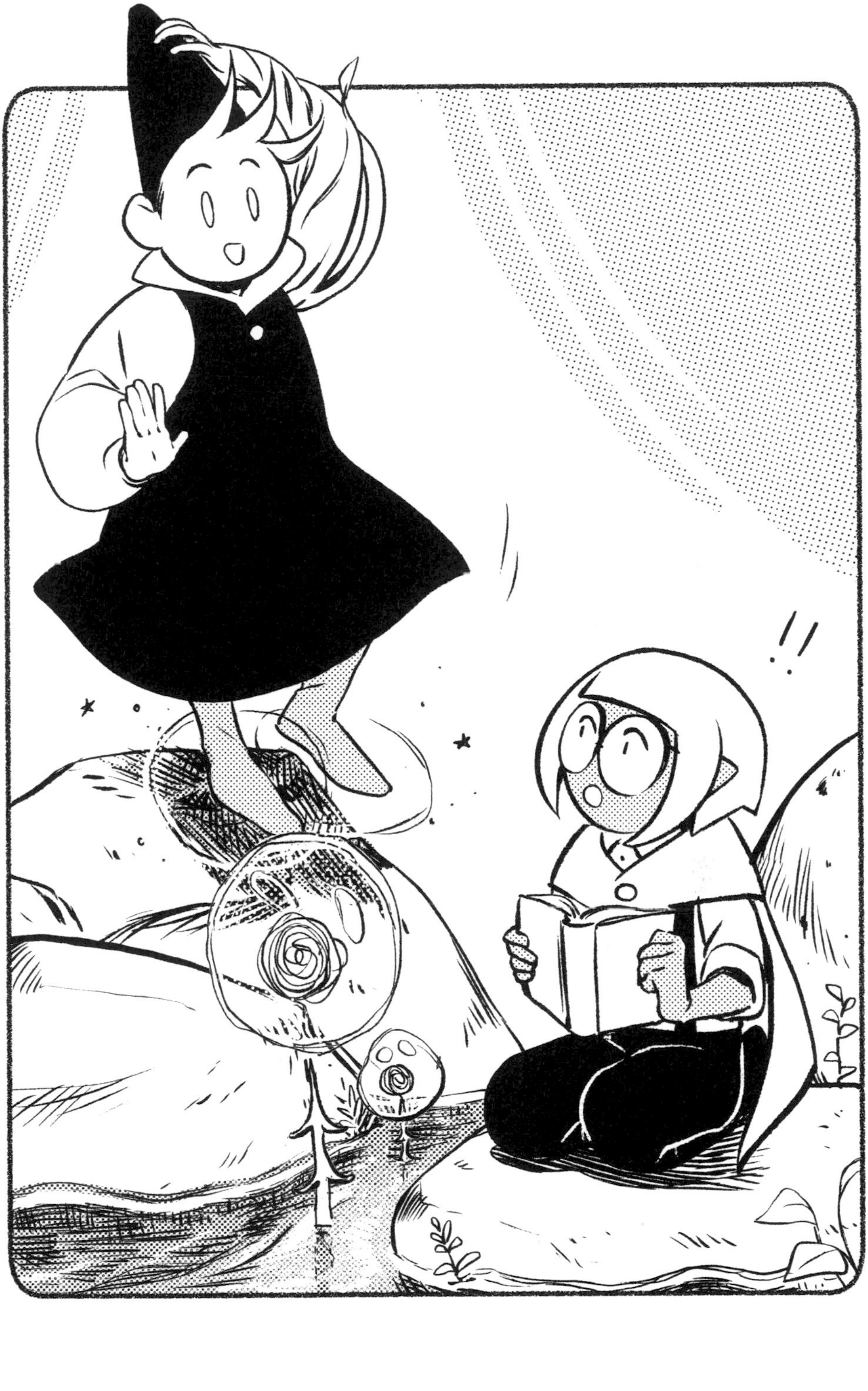
!!

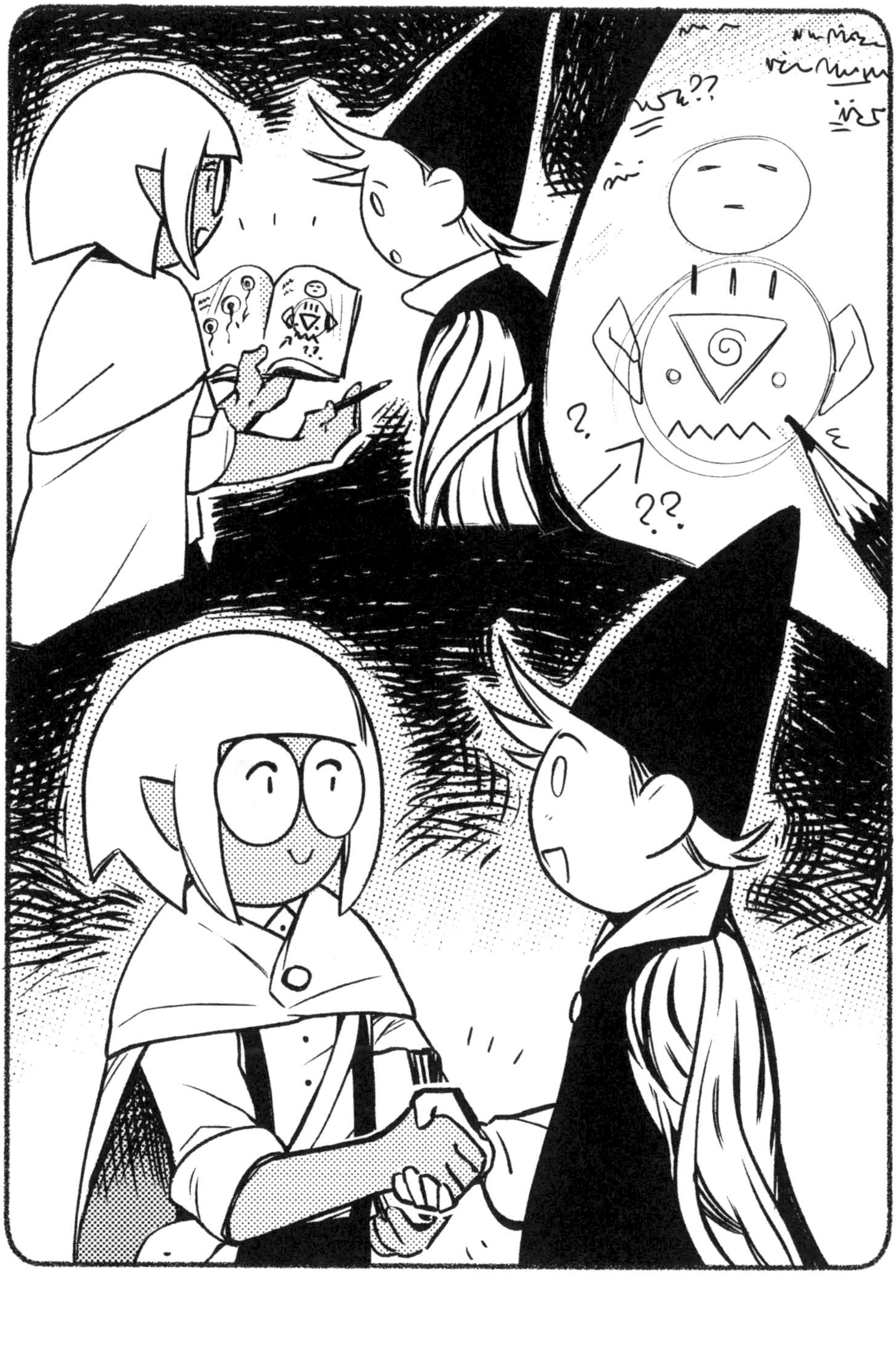
?
??

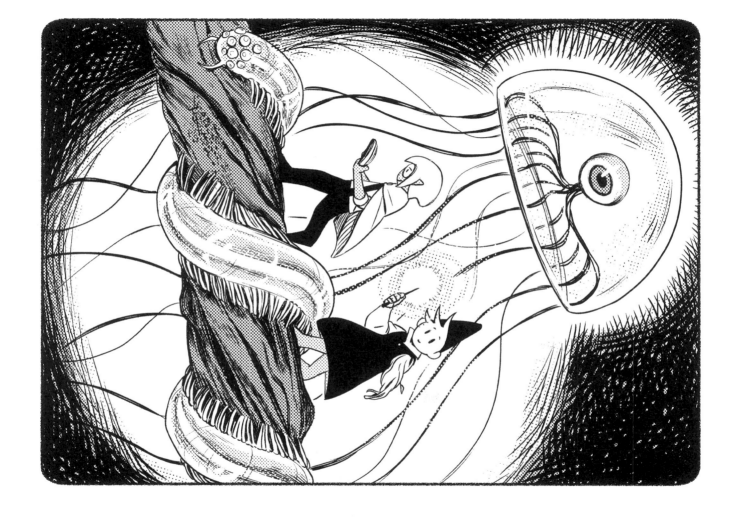

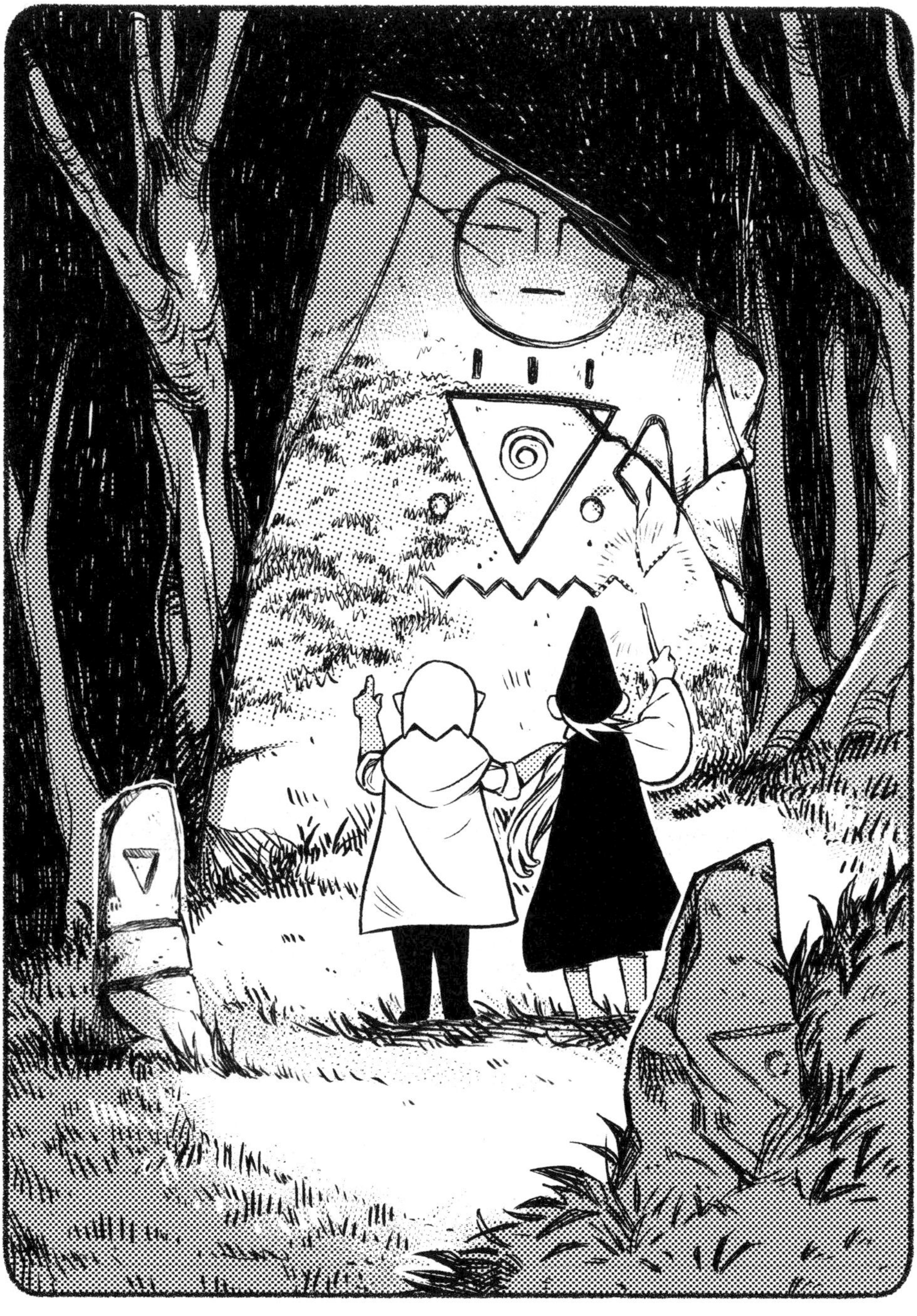

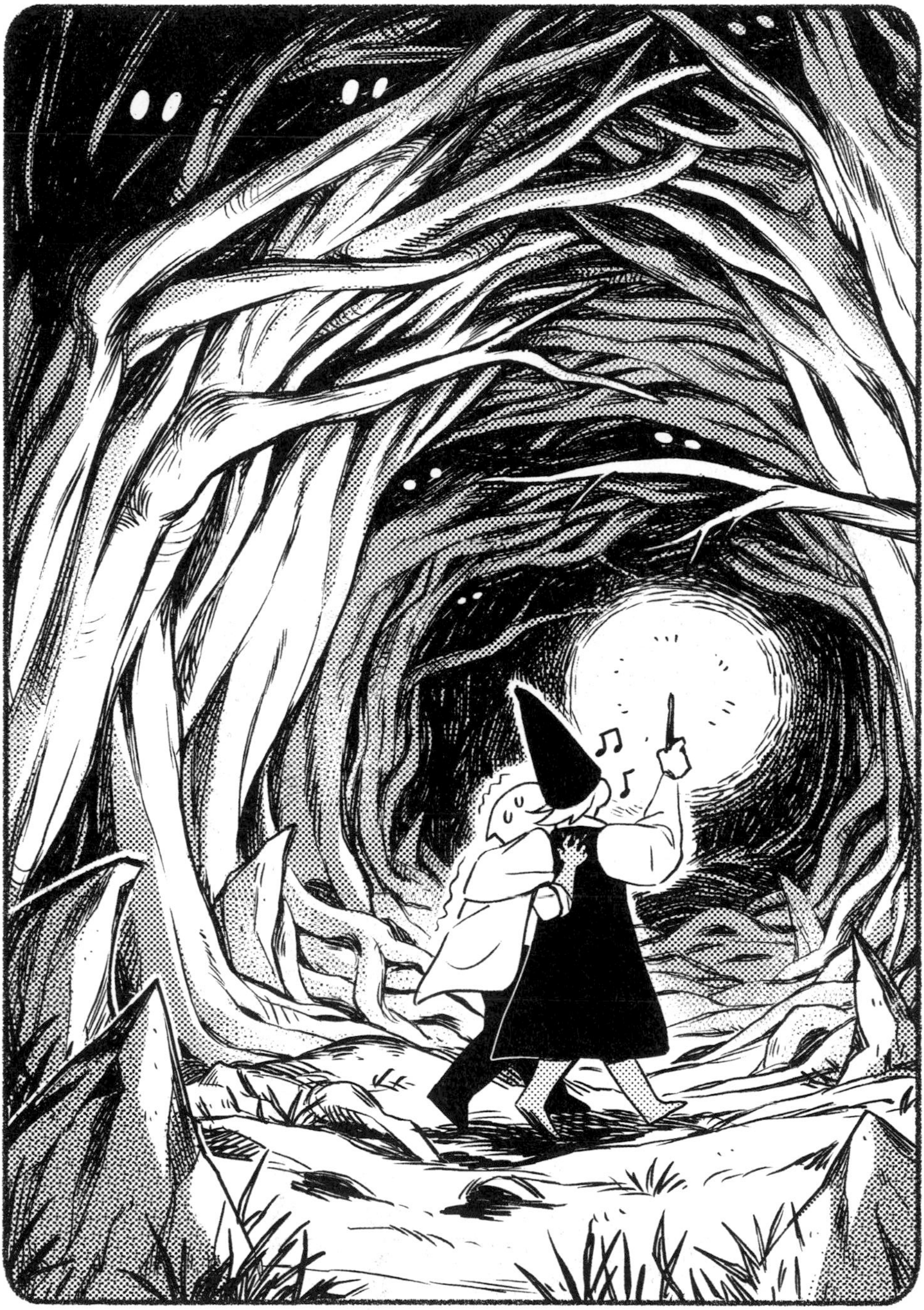

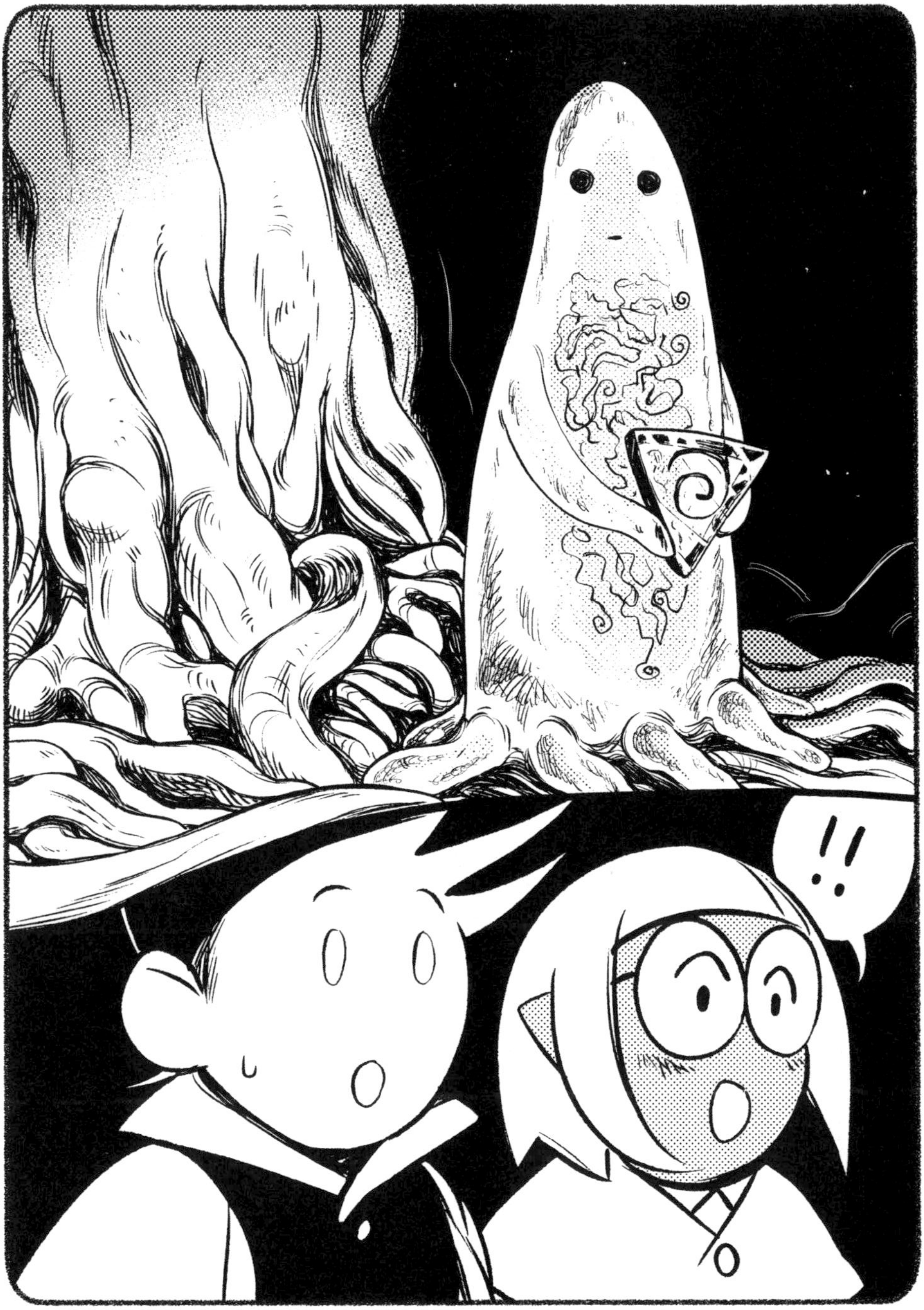
!!

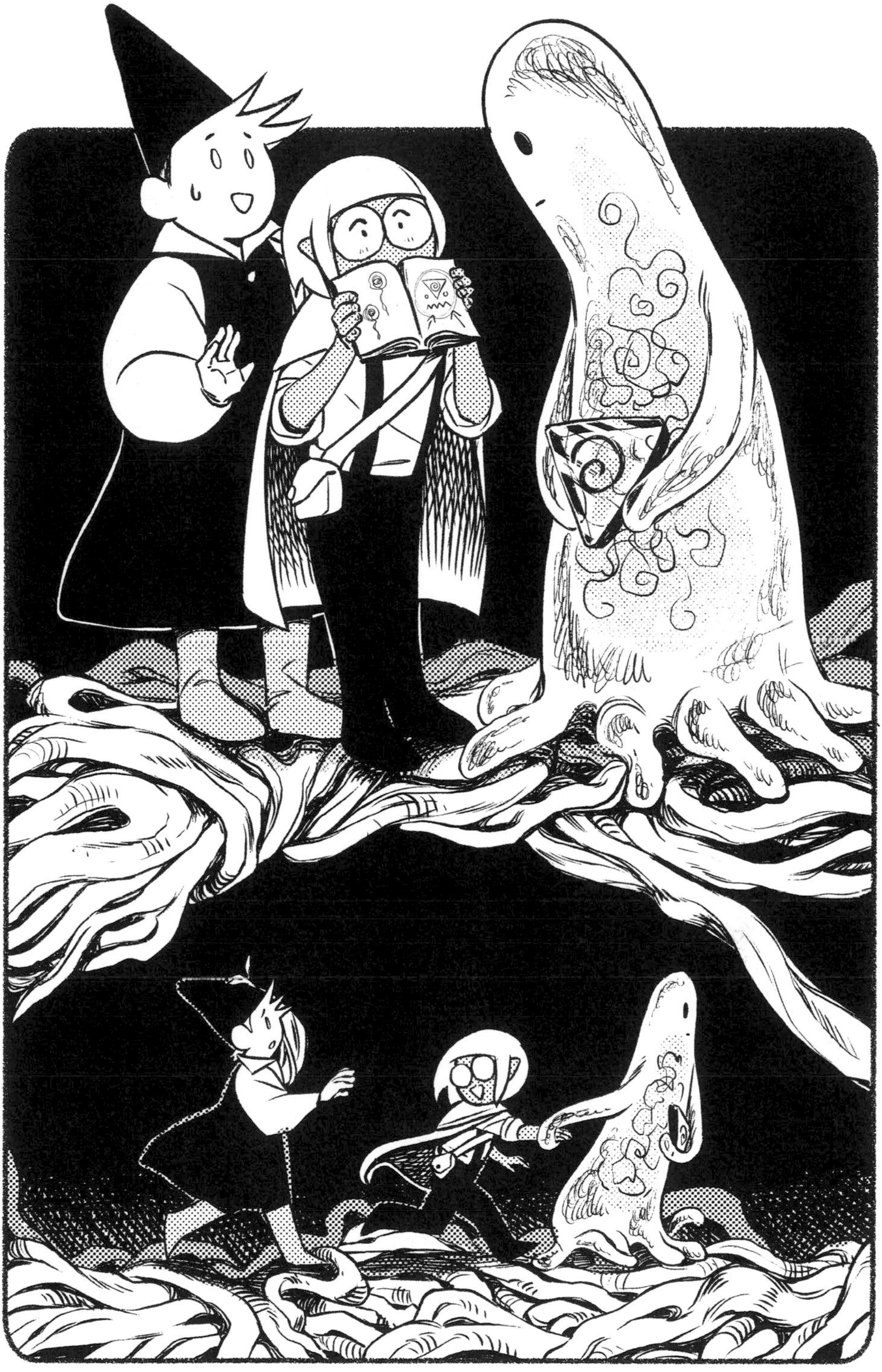

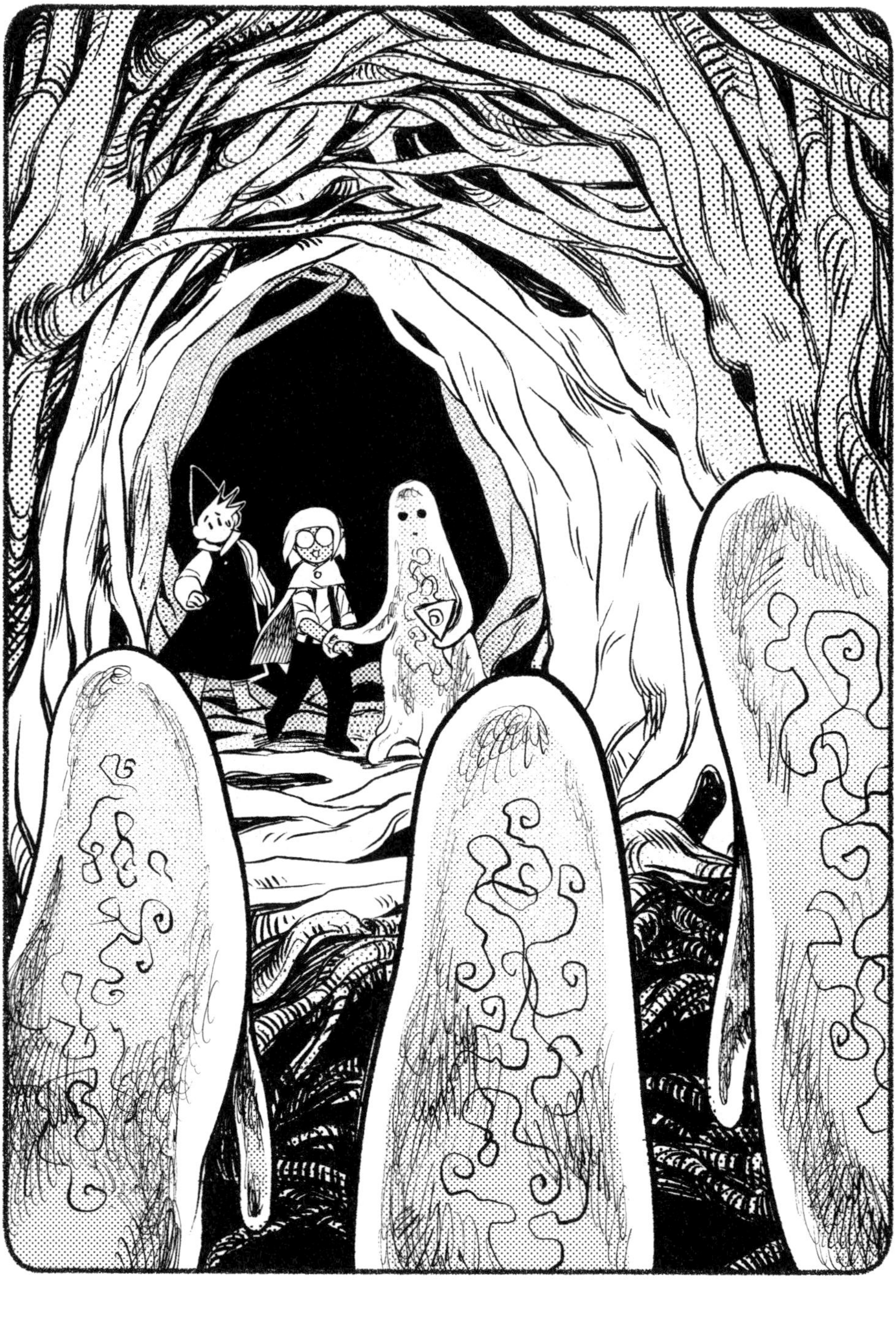

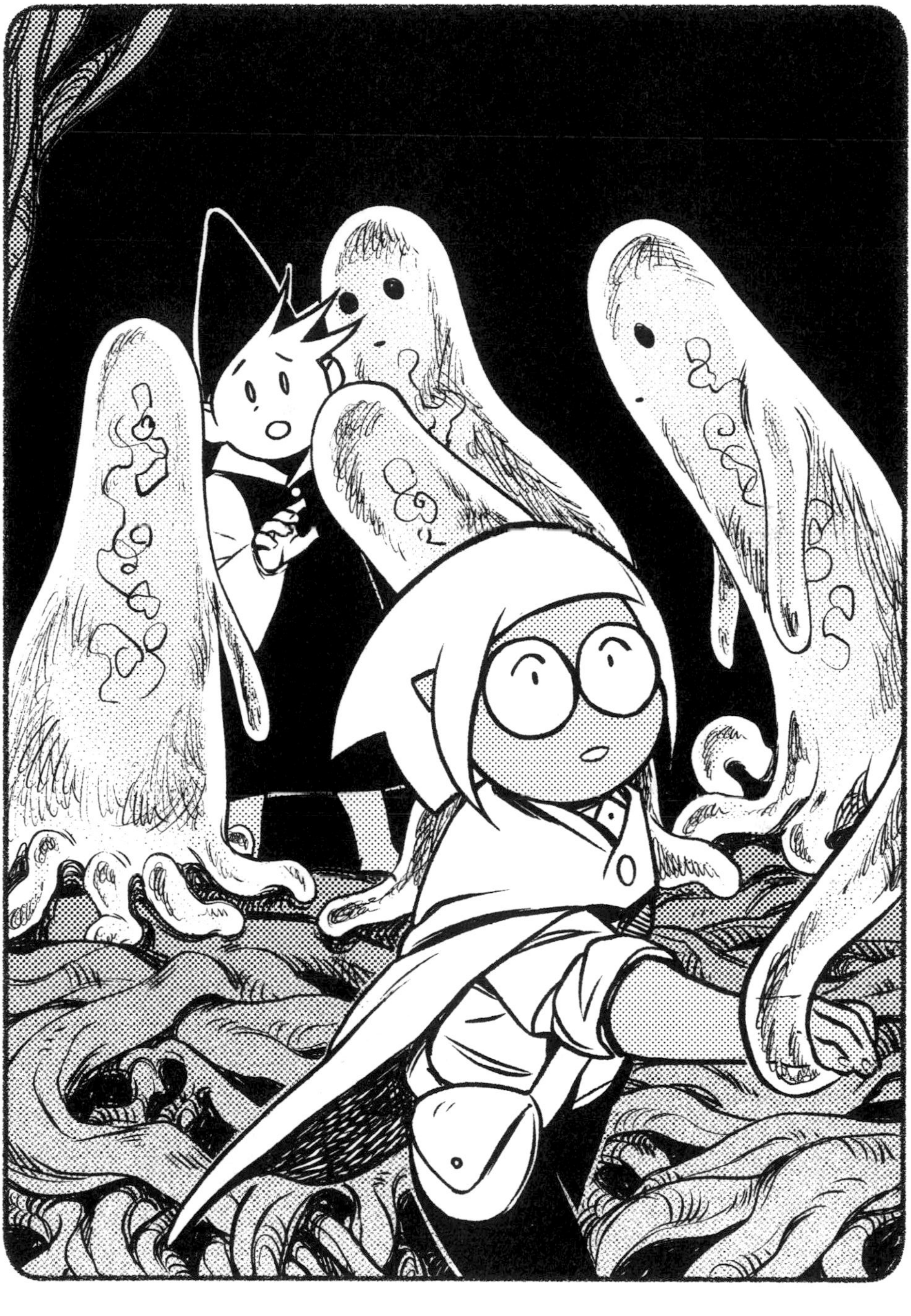

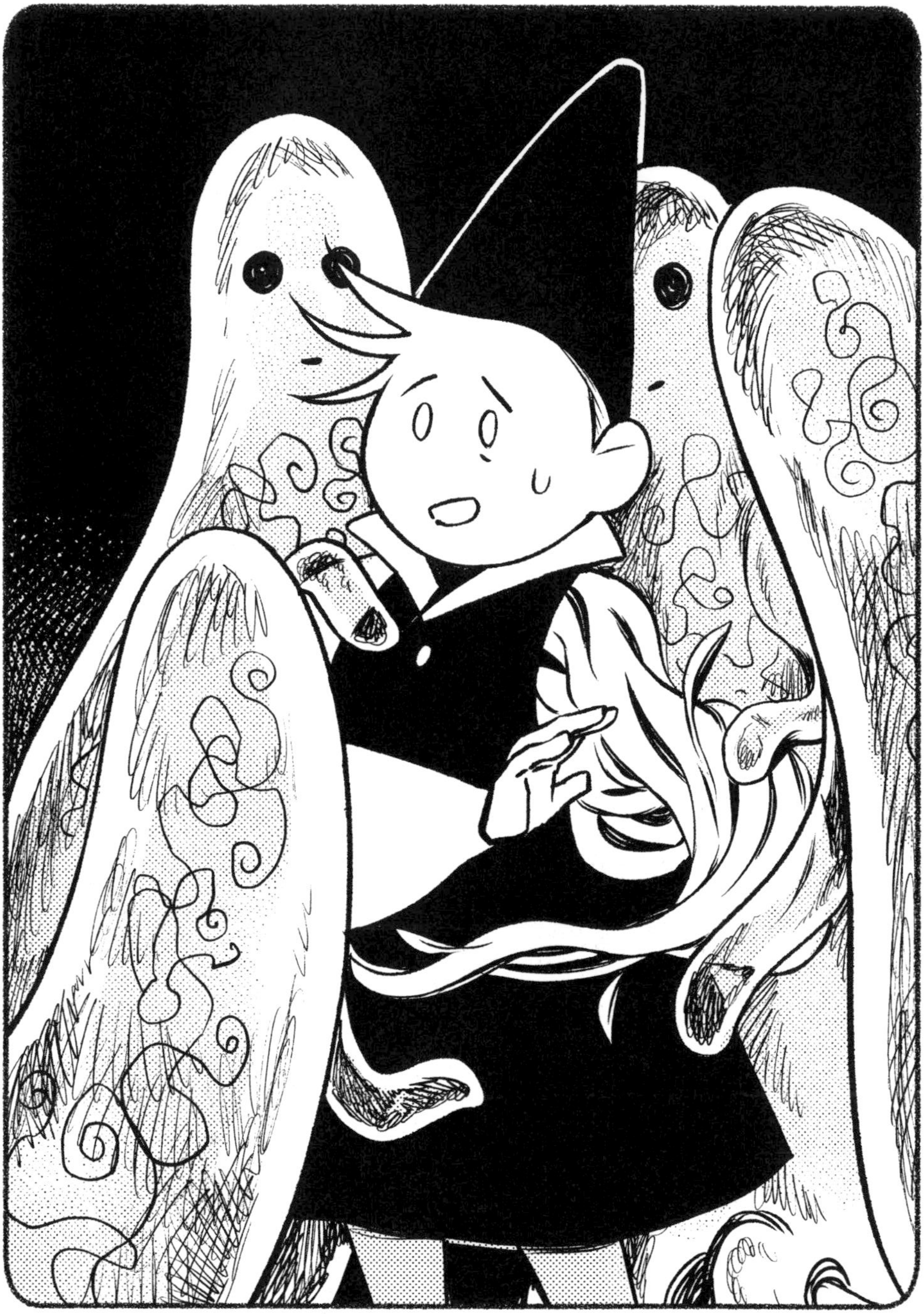

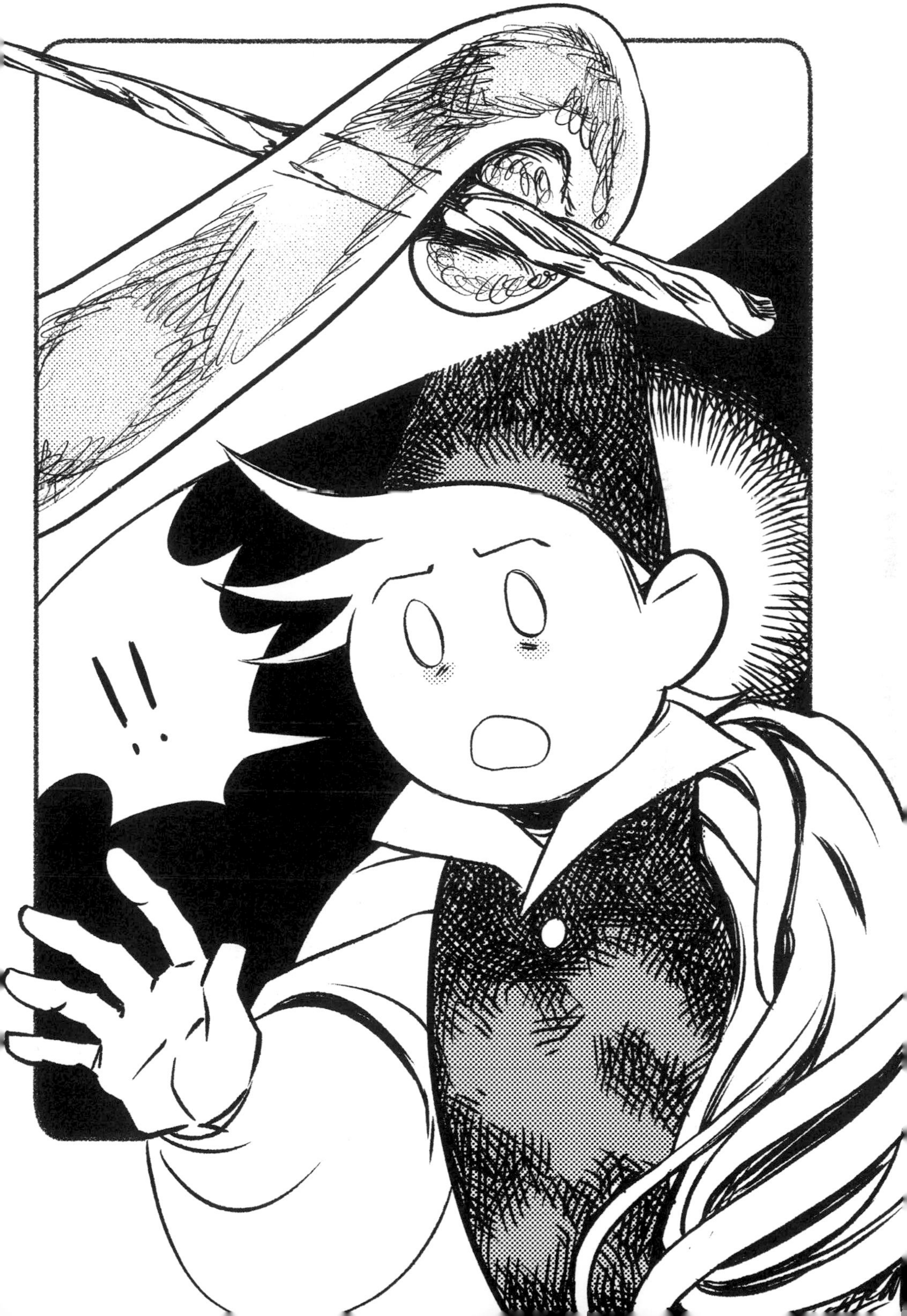
!!

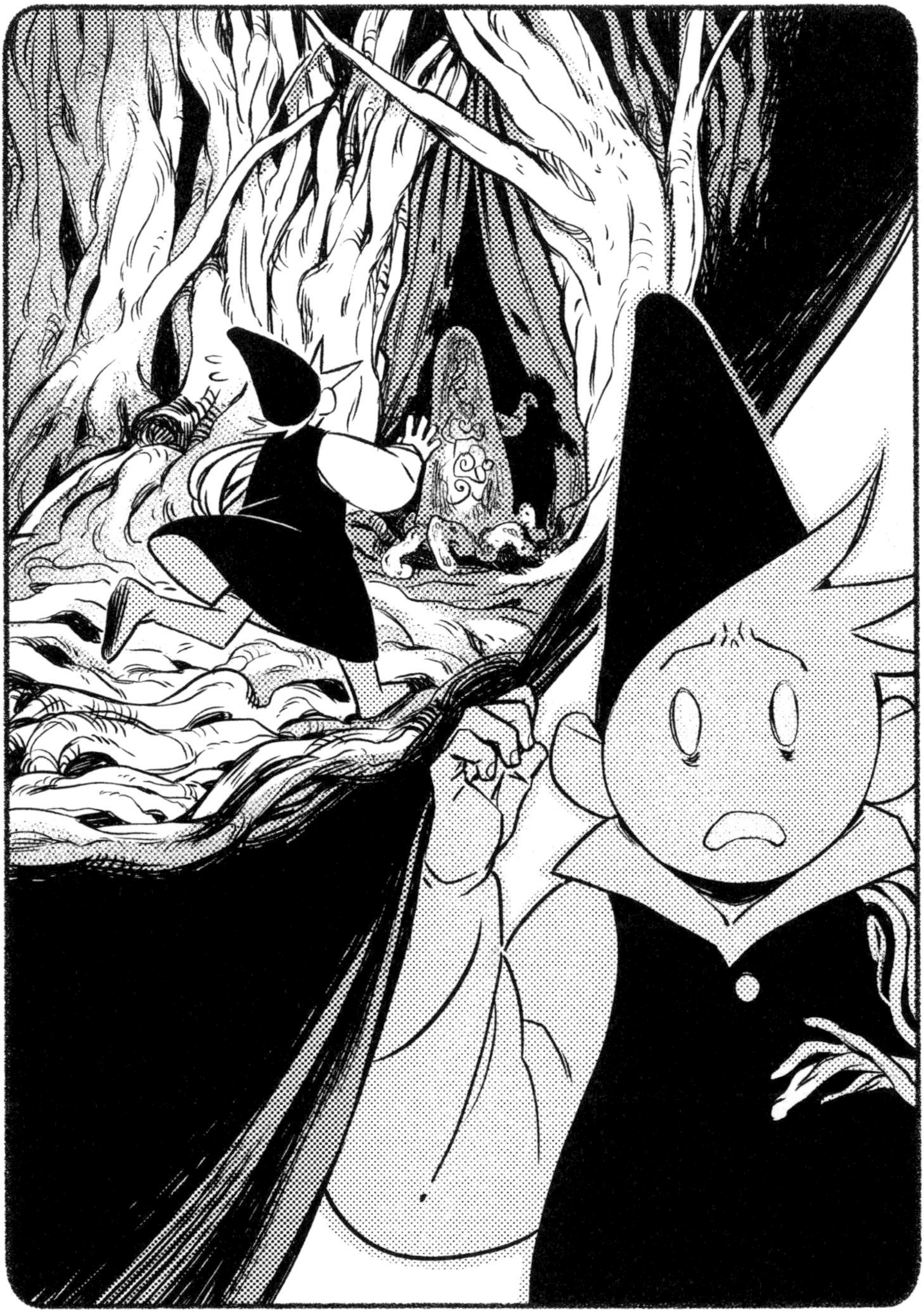

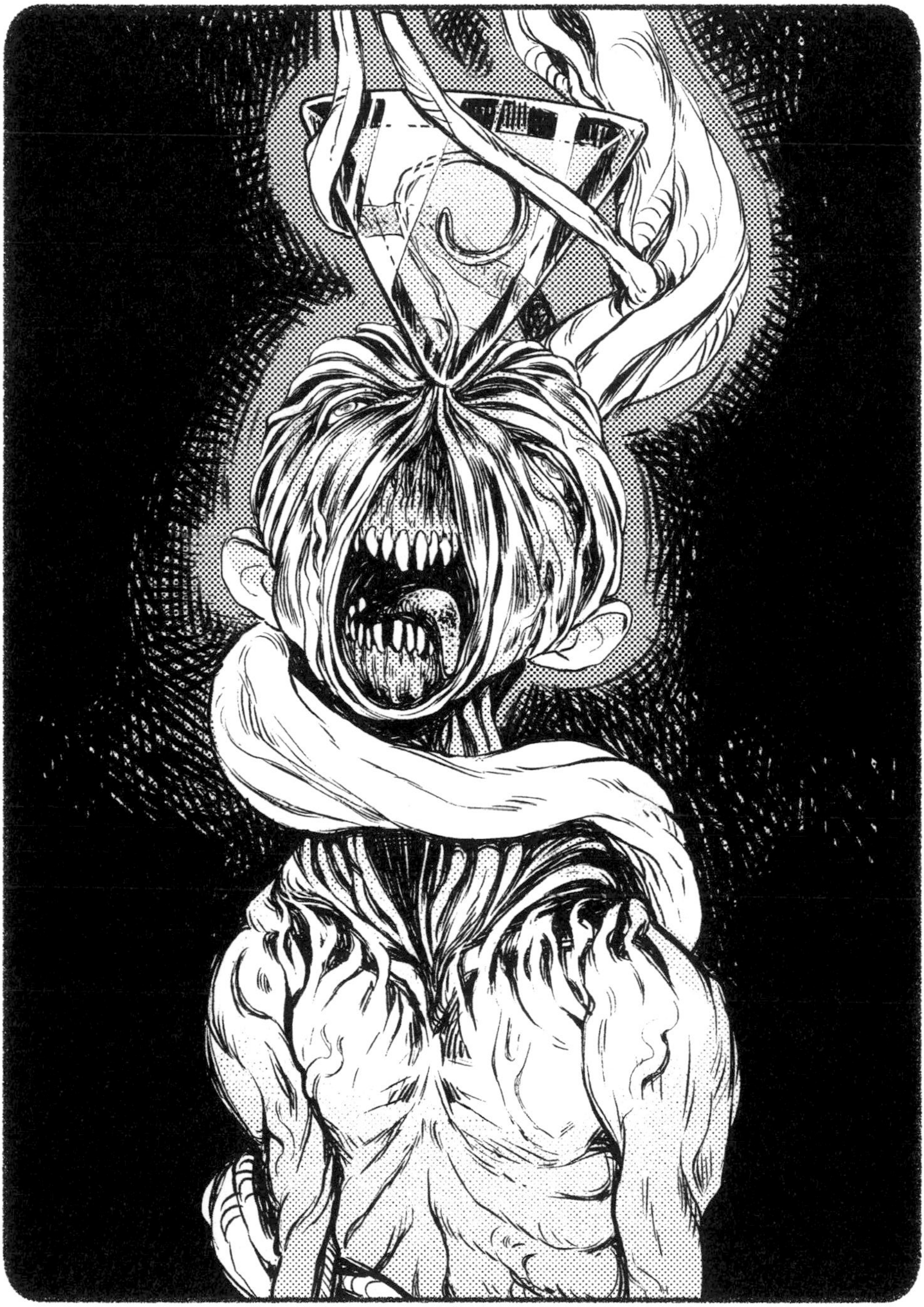

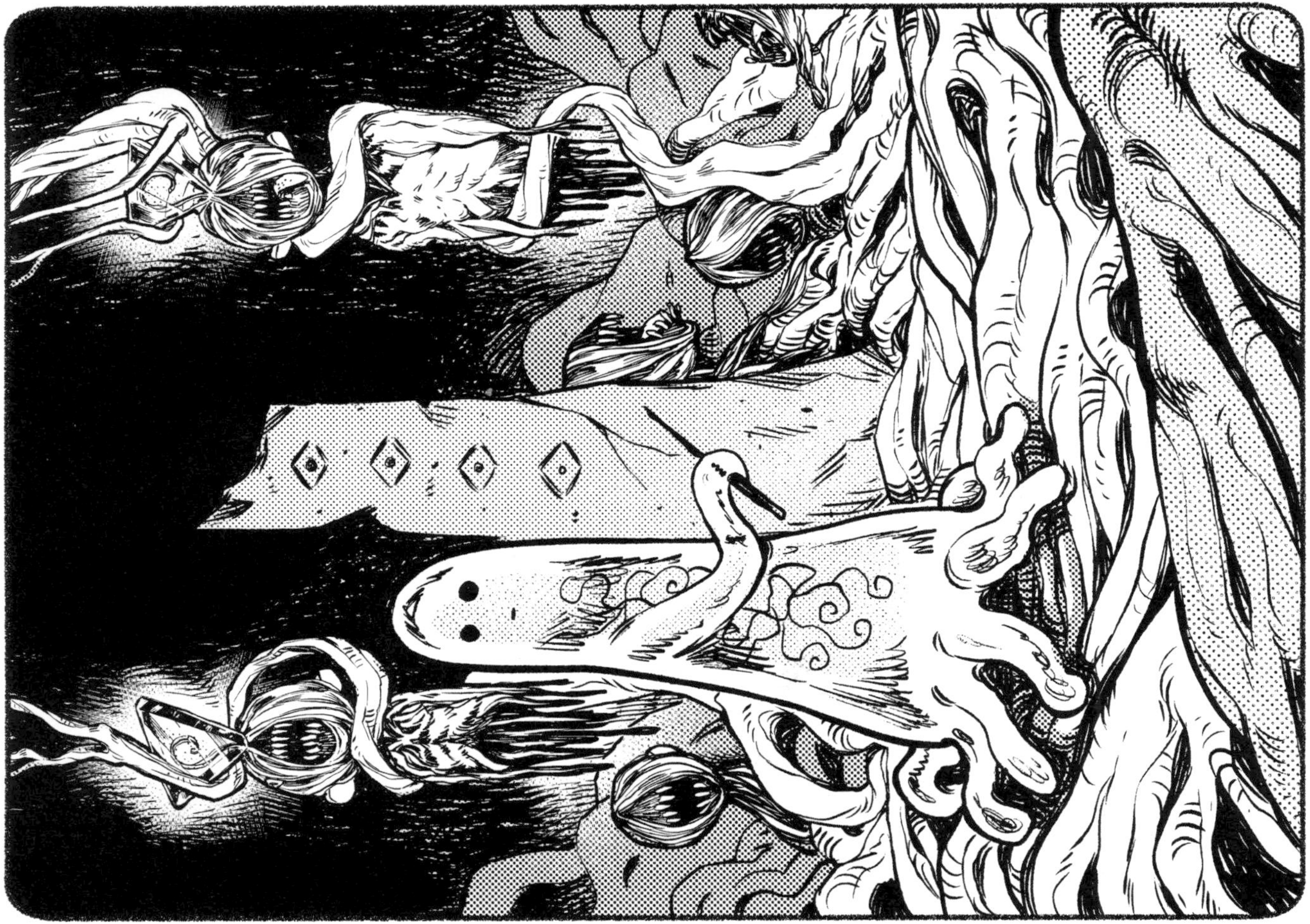

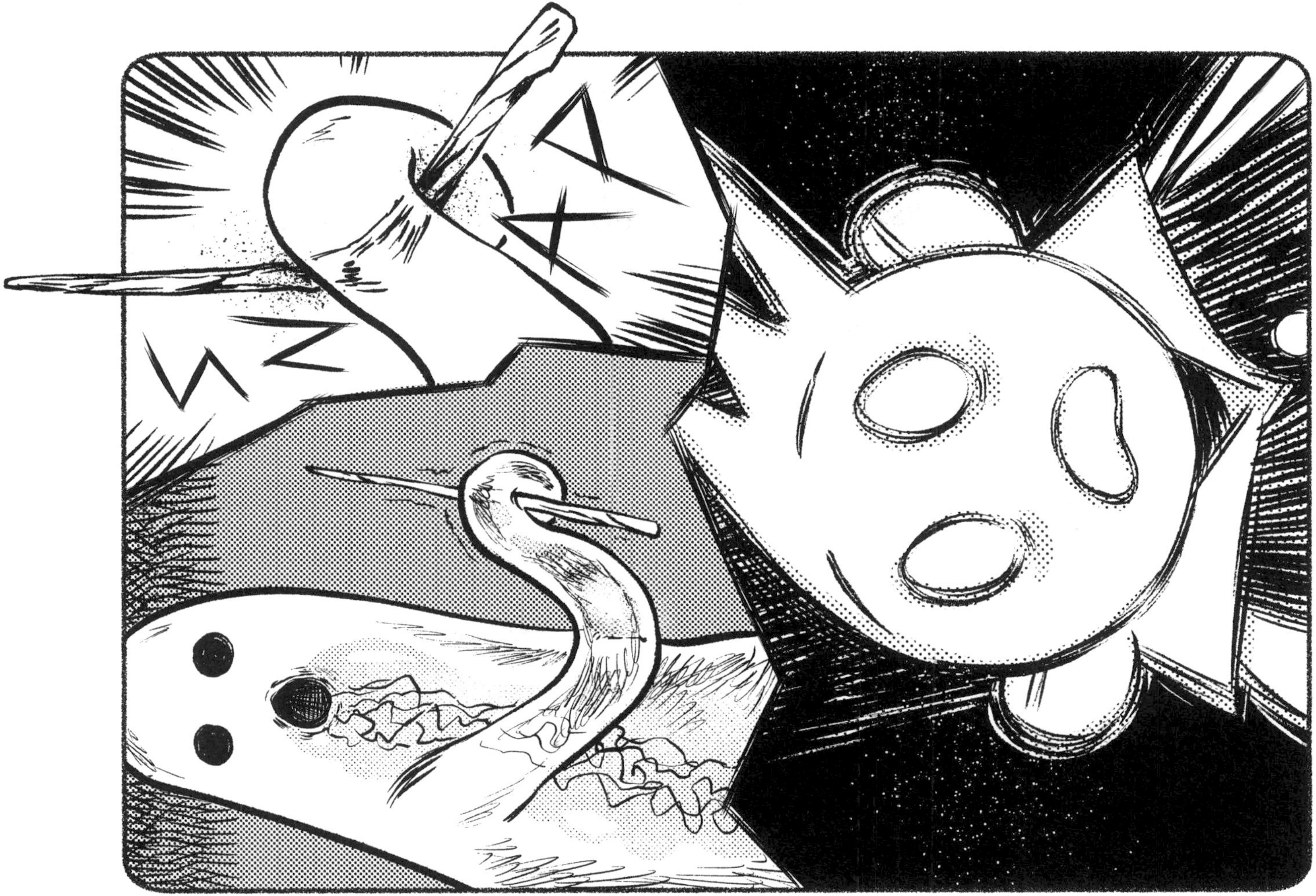

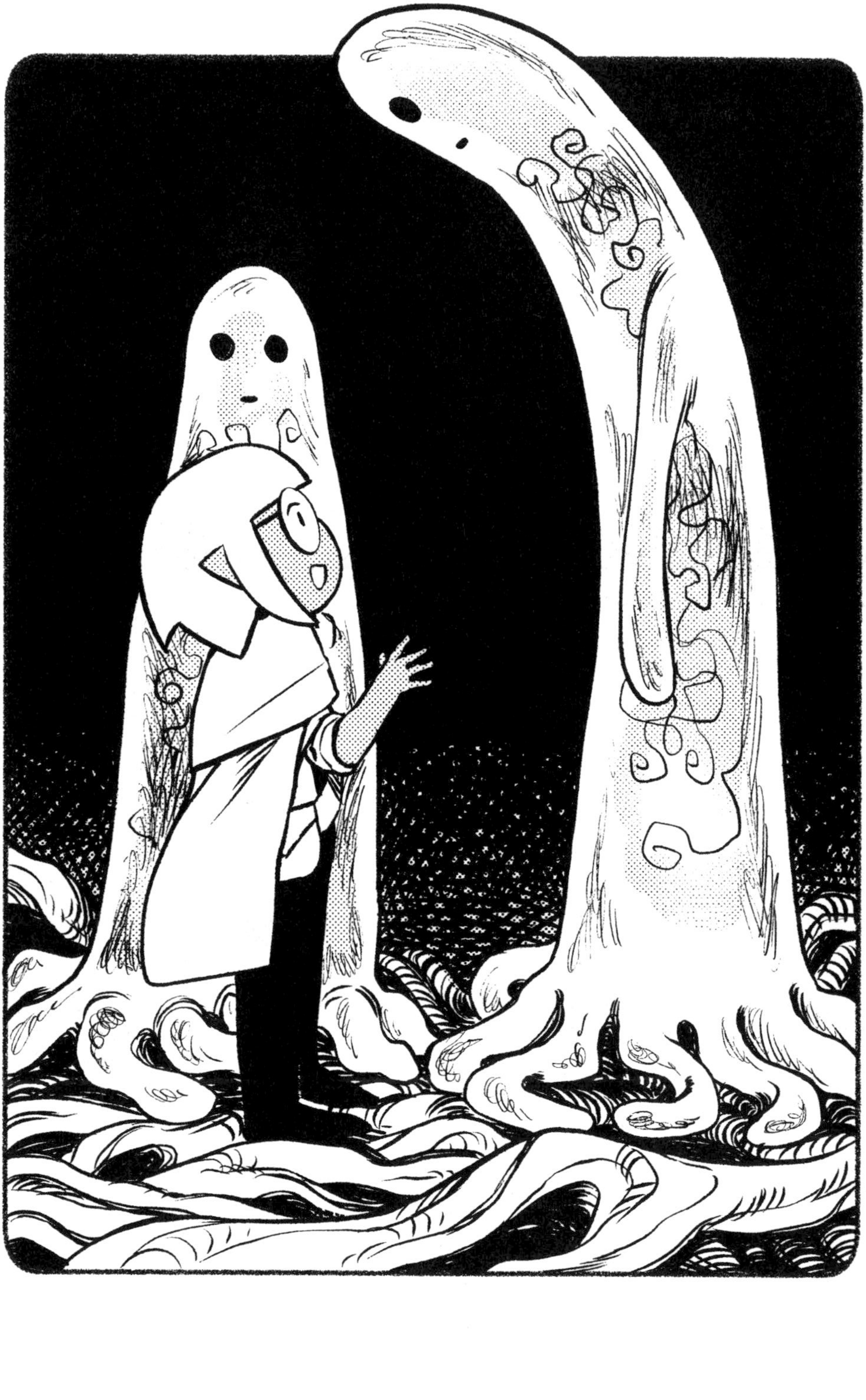

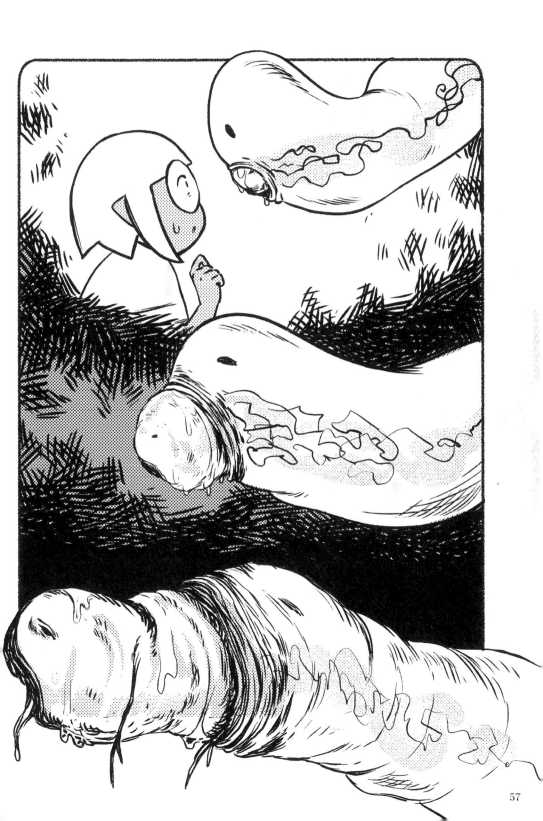

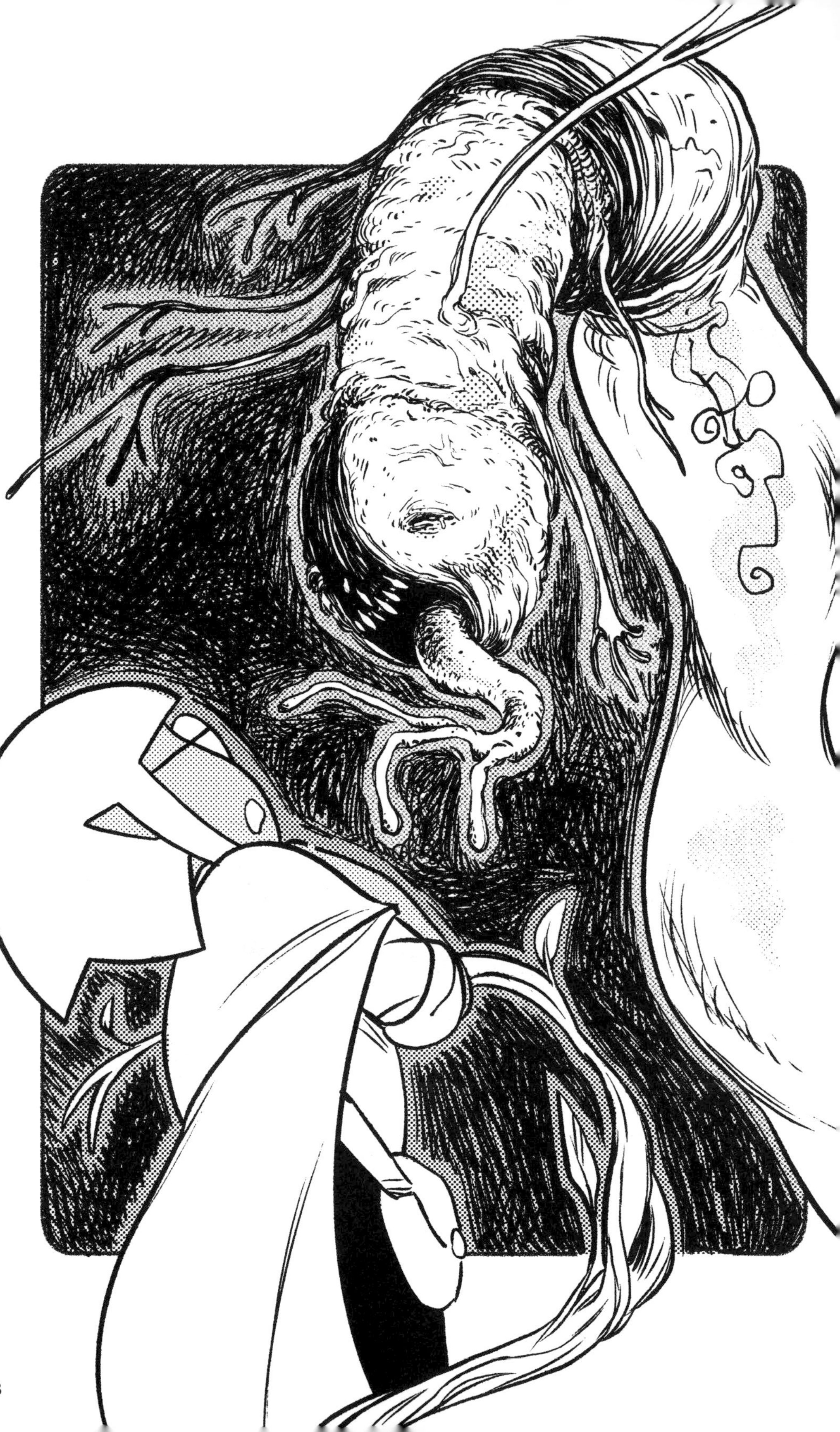

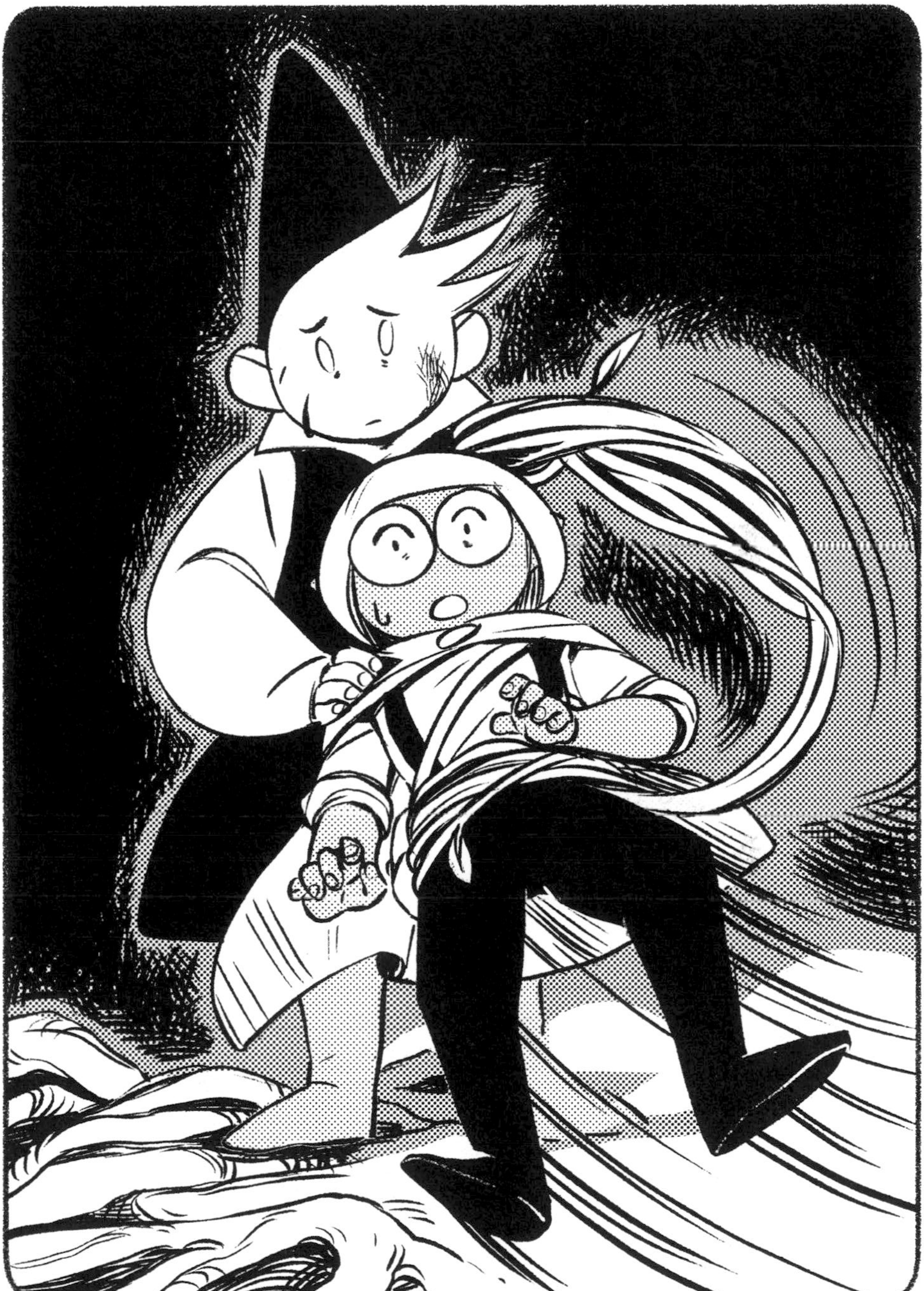

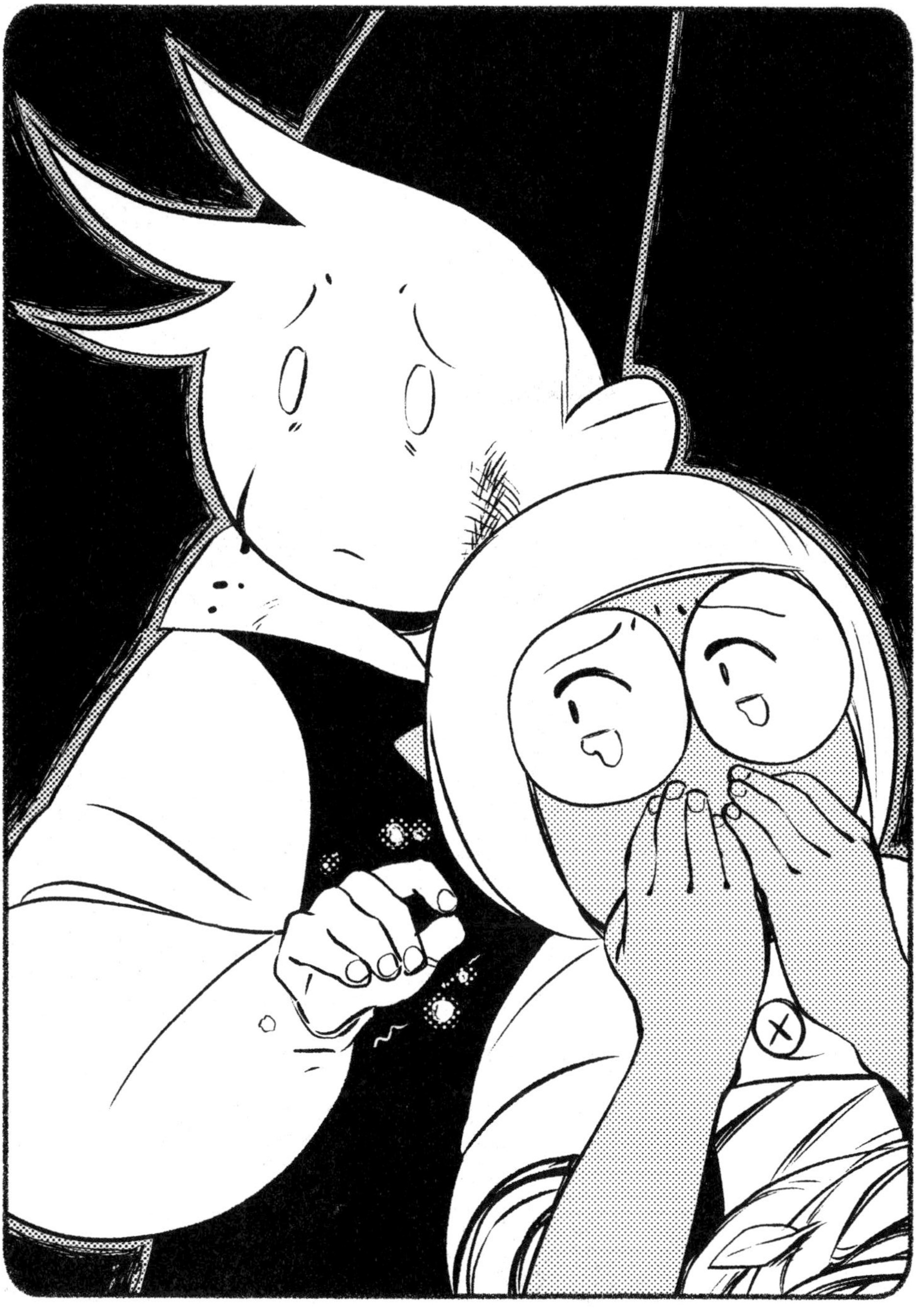

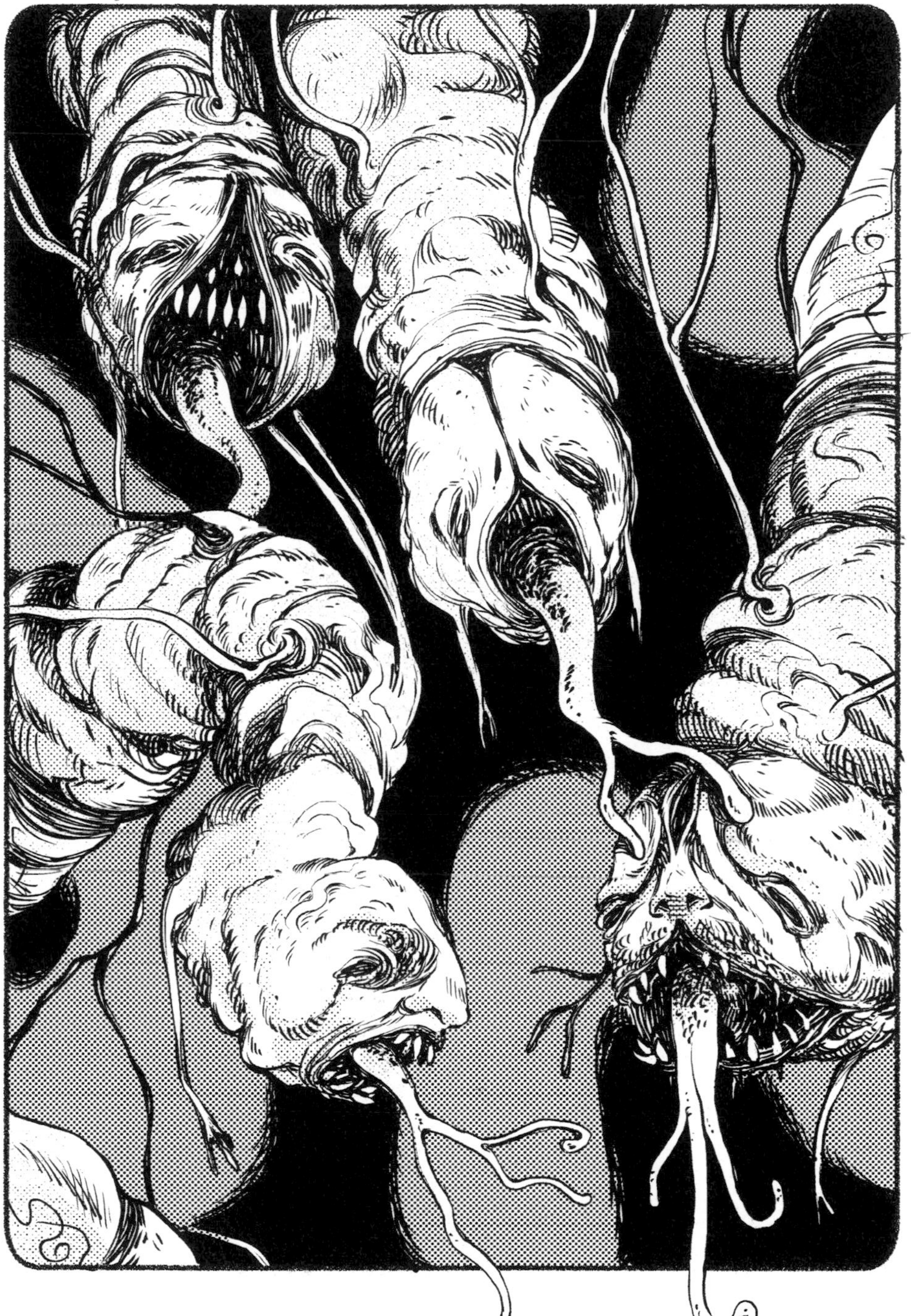

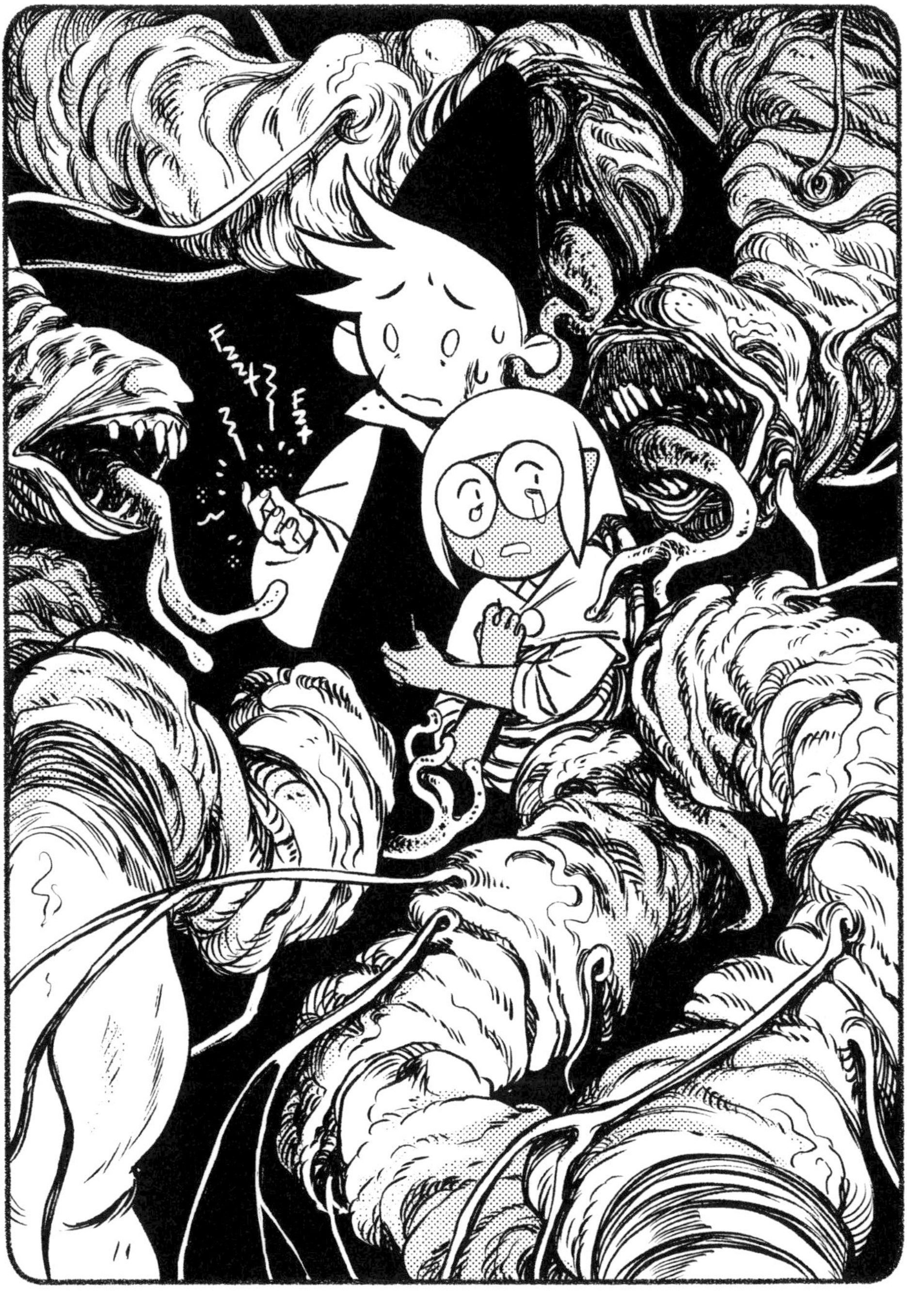
Fzzzt
Fzt

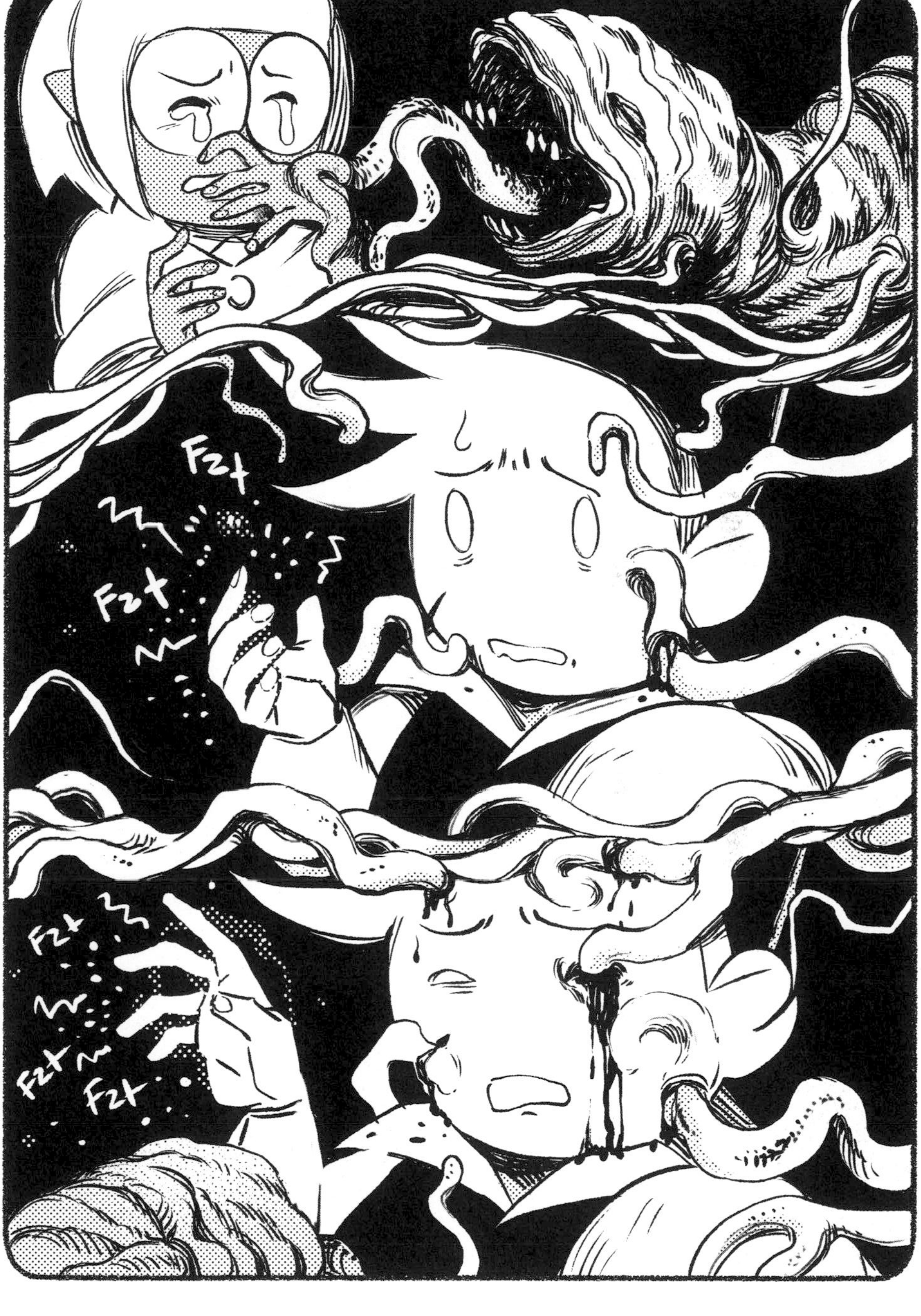
Fzt
Fzt
Fzt
Fzt
Fzt

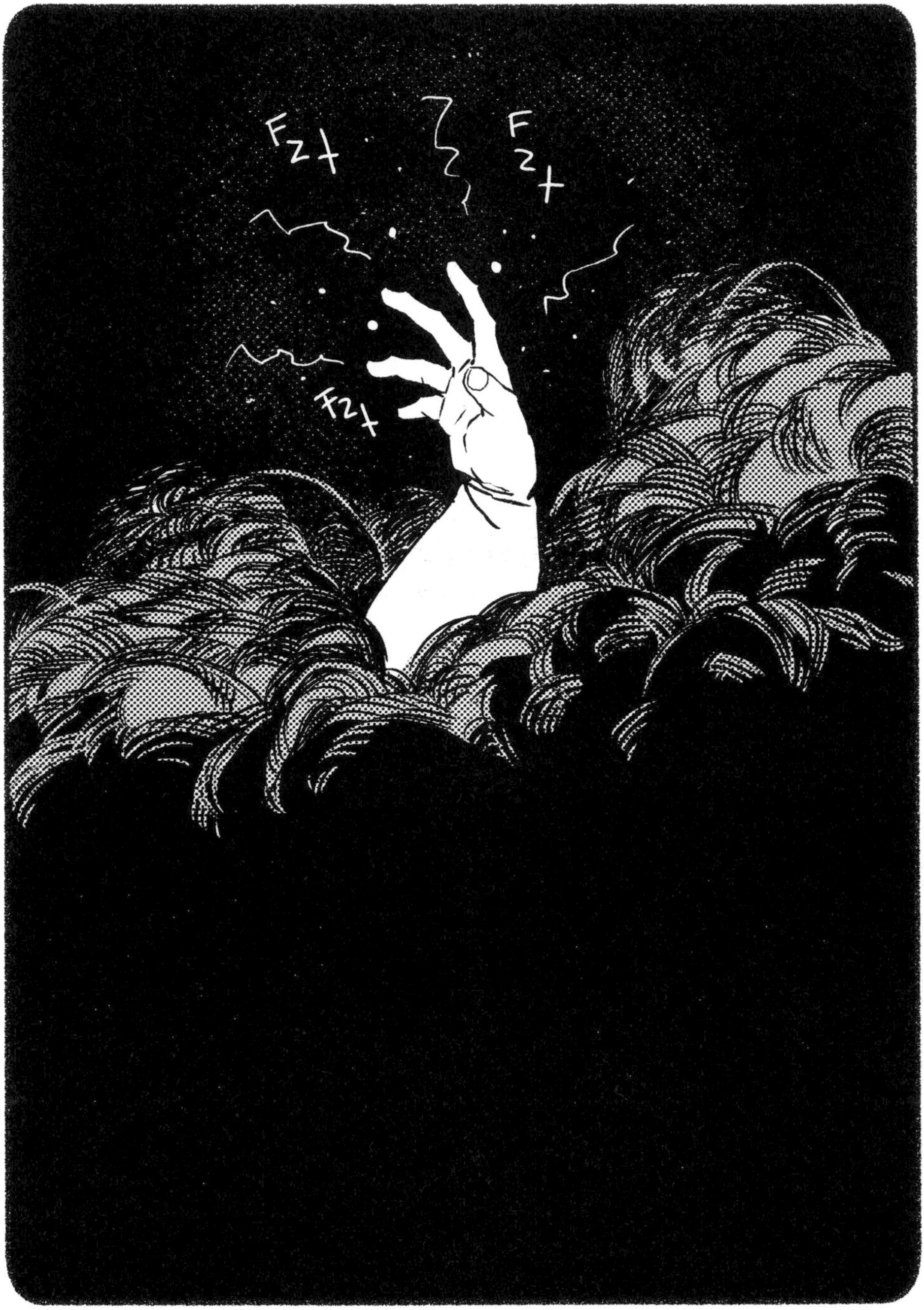
Fzt
Fzt
Fzt

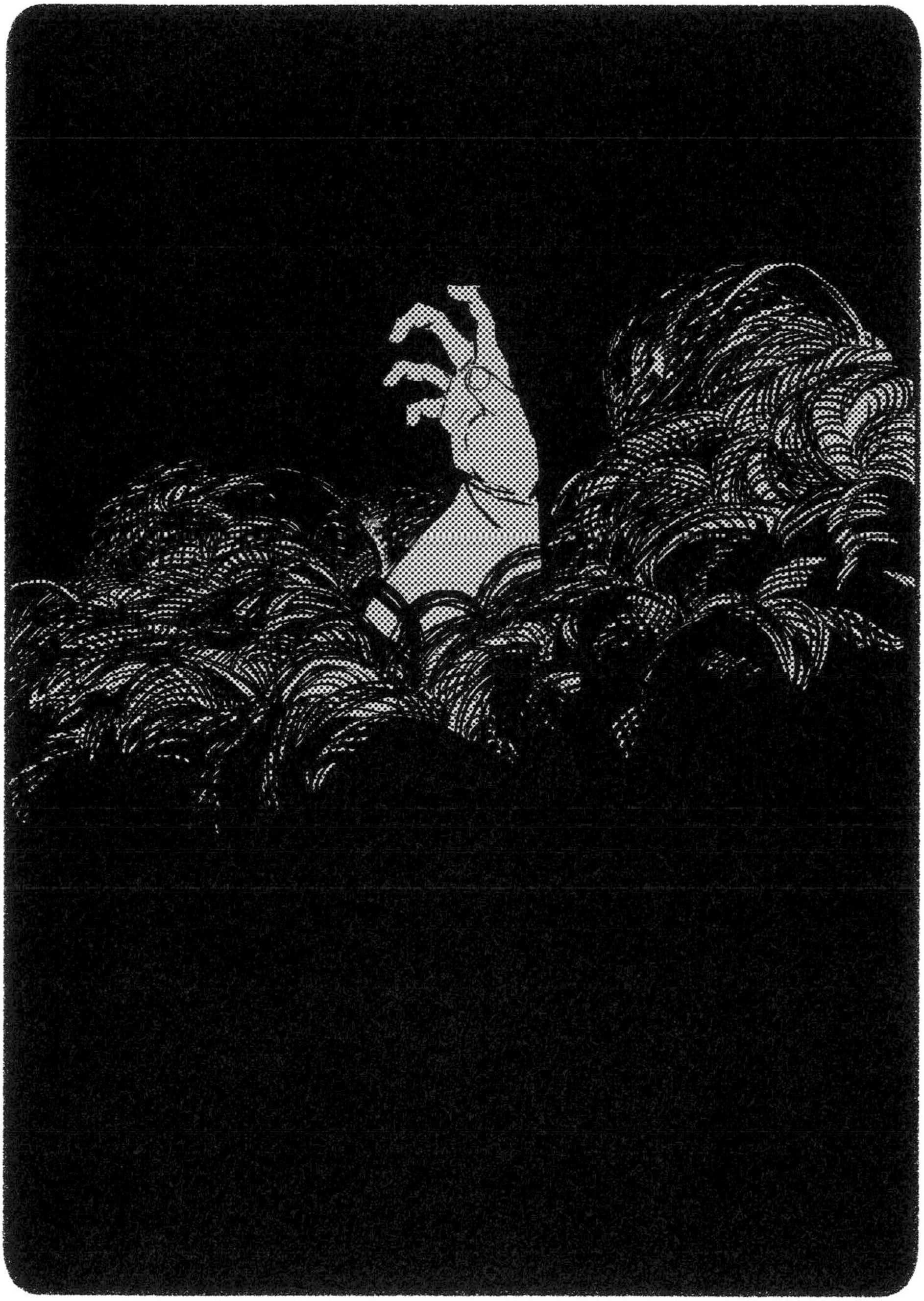

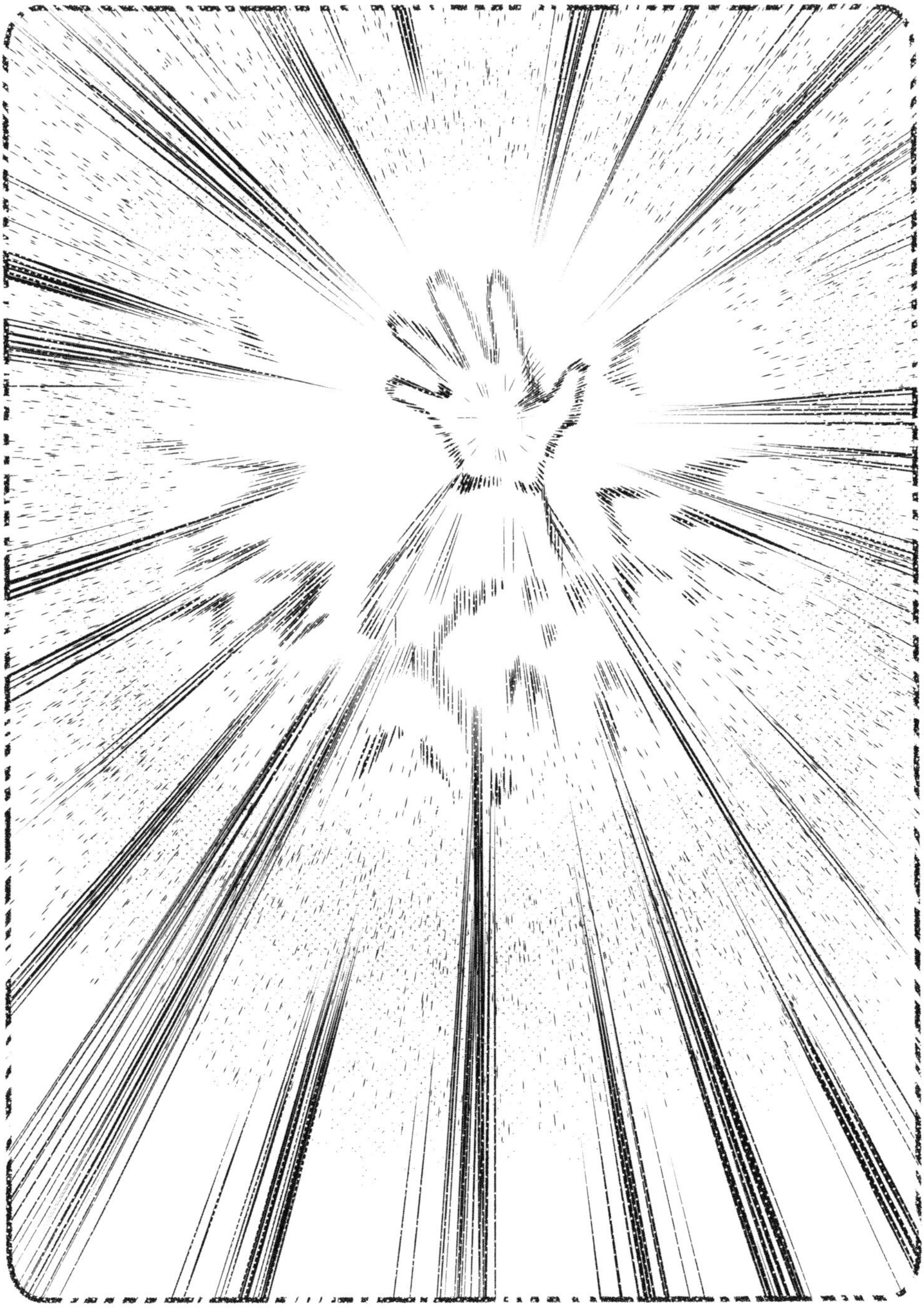

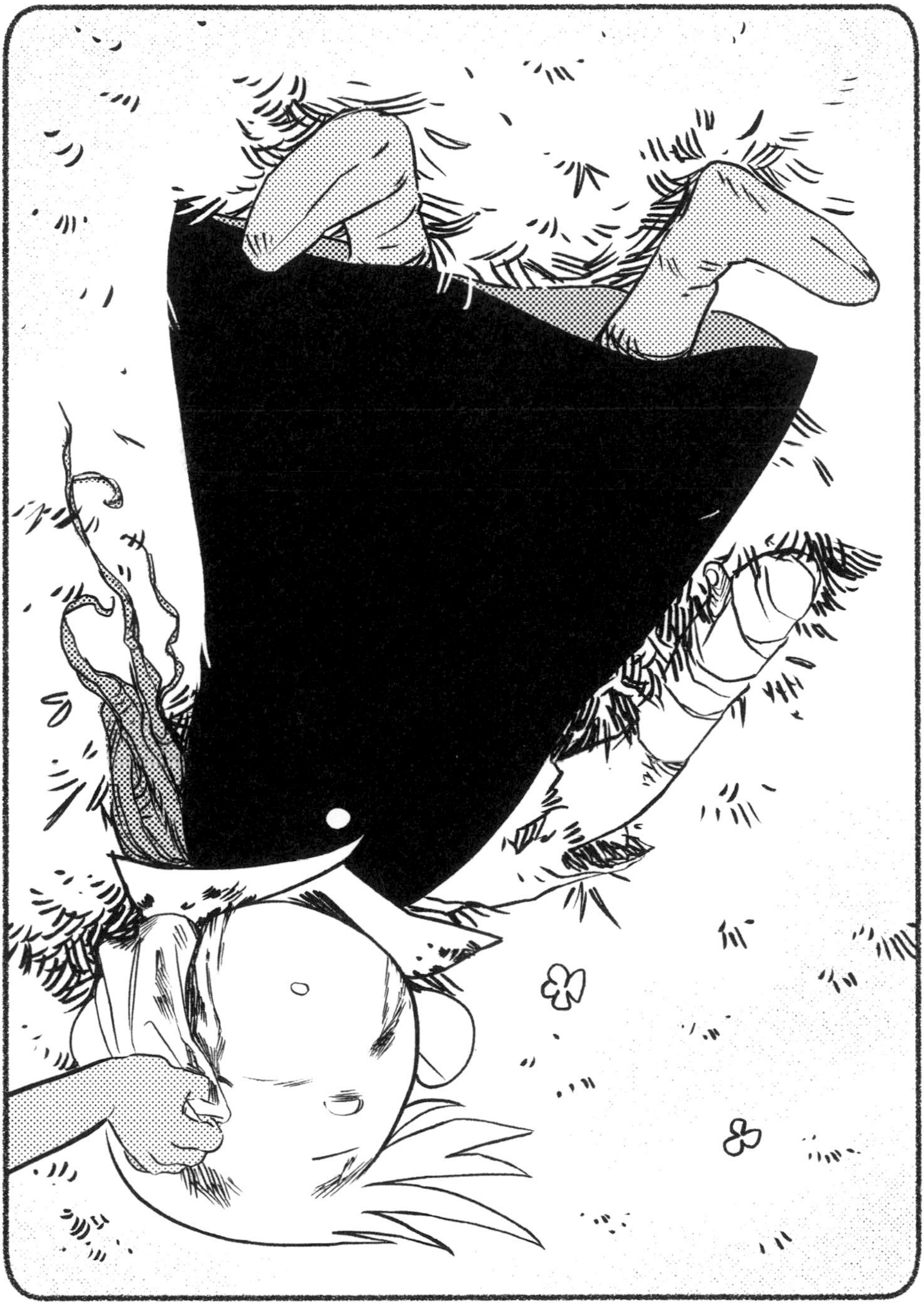

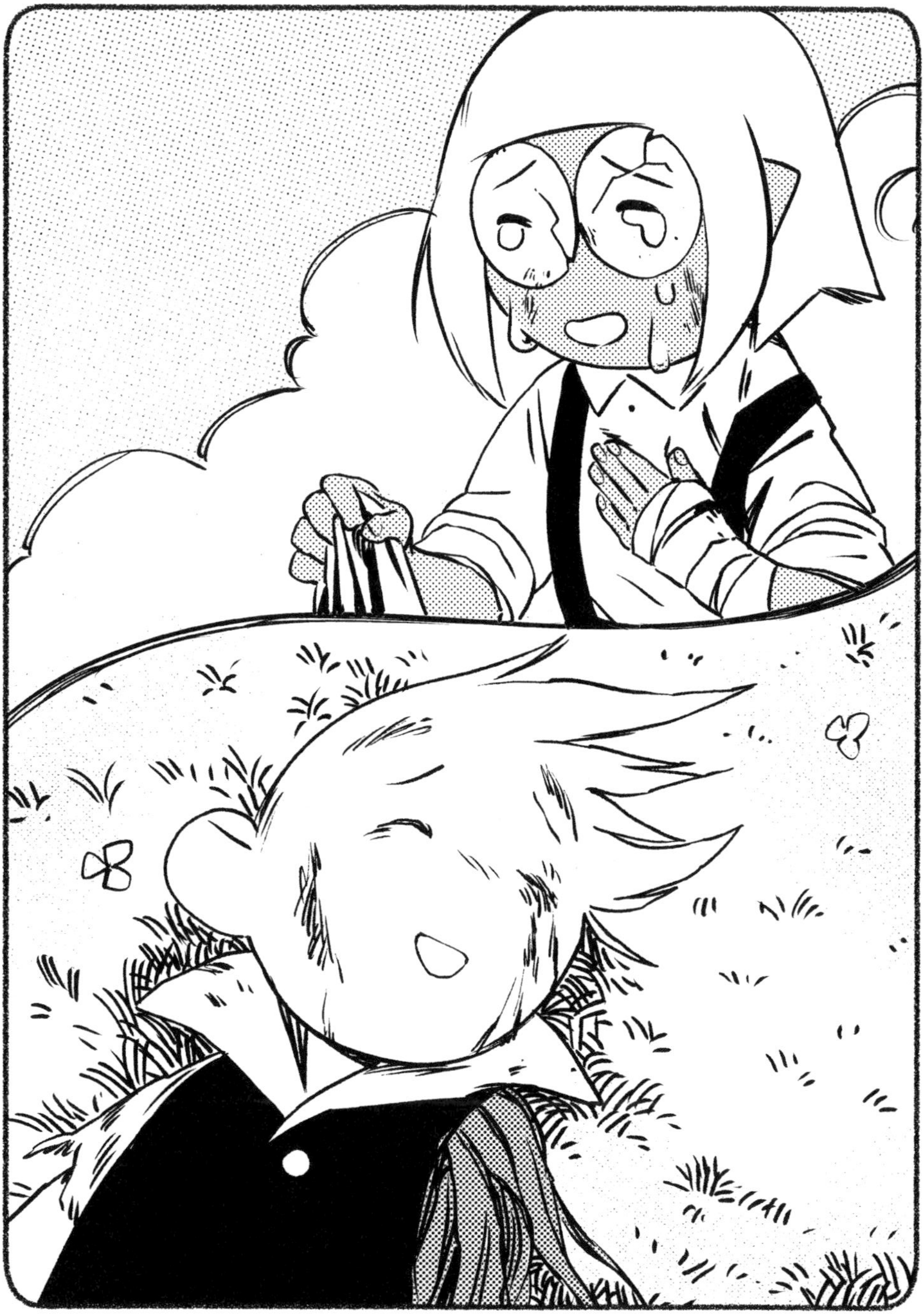

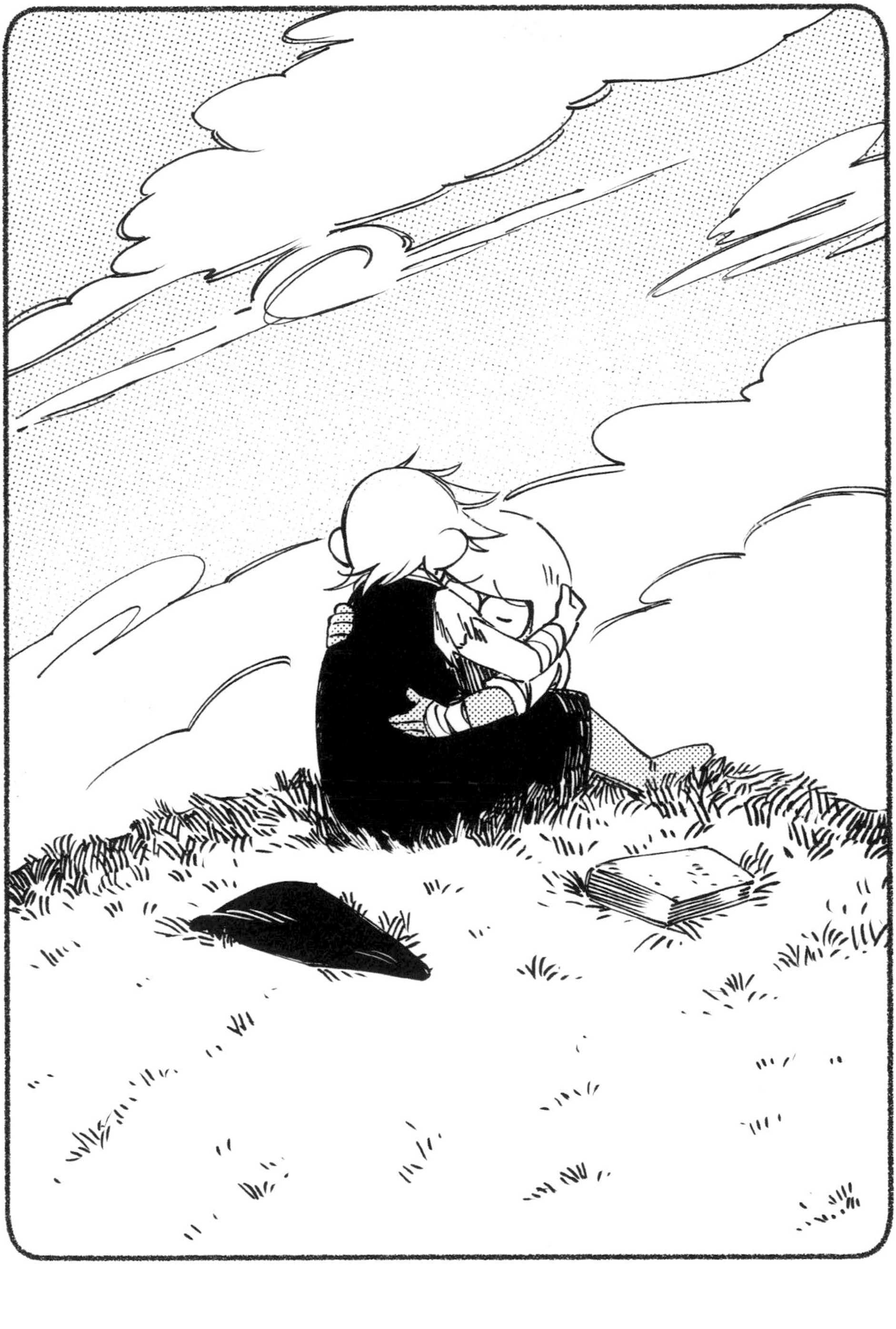

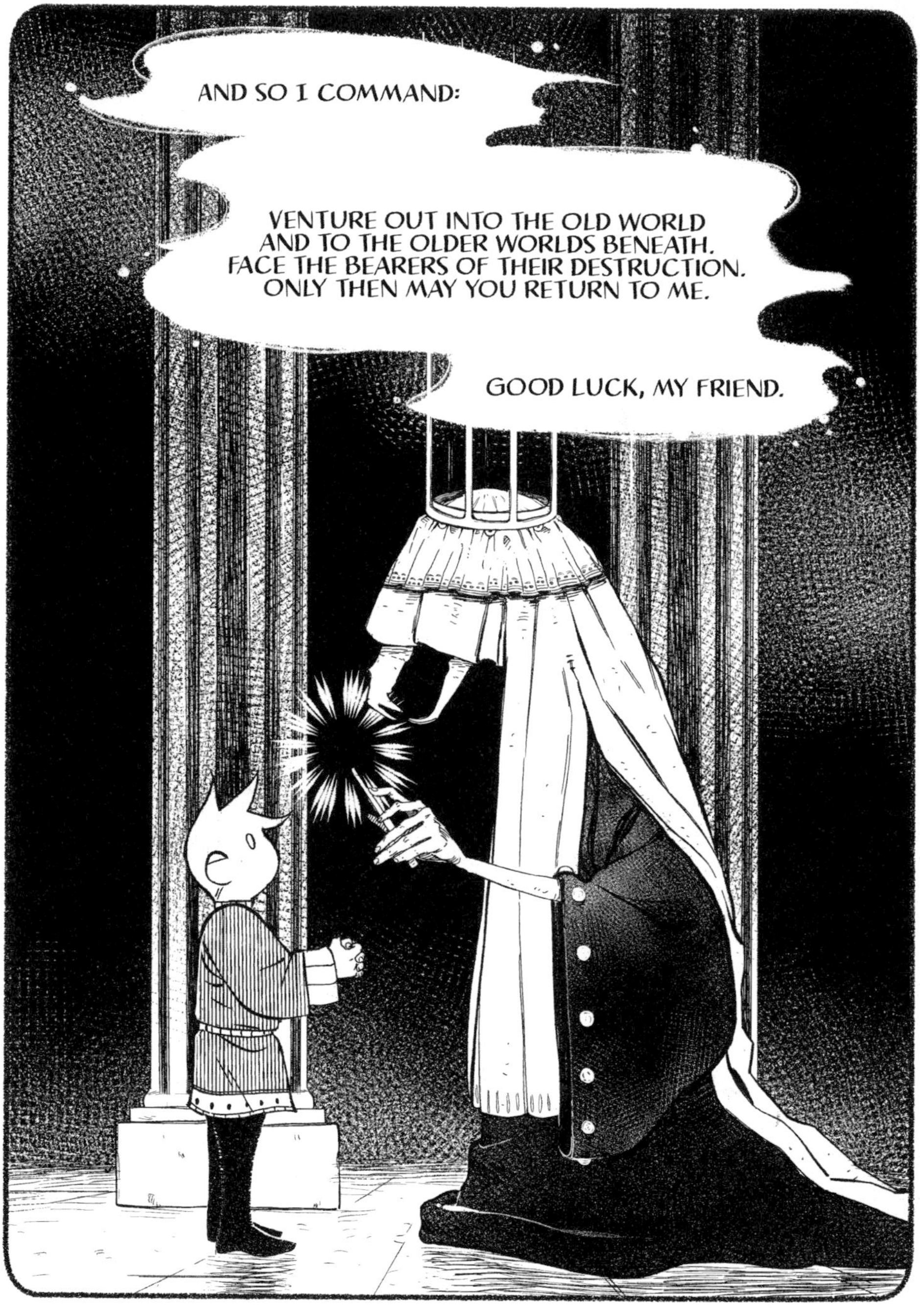
AND SO I COMMAND:
VENTURE OUT INTO THE OLD WORLD AND TO THE OLDER WORLDS BENEATH. FACE THE BEARERS OF THEIR DESTRUCTION. ONLY THEN MAY YOU RETURN TO ME.
GOOD LUCK, MY FRIEND.

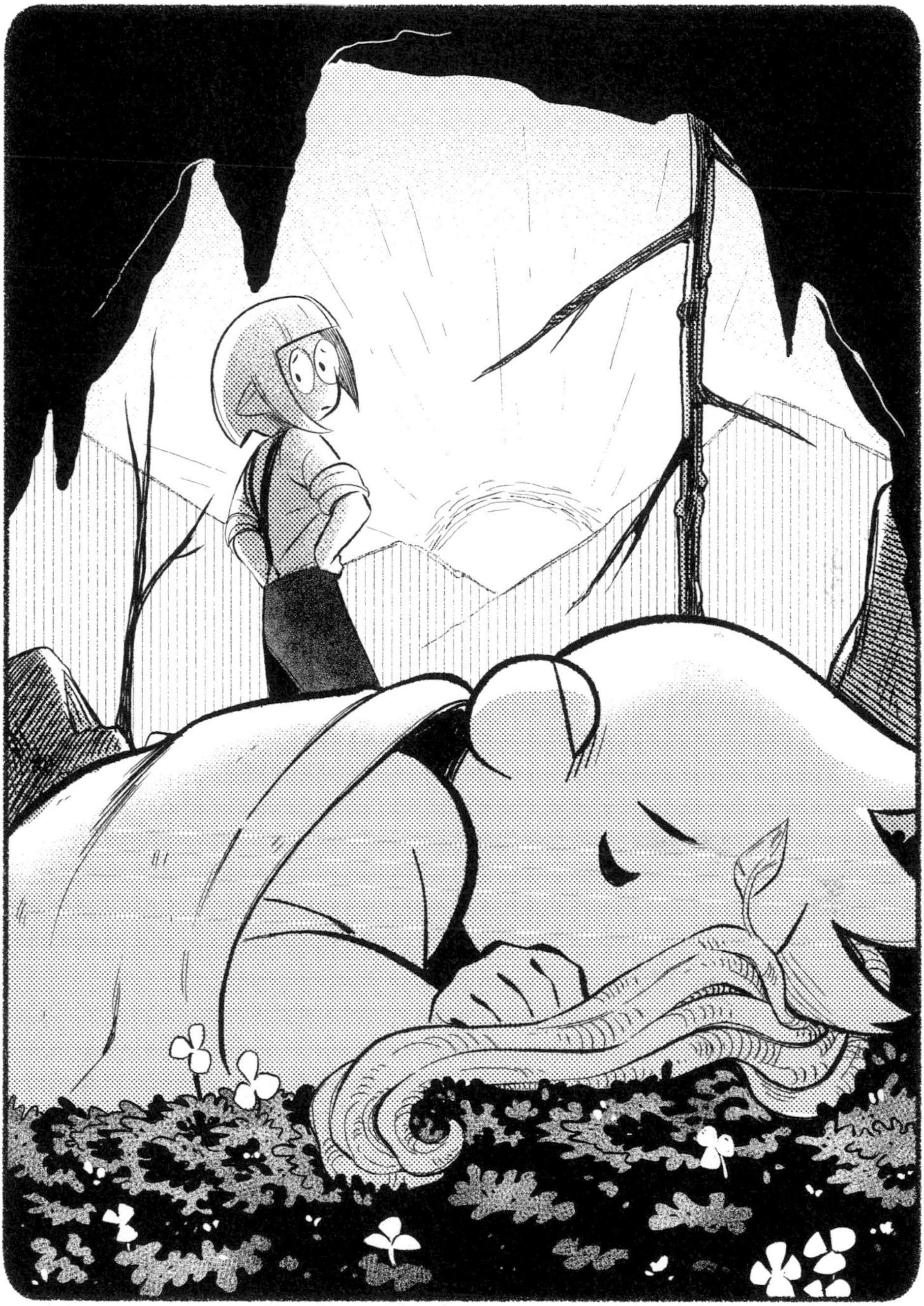

PART THREE

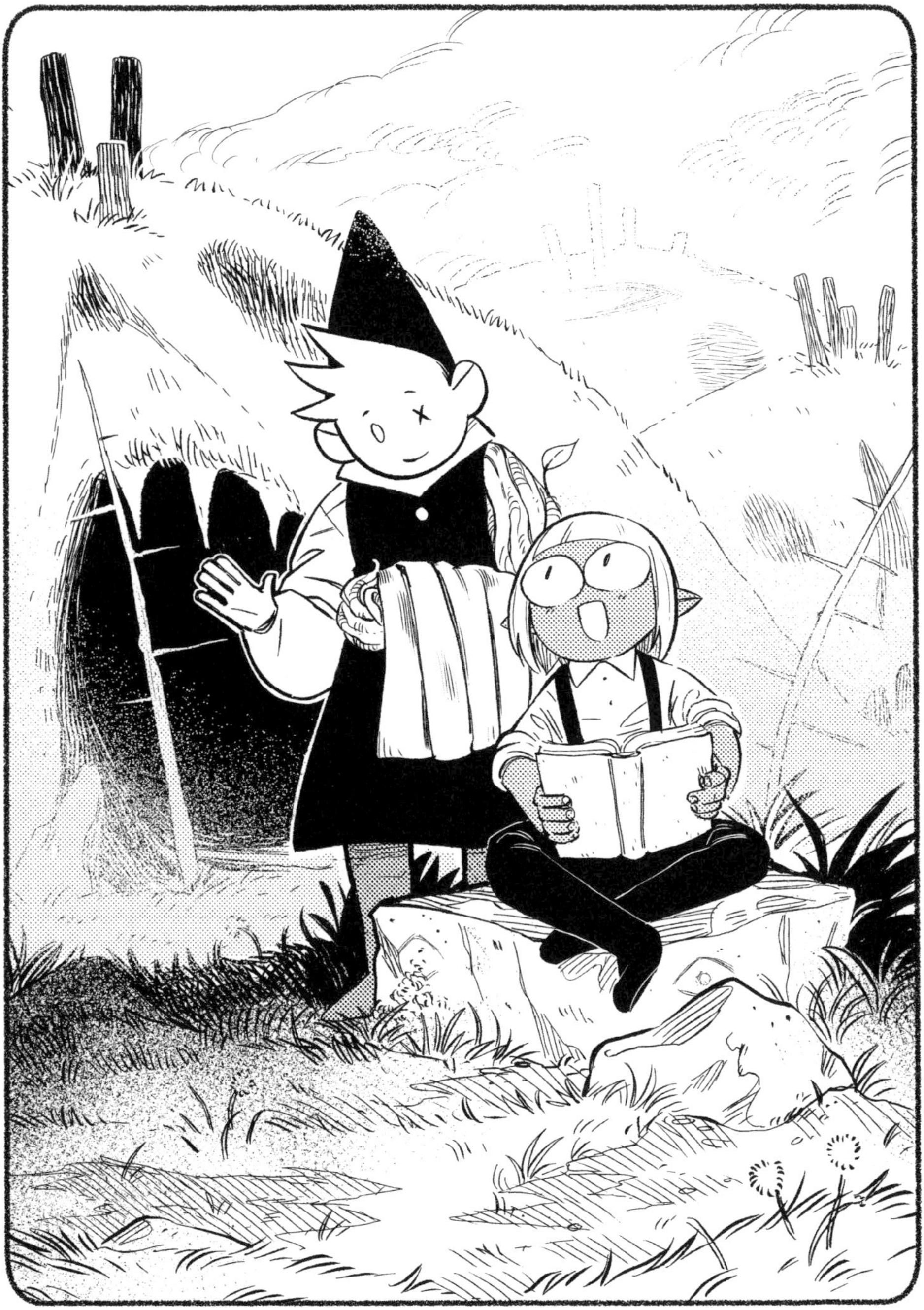

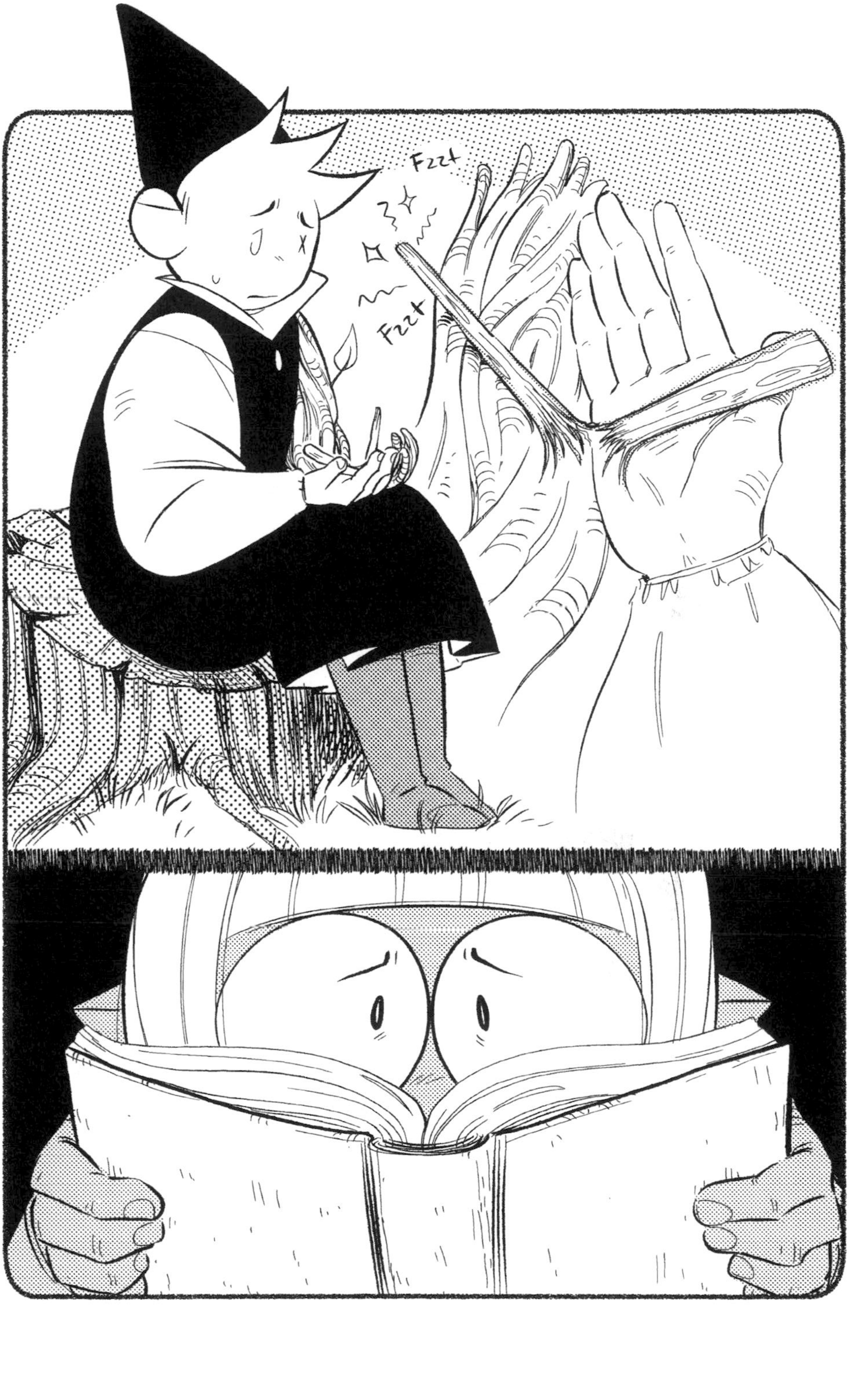
Fzzt
Fzzt

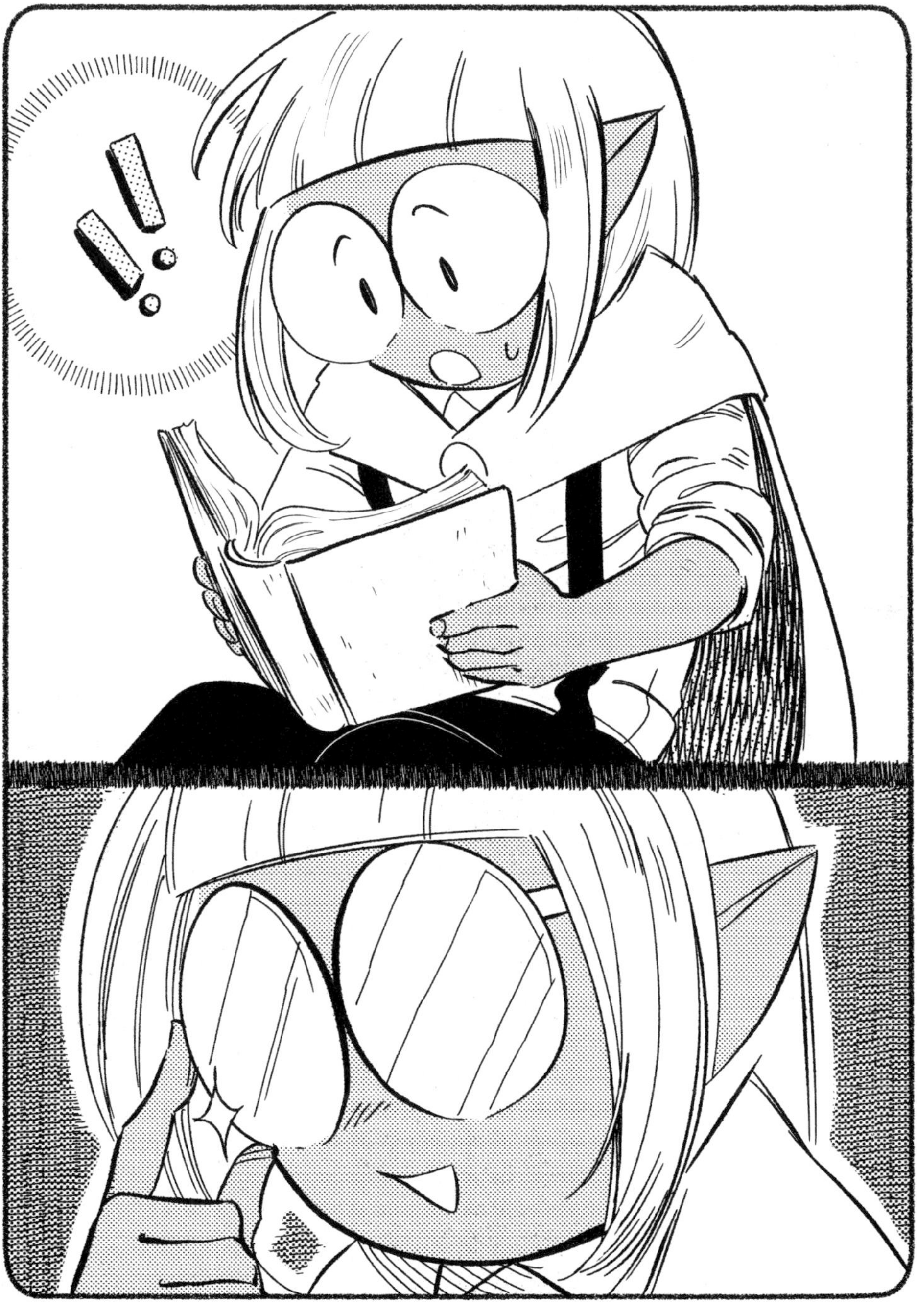
!!

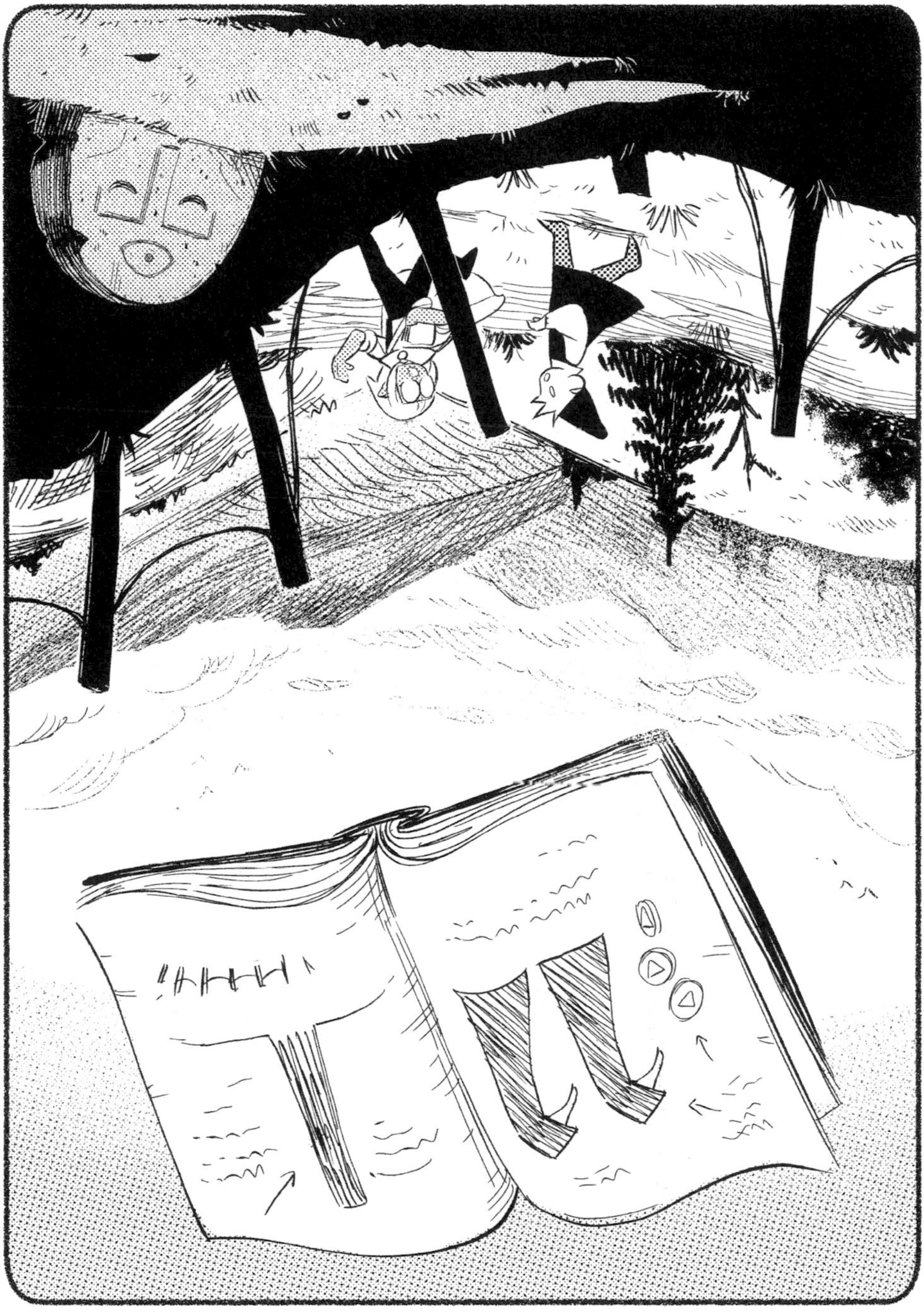

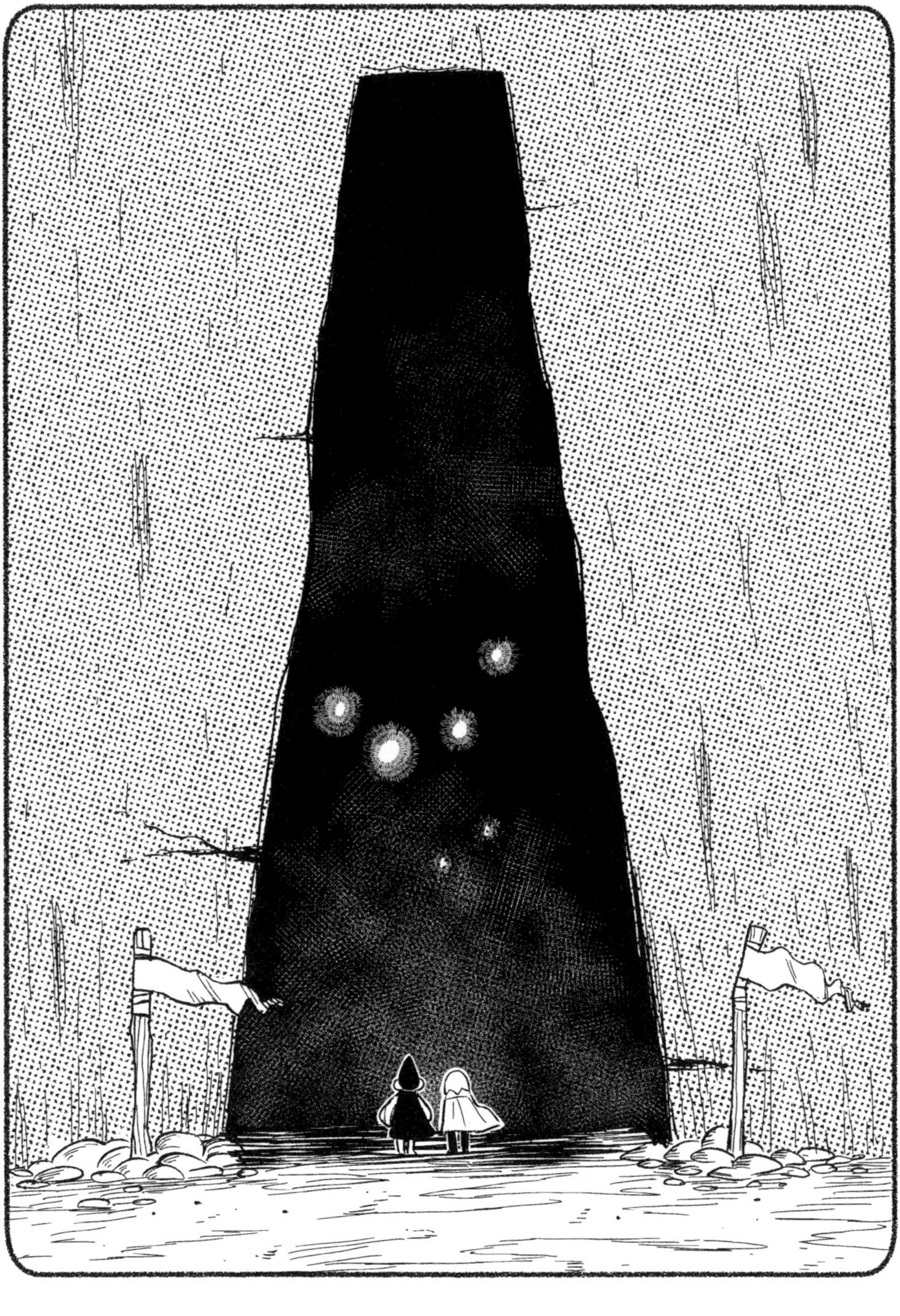

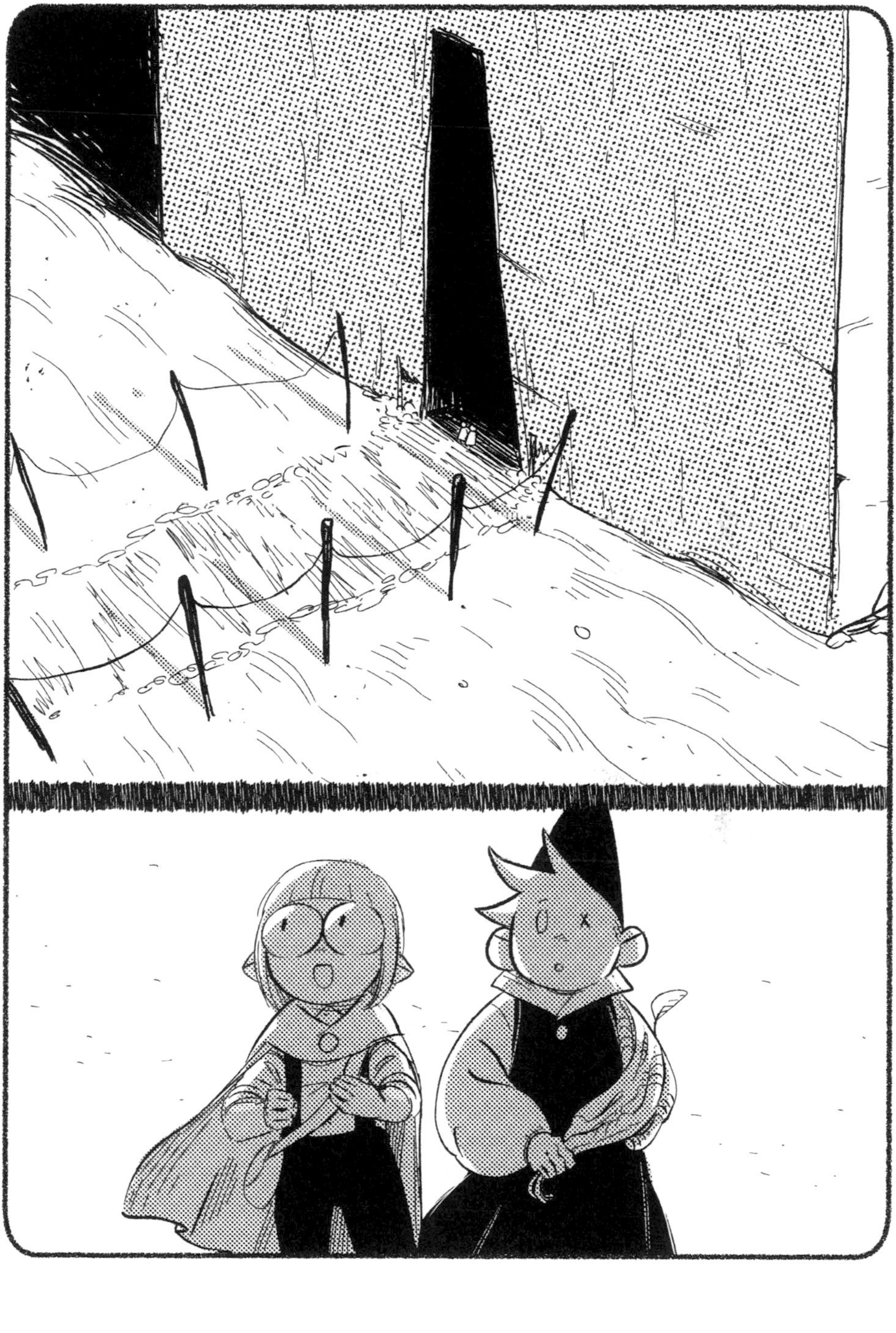

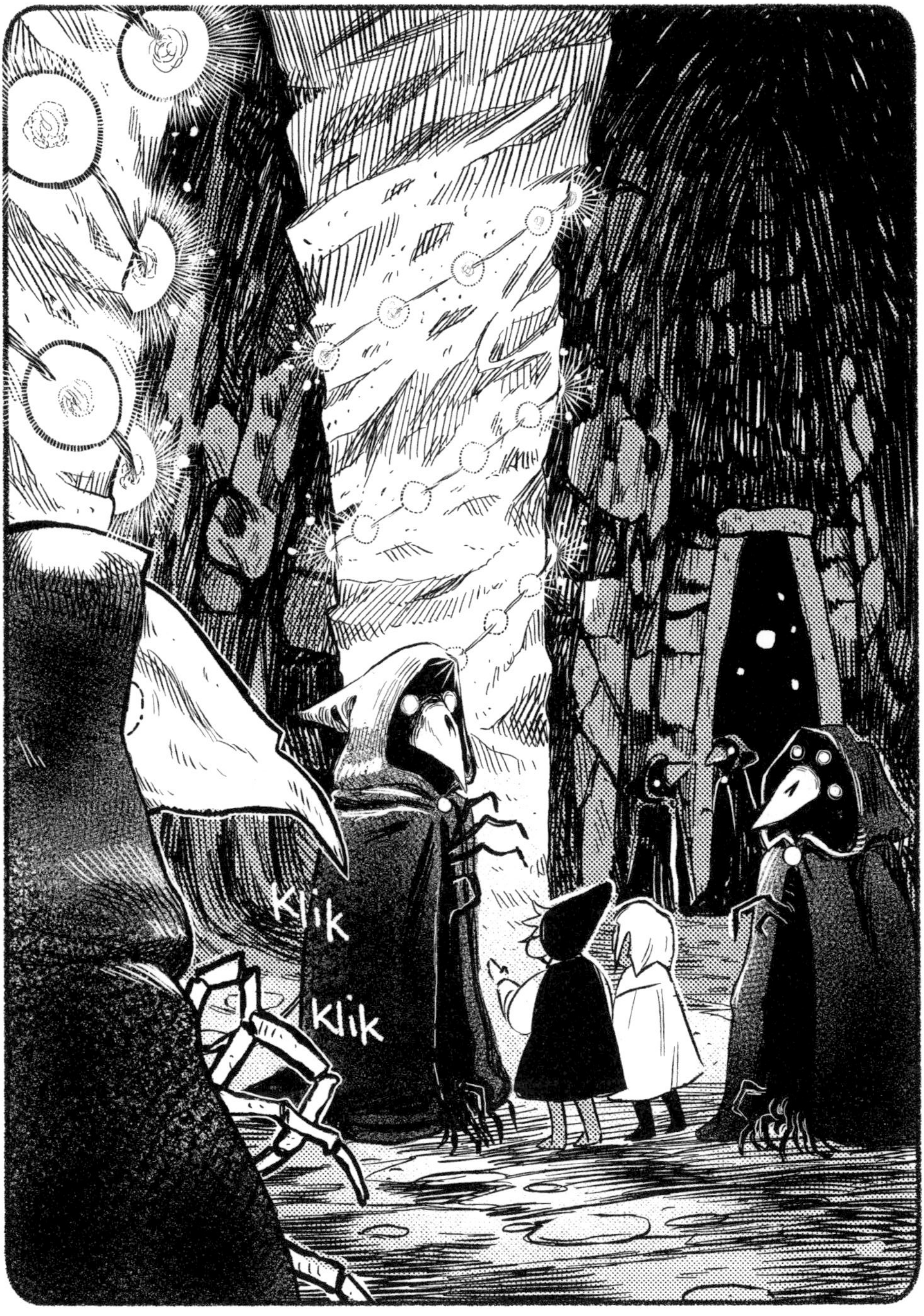
Klik
Klik

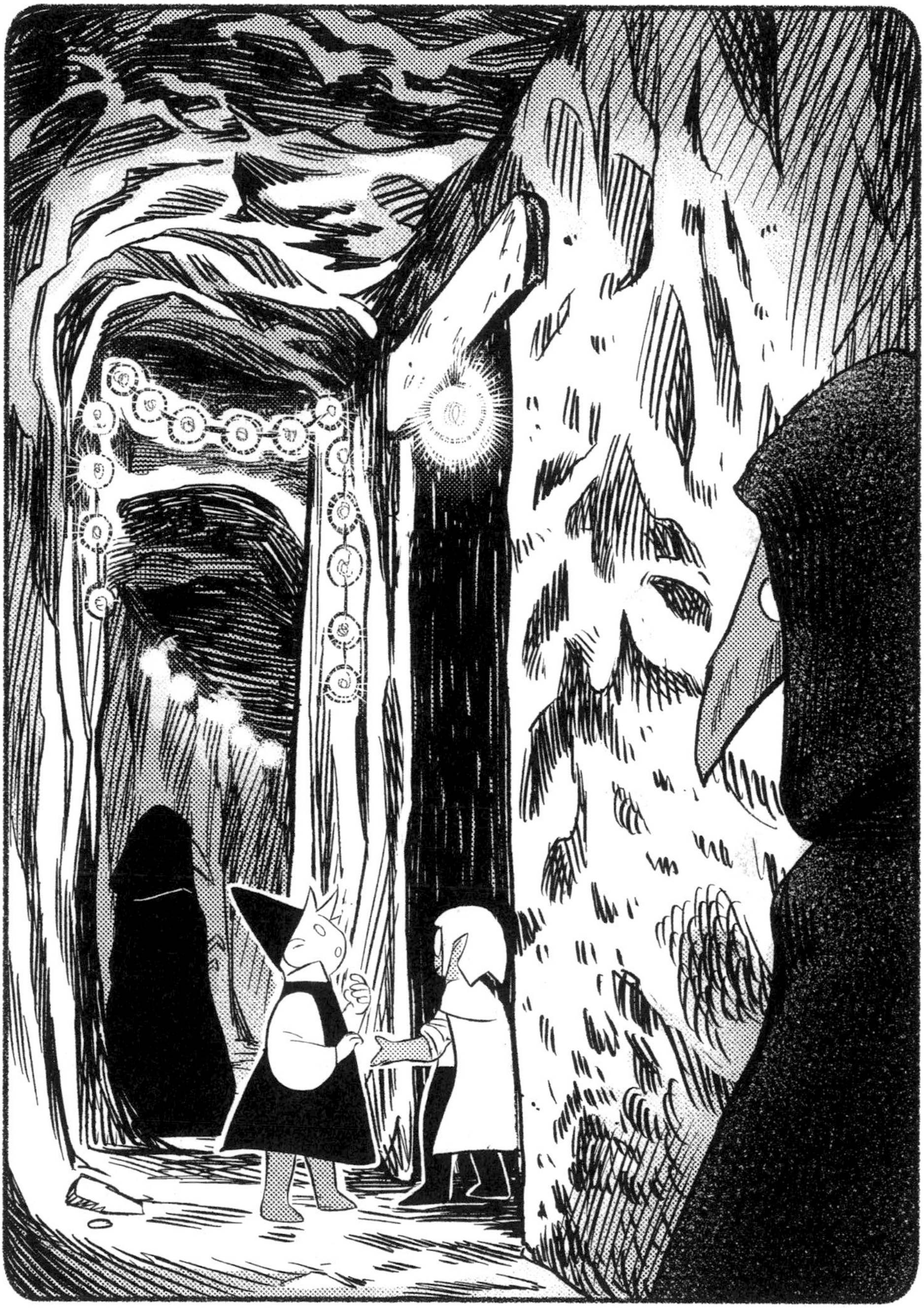

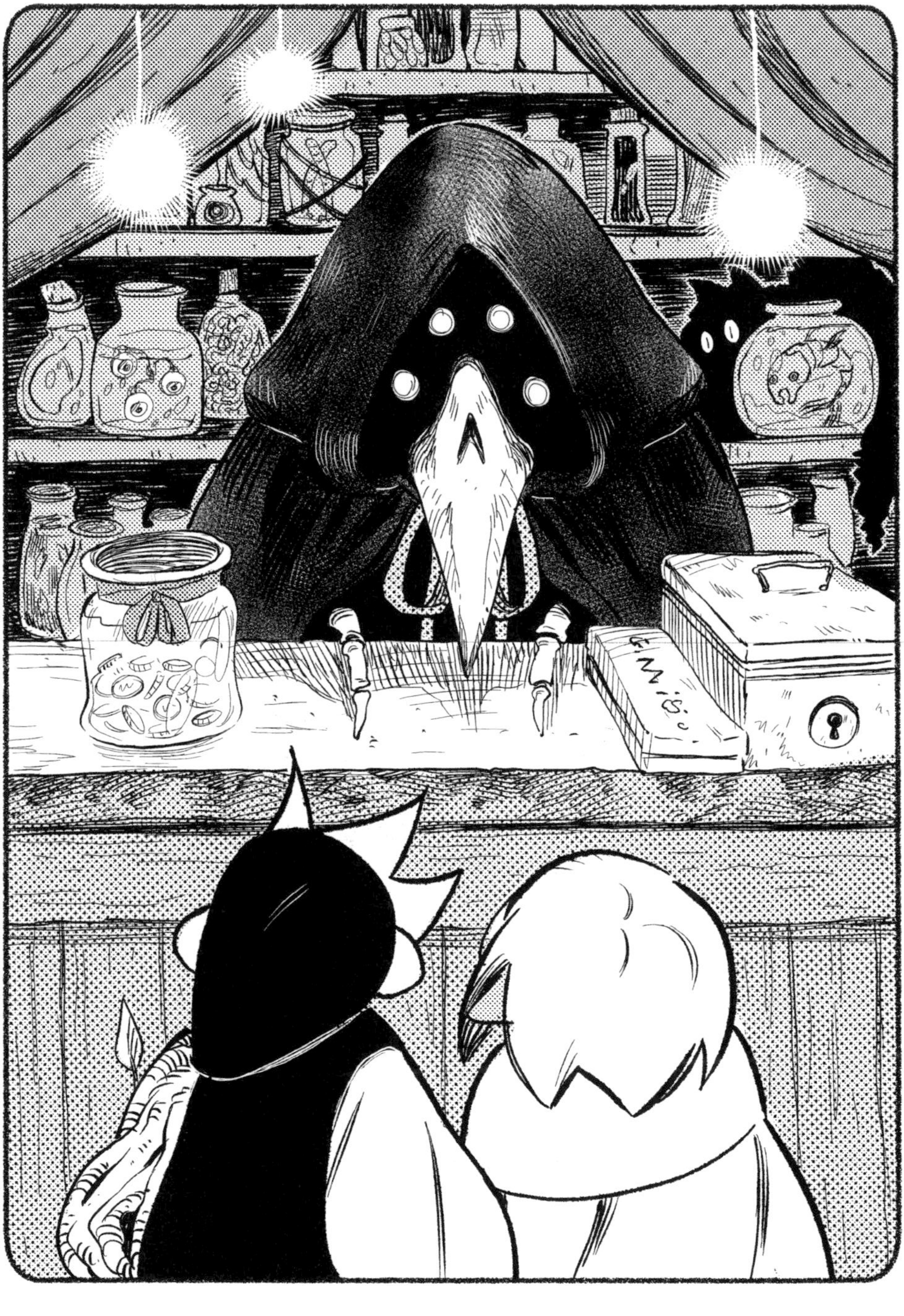

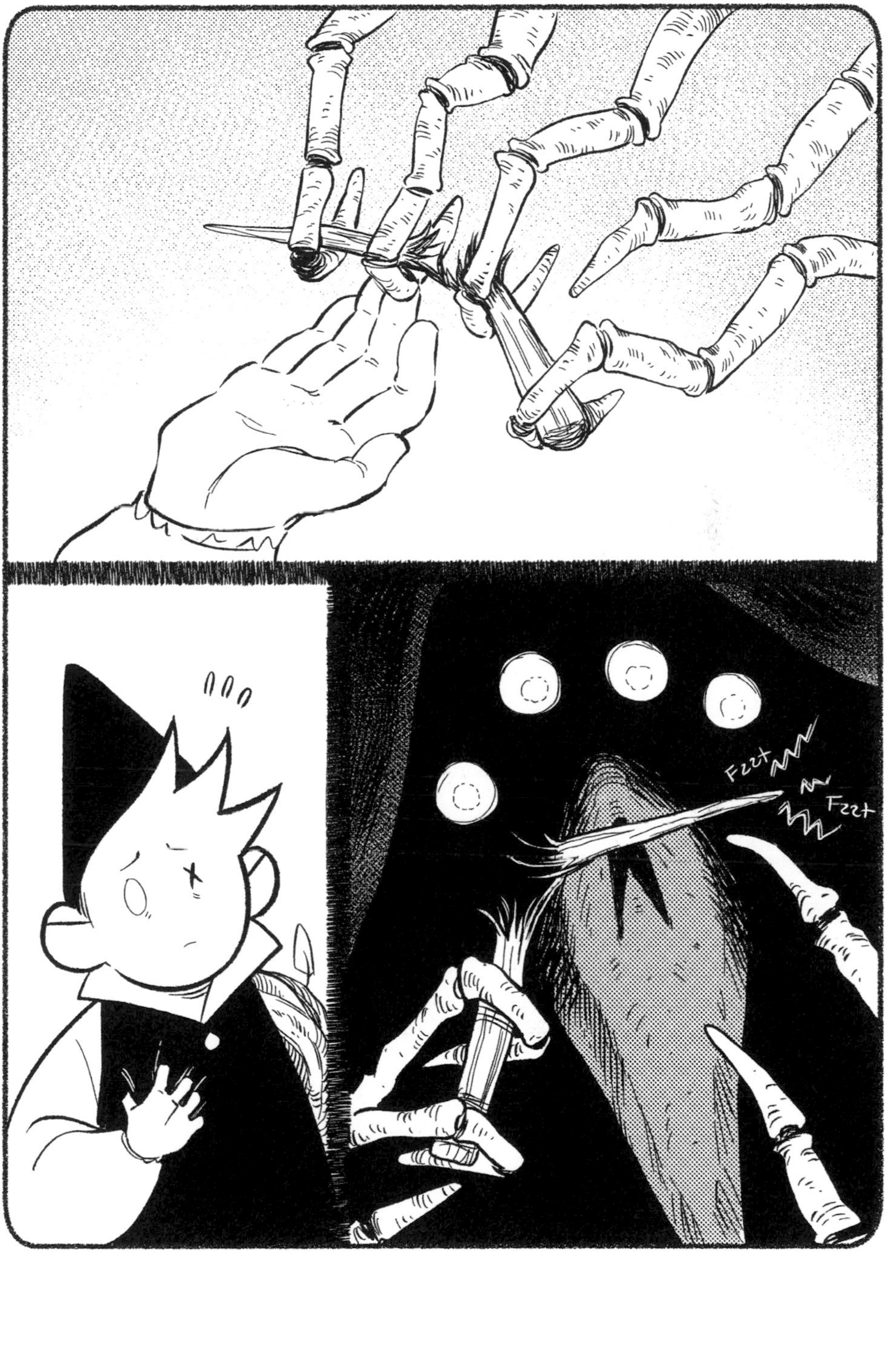
Fzzt
Fzzt

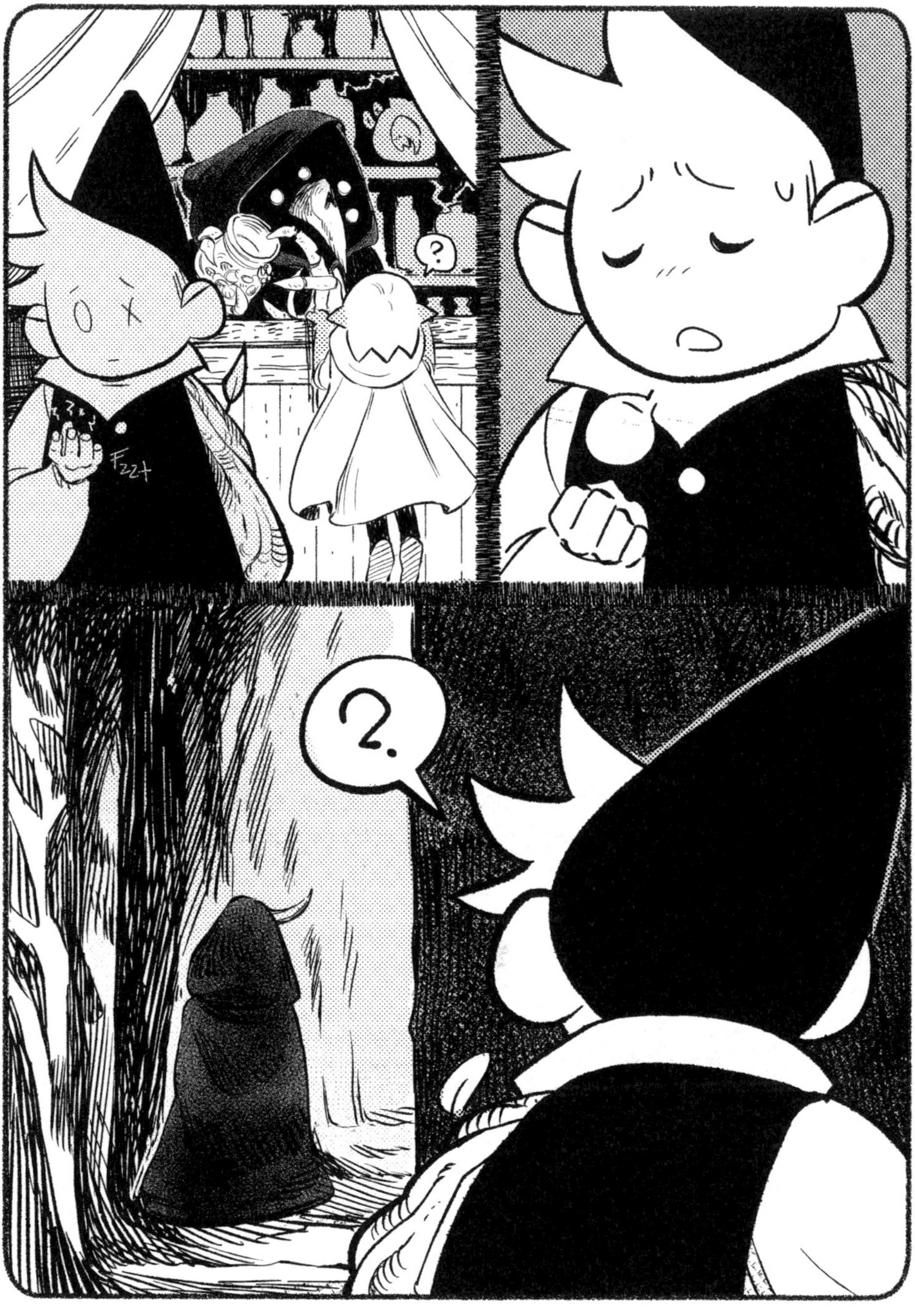
?
Fzzt
?

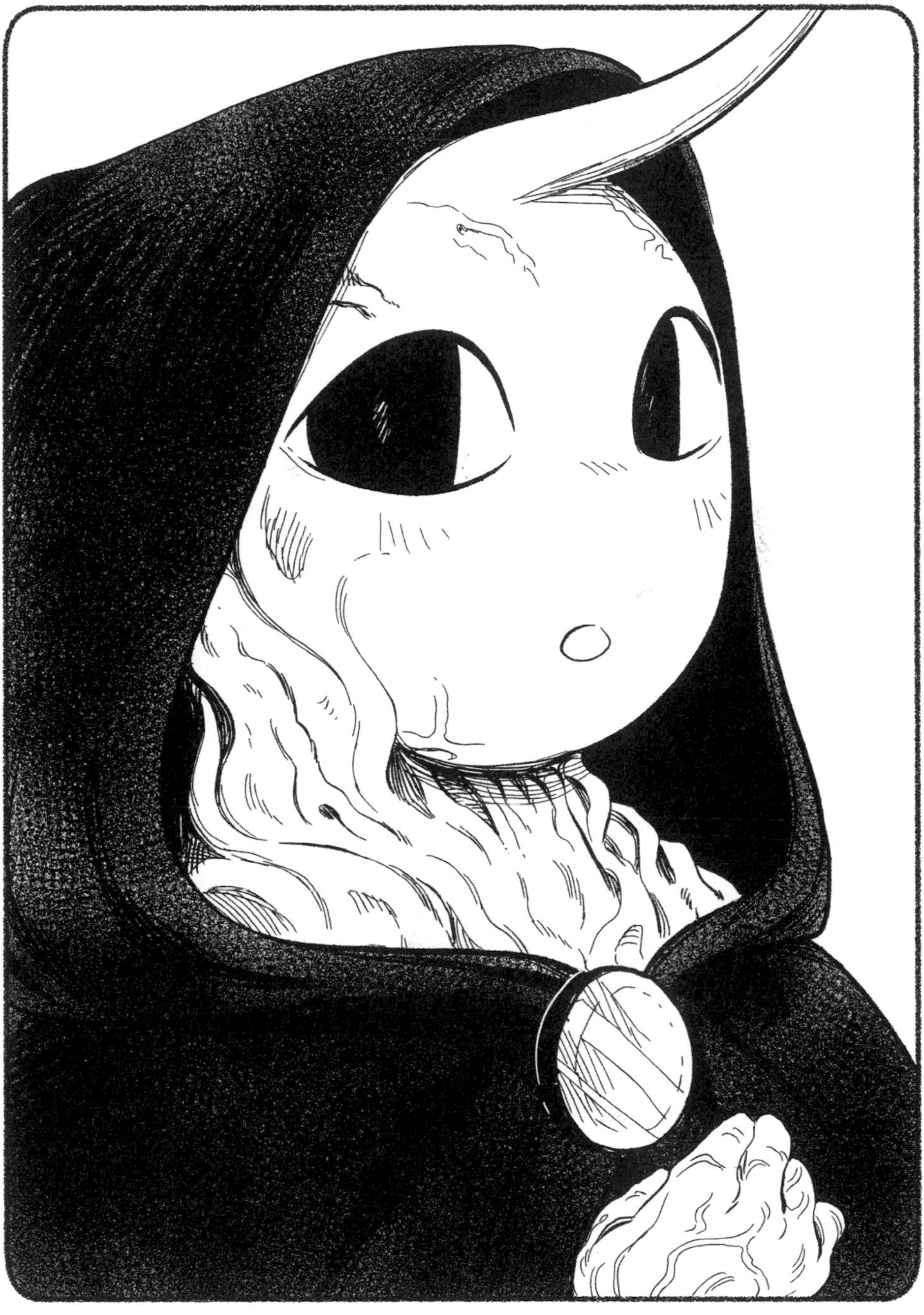

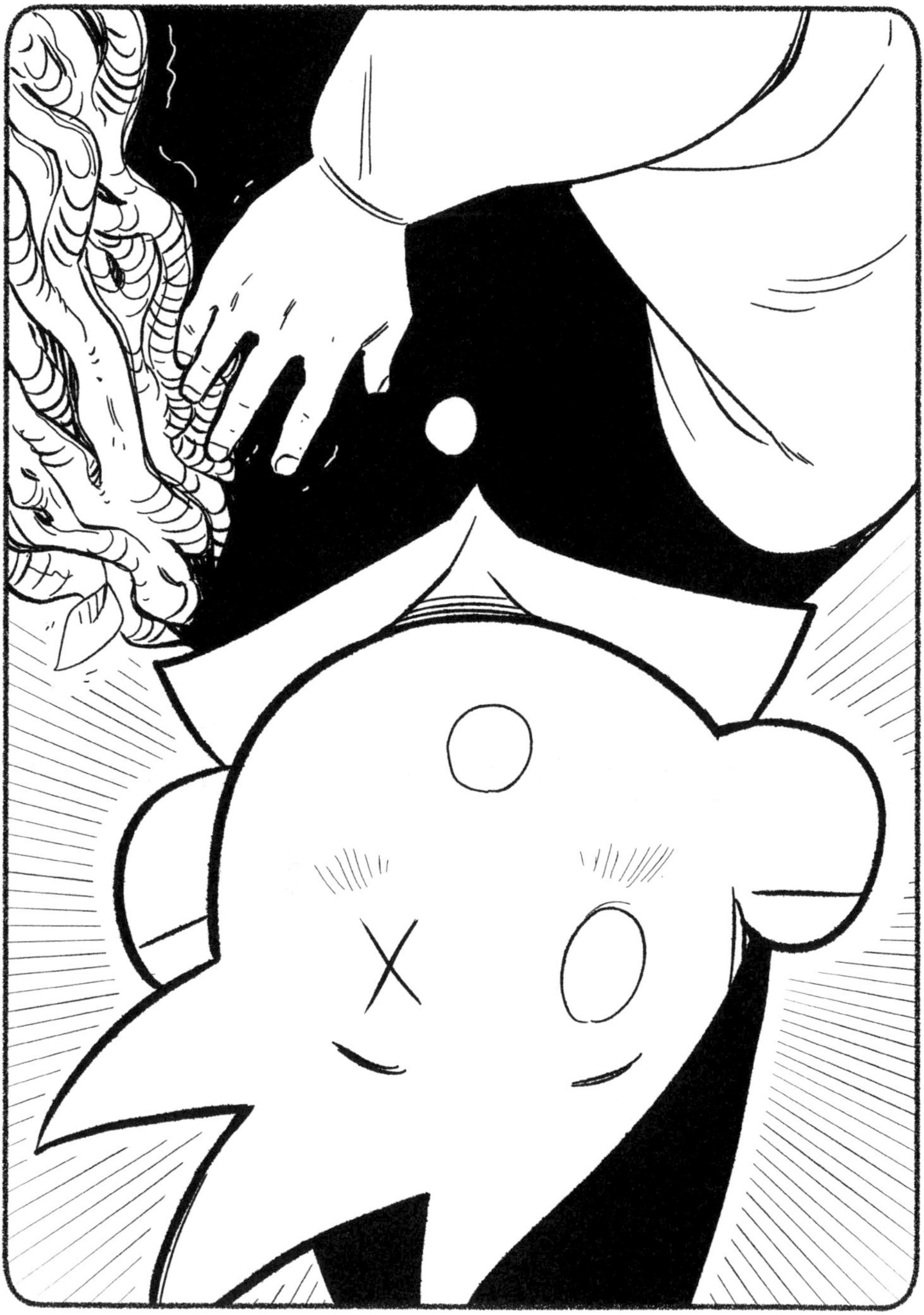

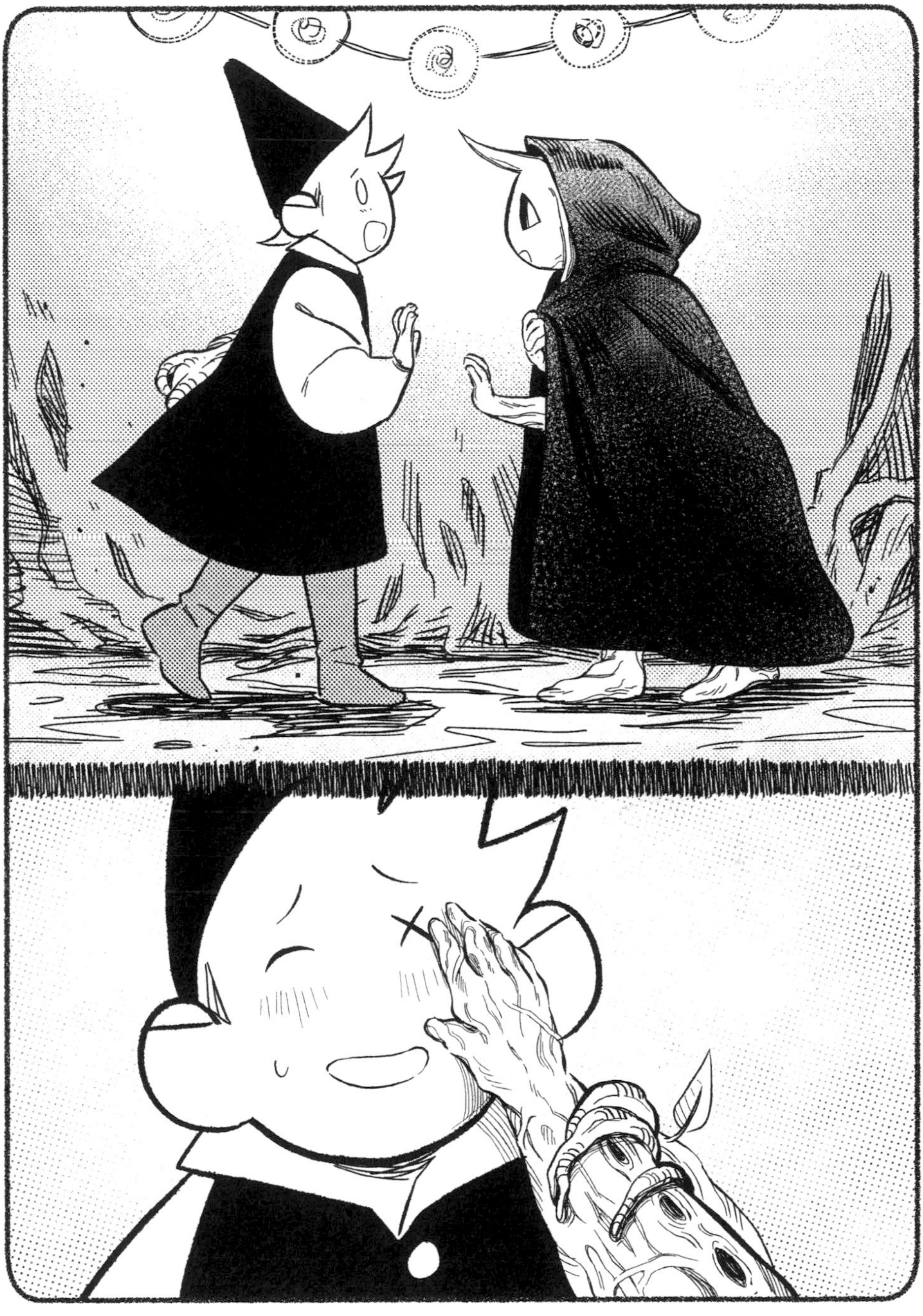

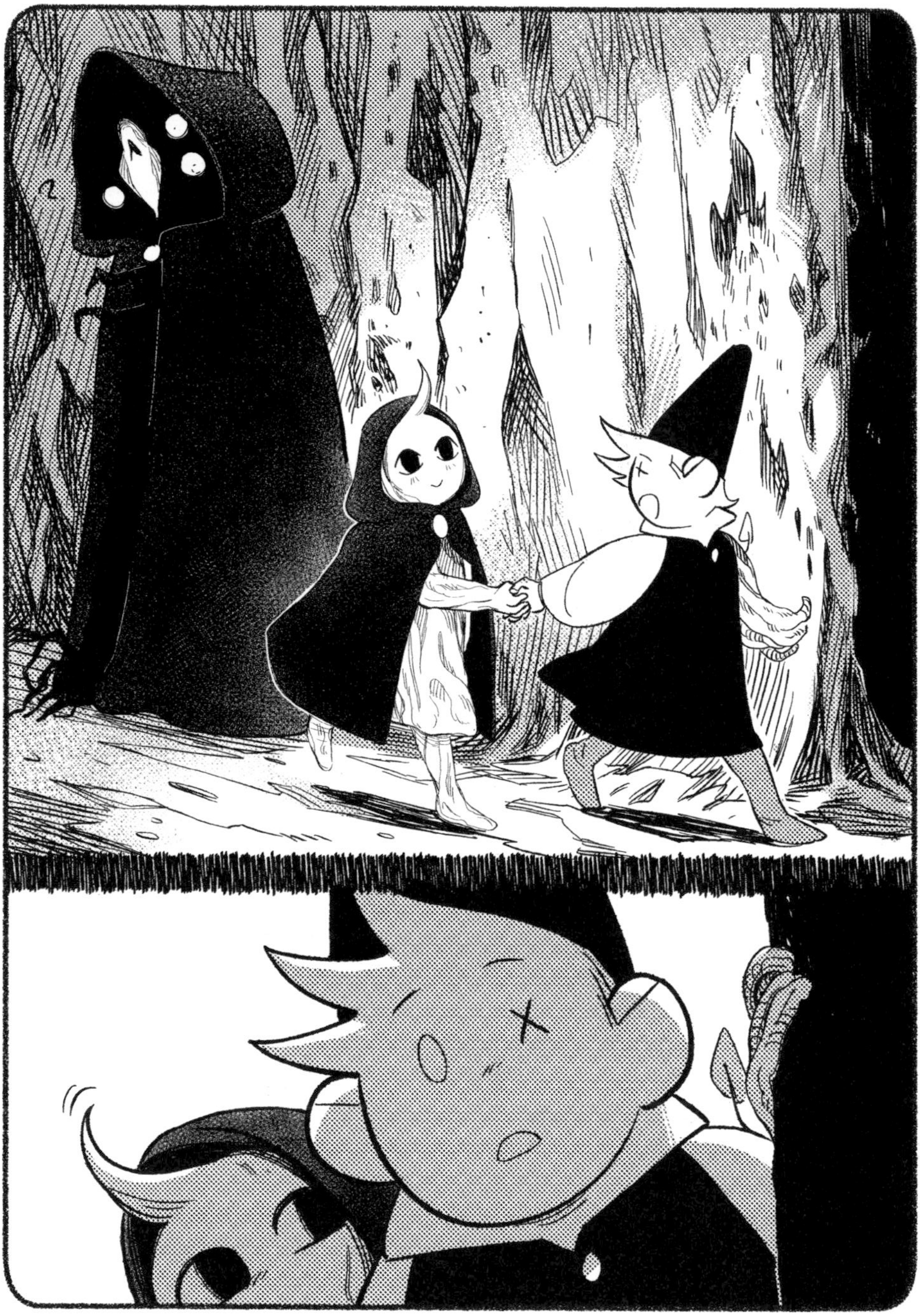

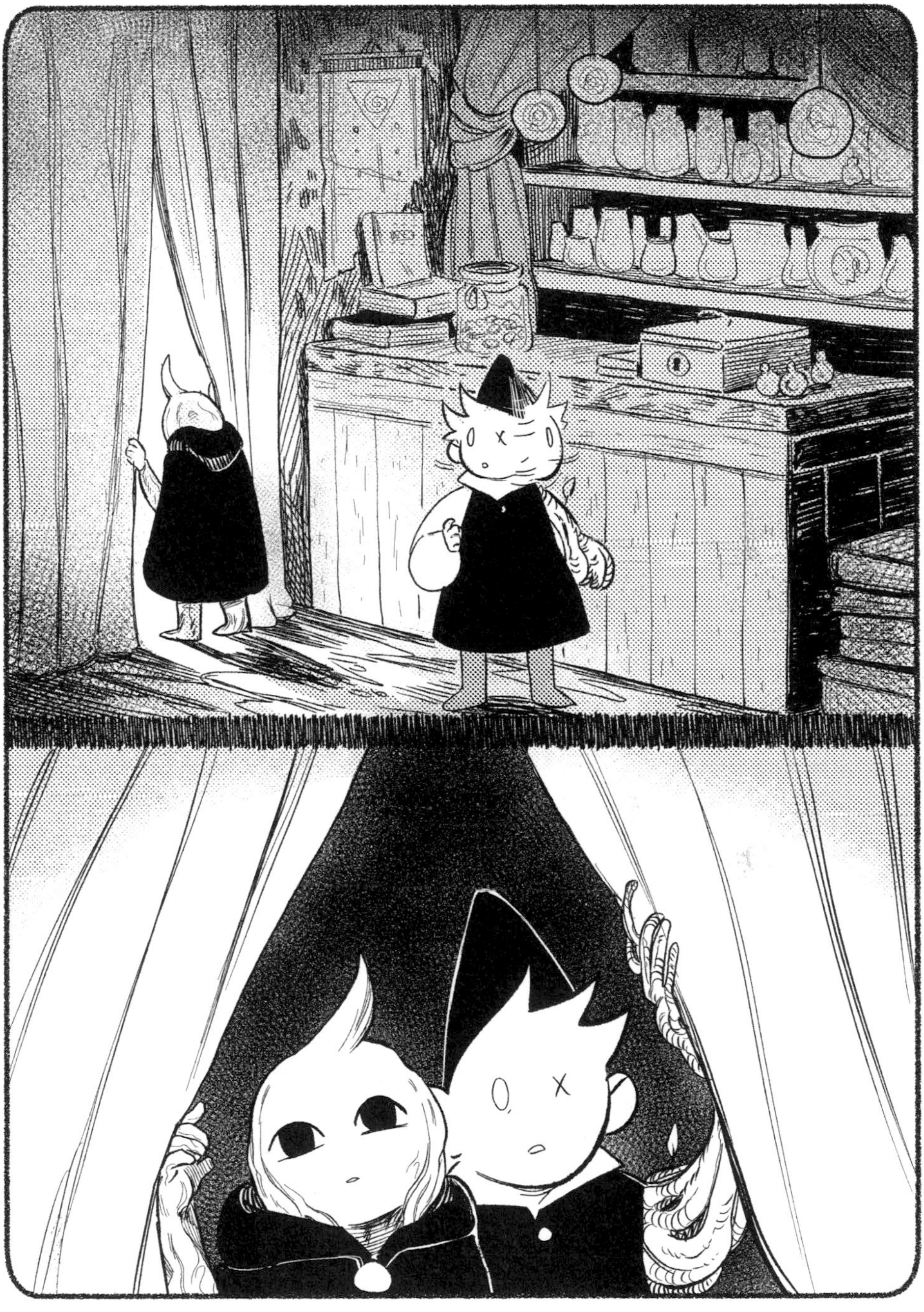

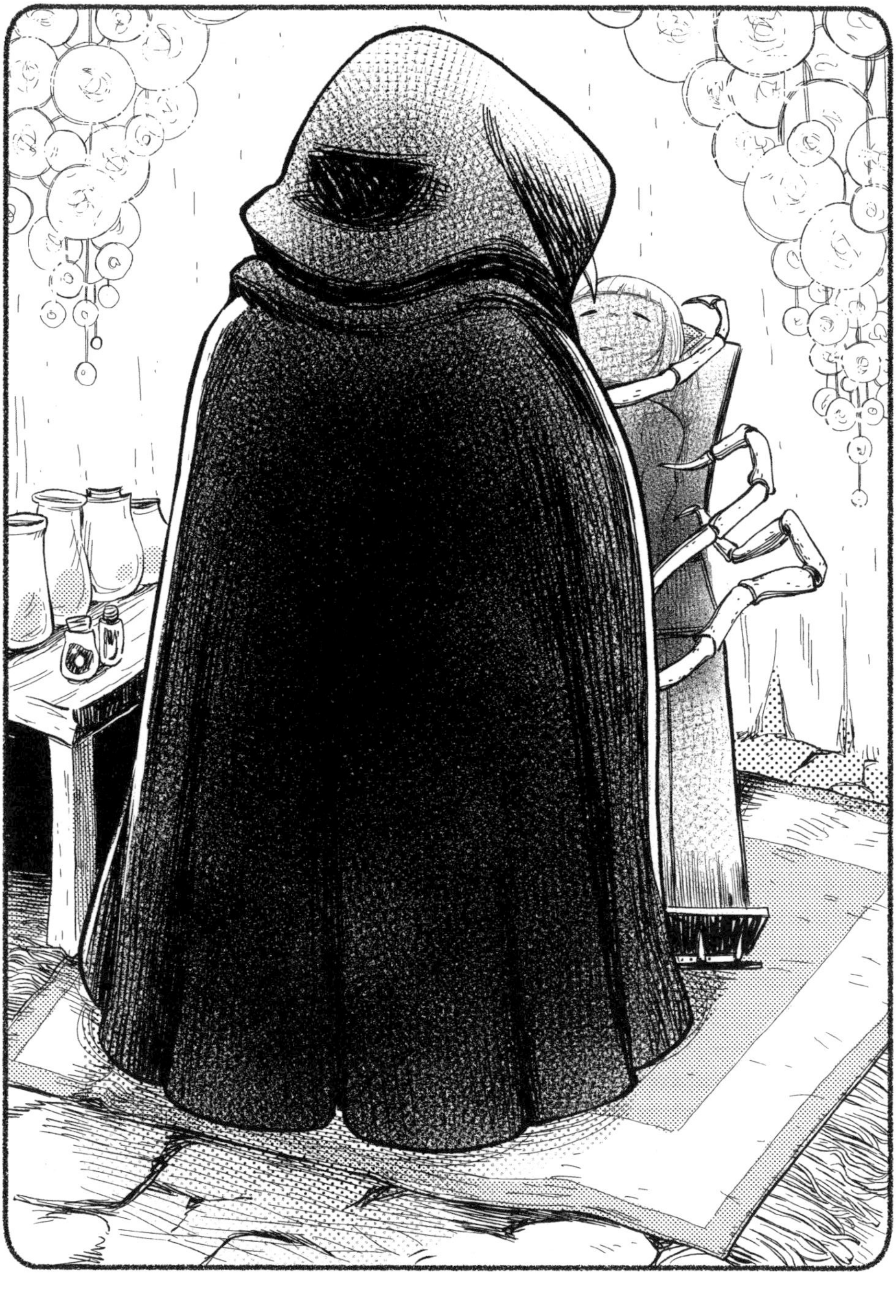

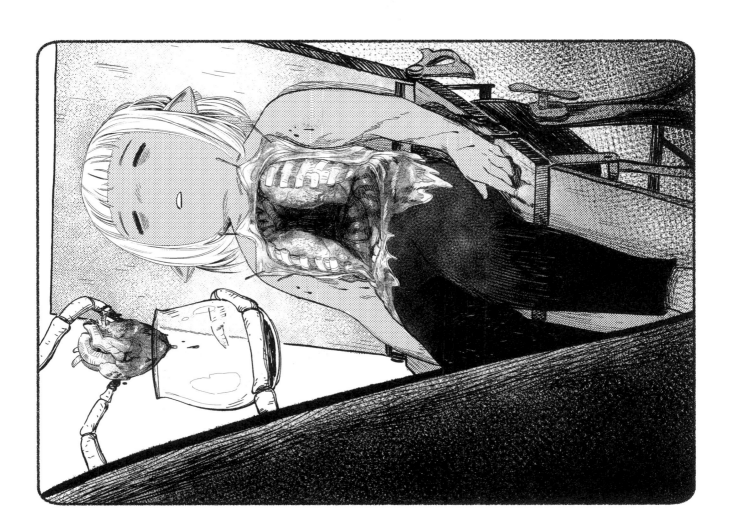

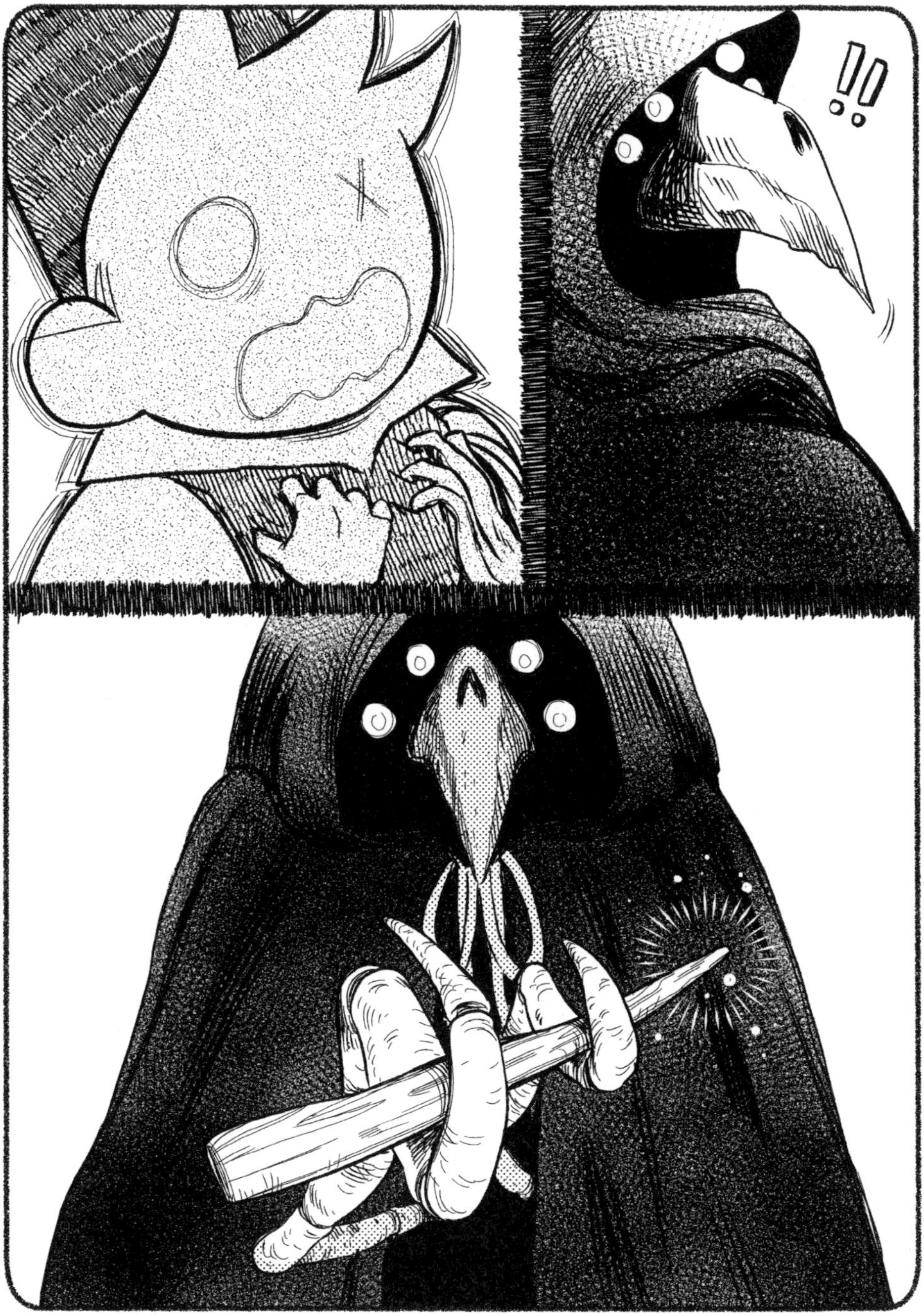
!!

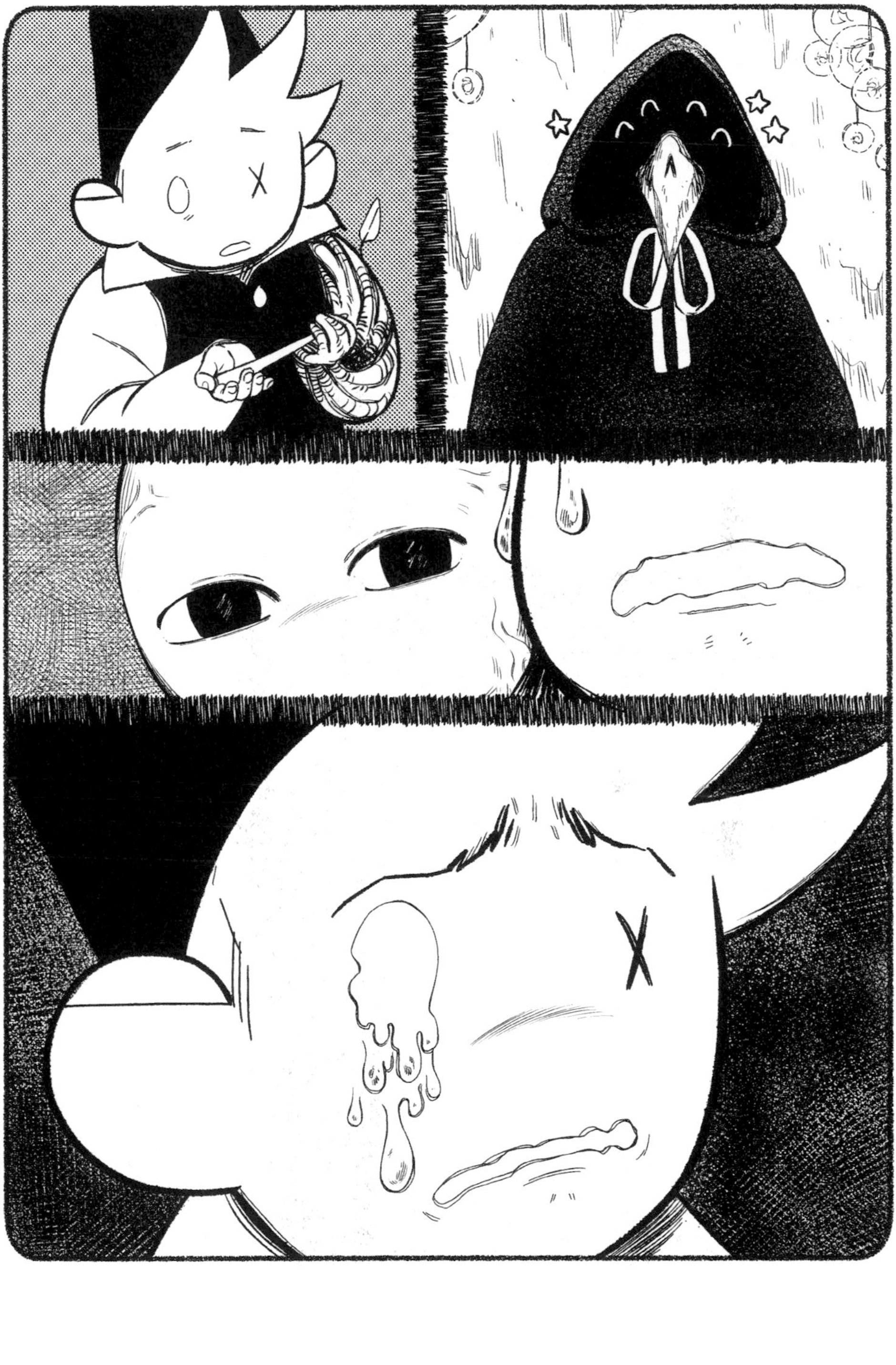

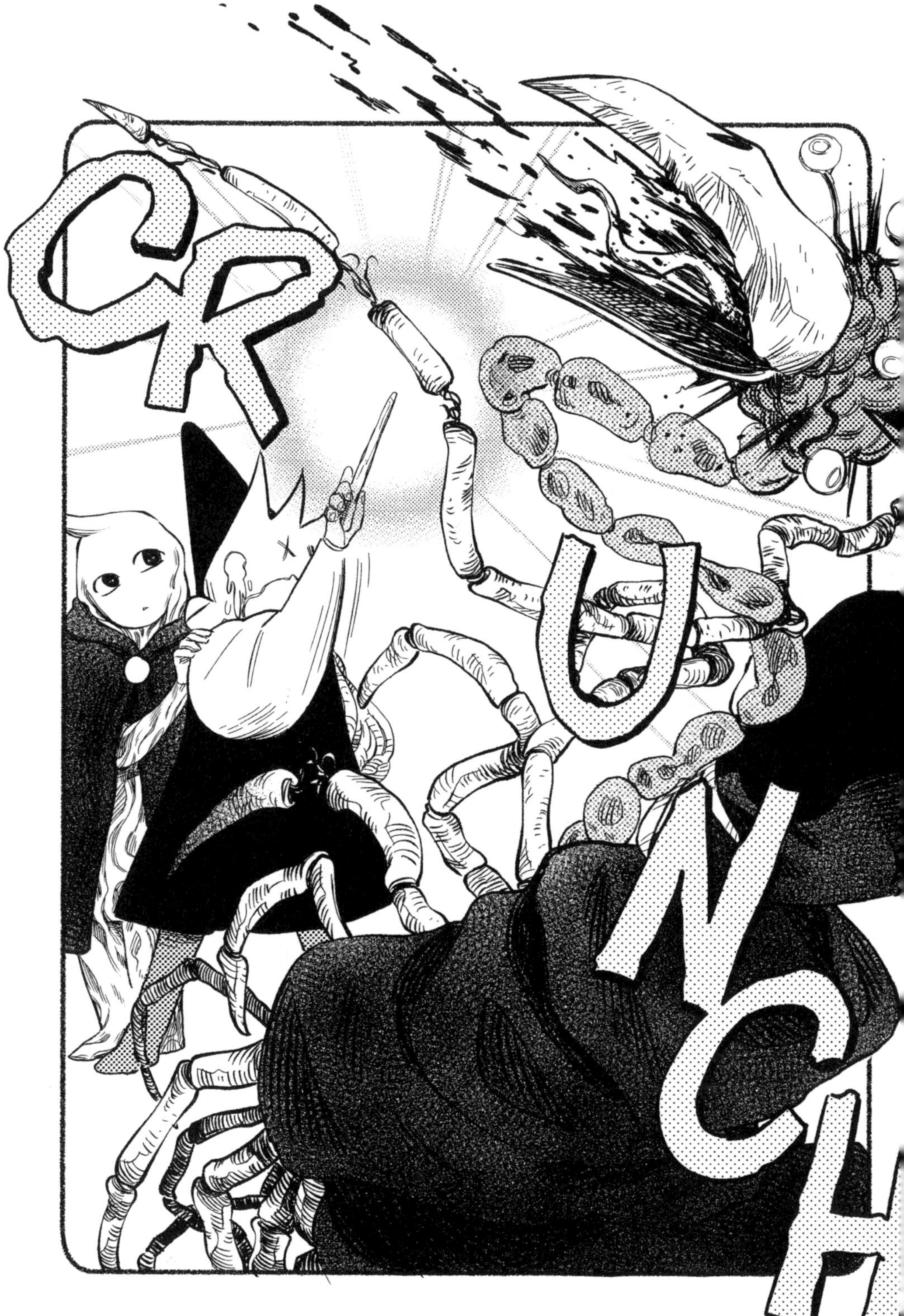
CRUNCH

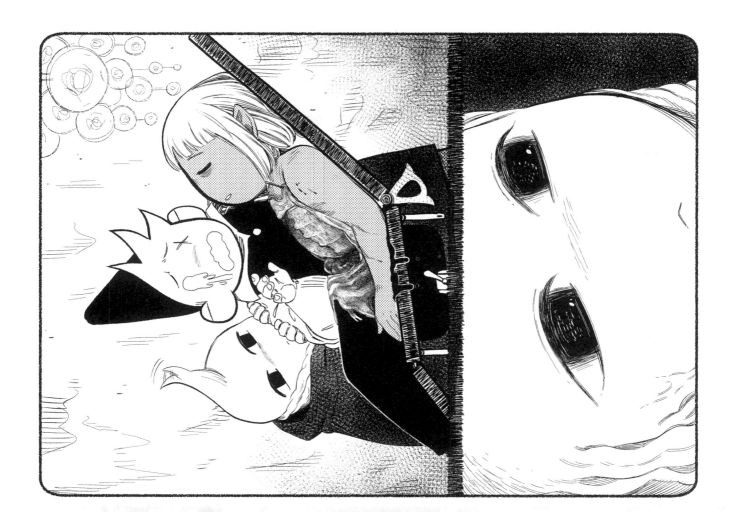

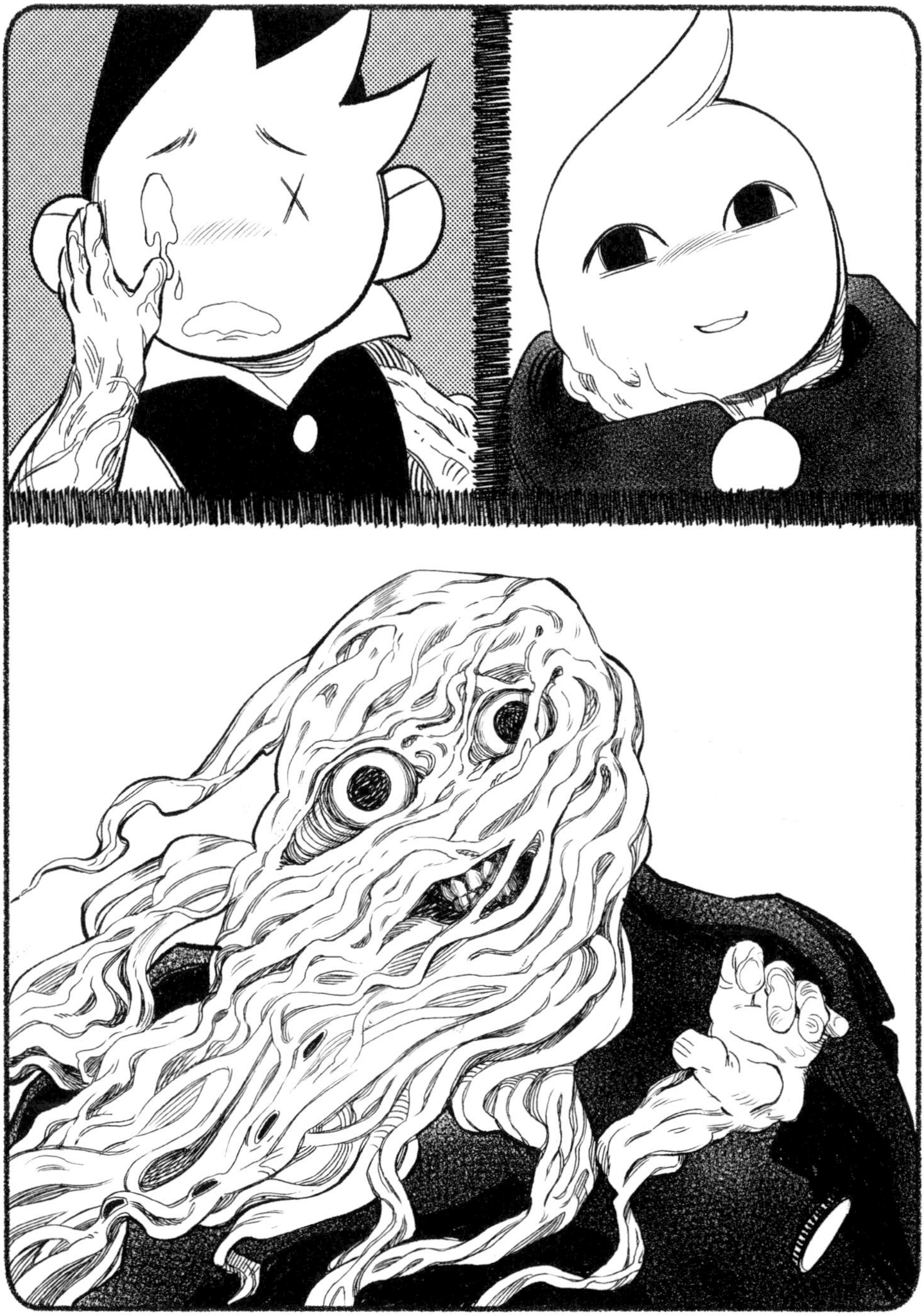

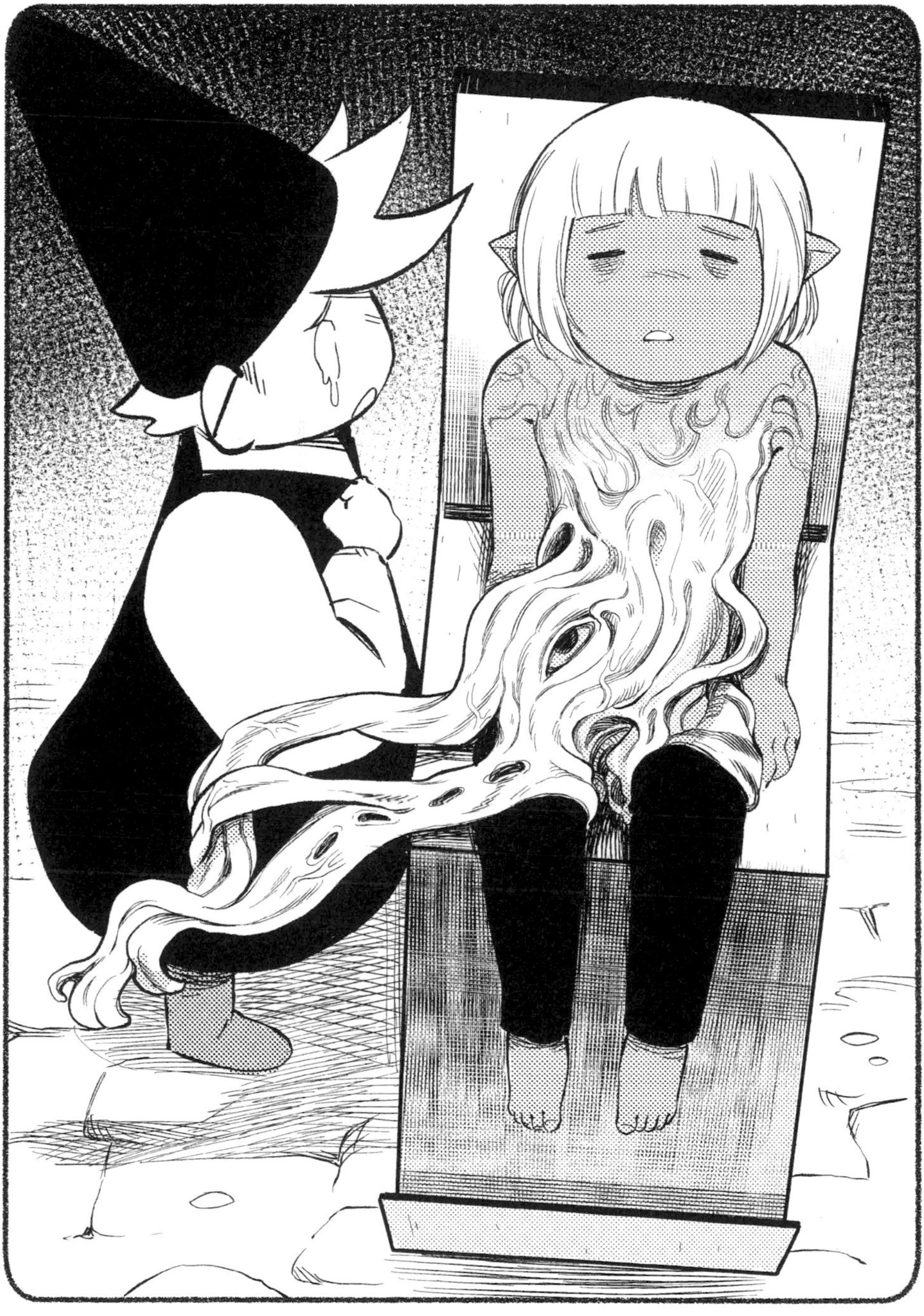

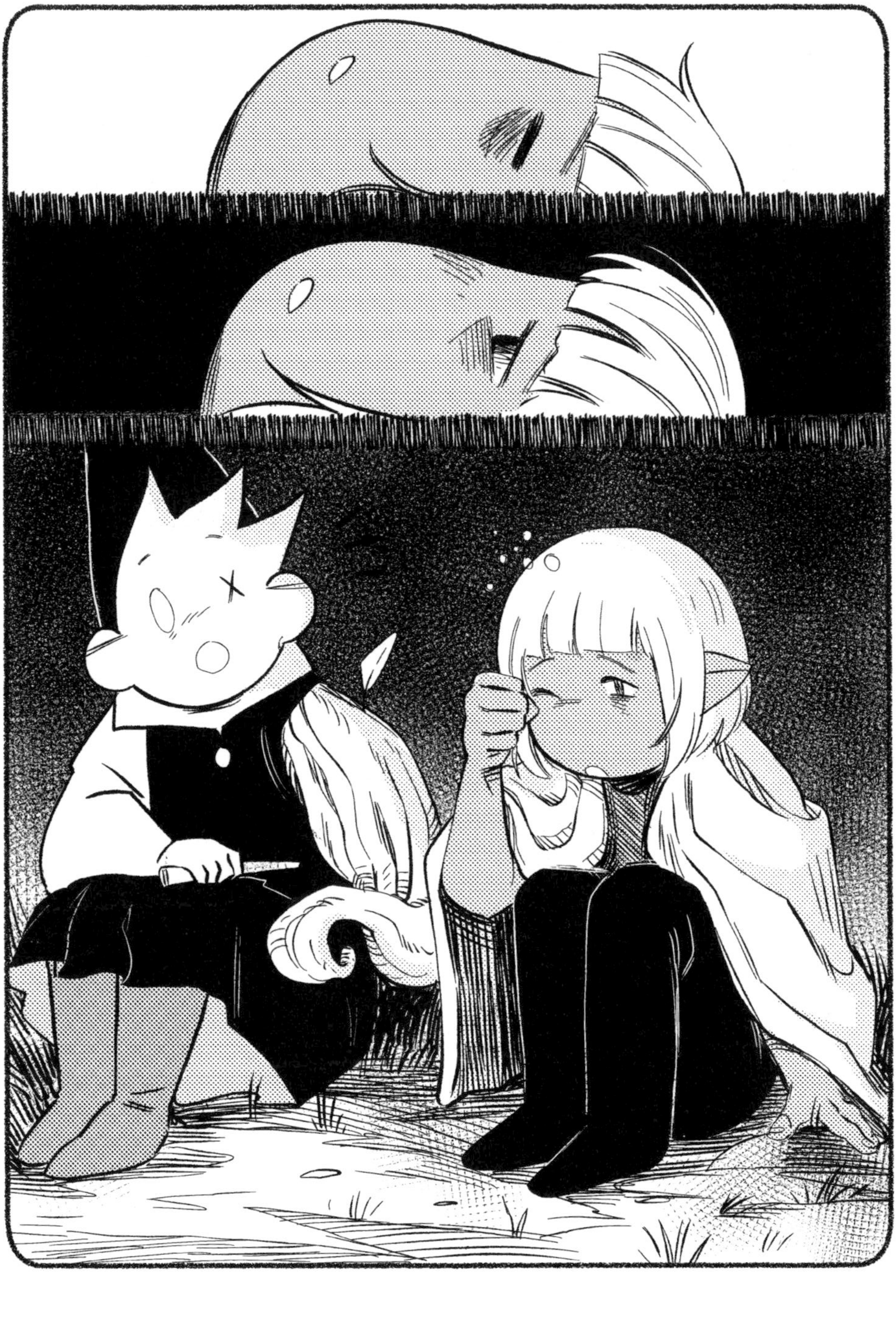

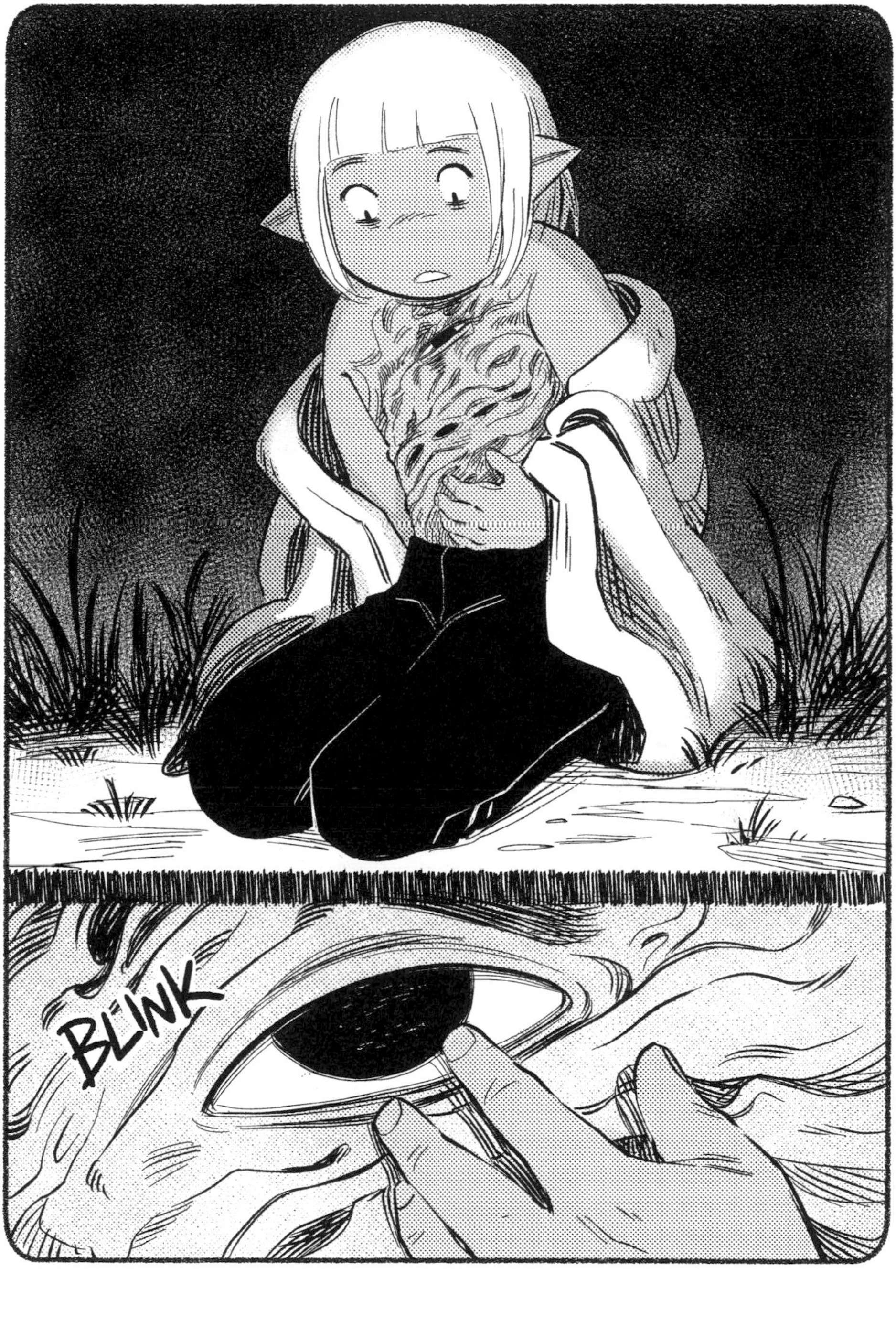
BLINK

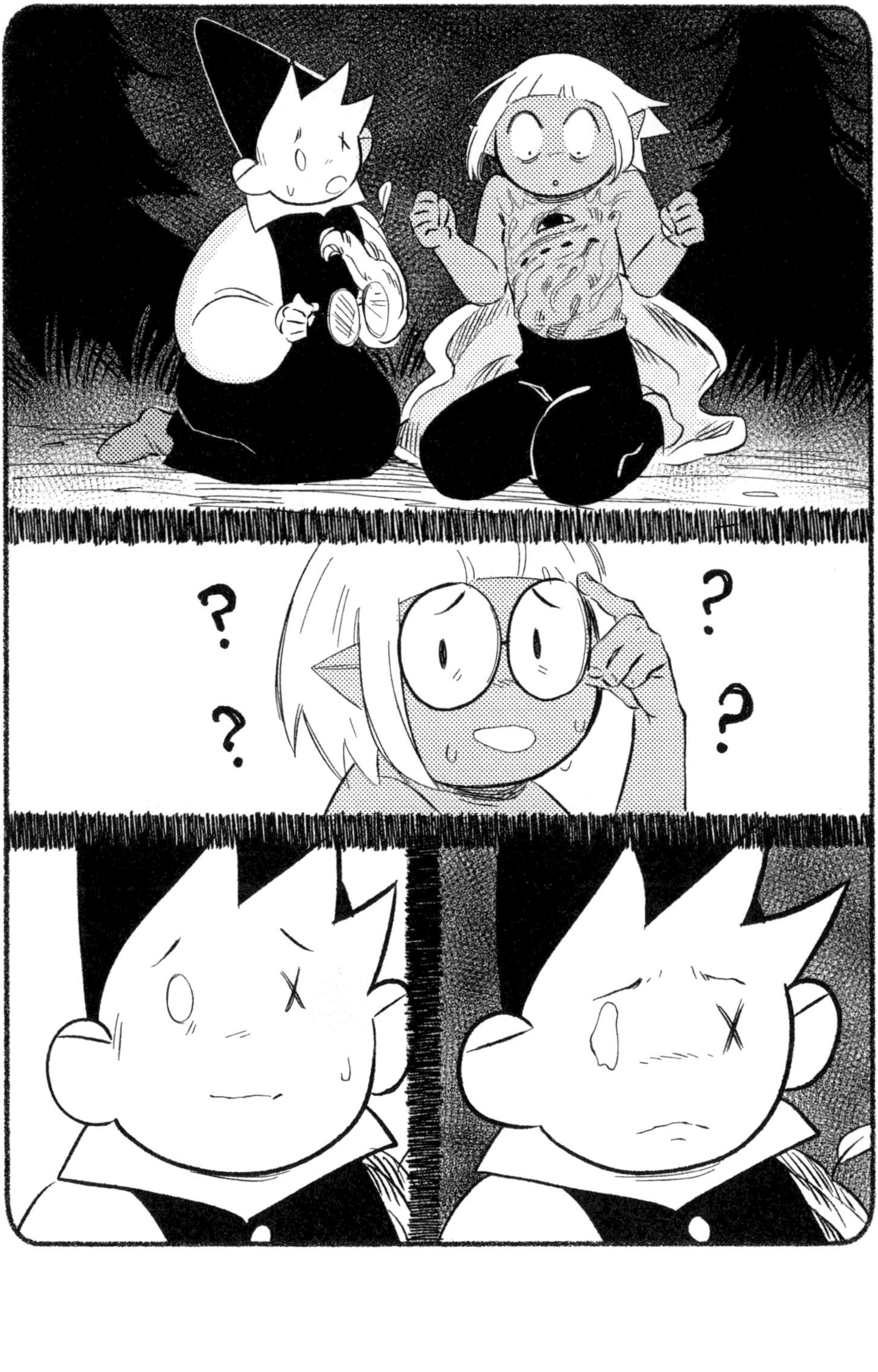
?
?
?
?

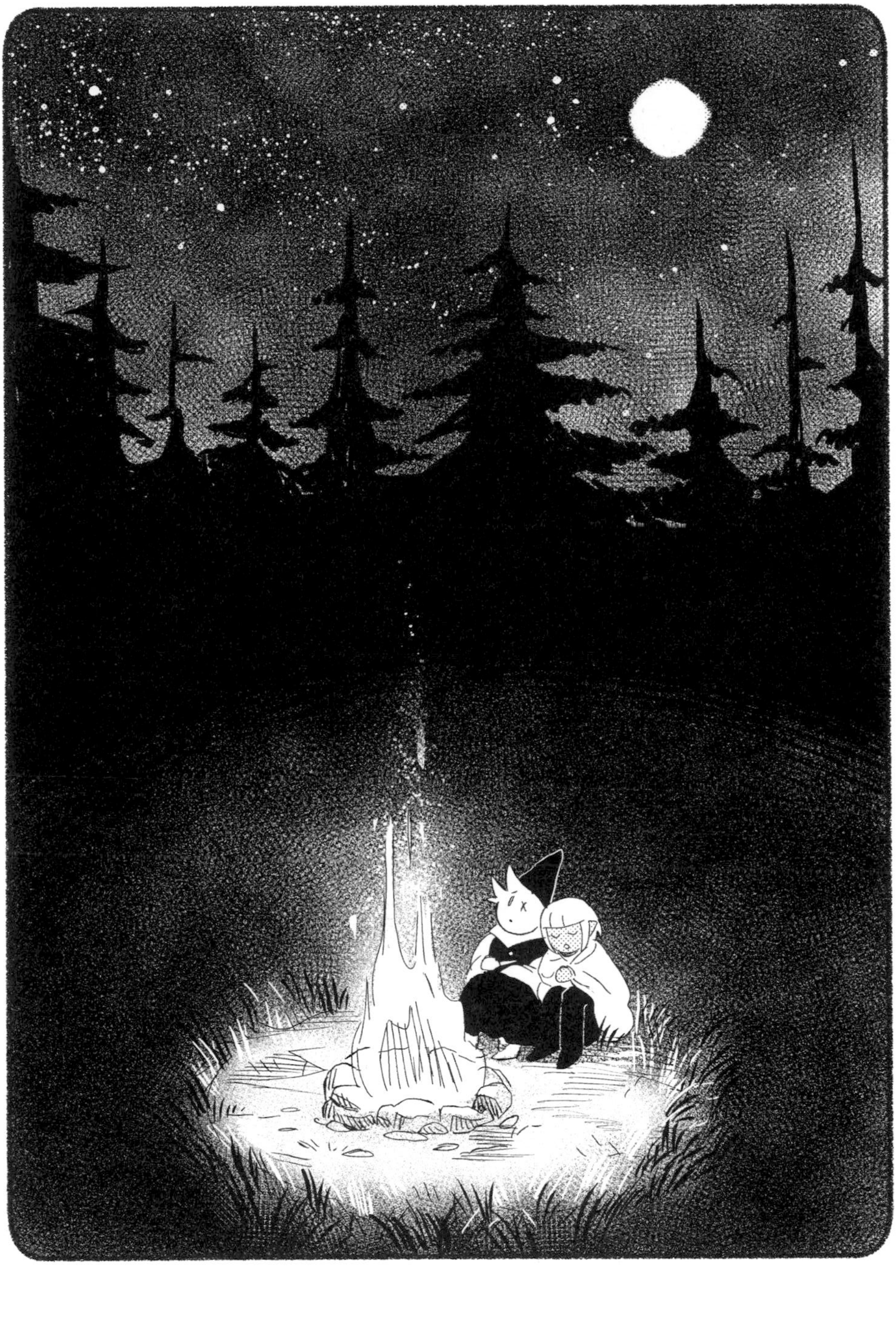

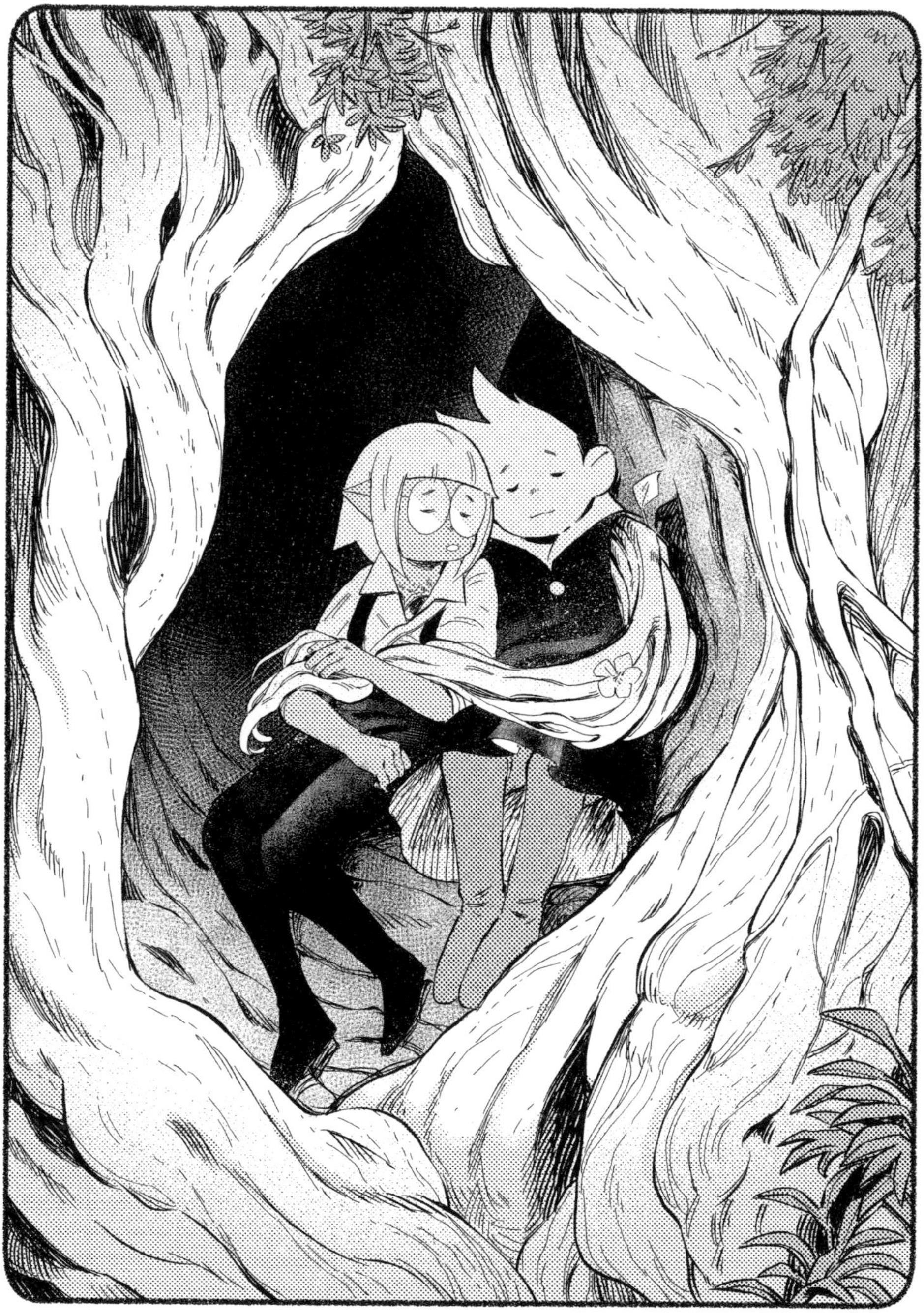

PART FOUR

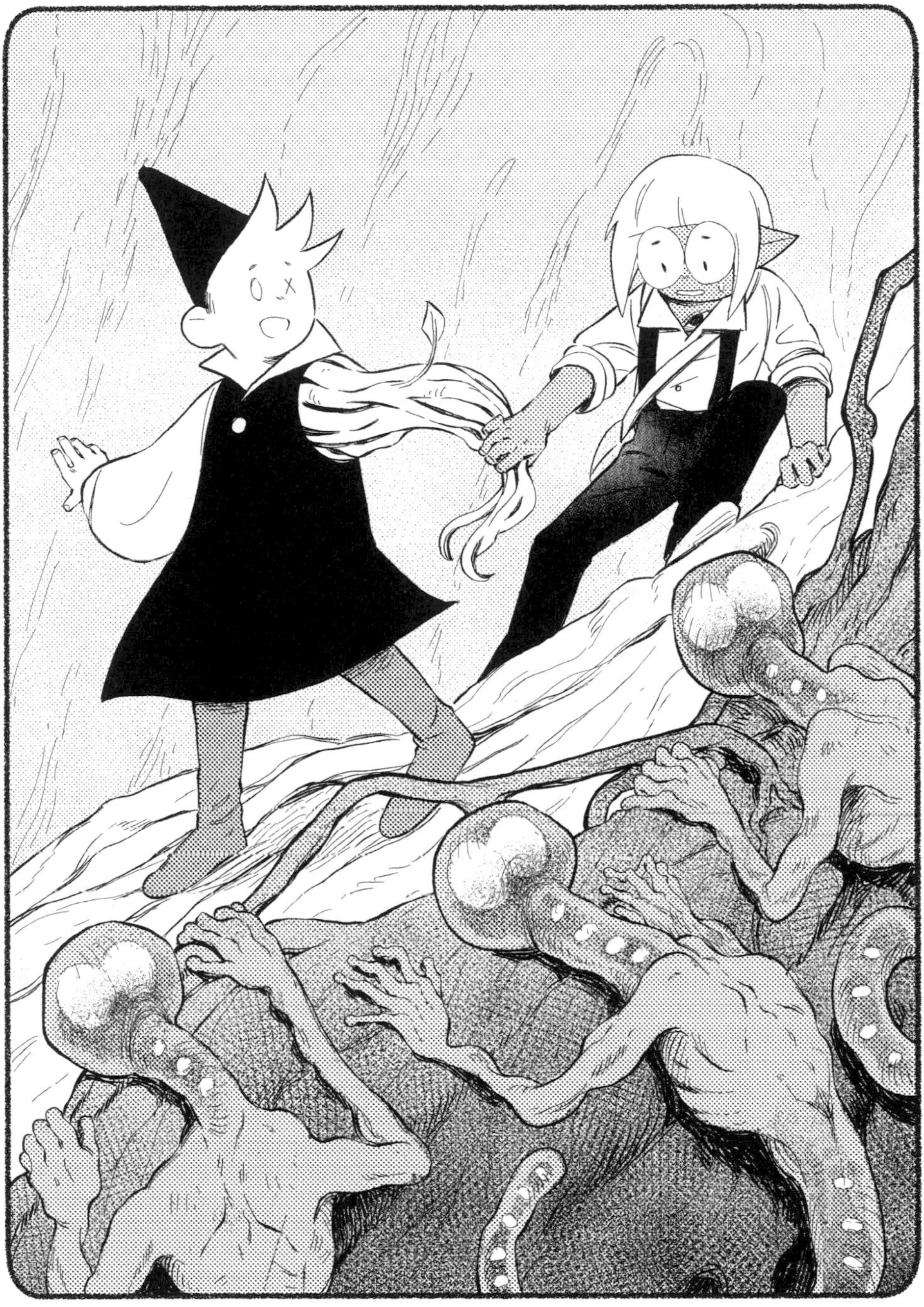

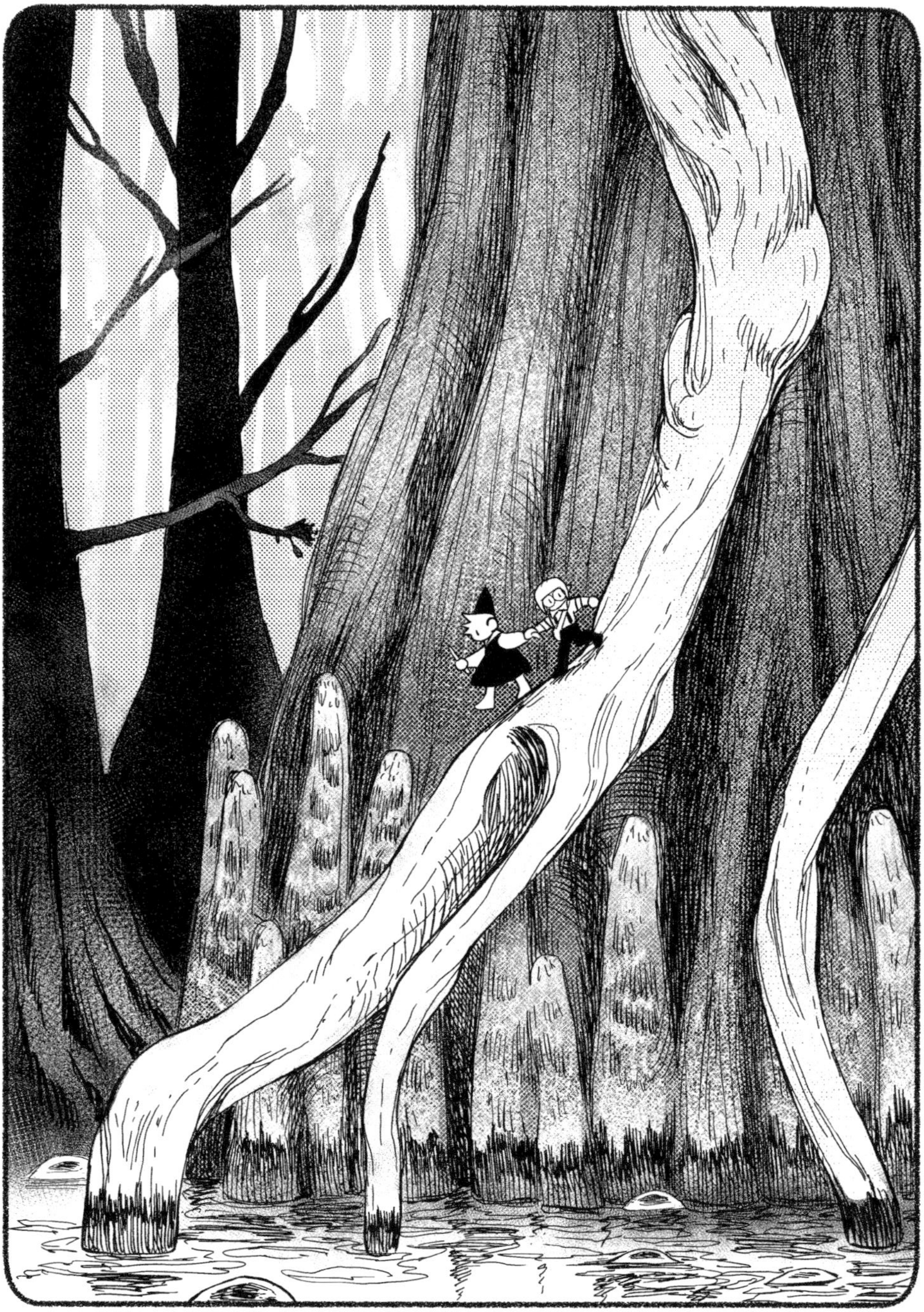

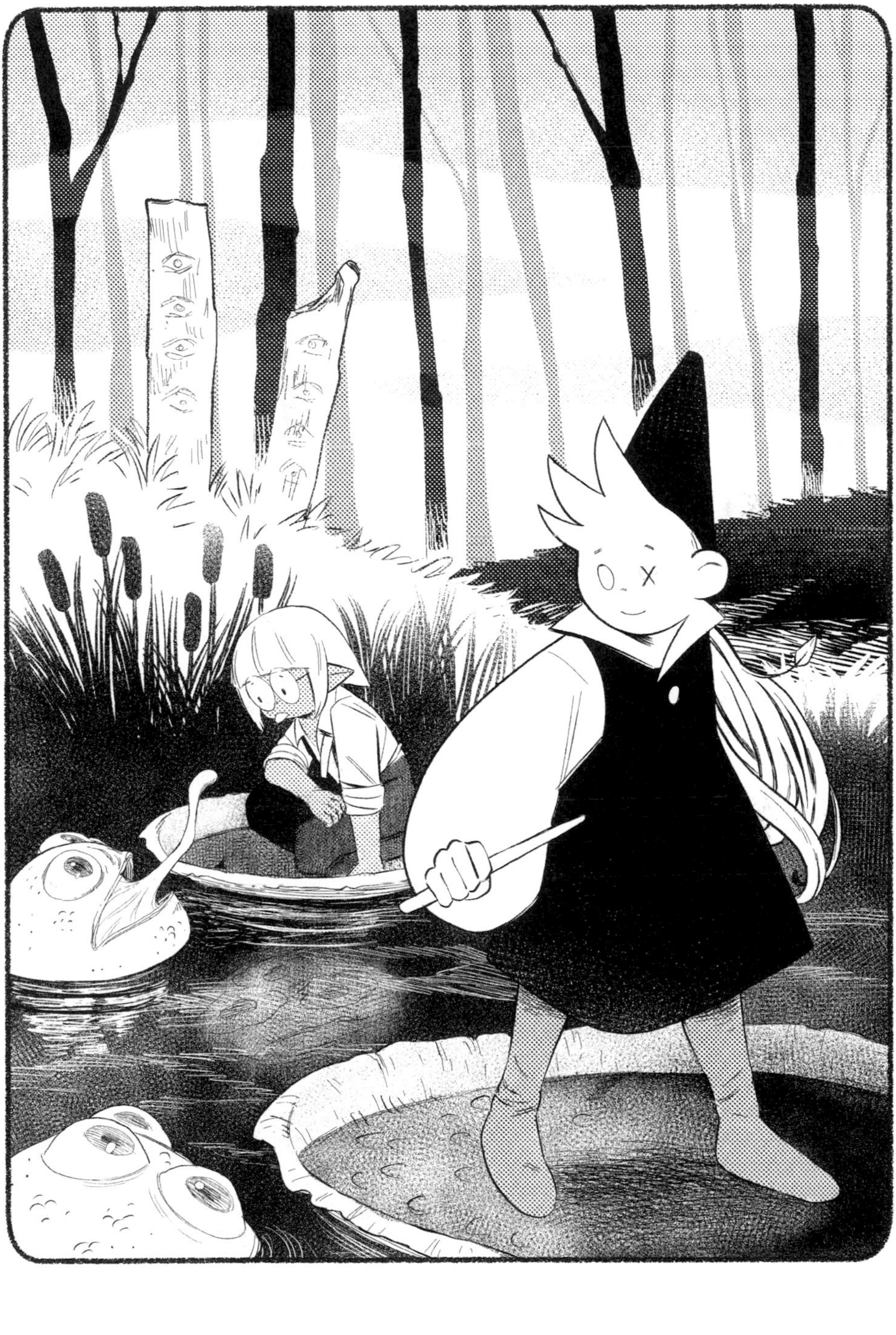

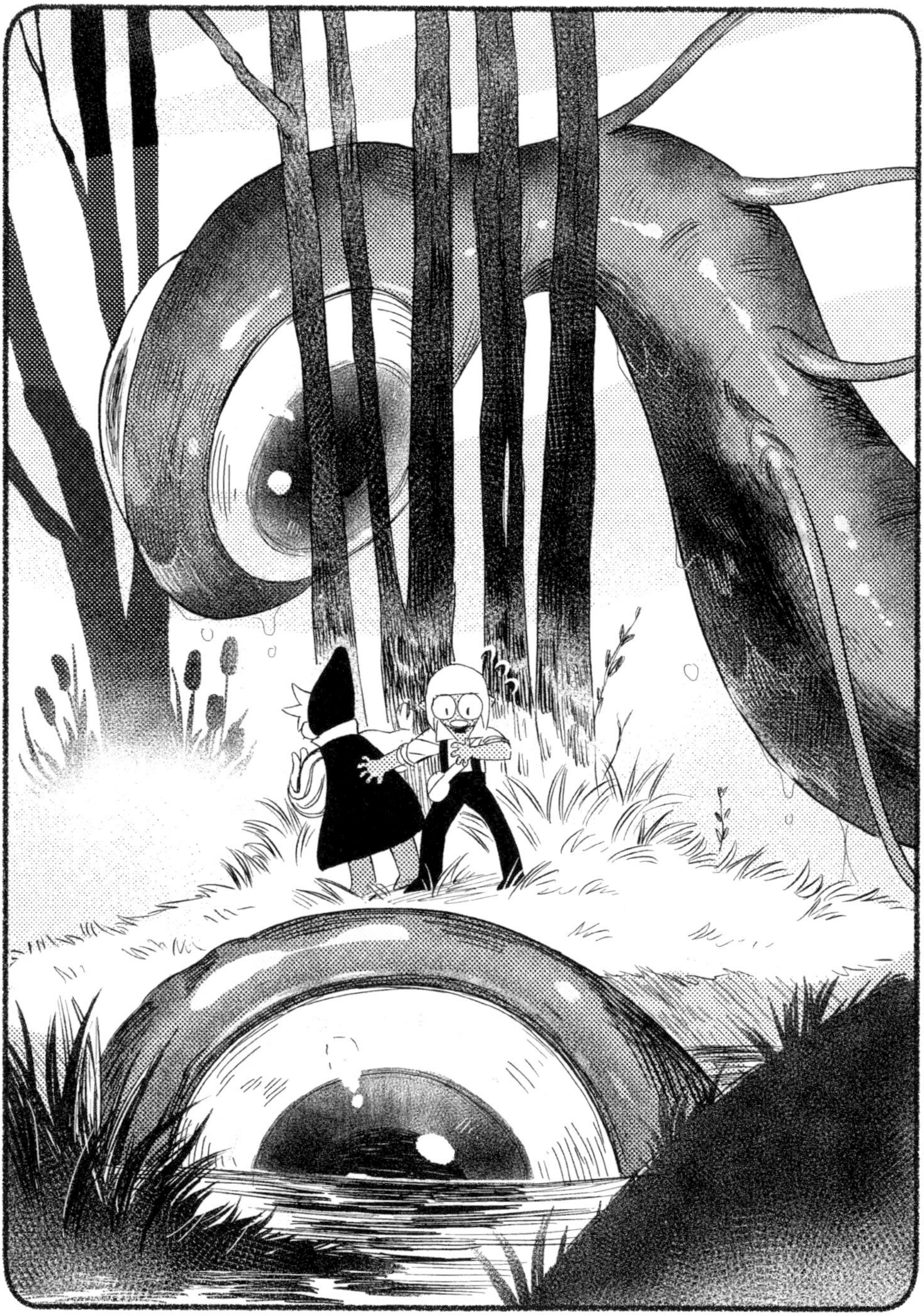

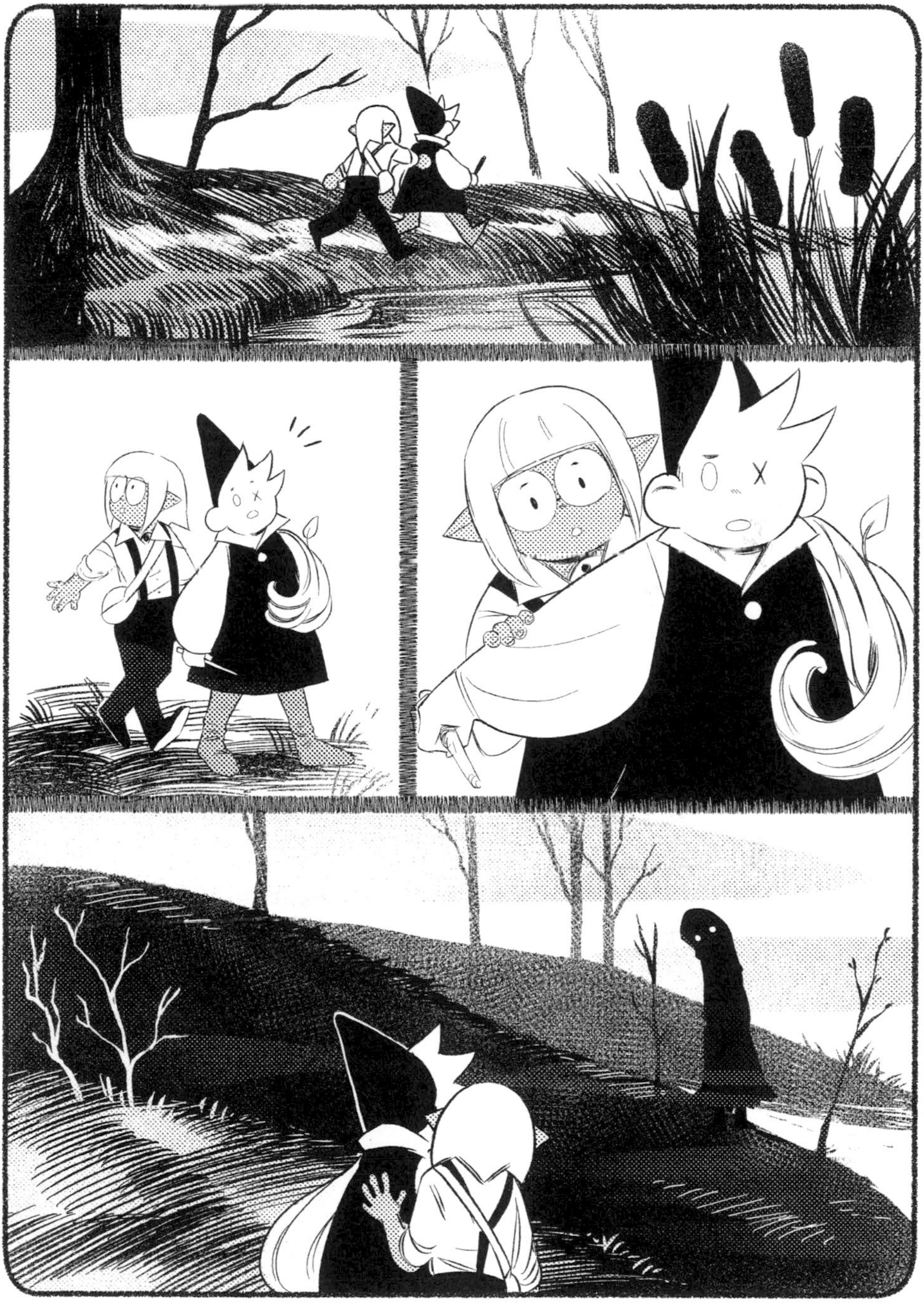

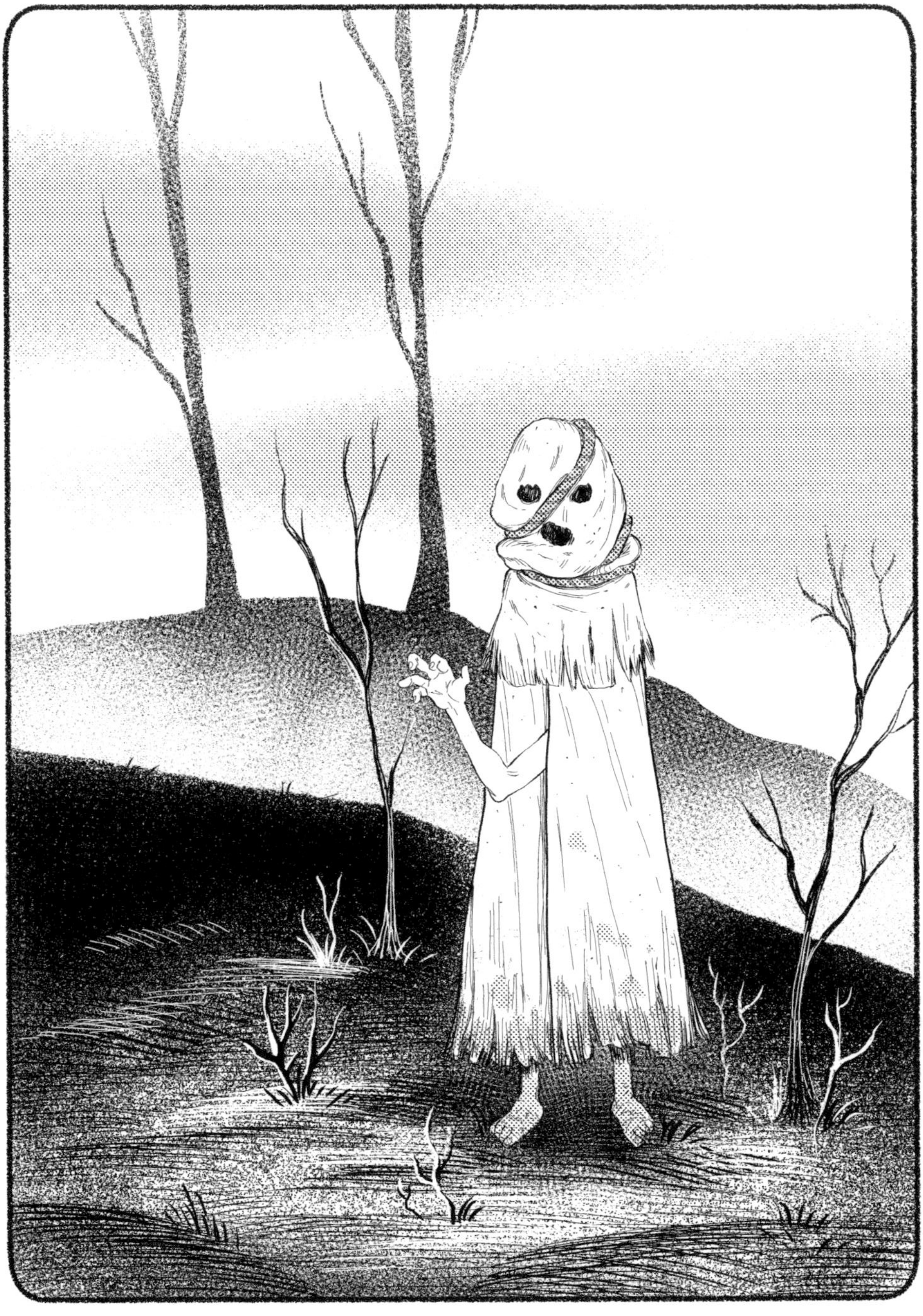

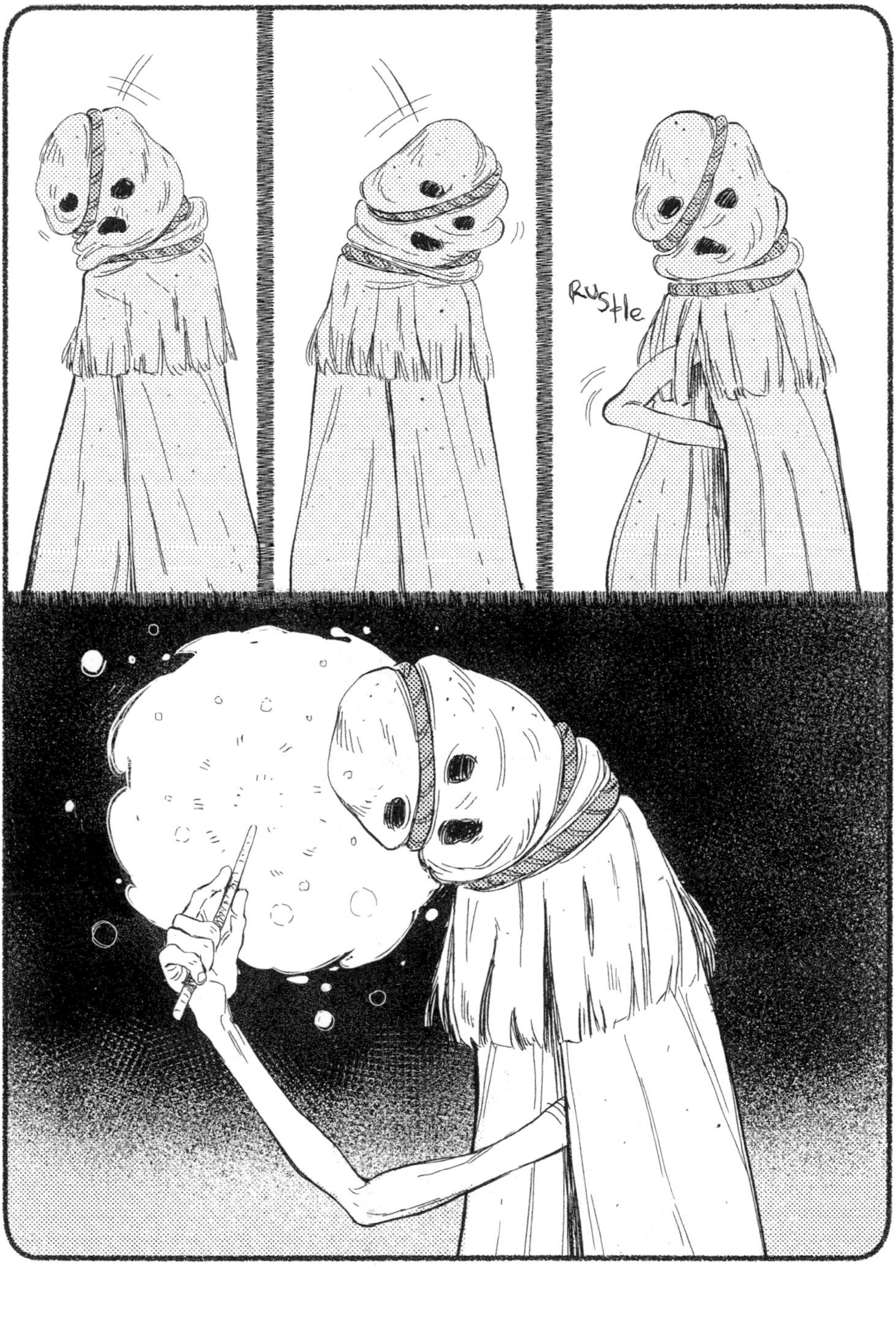
Rustle

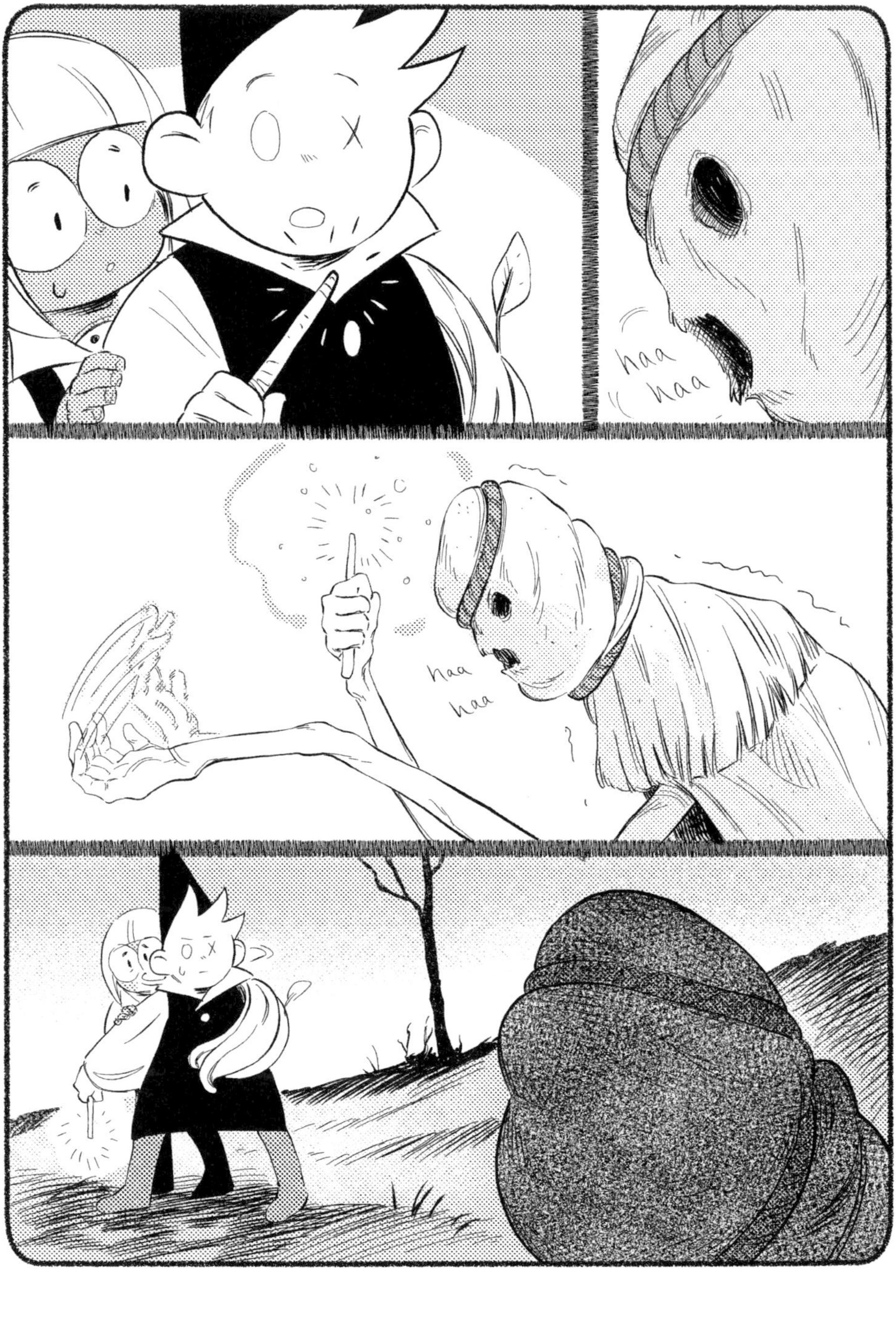
haa
haa
haa
haa

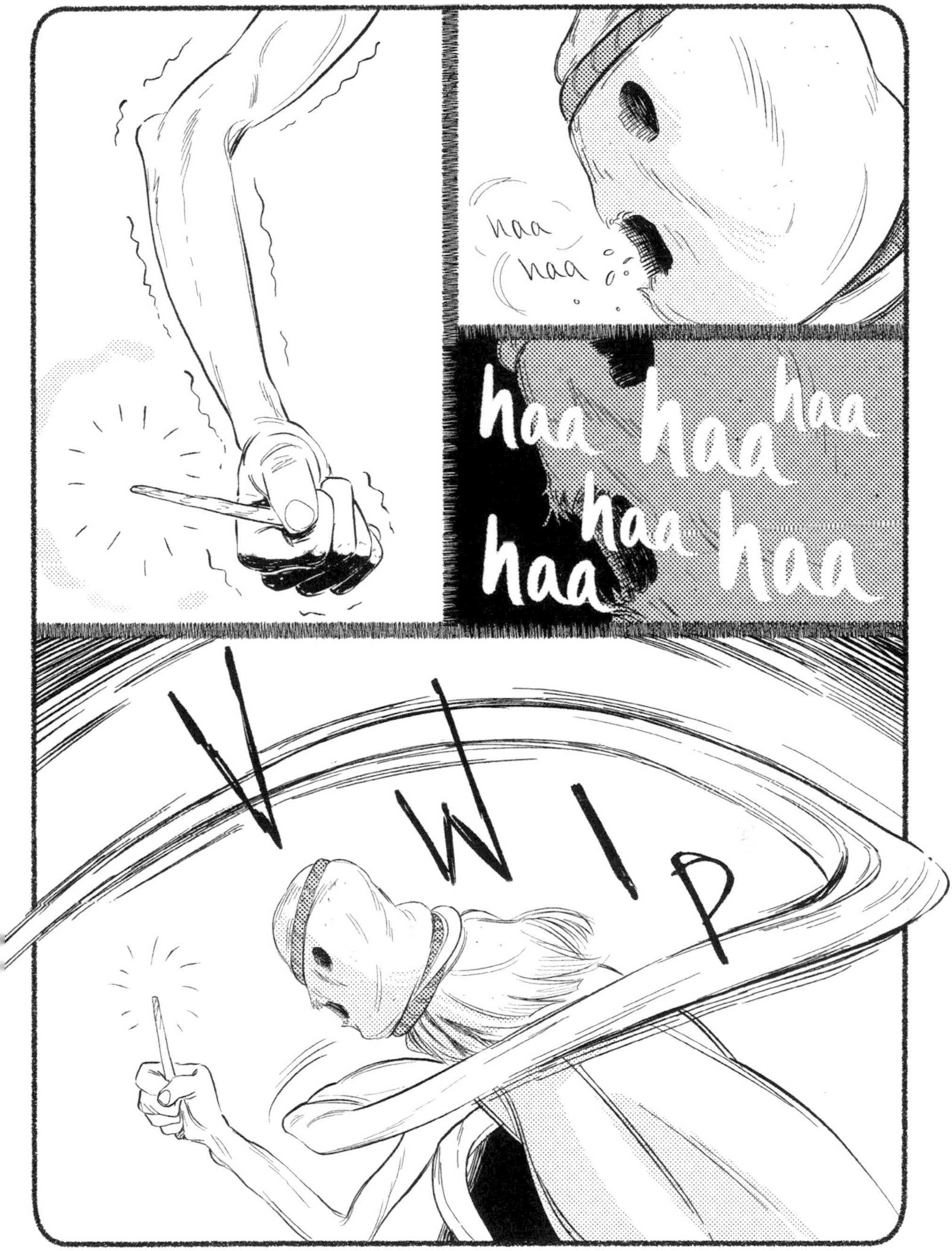
haa
haa
haa haa haa
haa haa haa
VWIP

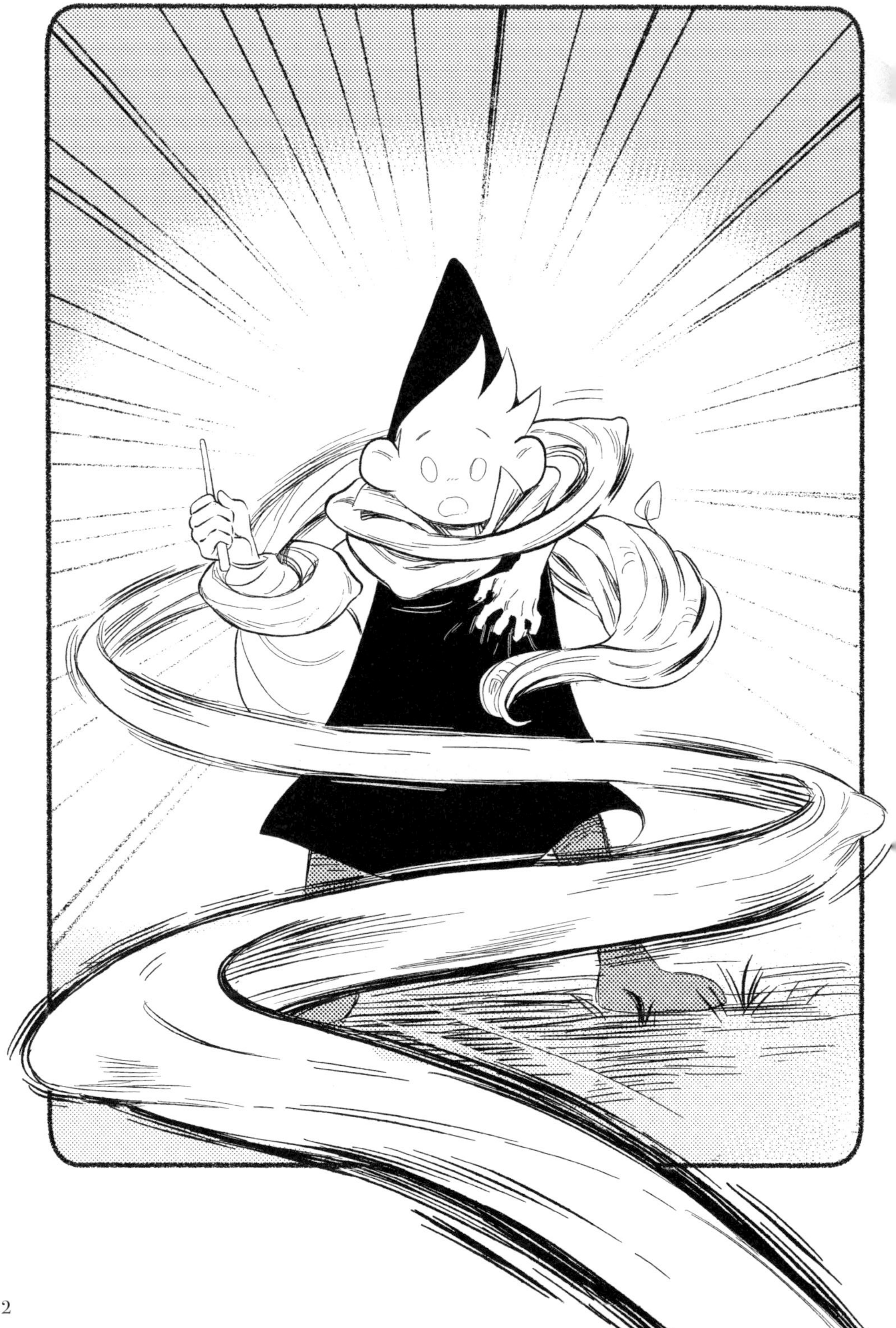

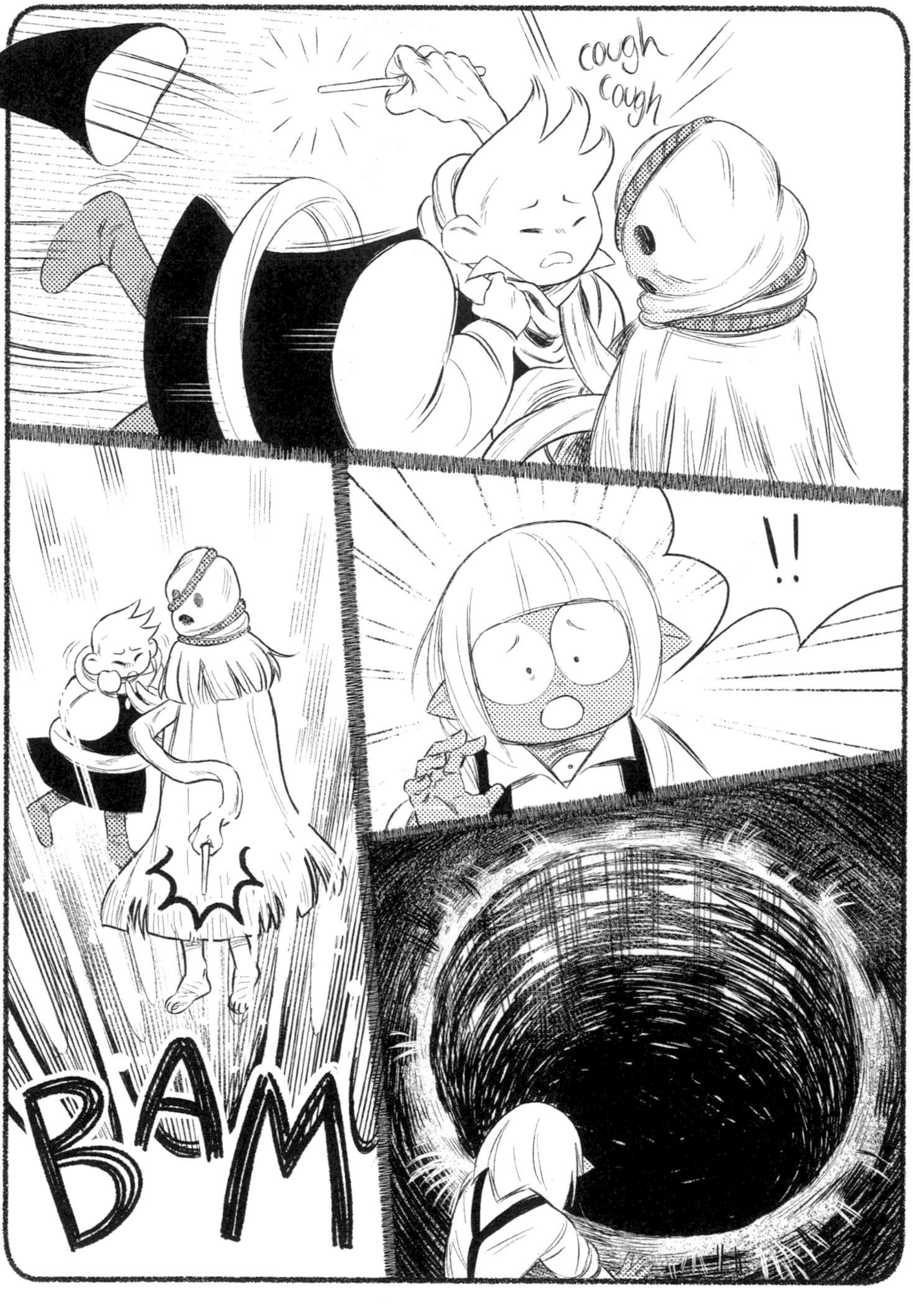
cough
cough
BAM
!!

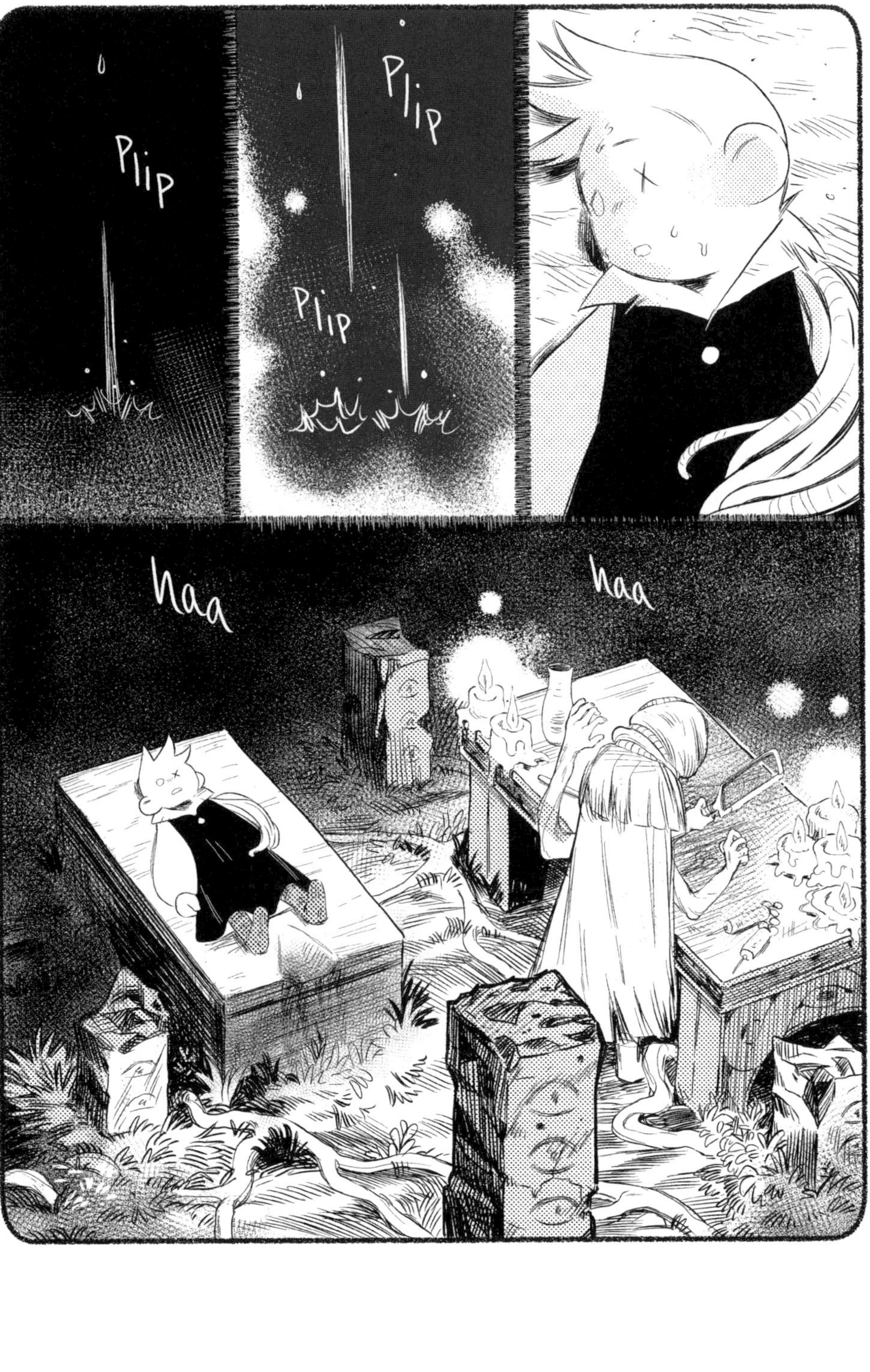
Plip
Plip
Plip
haa
haa

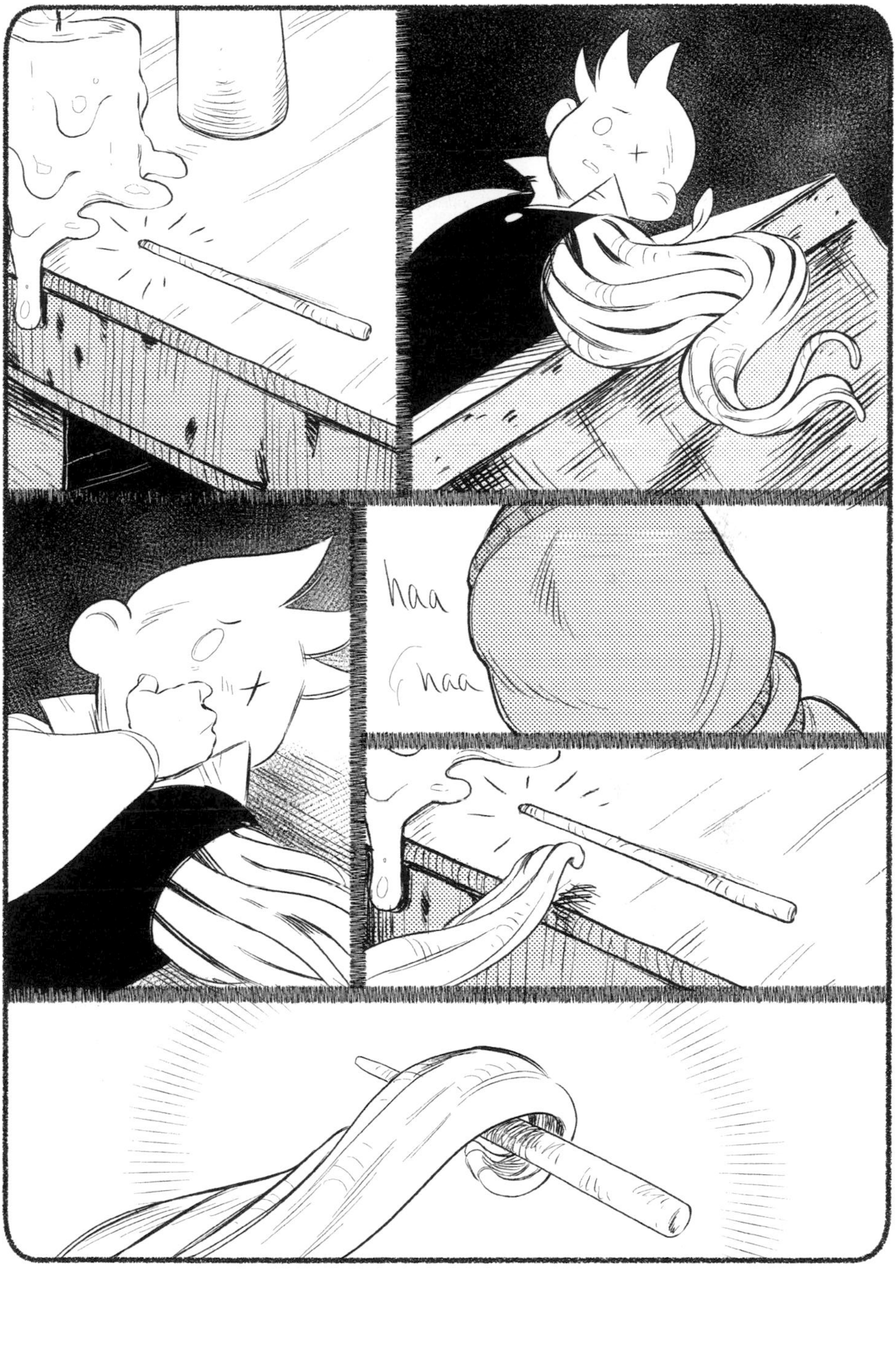
haa
haa

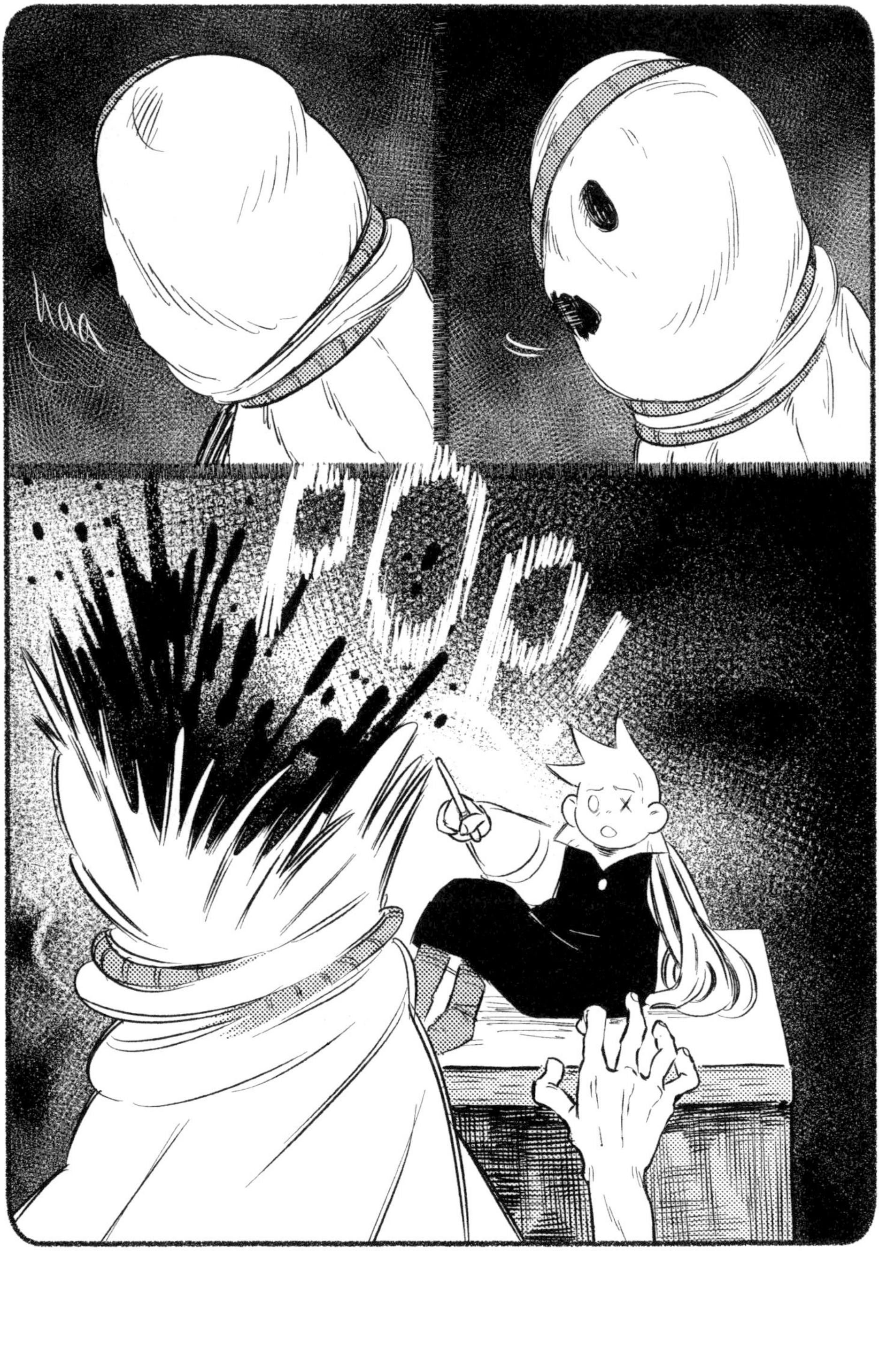
haa
POP!

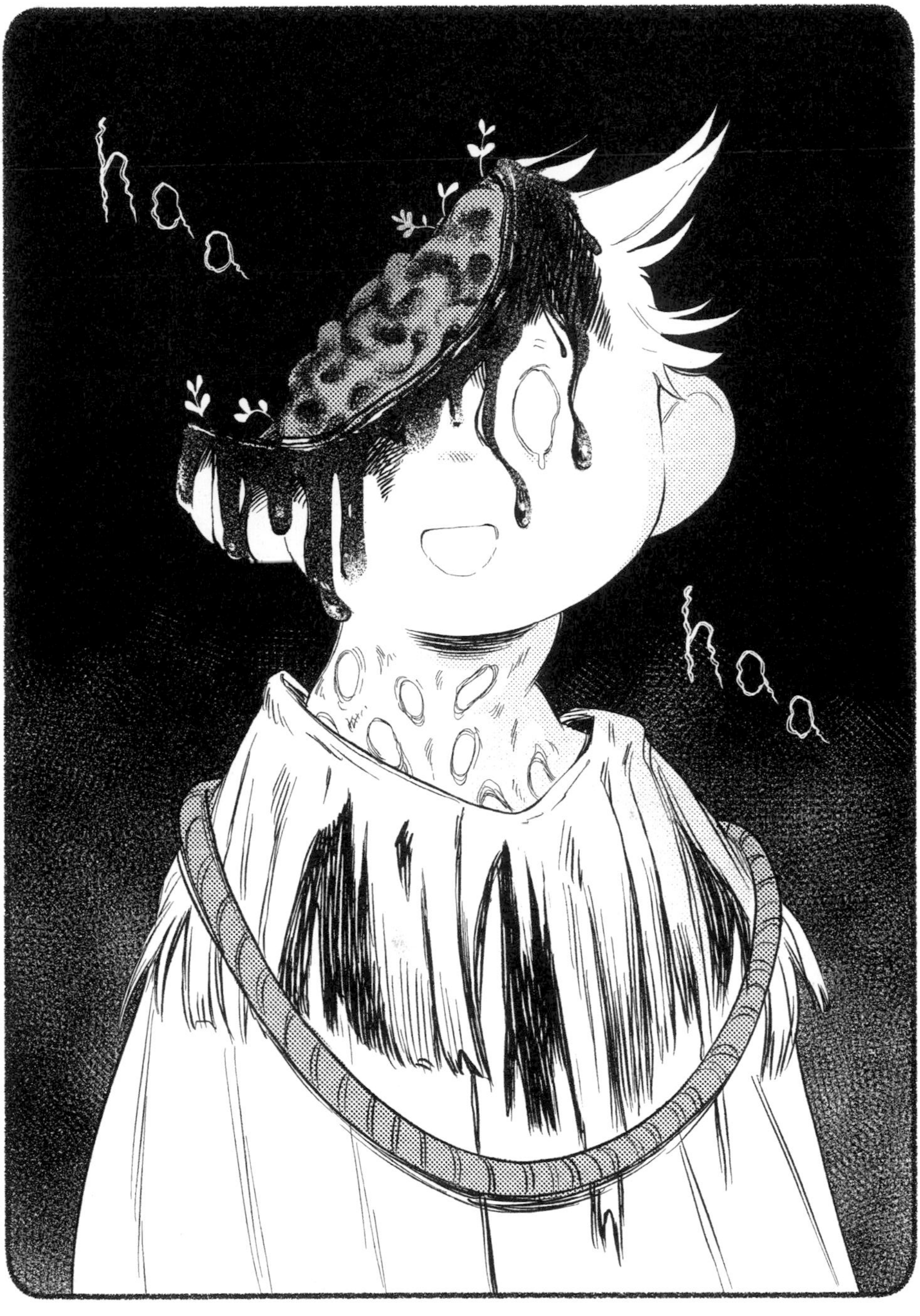
haa
haa

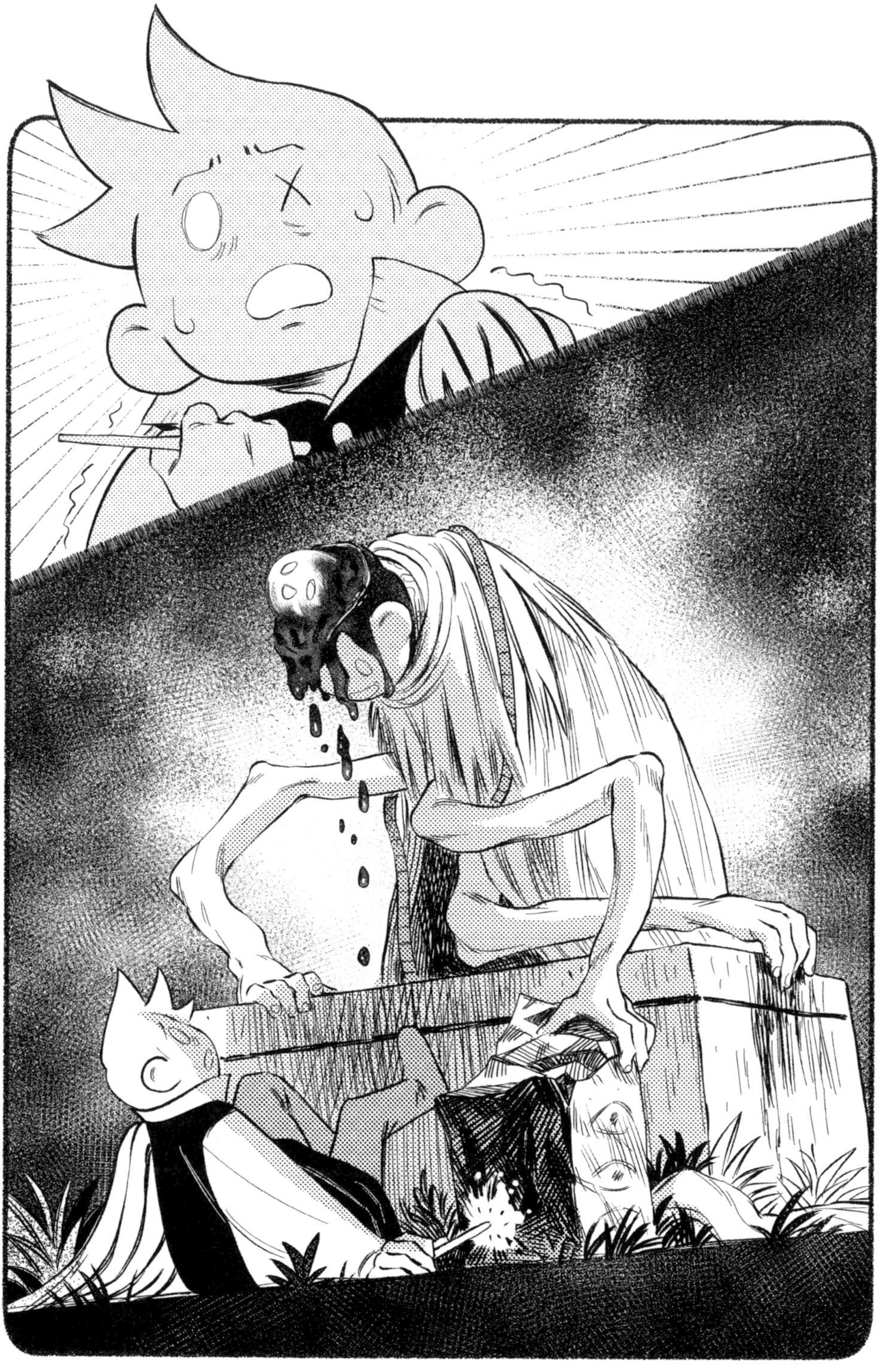

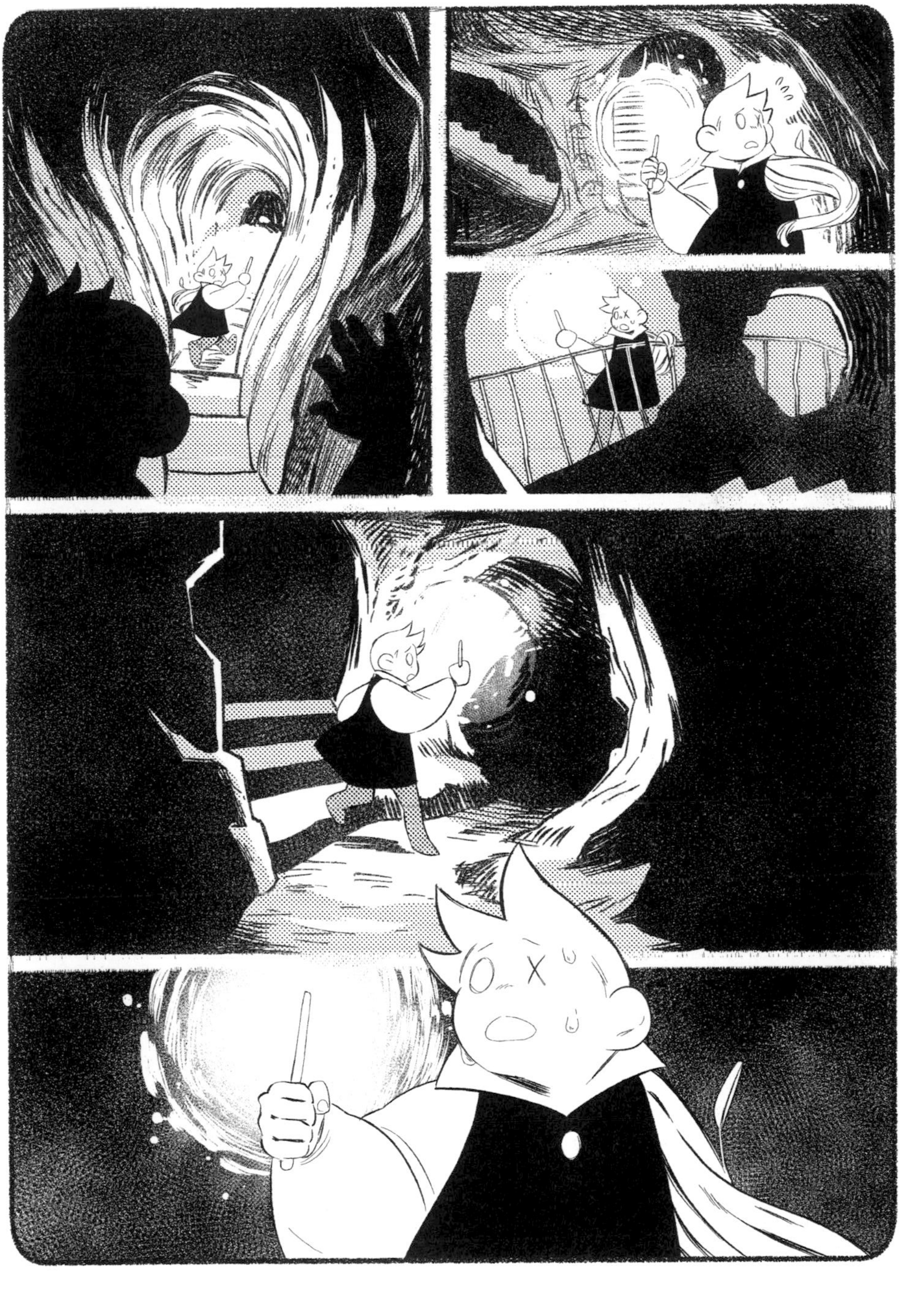

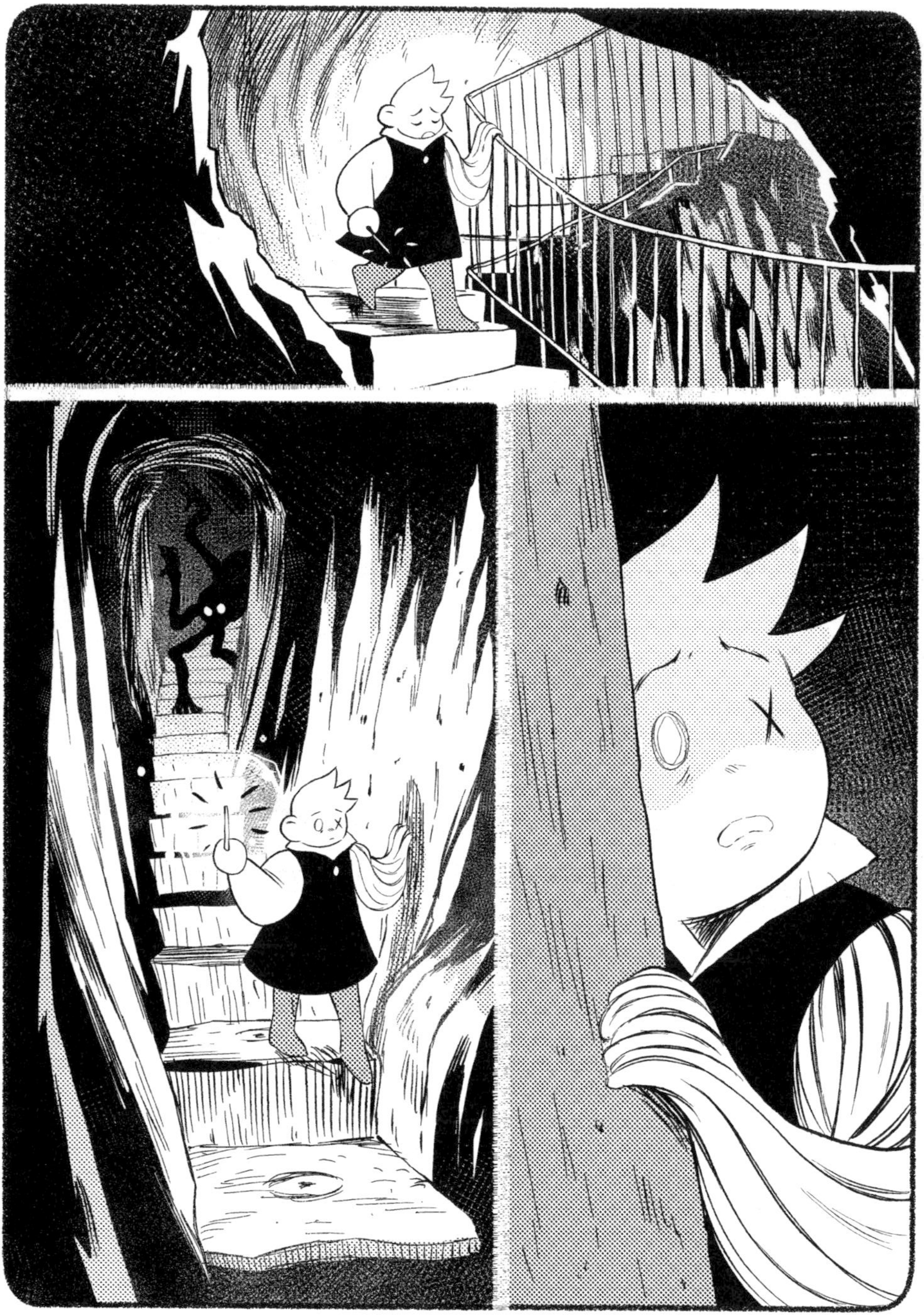

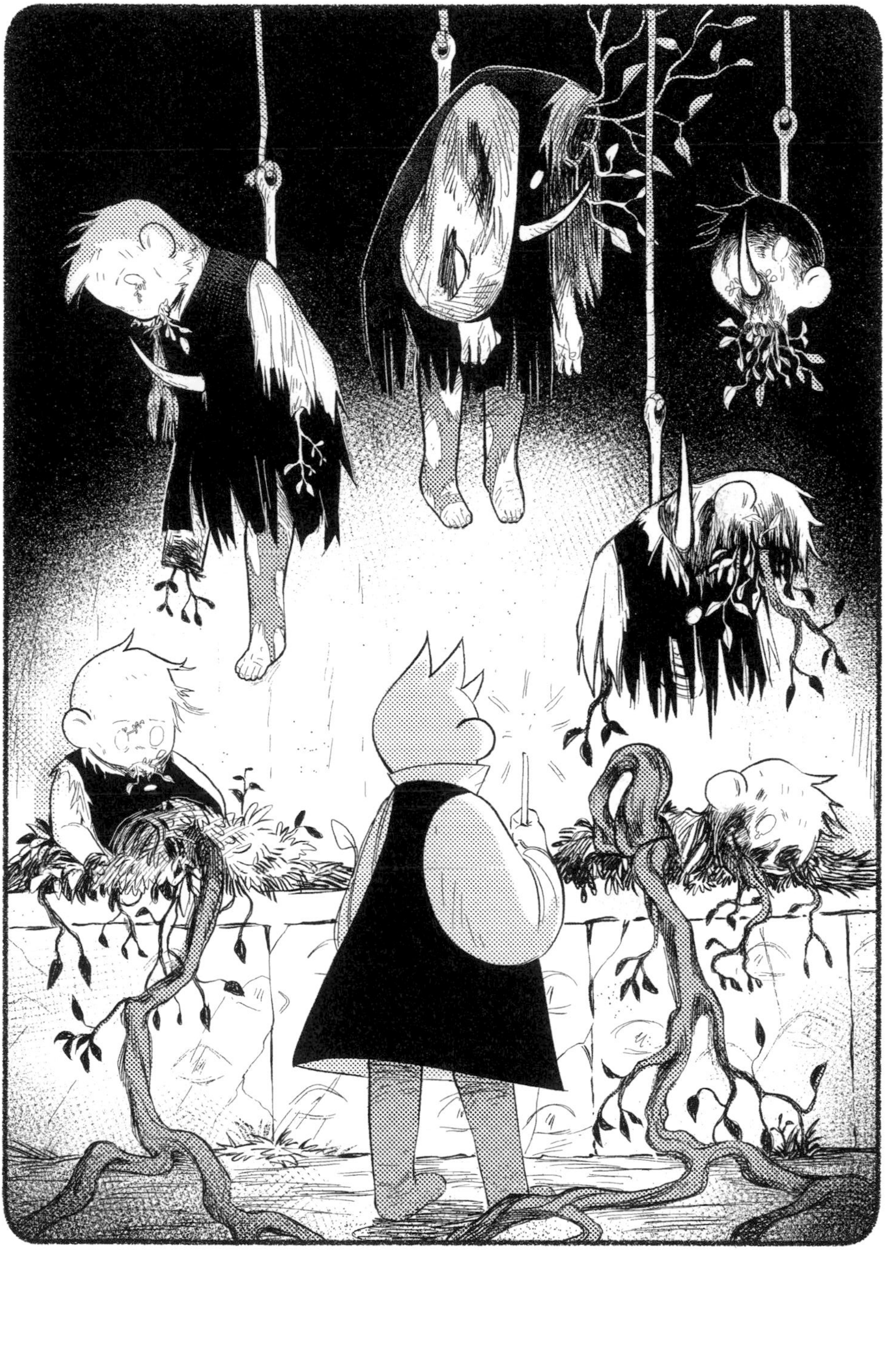

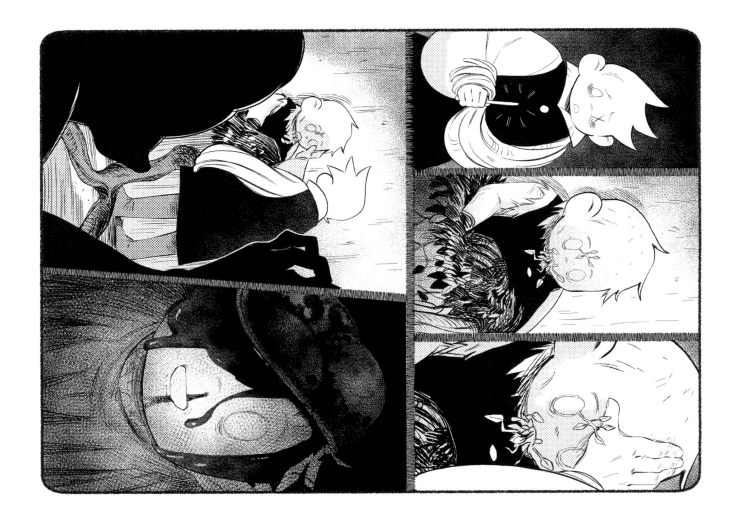

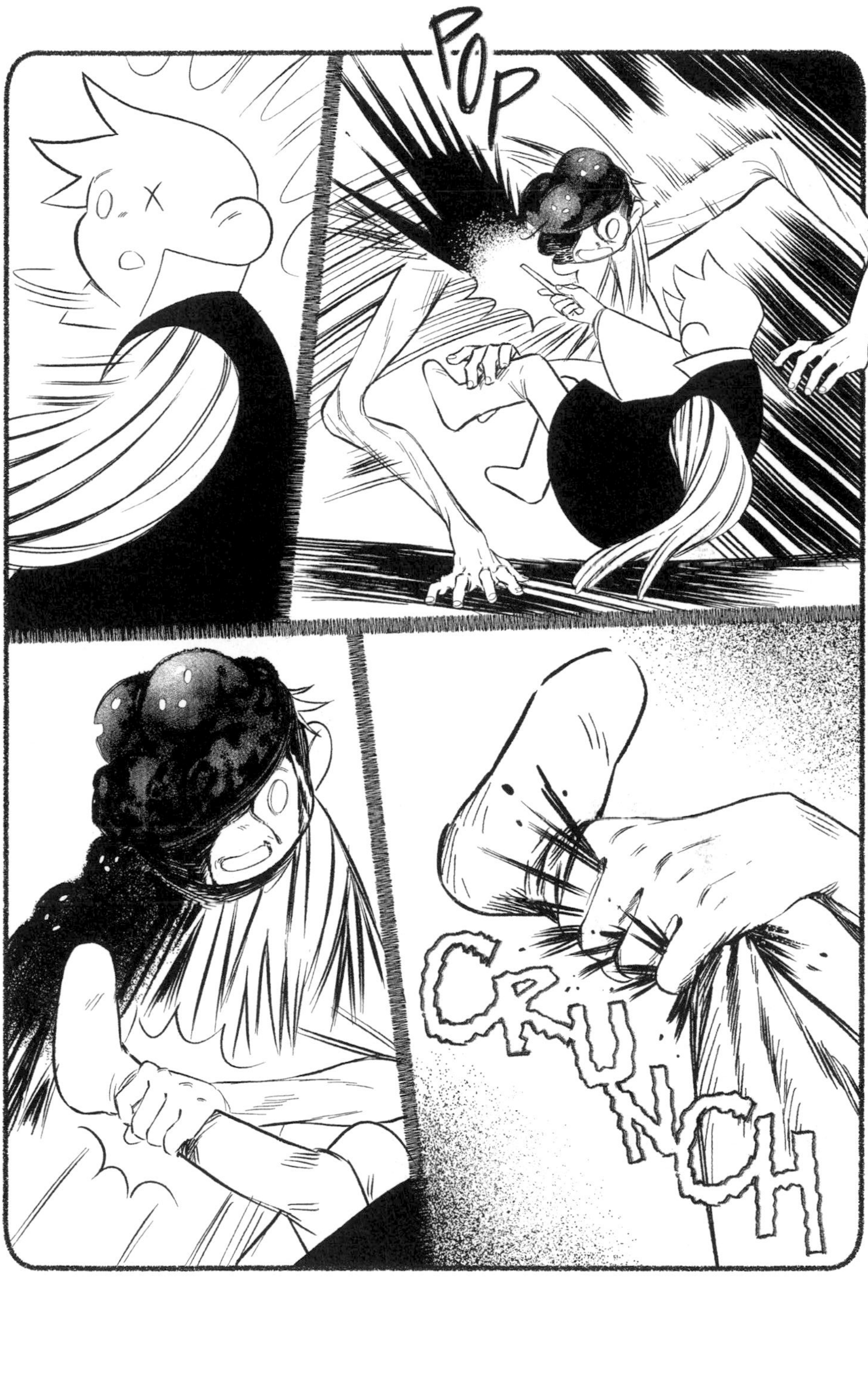
POP
CRUNCH

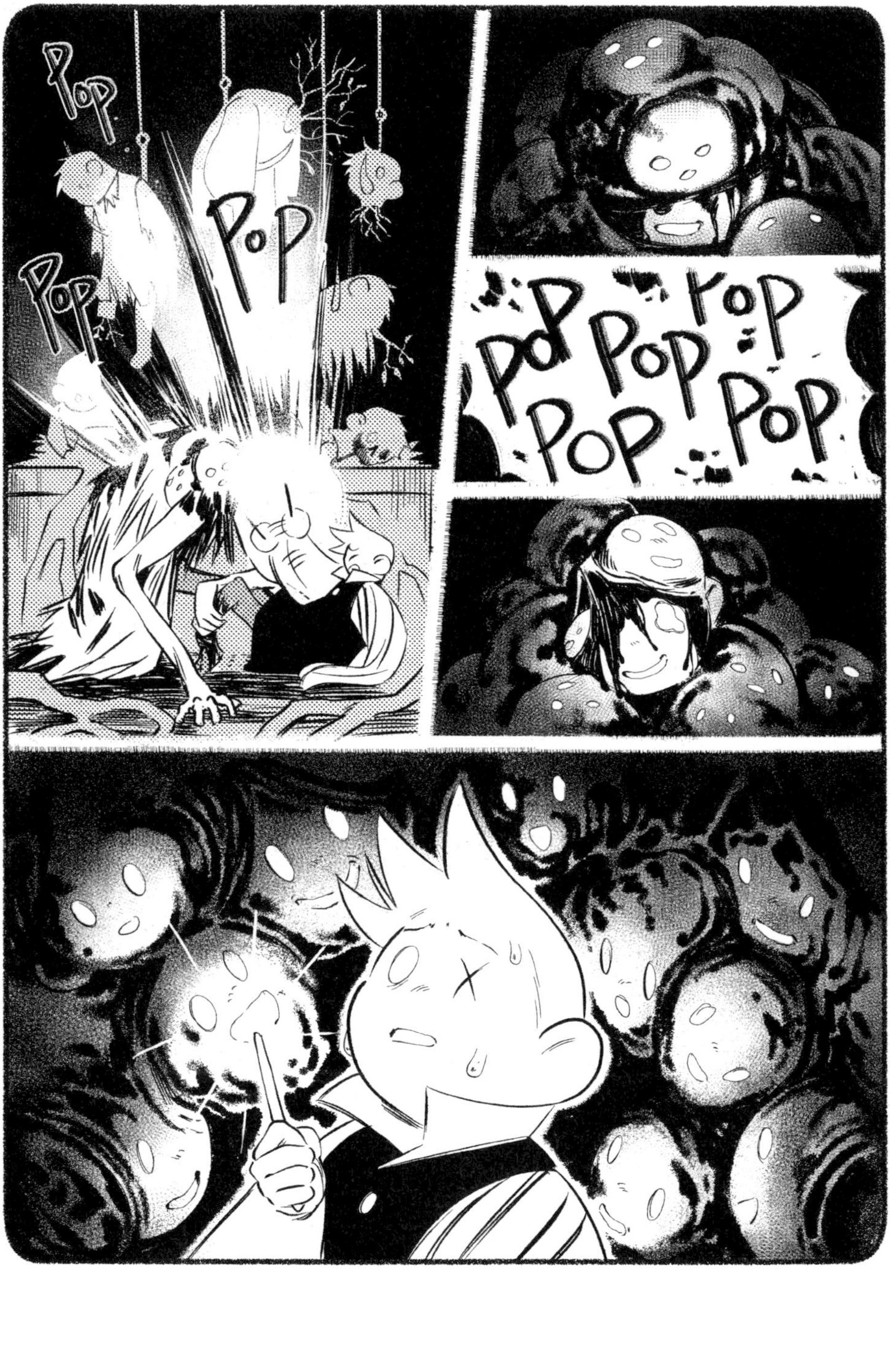
POP
POP
POP
POP POP POP POP POP POP

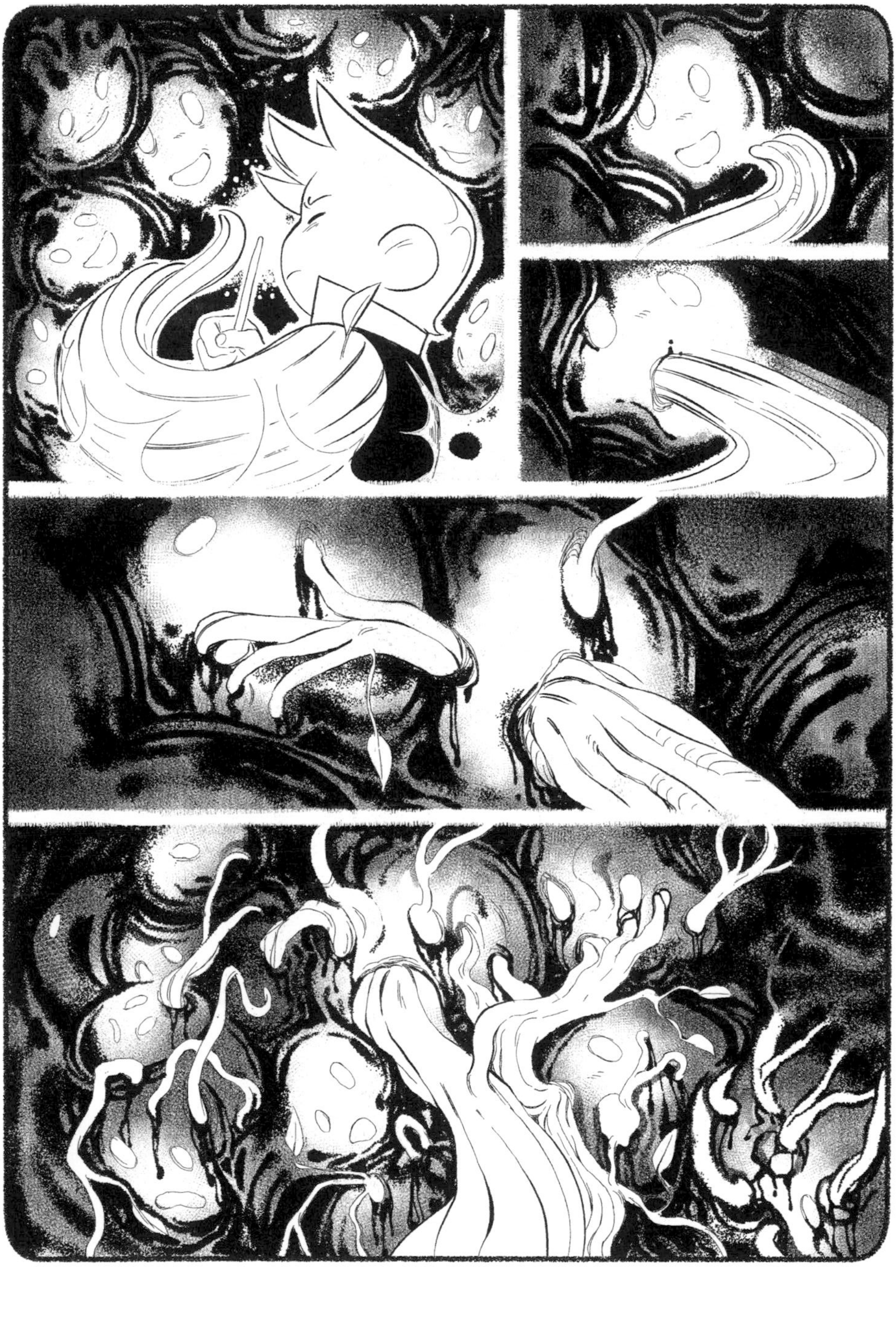

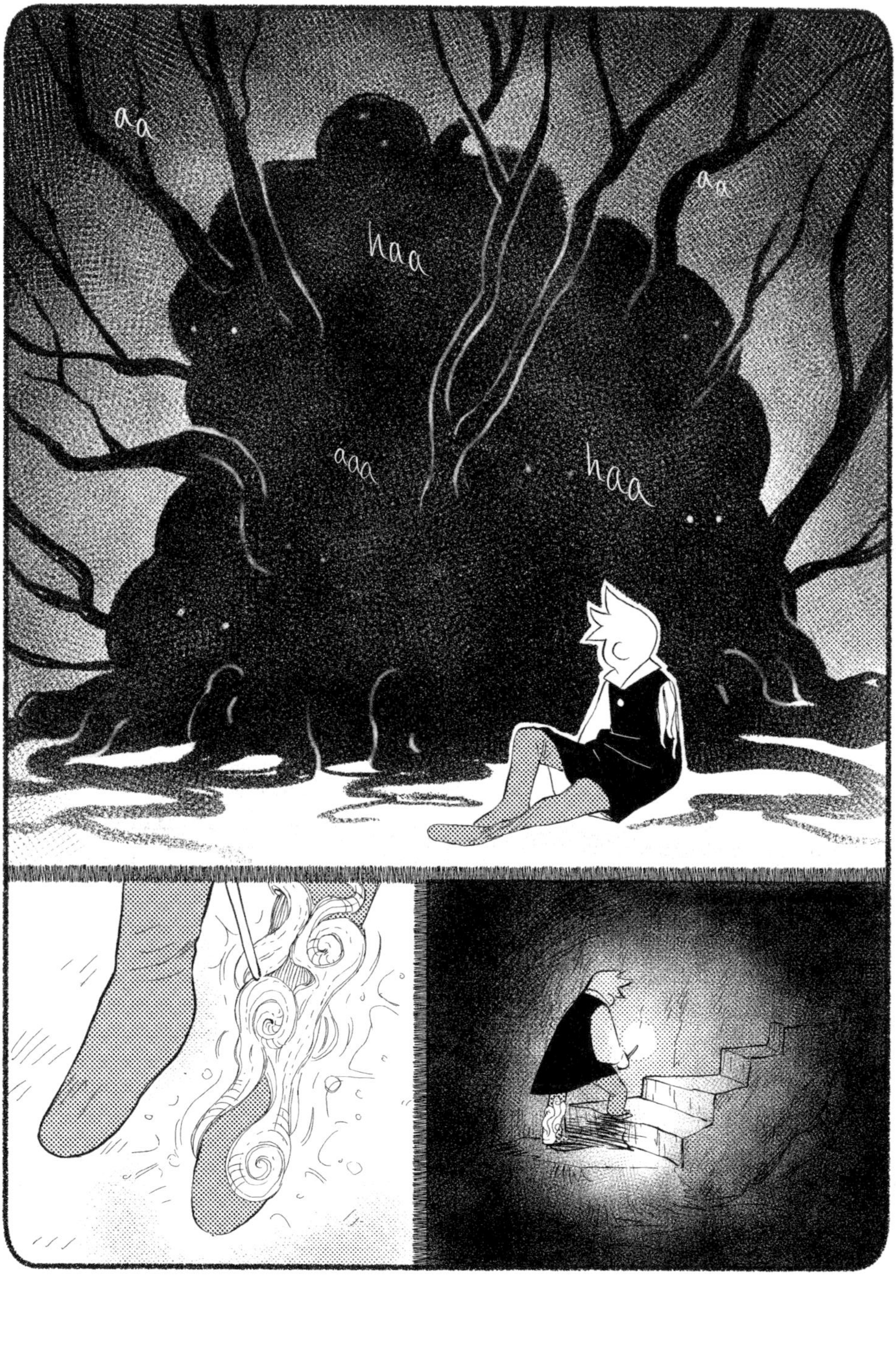
aa
haa
aa
aaa
haa

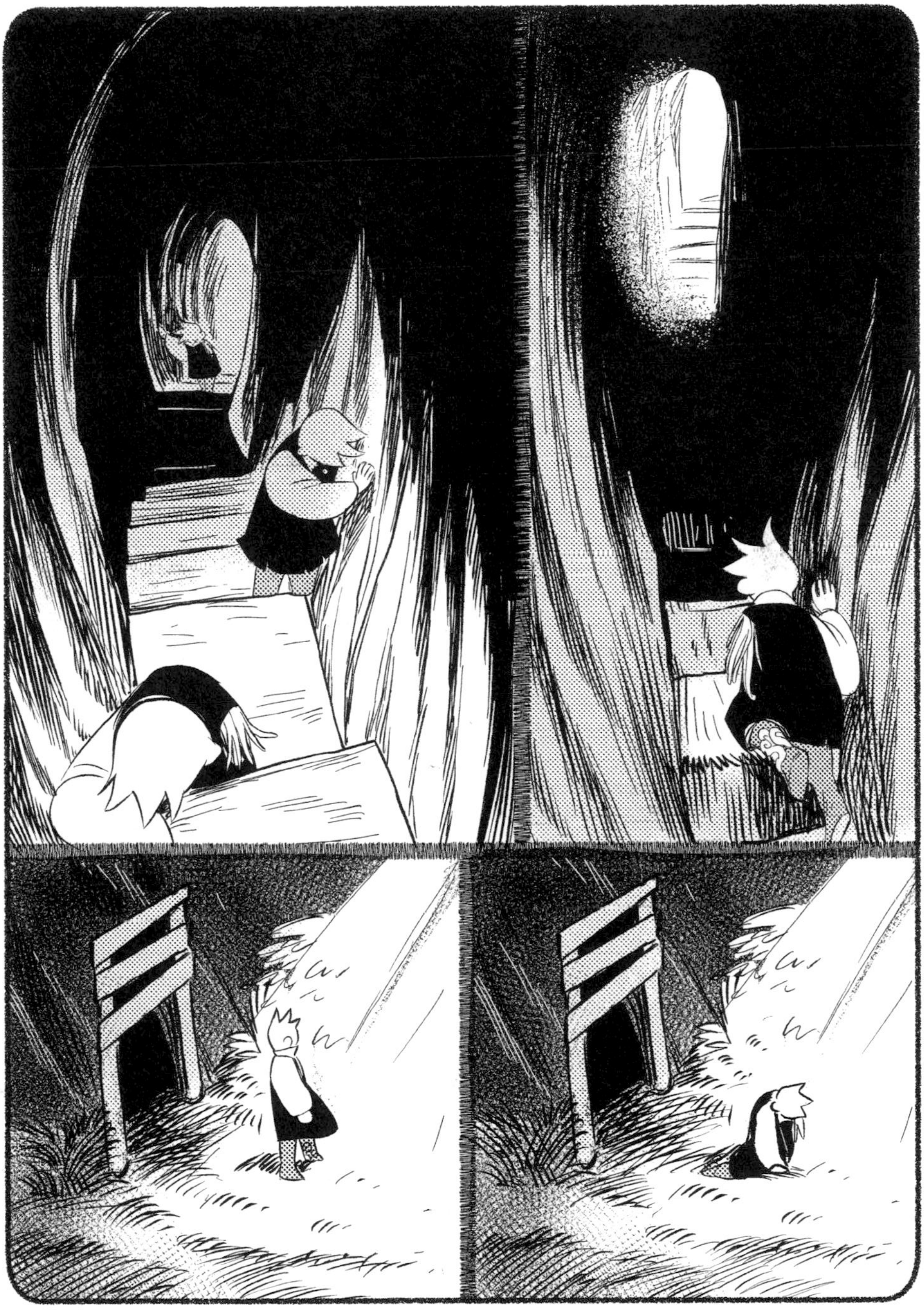

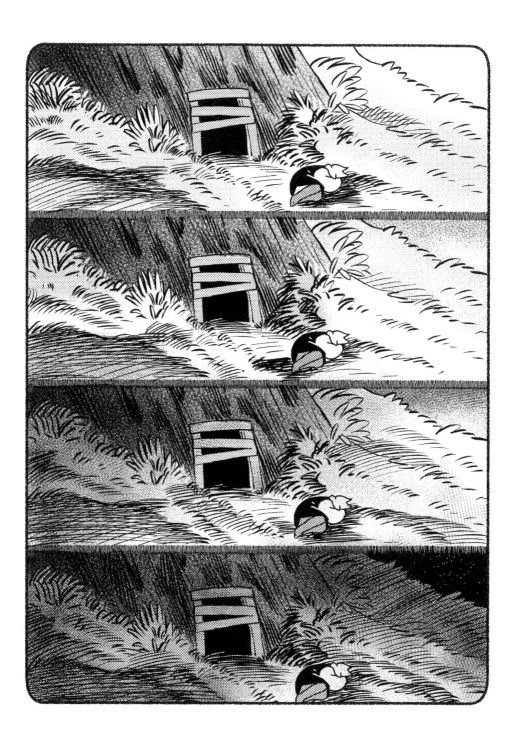

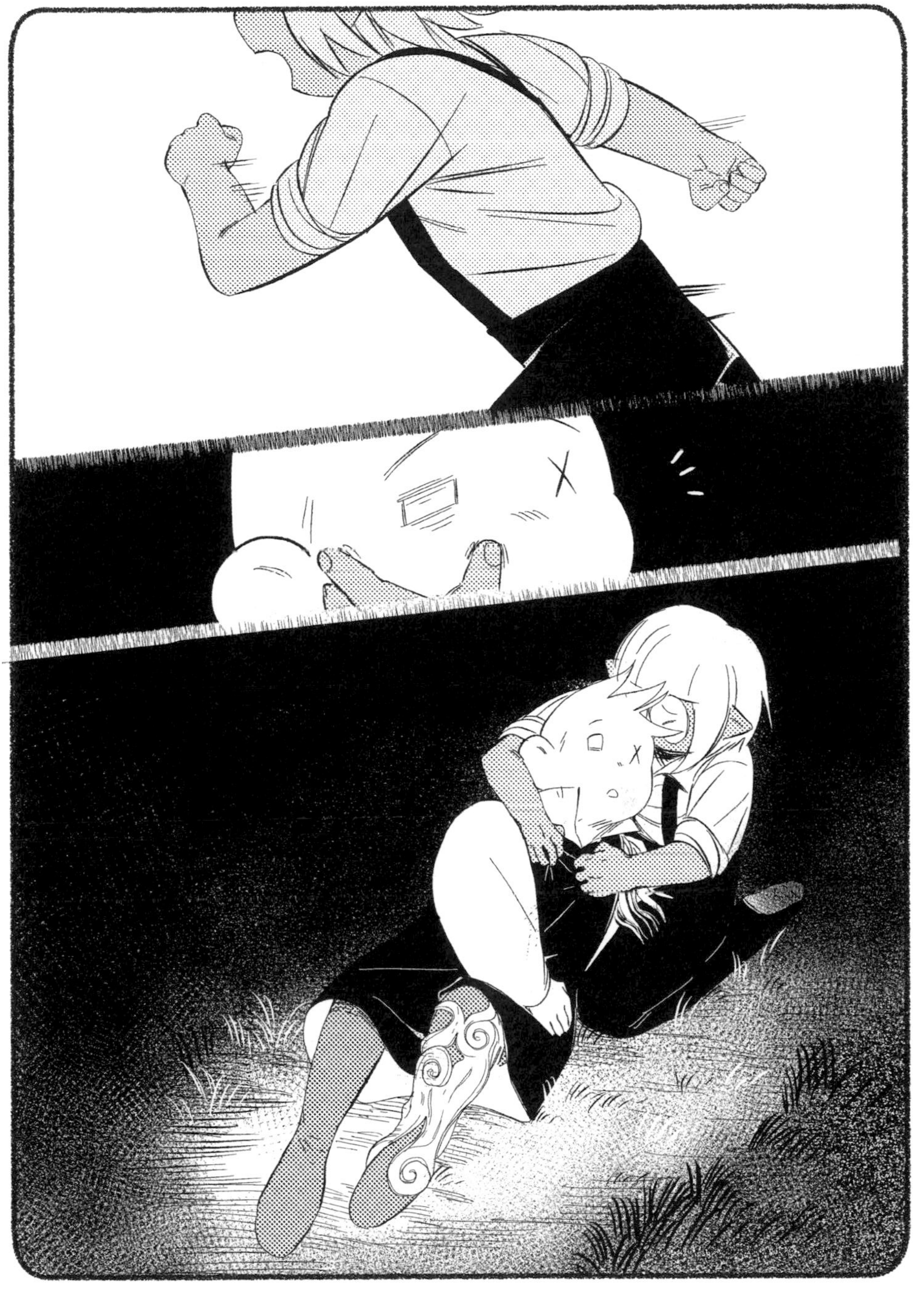

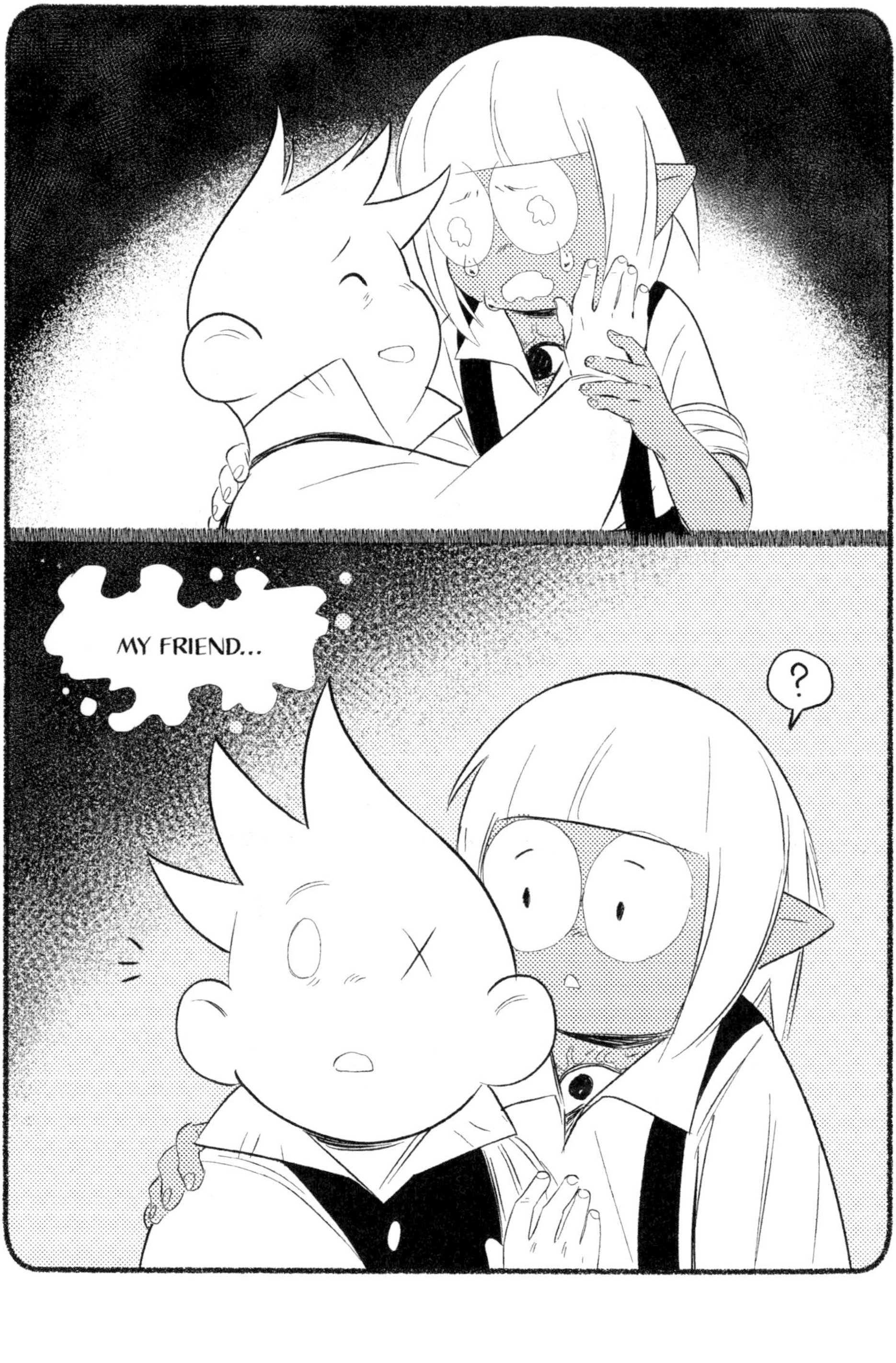
MY FRIEND...
?

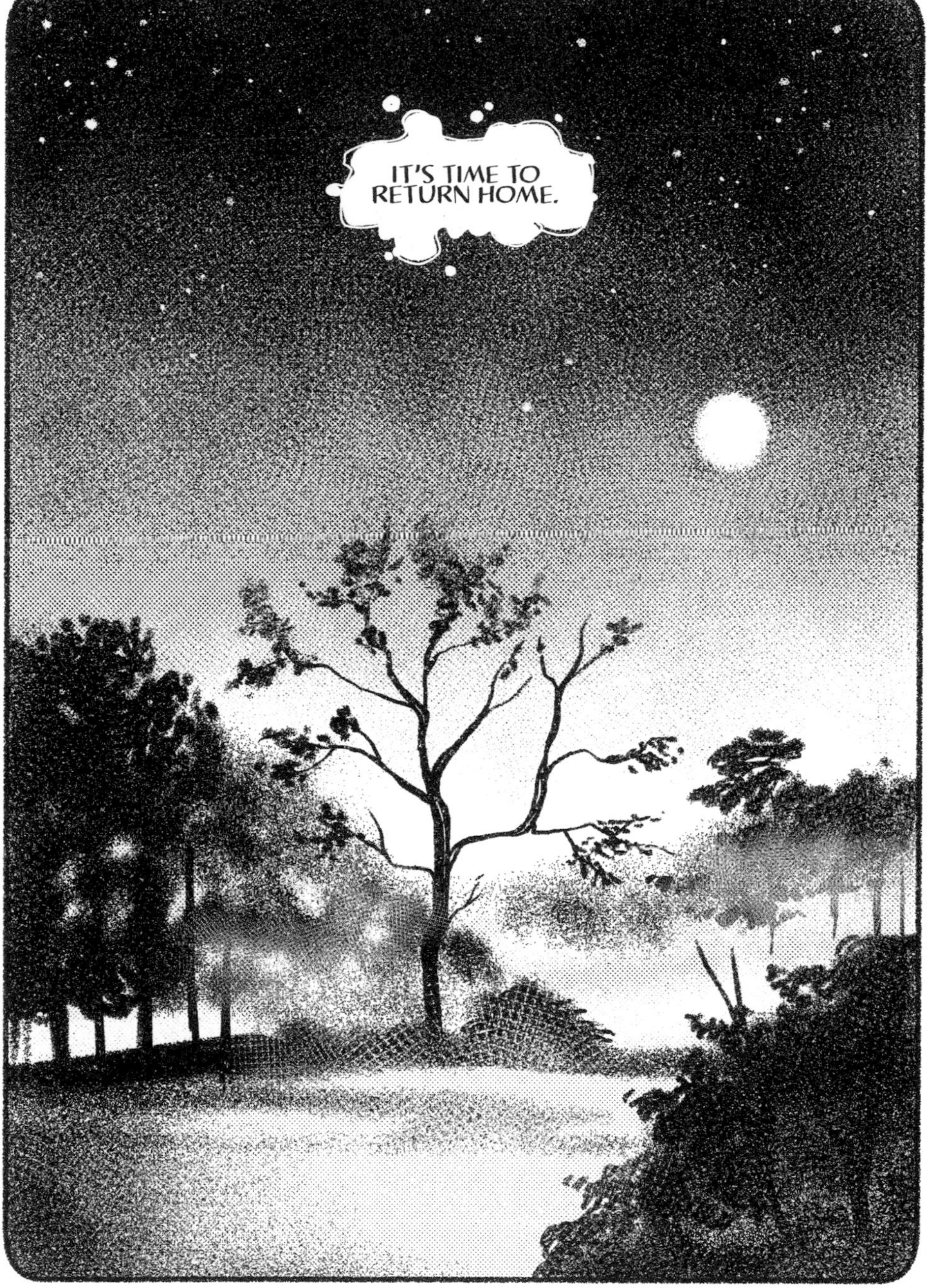
IT'S TIME TO RETURN HOME.

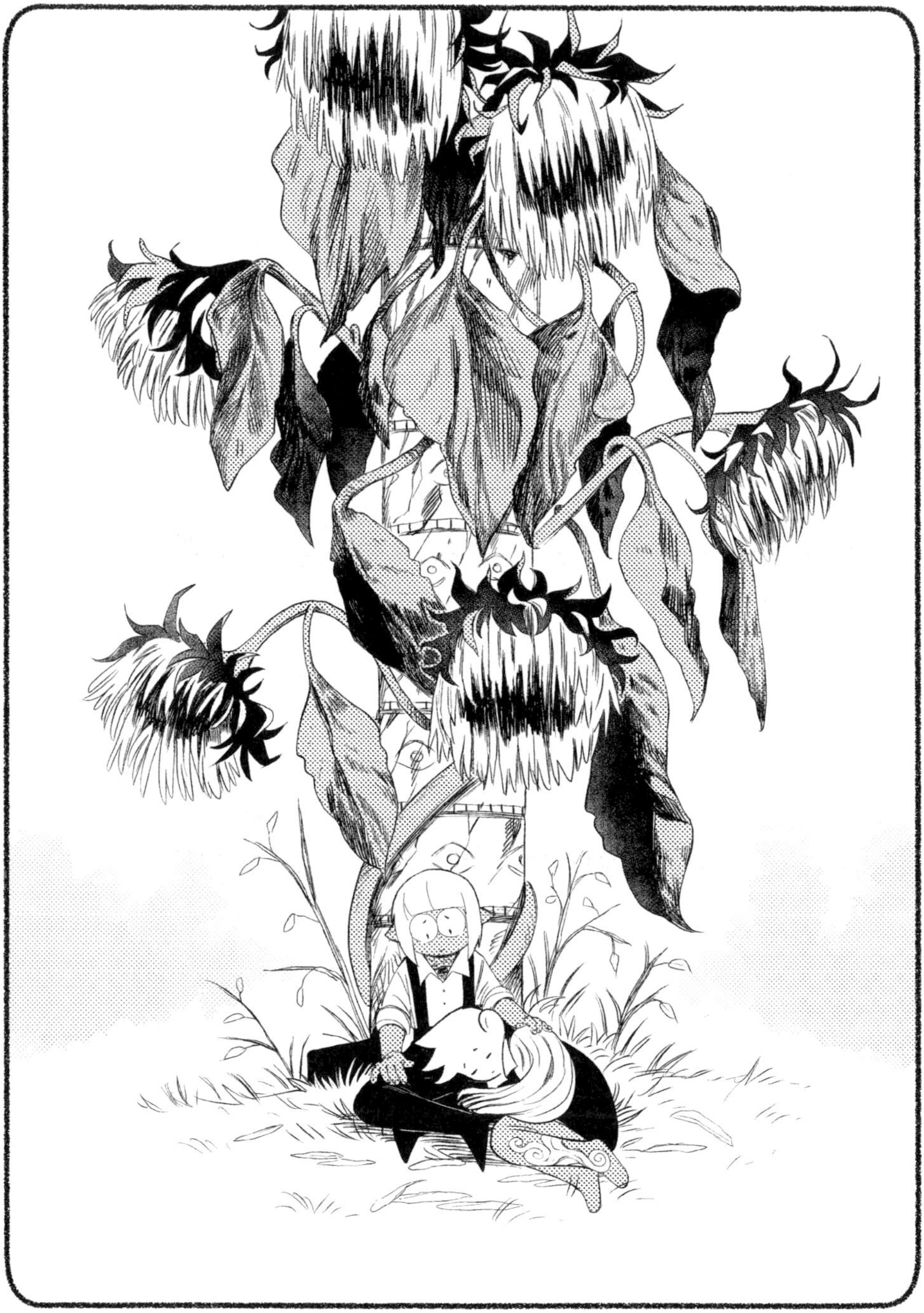

PART FIVE

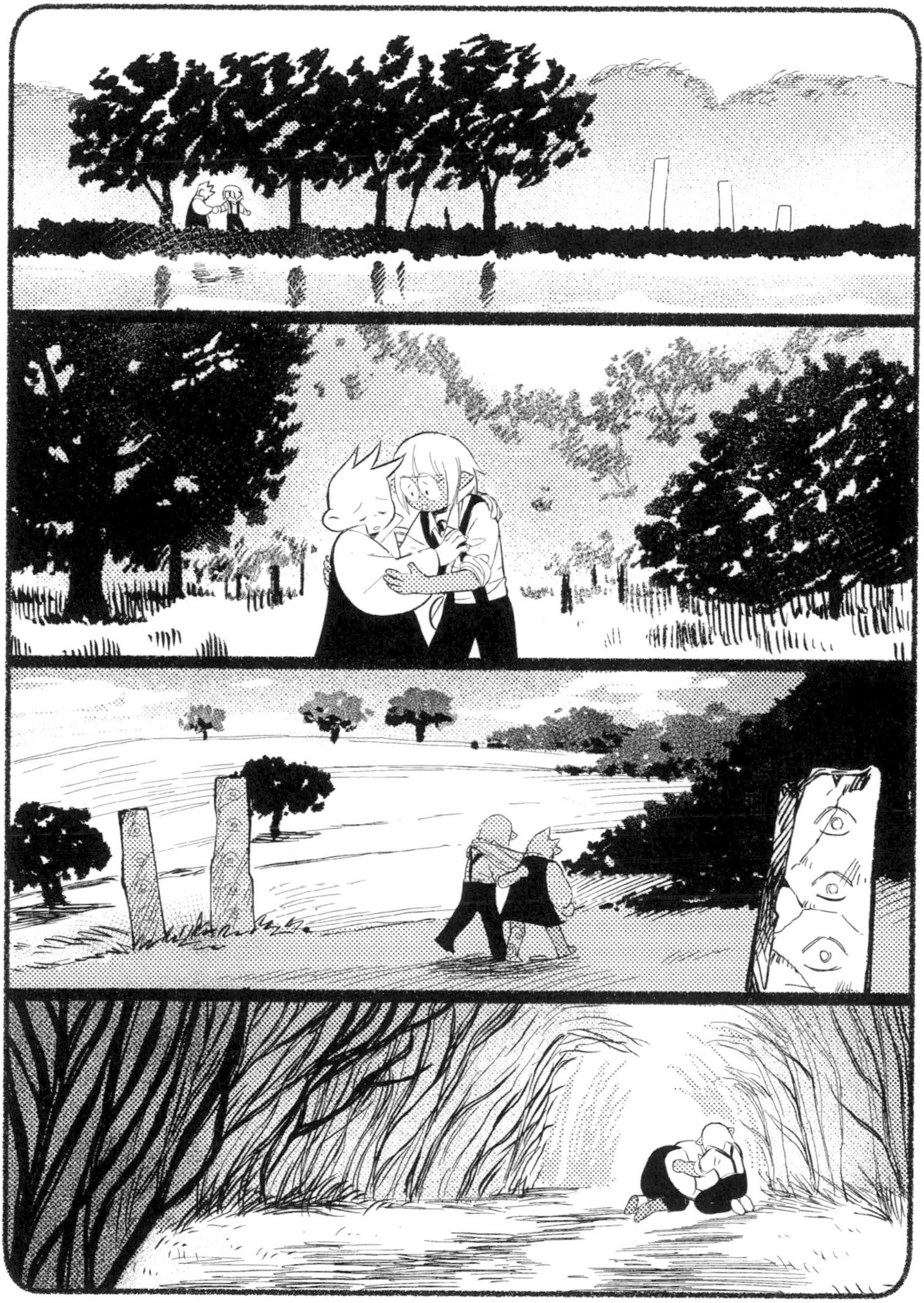

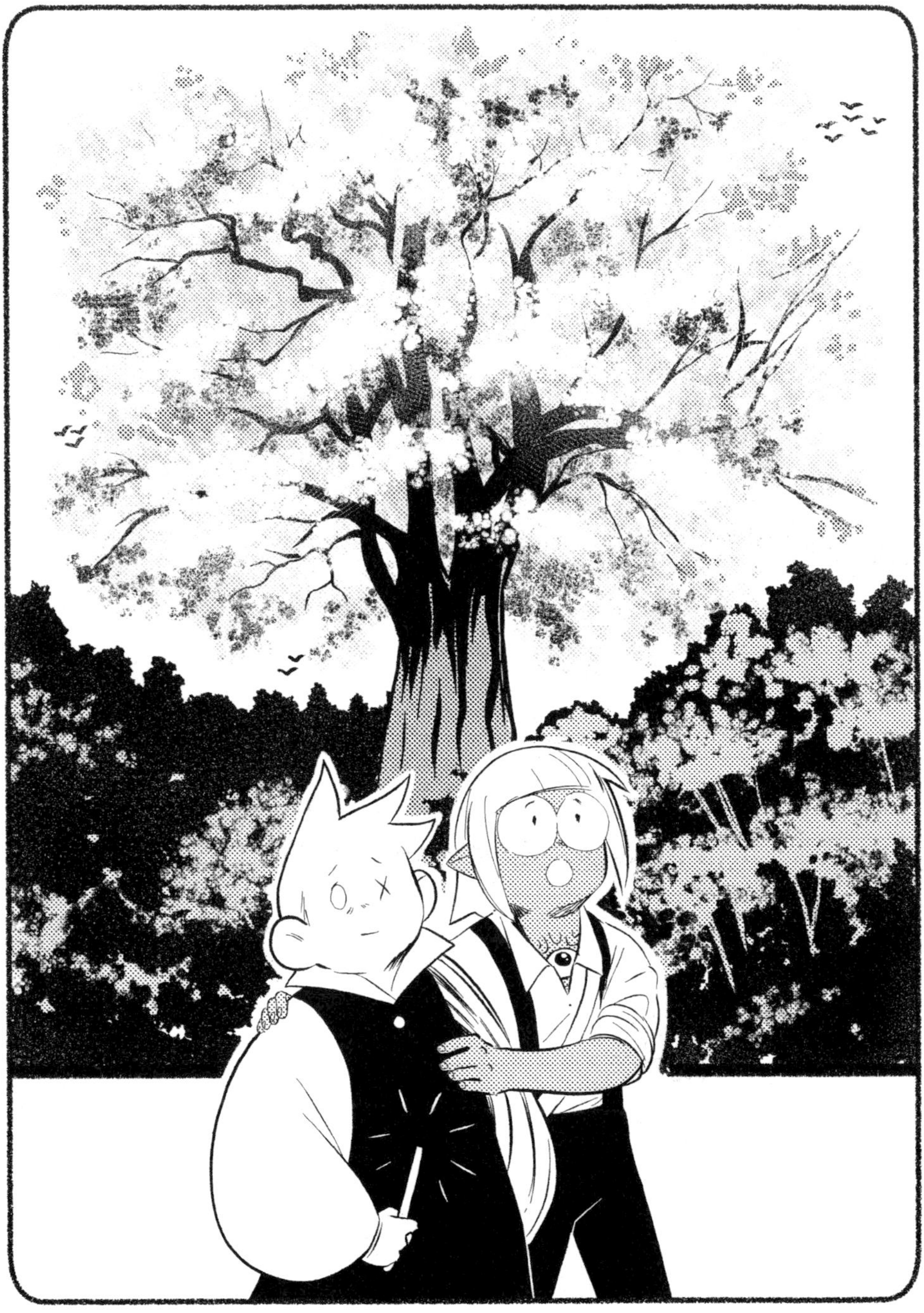

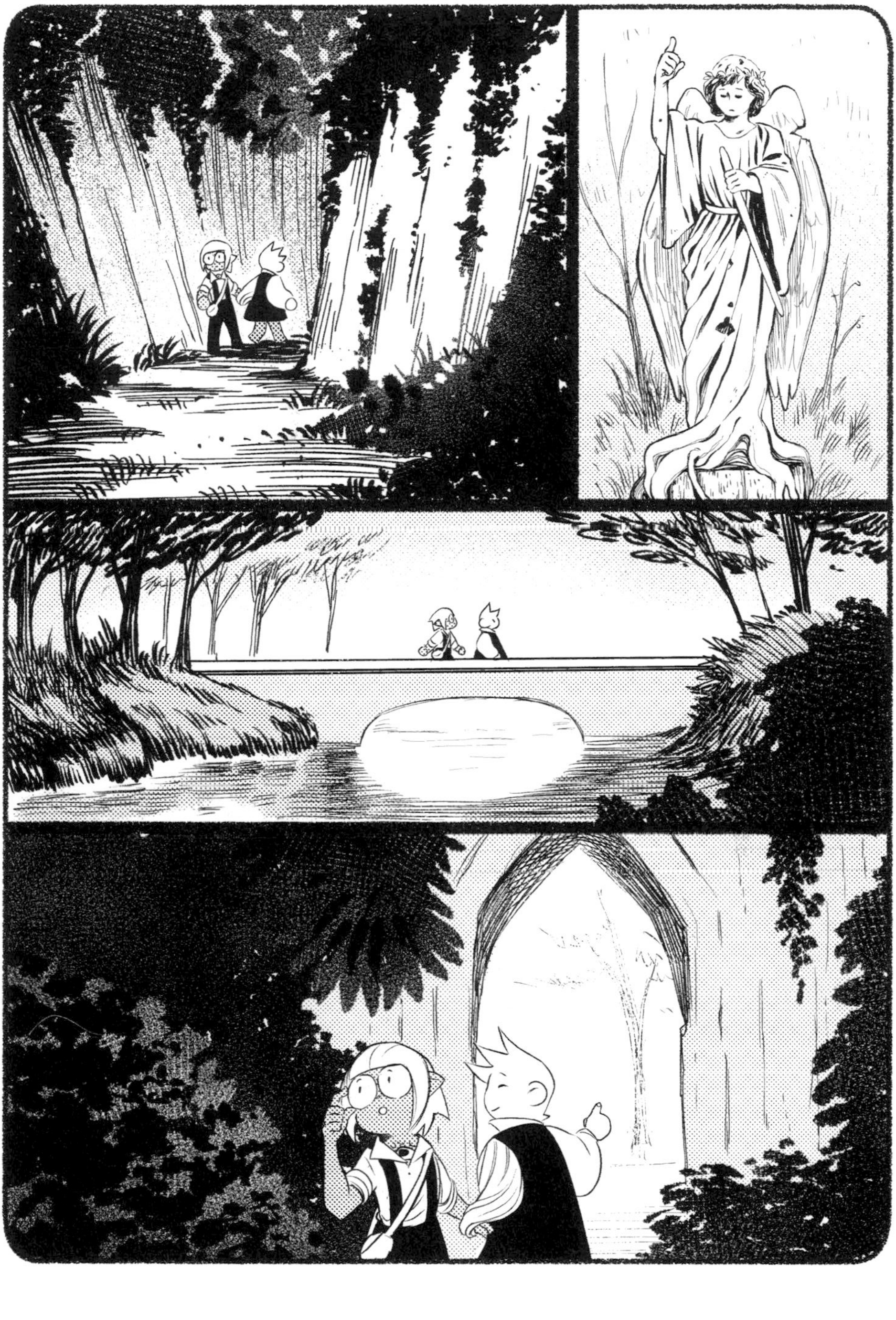

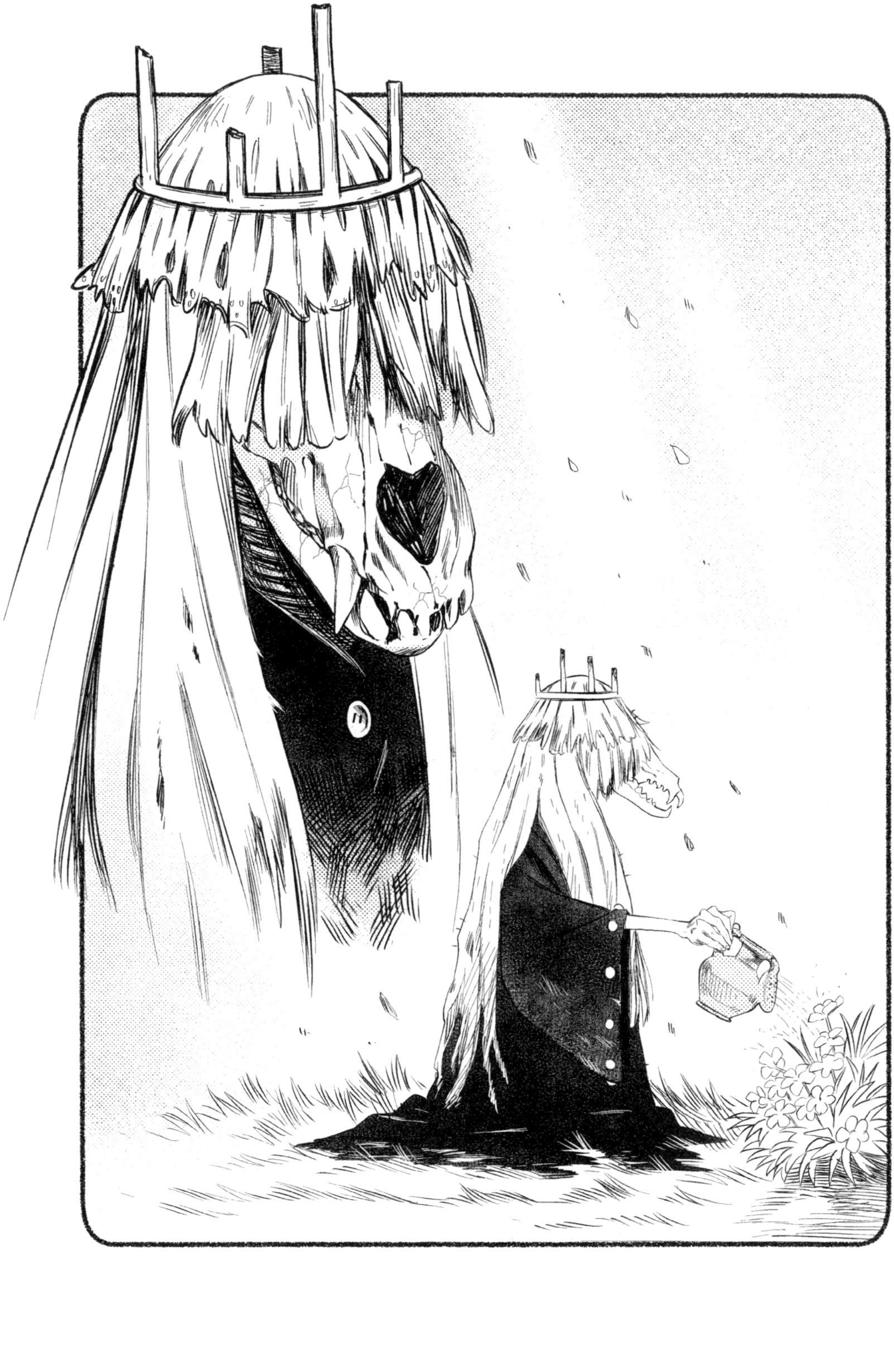

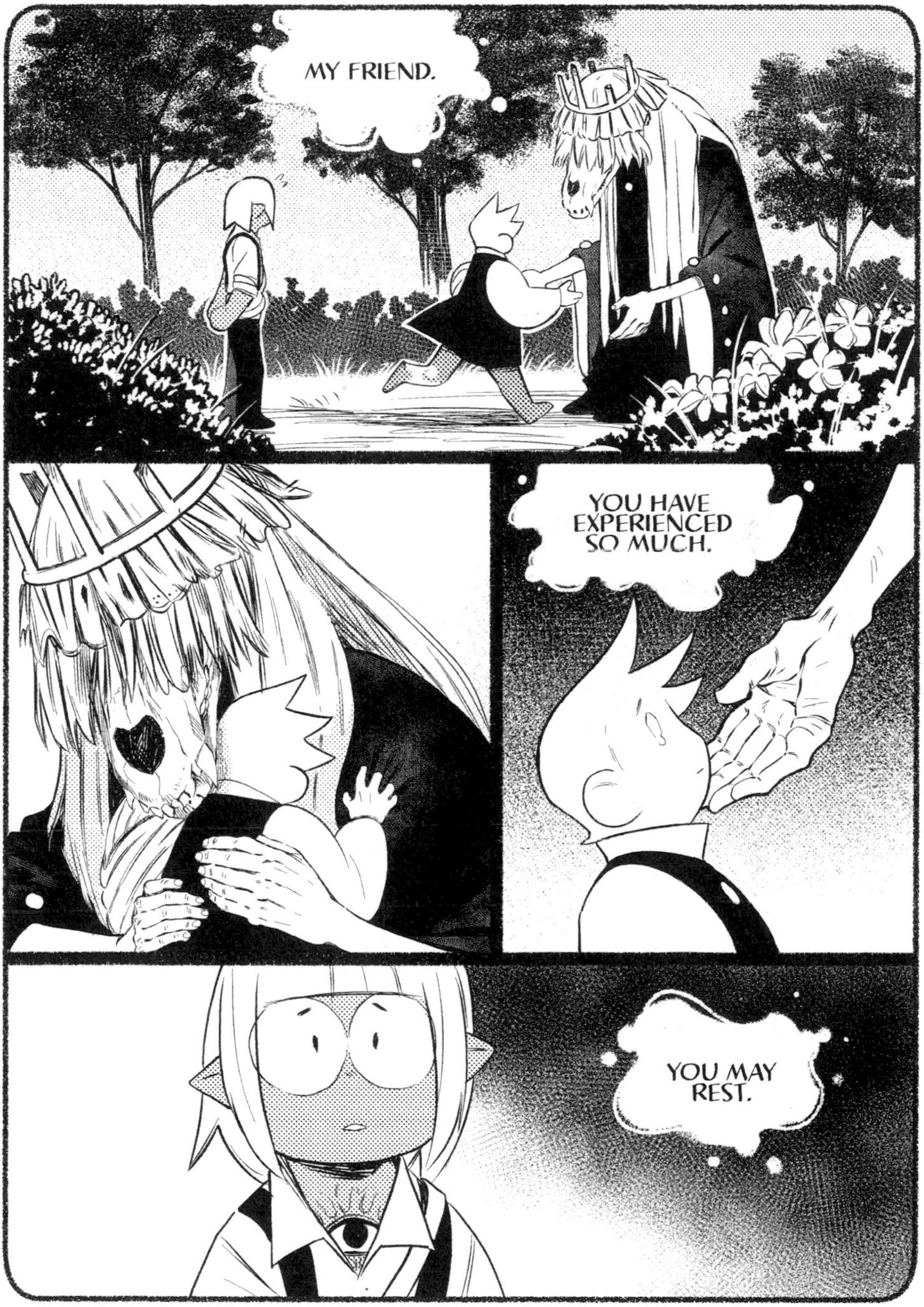
MY FRIEND.
YOU HAVE EXPERIENCED SO MUCH.
YOU MAY REST.

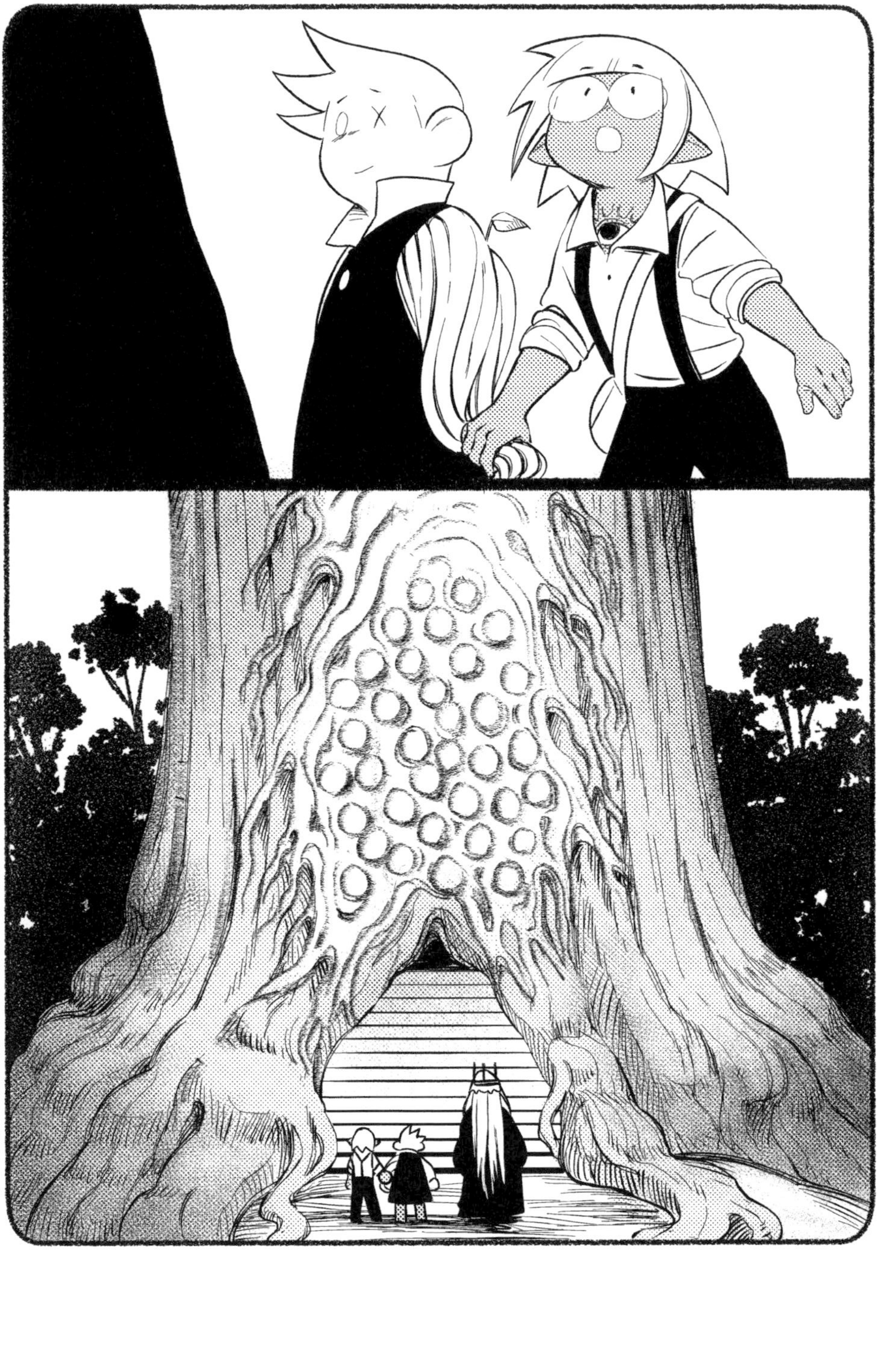

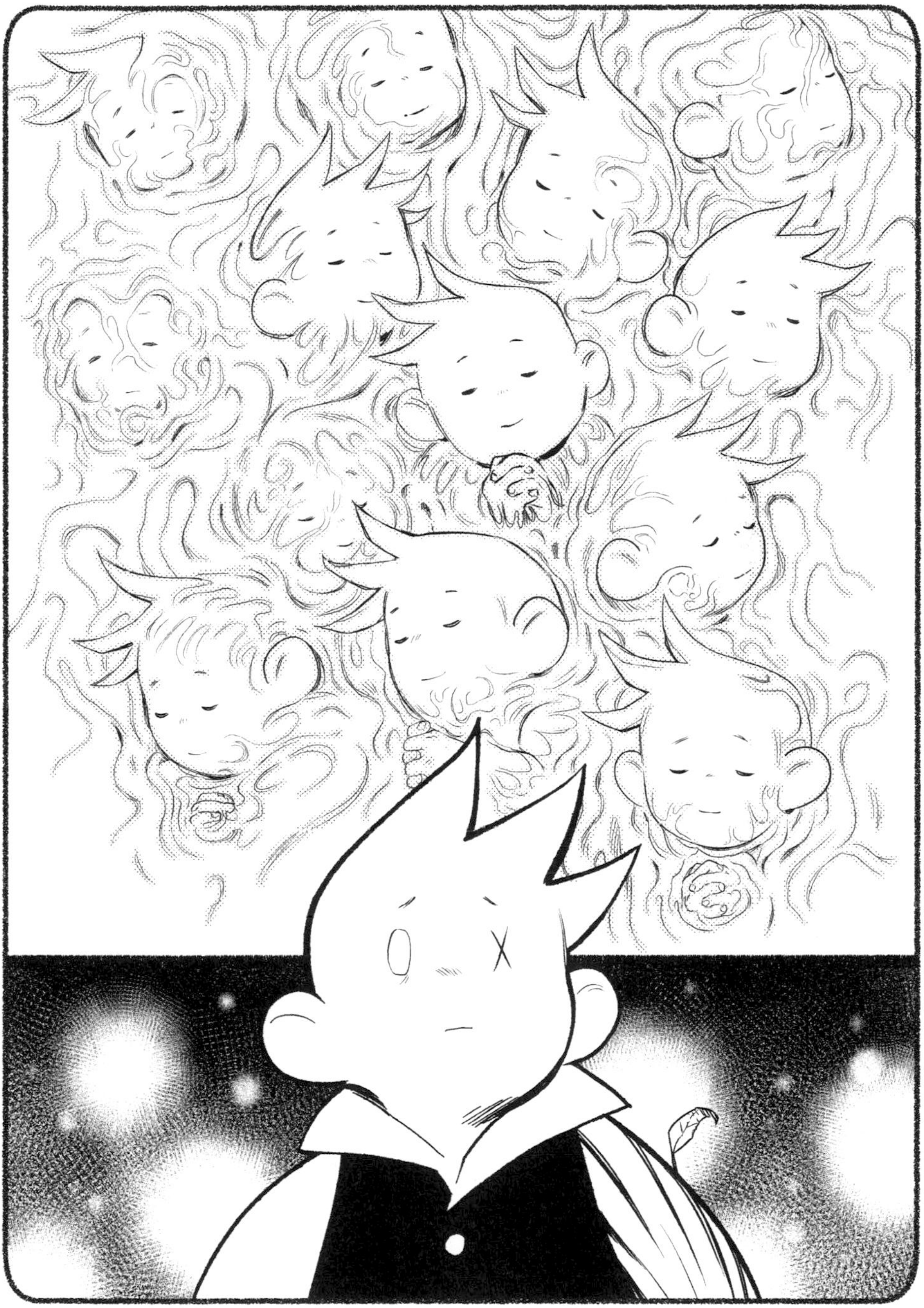

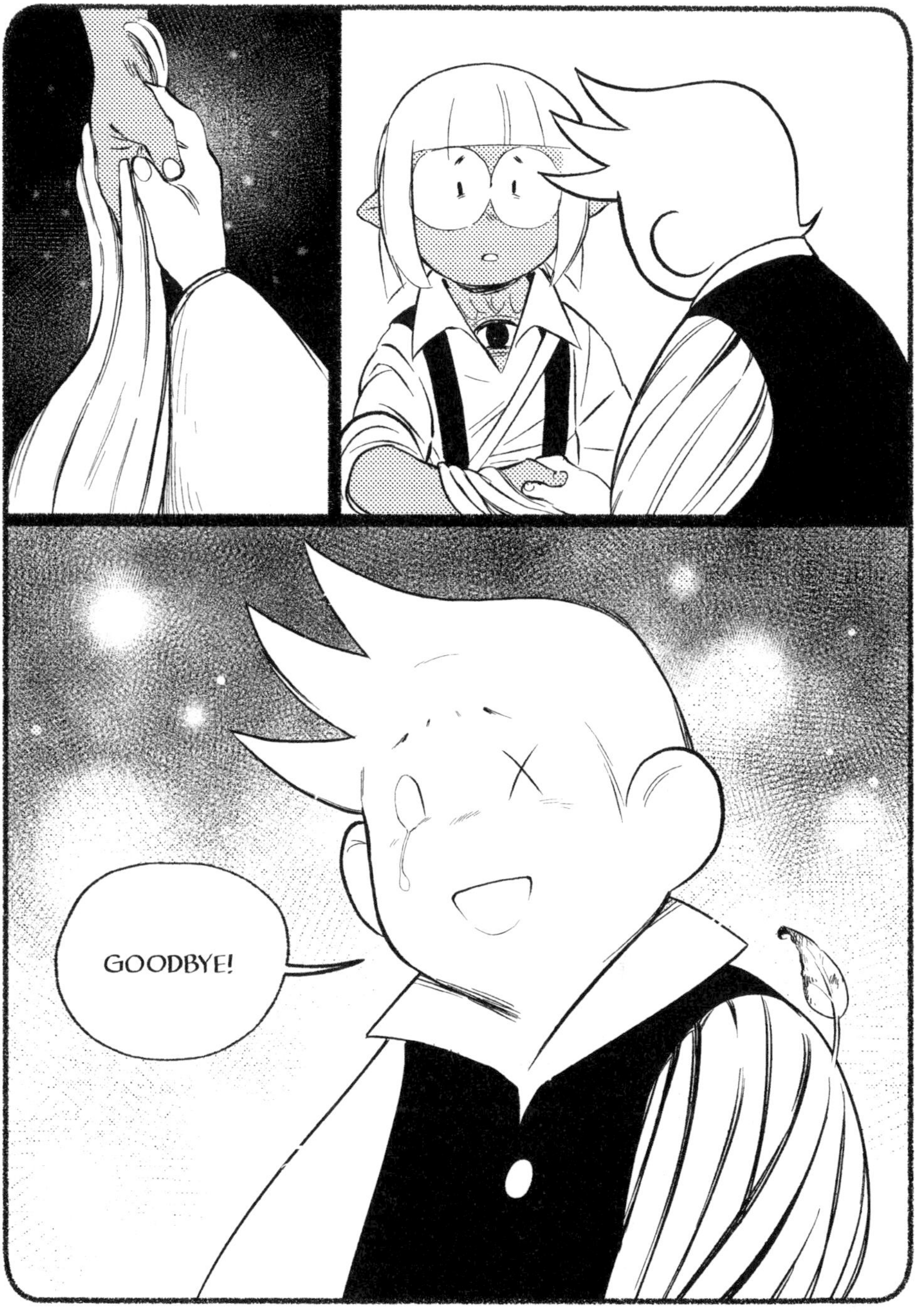
GOODBYE!

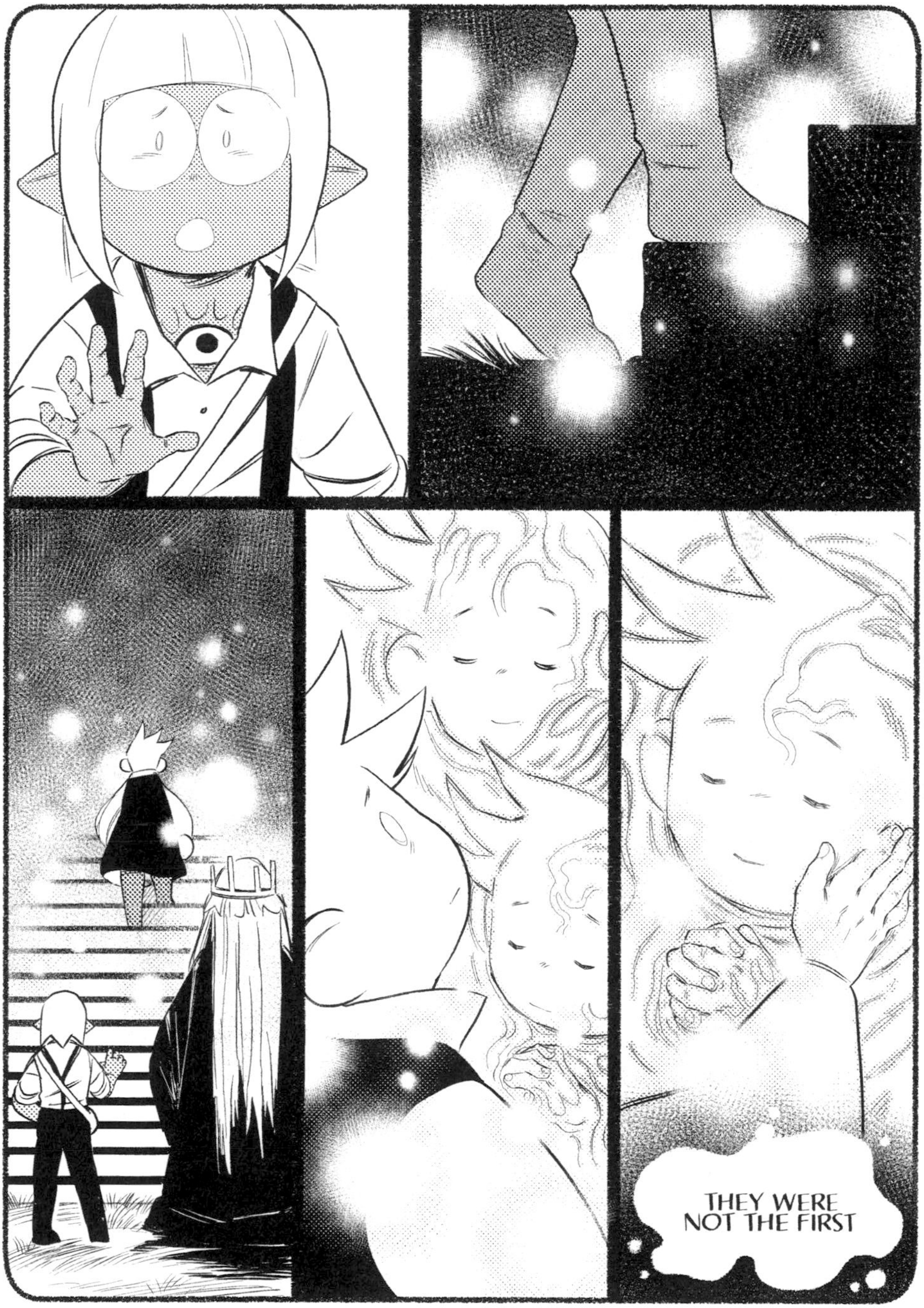
THEY WERE NOT THE FIRST

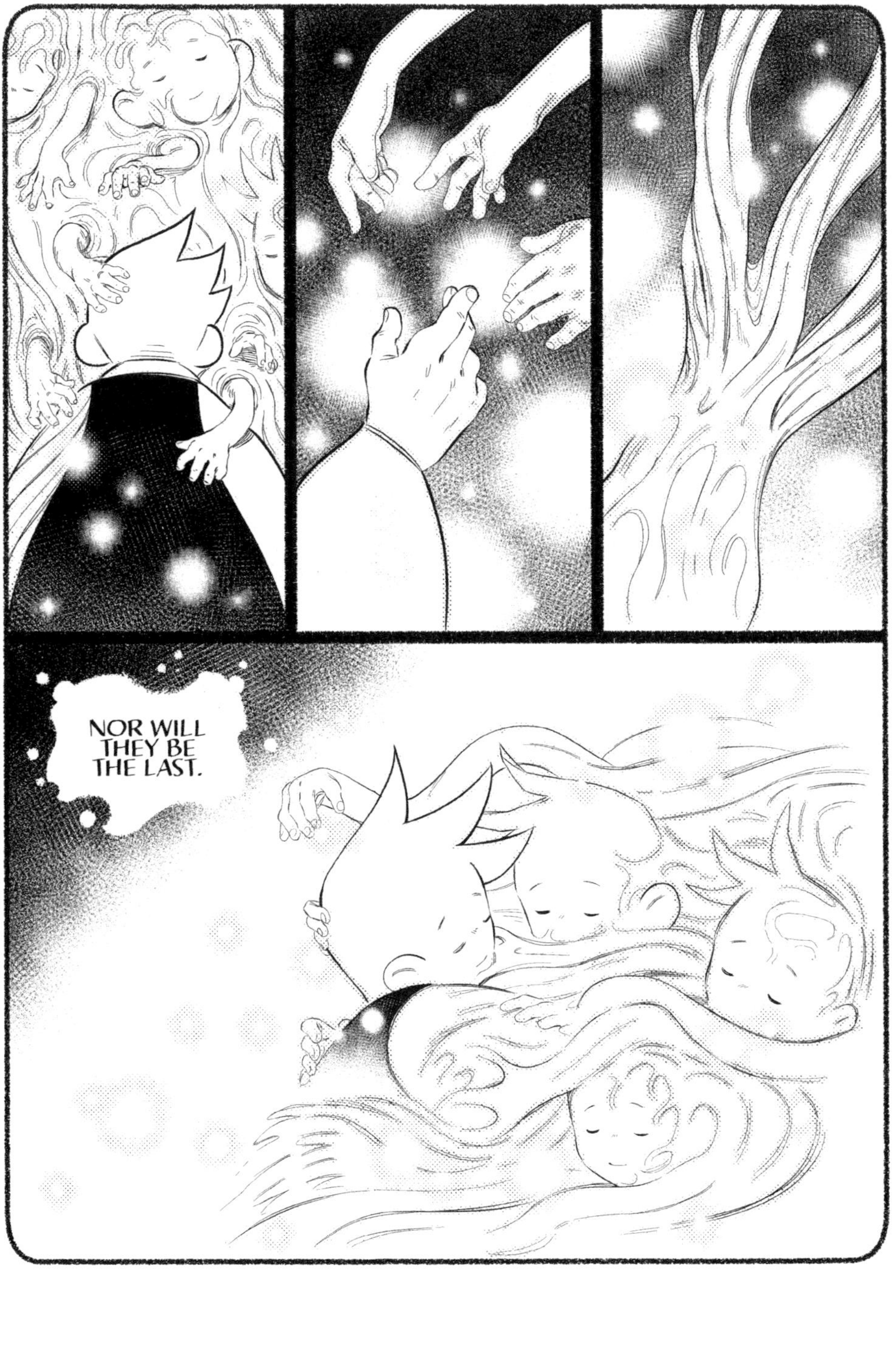
NOR WILL THEY BE THE LAST.

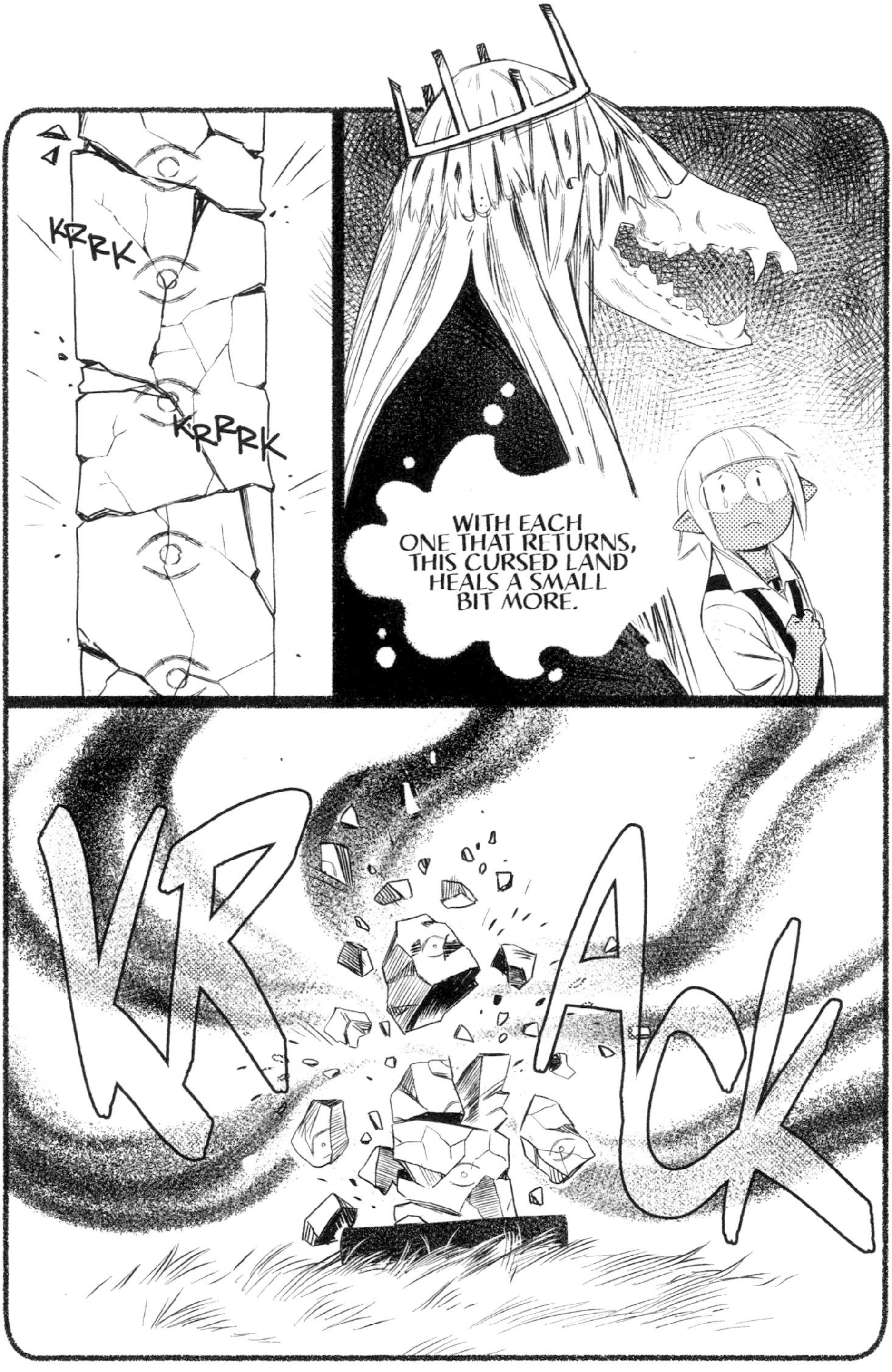
KRRK
KRRRK
WITH EACH ONE THAT RETURNS, THIS CURSED LAND HEALS A SMALL BIT MORE.
KRACK

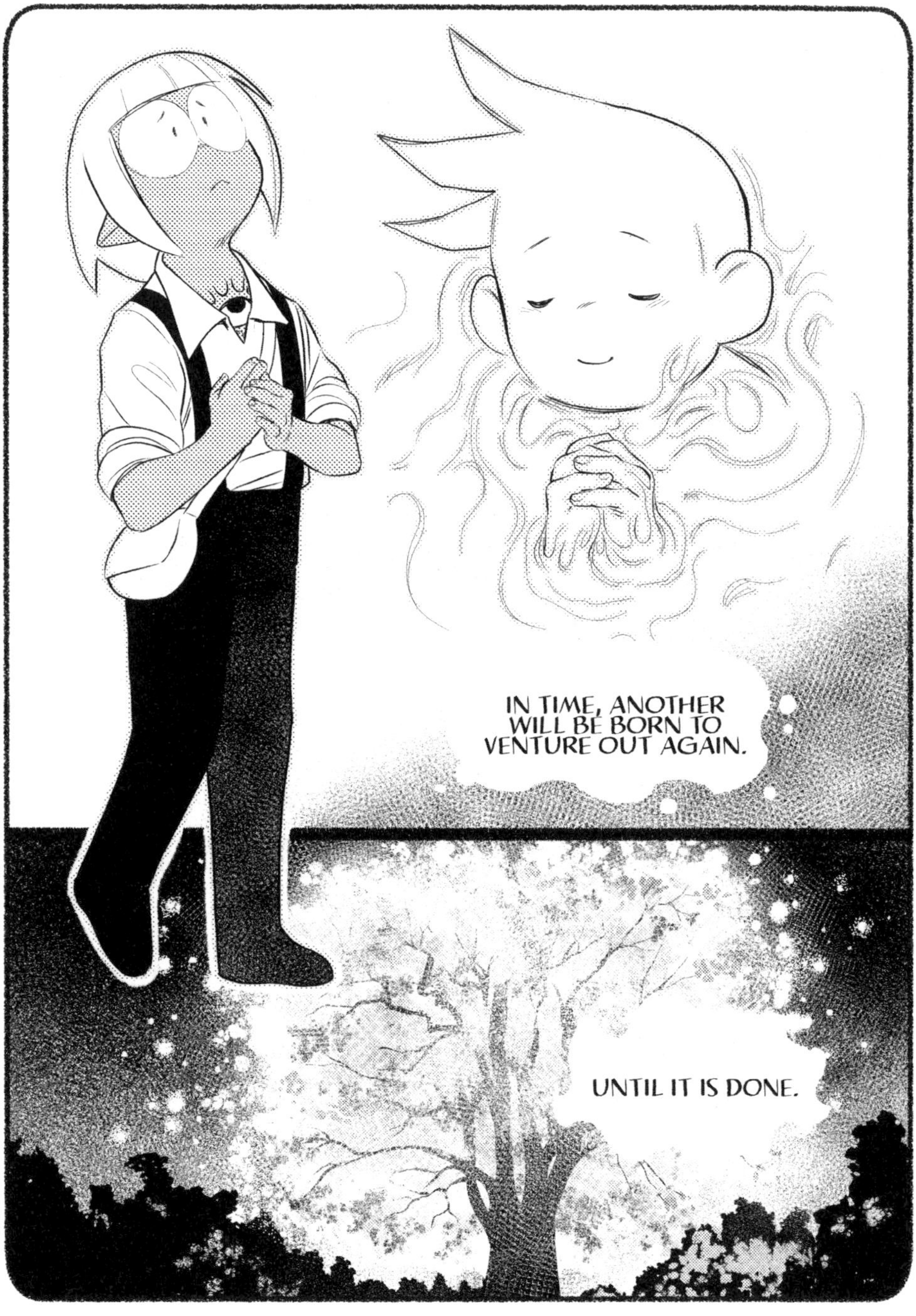
IN TIME, ANOTHER WILL BE BORN TO VENTURE OUT AGAIN.
UNTIL IT IS DONE.

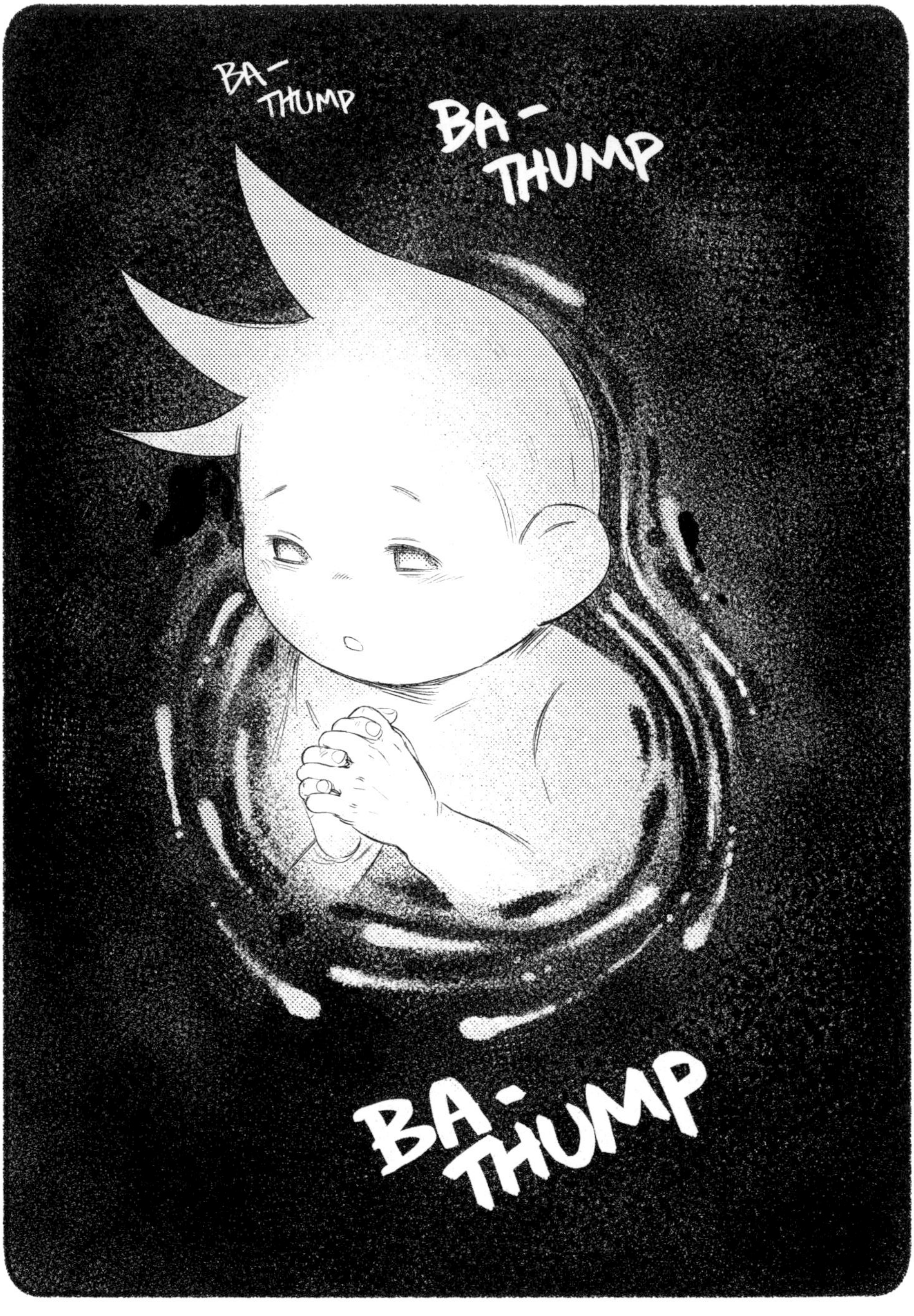
BA-THUMP
BA-THUMP
BA-THUMP

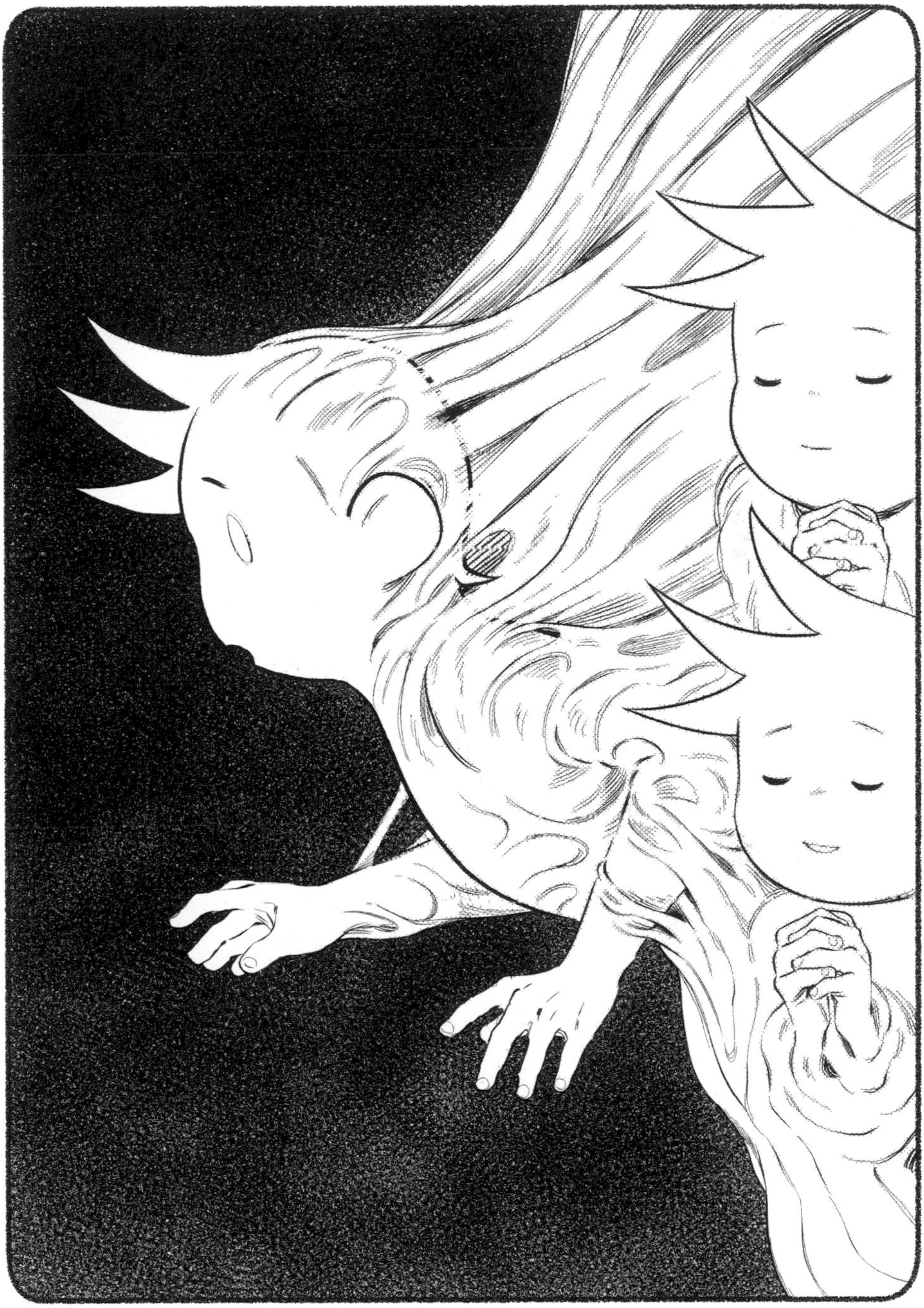

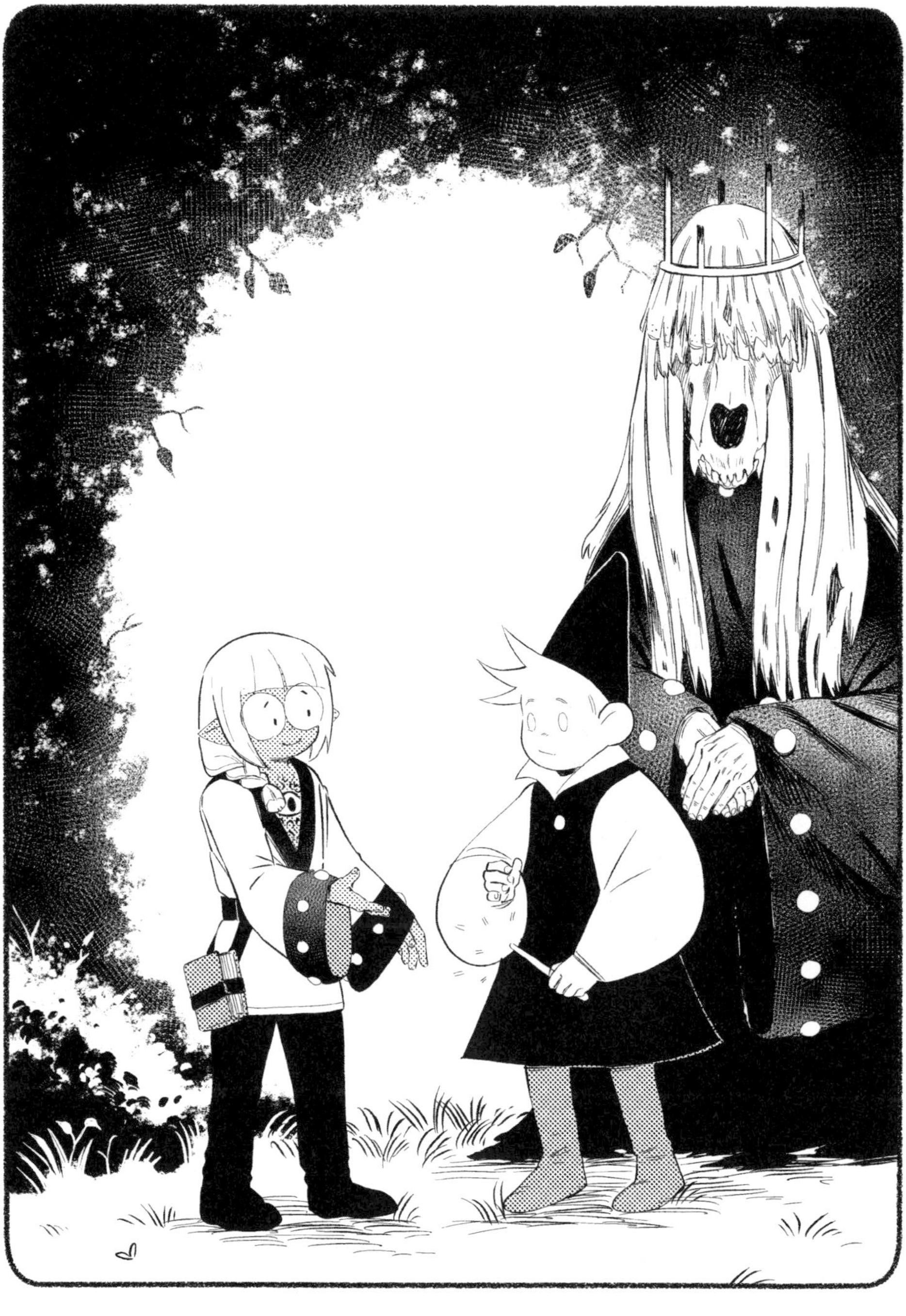

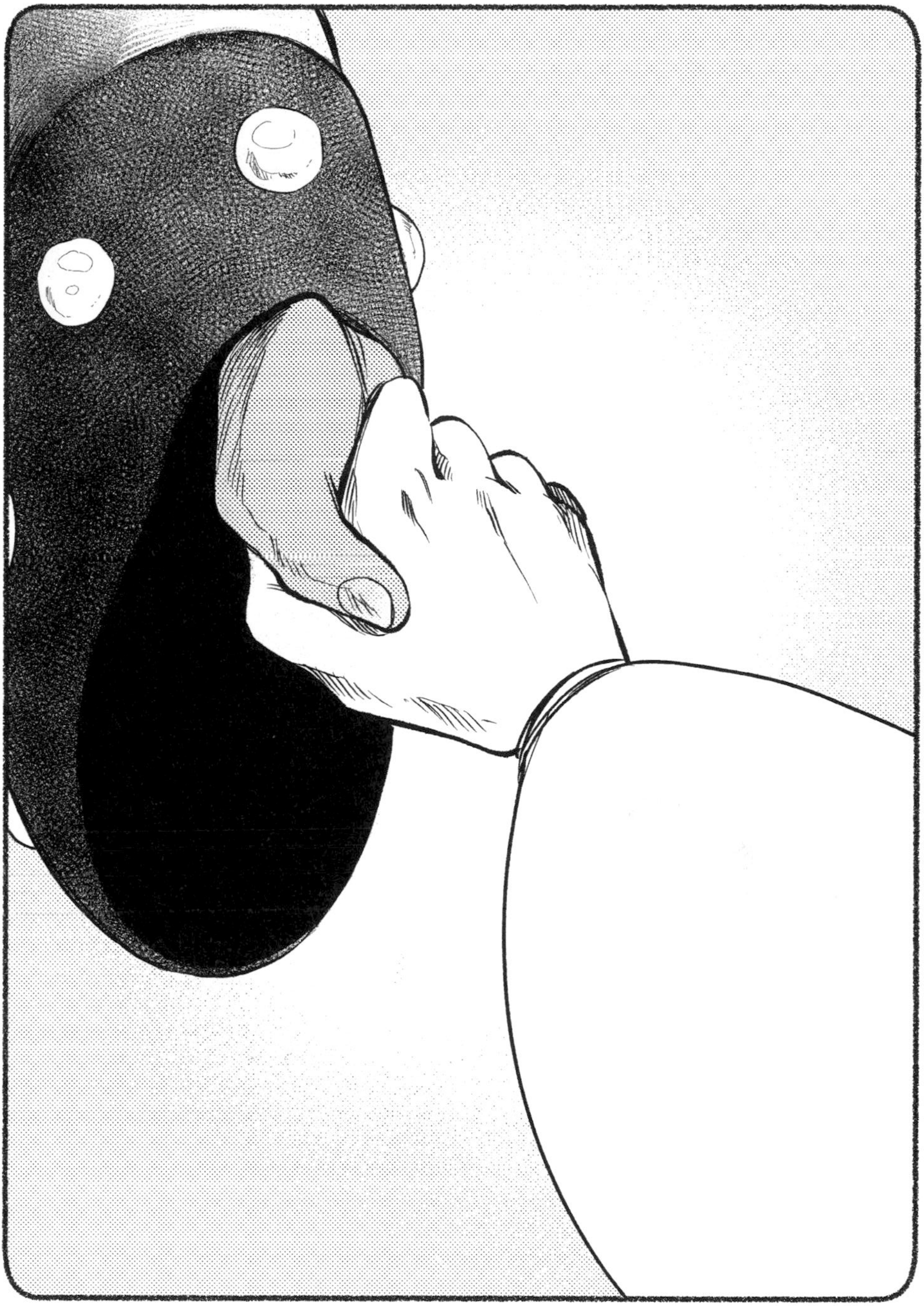

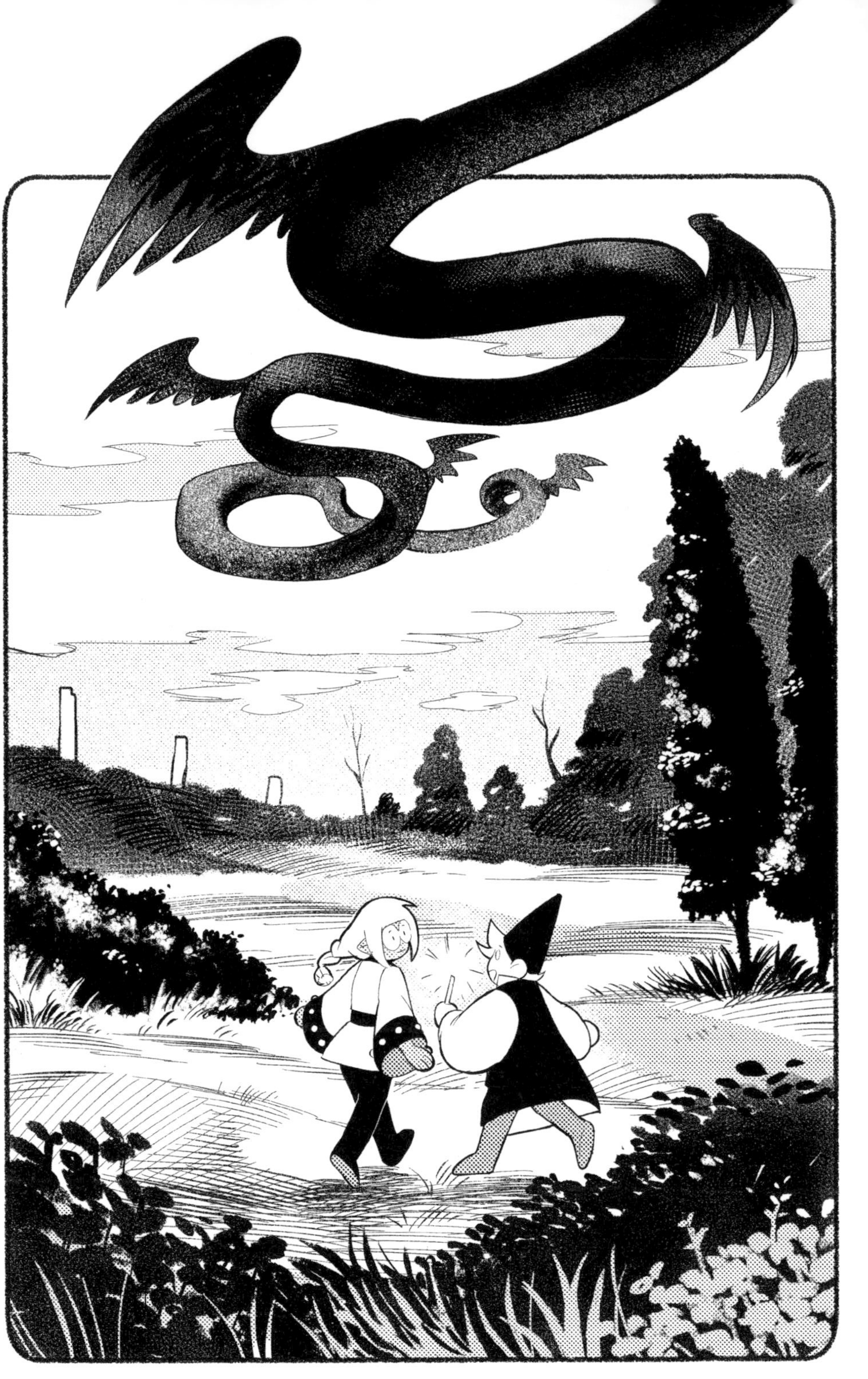

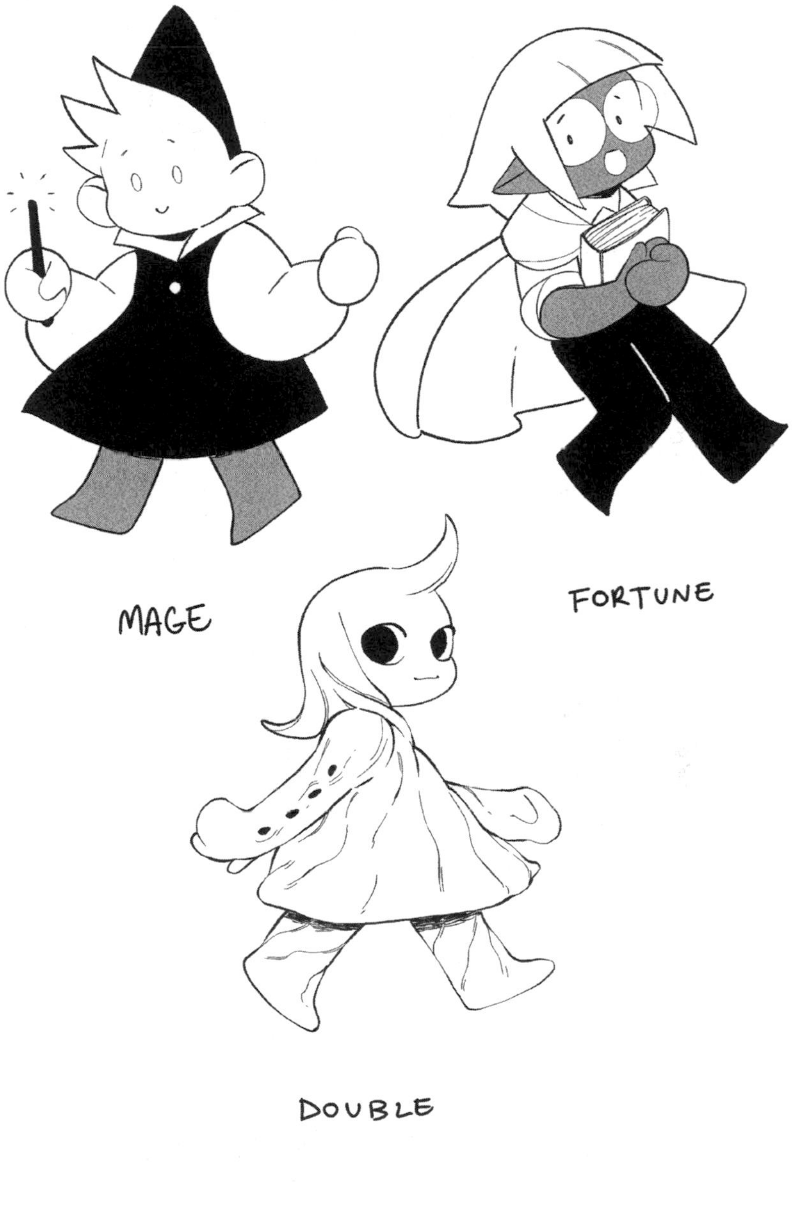
MAGE
FORTUNE
DOUBLE

SJMILLER

is a cartoonist and illustrator
based out of Las Vegas, Nevada.

They're interested in stories about the
corruption of the body and dread of the inevitable.